I0637035

DOGSH*T!

DOGSH*T!

HE WANTS TO SAVE OTHERS. HE NEEDS TO SAVE HIMSELF.

PHIL COBB

Dogsh*t!

He Wants to Save Others. He Needs to Save Himself.

By Phil Cobb

Published by Phil Cobb

Copyright © 2024 Phil Cobb

All rights reserved.

No portion of this book may be reproduced in any form or stored in a retrieval system or transmitted in any form without permission from the author.

This is a work of fiction. Characters and events are products of the author's imagination. Any resemblance to actual persons, living or dead, is purely coincidental.

Cover design by Donika Mishineva

www.artofdonika.com

ISBN 979-8-9887137-2-2

✿ Created with Vellum

PHIL COBB

CONTENTS

PART I

WHO'S YOUR HERO?

1

THE LESSONS OF MR. PROFESSOR

Whiskers had a suspicion that he was no longer the happiest dog in the world.

He had gone to sleep on the sofa listening to his human's voice. When the white Schnauzer with brownish ears awoke from his nap, the man he called Mr. Professor wasn't talking.

That wasn't completely unusual, because there were times when the daytime drinks would get the better of the ex-university instructor and he would lean his head back on the top of the sofa, close his eyes and begin snoring.

This time there was no snoring, nor was his head leaned back. It was drooped forward, chin on chest.

Whiskers stared at the unusual position, then barked, "Mr. Professor, wake up."

No reaction.

Whiskers uncurled himself, sat up and lightly scratched Mr. Professor's right hand. When he didn't get a reaction, he stood up and pushed both front paws against the man's shoulder. Mr. Professor toppled against the arm of the sofa and stayed there motionless, his head now hanging facedown to the side.

Whiskers jumped down to the floor and curled up tightly, feeling very unwell. The worst of all possible things had happened in a world that used to be the best of all possible worlds.

Mr. Professor was dead.

Did somebody sneak into the house to harm him? Not likely. A great watchdog like myself is always on the alert, especially when sound asleep. Besides, I'm sure that even strangers loved him as much as I did.

What Whiskers didn't know is that many people used to have pleasant daydreams about doing away with his best friend.

That's because, although Mr. Professor was very kind to Whiskers, he didn't treat others too kindly, particularly when he had been employed at Codswallop University in Blathersfield, Ohio. Mr. Professor had a very high opinion of himself, which made him overbearing when interacting with other professors and university administrators.

Tall and thin with slicked-back, black hair graying on the sides, Mr. Professor's haughtiness came from being a Renaissance man. He loved to argue points in a patronizing way that left his academic colleagues feeling belittled, confounded and floundering in their own fields of expertise. He also loved to drink and took great inebriated delight in showing off in front of his colleagues at social gatherings, leaving them sputtering in anger. He particularly pissed them off by saying that the only reason he drank so much was to dumb himself down to their level.

As time went on, the anger reached critical mass. A special meeting was convened at which the entire faculty and administration voted to drum him out of the university. After the last "Aye," the president of the university jerked the mortarboard off Mr. Professor's head, threw it on the floor and stomped on it.

But Mr. Professor wouldn't go quietly and gracefully from

what he called the University of Petty Jealousy. He began to berate everyone present, cursing at them in Carthaginian, Phoenician, Hieroglyphician, Esperanto and Pig Latin.

"I'm sorry," he said in English, "that you ignoramuses probably didn't grasp a word of those languages, so let me put it in terminology you might understand."

With that, he turned his backside to the jeering collegium, leaned over to flip up his academic gown, found his naked butt with both hands, pulled the cheeks wide and bugled out the first notes of Beethoven's "Fifth Symphony."

"Ask someone in the Modern Languages Department for help in translating that," Mr. Professor chortled.

As the football coach and the women's basketball coach manhandled him out the door, he yelled back, "You're all idiots. You can't stand it that I'm smarter than you. Even my dog is smarter than you. At least he will be after I teach him everything I know, and then he'll start his own university, and it will be the best of all possible universities, and when you apply for jobs he'll bite every one of you in the ass!"

After the coaches threw him down the steps, Mr. Professor trudged home to the small house with peeling gray paint and knee-high weeds. There was no understanding wife to greet him. Actually, there used to be one, and she had tried very hard to understand him. But instead of opening up to her, he would take another drink and say, "You don't understand me. Only Whiskers does."

Eventually, she became so fed up with a man who talked only to the dog that she ran away with a traveling toilet brush salesman.

Although he had been ousted from academic life, Mr. Professor retained a deep-seated, compulsive need to talk, to explain, to lecture. Without his captive audience of students, though, there was no one to enthrall with his knowledge. No one, that is, except Whiskers, a typical Schnauzer except for the brownish ears due to some randy interloper in his family ancestry.

So, day after day, all day long, with his audience of one, Mr. Professor held forth on subject after subject with detailed explanations and multiple digressions, even while shaving or carrying out other ablutions.

Whiskers' preference was to stretch out on the sofa with an ear being twiddled as channels were changed from science to cooking to history to sports to politics to fashion to war to religion to lifestyle and movies on the large thing called the boob tube, all the while with Mr. Professor expounding on the content and sarcastically assessing humanity's progress, complexities and inanities.

At first, the onslaught of words was just background noise to Whiskers. But the constant repetition began to have an effect. The words started to stick in a form of understanding.

Not everything Whiskers heard, though, was correct. Mr. Professor liked to pontificate with a bottle or glass of enhanced inspiration in hand, so his words were frequently misspoken. His articulation would become more and more imprecise and sometimes just plain sloppy.

Throughout his tipsy monologues, Mr. Professor would intersperse comments such as "Whishkers, you'rsh the only one who e'er unnershtuud me" and "You'rsh the shmarshesh dog in the vorld" and "You'rsh e'en shmarter than people. E'ery damn shtinkin' finkin' one uf 'em."

Whiskers liked that. Being so smart was something to be proud of, to boast about, to let other dogs know.

Whiskers also enjoyed hearing Mr. Professor talk about heroes like Sure Lunchalot and Hurtyourknees. They were wonderful. But even better was having been saved by a real hero.

Whiskers had often reminisced about that day. He was a

small, lost puppy, not knowing how to get back to his parents and littermates. But he forgot about his sadness upon finding a juicy, meat-loaded steak bone on the ground beside a restaurant's dumpster. Just as he was ready to tuck in, a Dachshund dashed down the alley to challenge him.

"Your bone or your life," the full-grown dog said.

Whiskers did not answer. He simply looked up, down and all around with a scowl on his face.

Growing impatient, the Dachshund snapped, "Well, what's it going to be?"

"I'm thinking, I'm thinking," Whiskers replied.

At that moment, a man rode his bicycle down the alley for his favorite Sunday afternoon recreation of dumpster diving, seeking treasures that fools had thrown away. Seeing the injustice about to take place, the man honked the horn on his bicycle and pedaled straight at the canine thug. Alarmed, the Dachshund yelped and ran away like a sausage on steroids.

"You're lucky that I happened by when you needed someone to save you," the man said. "And it looks to me like you're lost, but you're not lost anymore."

He picked up Whiskers along with the steak bone and placed both in the bicycle's basket.

While pedaling back home, the man said, "With those long whiskers, I'm going to call you Whiskers. And you can call me Mr. Professor, because that's what I am, a professor."

There were other heroes.

Being a dog, Whiskers especially identified with those who were canines. Mr. Professor would say, "Here's something special for you" and explain what was happening in shows featuring Grin Chin Grin, Sassie, and War Dogs of the Pawcific.

Whiskers figured that if those dogs could be heroes, so could he. So what if he was just an average-size dog?

Size doesn't matter. All I have to do is bite the bad guy in the butt.

Thus inspired, and until he actually did something, Whiskers became a hero in his own mind. Combining that with his natural terrier propensity for feistiness and a good dose of hardheadedness, he developed an extremely elevated opinion of himself. And a lesser one of others.

Besides, who needed others? Not him. Not when he had the best human in the world. Not when they lived very well on something called Social Insecurity while happily sharing Yummy Gutz dog food.

Now, though, that wonderful life was over.

The smartest man in the world had pickled himself.

At the moment, Whiskers wasn't sure what to do except wait. Maybe somebody would come by. Then he realized that nobody was going to come by. Nobody had ever come by. No family, no friends, no neighbors. And that was a problem because...

Humans want to be buried like a bone, but even if I could drag him into the backyard, my toenails and pads would wear off before I could dig a big enough hole. Or maybe I could do like Sassie and run in circles in front of people and bark at them until they came to help me dig. But what if we get done and they try to take me away?

Mr. Professor had often said, "They took everything from me, but I'll never let them take you." That always sounded very bad.

More time went by. Whiskers was hungry. He stared at the refrigerator. The door was closed, and it was going to stay that way.

It was obvious what he had to do. He had to leave the house and the human that he loved.

Unlike people, though, Whiskers wasn't afraid.

Throw the average person in the woods, and he would whine and cry and fall down and die on the spot. Throw the average dog in the woods and he would do just fine, thank you.

Whiskers, however, was not an average dog. Mr. Professor

had told him many times that he was the best and smartest dog in the world.

Not only that, he was a terrier. A terrier with attitude. And, most probably, the bravest of all dogs.

So Whiskers was prepared to go out into the world with the best of all possible humans as his life example.

After giving Mr. Professor a final lick goodbye, Whiskers stood at the doggy door, having no doubts about what he would be.

I'll be a hero.

2

A REAL CHAMPION

"A storm is coming! The sky is going to break!" squealed Whiskers.

Terror flooded through his brain, producing absolute panic that was impossible to control. Nothing filled Whiskers or any other dog with such mindless fear as a storm.

Instinct had hard-wired him to run and pee and bark for all he was worth and not stop. At the house of Mr. Professor, he would tear around the backyard as lightning cracked and thunder boomed and heavy rain beat on his pathetically drenched body. If in the house, he would run in circles around the den, jumping on and off stuffed chairs, the coffee table and the sofa, peeing and barking and refusing to stop even when Mr. Professor appeared and tried to calm him.

Whiskers wasn't embarrassed then and not now. As any fool could plainly see, this was the end of the world. The thunder said, "Death is here." The lightning said, "There he is." The rain said, "Drown him."

The only protection was to keep running from a storm until it was left behind.

Now, he ran blindly through sheets of water while the

thunder and lightning proclaimed every step of the way they were going to kill him. After a while, he could hear other dogs barking, squealing, screaming.

Drawing nearer, Whiskers made out glowing points of light rapidly bobbing up and down with each lightning strike. They were the eyes of barking dogs going insane on a night of terror.

Whiskers ran toward them.

"I'm coming," he said. "I'm Whiskers."

The moment he barked his name, the lightning and thundering ceased. The downpour changed to a gentle rain. By sheer luck, Whiskers trotted into a camp of terrified hobo dogs at the perfect moment.

"Storms don't bother me," he said triumphantly. "I was taking a stroll to enjoy the rain, the thunder and the lightning. But I could hear how scared you were, so I chased the storm and bit it in the ass and it ran away."

All the dogs in the camp looked at Whiskers in amazement. They had never heard of a dog or any kind of animal that wasn't afraid of storms. And how could you bite a storm in the ass? In fact, where was its ass? They couldn't even see the head of a storm, much less its ass.

Highly impressed, the hobo dogs crowded around to introduce themselves, but Whiskers said he had a better way.

"Everybody get in a circle with your muzzles looking in and your butts pointing out. Then I'll run around the outside while you bark your names and try to toot in my face."

Whooping and hollering, all the dogs eagerly formed the bassackwards ring.

"Ready, set, blow," Whiskers yelled.

He took off running around the outside of the circle. As he came past, each dog did his or her mightiest to produce the most pungent air possible.

"This is a blast, Whiskers," yelled Bubba, a Coonhound.

"I know," huffed Whiskers as he flew by, "and I'm enjoying every whiff. It's a really efficient way to get to know all of you."

"Where did you come up with this idea, Whiskers?" asked Buster, a Bulldog.

"I saw it with my human, Mr. Professor, when we watched something called the Tour de Farts on YourPeein TV, except people were riding past each other on tall, skinny things while pumping their legs up and down real fast to make as much gas as possible."

After that introduction, Whiskers settled in with the hobo dogs and became very comfortable with their lifestyle, which consisted of lazing about and telling stories. One of their favorites was about something that made all dogs drool.

"I tell you," said Lola, a Cocker Spaniel, "the Big Bone is the greatest bone of all. It's so big that it would take a team of Huskies to carry it."

Duke, an Airedale, jumped in excitedly, "It always has meat on it! That's because when you chew meat off, new meat appears. It never gets old and dry, so it never loses flavor, which is the most delicious that any dog ever tasted."

Hmm, that Big Bone sounds mighty fine, even better than the dog food that Mr. Professor and I loved so much. I'll just ask these dogs where it is and go get it.

"The only problem," said Ratsy, a Rat Terrier, "is that no one knows where the Big Bone is."

"Maybe it doesn't exist," chimed in Boomer, a mutt of no discernible lineage. "Maybe that's why nobody ever says they actually got a piece of it. It's always somebody saying that it was a friend of a friend's friend who saw it."

"Whether it exists or not," snorted Bandit, an old country hound, "I'm gettin' darn hungry just listenin' to you all jabber about it, so talk about somethin' else."

That ended the rhapsodizing about the Big Bone, so the

dogs moved on to another favorite topic—fighting. Soon they were arguing about who had been the greatest fighting dogs and which of the tough old-timers could whup today's soft pretenders.

The more Whiskers listened, the more annoyed he became. He didn't want to hear about other dogs. He wanted to hear about himself, even if it had to come from himself.

"That's nothing," he said when one old dog finally finished extolling the fighting skills of a long-ago champion. "I've been fighting all my life, and not just dogs."

The others eyed him skeptically. He didn't look like a fighter.

"What's the toughest animal you ever fought?" asked Queenie, a Doberman Pinscher.

"The toughest? They're all tough, but the most unusual animal I ever fought was a hippo."

"A hippo? What's a hippo?"

"That's what people call a hippopotawatamus. It's real big and real fat, like a big pack of dogs all stuck together."

The hobo dogs couldn't figure that out. How many heads does a hippowhatsit have? How many legs? How many tails? Can it run in all directions at the same time? It must make a huge noise when all of its heads bark at once. Imagine all the teeth it must have.

"You really fought one of those?" Queenie asked, skeptically.

"Yes, I did," Whiskers said proudly.

"Where?"

"At the zoo. That's where they keep all the wild animals that people are afraid of. Mr. Professor would take me there to fight them in their cages."

"How did you fight that hippo?" Bubba asked.

"They live in water," Whiskers said, relishing the opportunity to educate his unschooled audience. "I jumped headfirst into the hippo's pond and went under the water. When I opened my eyes, I saw an enormous body with legs as big as tree trunks. Then I came up to the surface and almost pooped the biggest poop of my life. The hippo's huge mouth was wide open in front of my face, and the waves in the water bounced me up and down and rolled me into it."

"Did he eat you?" Lola asked.

"He tried!" Whiskers said, wiggling and jerking his body and legs to and fro to convey his desperate struggle.

"His breath was so hot that my fur caught on fire, but the water in the pond splashed over me and put it out. Then he slammed his mouth shut with me inside. His teeth weren't sharp like our teeth. They were like ham bones—big and thick and flat on the end from eating all the people and dogs who had lost their fights with him. He started grinding his teeth while his tongue was pushing me toward them."

"How did you get away?" asked Muscles, a Mastiff.

"I stood up and pushed against the roof of his mouth, trying to force his jaws open. But as strong as I am, his jaws were so big and heavy that I couldn't budge them. That's when I did something I knew he wouldn't expect."

"What was it?"

"What did you do?"

"Tell us, tell us!"

The hobo dogs skittered about, with shots of pee squirting out of the most excited ones.

"I jumped down his throat and swam into his stomach. Once I was in there, I dog-paddled as fast as I could through the poop in his intestines and shot out of his ass."

His listeners stopped their capering and stared at Whiskers, flabbergasted. They never would have thought of doing something so bold.

"Next, I turned around in the water, gripped the hippo's butt with my toenails and pulled myself up. I ran across his back, jumped on top of his head and bit him big-time in an ear, jerking it this way and that way, again and again and again," Whiskers said as he ran, jumped and snapped at the air to act out the story.

"Then what?" asked Buster.

"The big ninny let out a bellow of pain. He didn't know what to do. He had never been in a match with a water-fighting dog who knew all the tricks of the Navy Bean Seals. He was so scared that he started swimming for the other side of the pond so he could hide in his underwater cave. Just before he dove below the surface, I jumped off. Then I swam around the hippo's pond in a victory lap. All the people there were cheering because someone had finally beaten the hippo."

After hearing that tale, many of the hobo dogs knew they were in the presence of a real champion.

But others weren't quite so sure, no matter how authoritatively and confidently Whiskers talked. He was just another average-size dog. Besides, fighting on land was different from swimming out of a hippo's ass.

"Can you fight a bear?"

"Who said that?" asked Whiskers.

"I did," replied Iggy, a mixed-breed dog. "I never heard of that thing in your story, but I know bears are real."

The other dogs nodded their heads. They knew all about bears. Very bad business. You did not want to mess with a bear.

"They are huge," Iggy continued. "They weigh much more than all of the dogs here put together. They've got teeth and claws longer than your head. They can run as fast as a horse. They climb up trees to pull animals down. And then they eat them, crunching their bones into tiny pieces. When they fart, the smell carries everywhere, and it says to the other animals in the woods: 'I just ate so-and-so and you're next.'"

All the listeners winced, except one.

"I'm not afraid of a bear," Whiskers bragged.

"Maybe, maybe not," Iggy said, "but I know a dog who fought a bear for real, by himself."

Everyone's ears perked up. How could a dog fight a bear by himself and live? No dog could do that, not even a wolf. Only dogs in packs would even dare approach a bear.

"What kind of a dog is he?" Lola asked.

"I don't know," Iggy said. "He's like no dog you've ever seen. There's no way to tell what he came from. He looks like all the fiercest breeds combined. He's so big and so ferocious that when he stares at you, you pee all over yourself."

"What's his name?" asked Buster.

"His name is Scut," Iggy answered.

"Why did he fight the bear?" Queenie asked.

"He did it for fun because he likes to fight," Iggy said. "He did it because other dogs are too easy for him."

"I'm not afraid of him. I'd fight him right now," Whiskers boasted, making a big show of peeing on a clump of crabgrass and kicking dirt behind him with his back legs. "I know the type you're talking about—big and stupid, the kind that's easy to outsmart as well as outfight. It's a good thing for him that he's not here."

Snorting and laughing, his listeners shook their heads from side to side.

"Laugh all you want," Whiskers grumped, "but I know a fighting skill that people use. Mr. Professor would jump around demonstrating it. It's called carrot-rotty. I used it to win all my fights at the zoo, and now I'm ready to take on anything."

A number of the hobo dogs rubbed their paws against their heads and over their eyes. They weren't sure what to believe. Either Whiskers was a champion fighter or he was a champion liar.

Then Whiskers did something marvelous.

He stood up on his hind legs and began pawing at the air, making weird noises in something he called Jumponknees while squirting out a little pee for macho emphasis. The hobo dogs' mouths fell open. They had never seen any dog stand up on its hind legs to fight.

Their respect for Whiskers grew immensely.

3

NO MORE DOUGHNUTS

Wincing as the sun's first rays jabbed through the van's windshield, Janvier squinted to survey the sides of the trash-filled alley. Hungry, but not daring to take a doughnut from the box beside her, she focused on finding a stray.

Looking for loose dogs at dawn had become a necessity. The best dog-catching spots had long been claimed. If she started to get close to one, the other dogcatchers would alert each other with their cell phones and block her van with theirs until she turned back. The only places they left for her were bare-dirt areas that offered very little to attract strays, so she had taken to getting an early jump on better pickings.

Why do they have to be so mean?

All she ever wanted was to be accepted as one of the team. And why not? Her father had been a dogcatcher, deeply respected for his ability to bring in the wiliest dogs as well as the most vicious ones. Some dogs he couldn't bear to turn in, so he built a private kennel where they lived until he found homes for them.

Janvier wanted to be just like him, working to protect the

community of Latte, California, from animals that shouldn't be on the loose while aiding the sweet ones. But not long after she joined Dog Catching Unit No. 9 an outraged animal lover forced her father's van off a freeway overpass. The crash killed him and all the dogs inside.

Each day at work Janvier saw her father when she passed by his photograph edged in black crepe on the wall. The other dogcatchers would stop by the photo, salute it, then look at her and shake their heads from side to side, making sure she saw them do it.

Jerks, jerks, jerks.

When her father was alive, they had behaved themselves. Now that he was gone, she not only had to put up with their sneers but also their leers.

Janvier was attractive with a good figure, striking ice-blue eyes, well-defined cheekbones and shoulder-length black hair. The guys exaggerated their leers, making them overly obvious and insulting on purpose, a coded way of reminding her that she was a woman intruding in their world.

Why can't we all just do our jobs? Why do they have to be such idiots?

She had complained to Human Resources, but they said not to make waves because they didn't want those knuckleheads to find out that a guy in another state had won a lawsuit by claiming that working with women caused him to think impure thoughts that hampered his concentration and therefore his ability to meet job expectations and so was legally entitled to retire on permanent disability pay, which he was using to purchase a timeshare on a Bimbo Lines party cruise ship so he could become even more disabled.

Not knowing what else to do, Janvier had begun bringing doughnuts for everyone, along with a smile, hoping that would soften their hearts. Morning after morning the guys took the doughnuts, but with smirks on their faces and comments like "legacy," "doughnut girl," and "at least you're good for something."

Ungrateful pieces of dog-dookie.

She had often thought about not bringing any more doughnuts, but she knew they expected them, so she didn't want to make the guys mad by stopping. Well, actually, she had tried once to stop, after the rookie joke.

The regulars would take a rookie to a woods at dusk, saying that a dog had been spotted inside. They explained that the rookie had to get in there and bring the dog out in order to pass the nighttime field exam.

Except, there never was a dog in the woods. The rookie would stumble around in the dark and become lost while being pricked by thorns, scratched by branches and smacked in the face by limbs. It was the dogcatchers' version of a snipe hunt.

But it was more than a prank. It was a test to see what a rookie was like, a way to be accepted as "one of the guys." All the rookie had to do was laugh it off as a good joke on himself.

But this rookie was a herself.

That factor had caused a lot of discussion as to whether they should even bother with her, but the men had to admit that Janvier had shown real balls by taking all their crap and not quitting. They agreed to give her a chance.

But fetch-the-doggy didn't go well.

Janvier had come out of the woods scratched and bleeding with one eye swollen to find the men laughing at her. When told that the test was only a joke, she didn't laugh. She just hung her head and walked away. It was more evidence that they were all against her, scheming to make her quit because she was a woman trying to do "a real man's job."

The next morning, Janvier had shown up empty-handed at work only to hear big-gutted Fred growl, "Hey, rookie, where are our doughnuts? You don't stop bringing them until we tell you to stop bringing them."

So here she was, driving down an alley with doughnuts hot and fresh out of the baker's oven so she could keep Fred and the other jerks happy.

Maybe I should start bringing day-old doughnuts. That would show them.

Movement in a tall pile of cardboard boxes interrupted that pleasant daydream.

Janvier inched the van forward twenty feet, stopped and rolled down her window. A rustling noise was coming from behind the pile.

Stepping quietly out of the van, she approached the pile slowly, holding a pole with an adjustable loop on one end. Moving cautiously up to the boxes and seeing nothing on the ground but spilled garbage, she started to walk around the pile to investigate and...

BWAHM!

The pile of boxes blasted apart as a dark figure flew out from the center and smashed against Janvier, knocking her to the ground.

She lay on her back, stunned after making such a dumb rookie mistake. Instead of standing away from the pile and jabbing at it with the long pole, Janvier had walked right up to an ambush.

Gasping for air, she inhaled the hot breath of the enormous dog whose forelegs had her arms pinned. The animal opened its mouth, letting saliva drip onto Janvier's lips. The dog's dark-brown eyes glared with hatred while a low, slow, powerful growl rumbled in its throat.

Squirming, Janvier raised her head and chest and twisted sideways to roll the dog off, but it weighed more than she did, and its heaviness bore her back down. Angered by her resistance, the animal snarled in vicious bursts and snapped its teeth an inch from her eyes.

Janvier stopped struggling. She didn't want to lose her face.

The beast then made a strange noise—not a bark, not a growl, not a whine, but something different, almost like a laugh.

New fear spread through Janvier.

He knows what I am!

The sound of her dogcatcher's van—a unique combination of engine noise and rattling equipment that signals the end of canine freedom—had betrayed her.

Helpless under the huge dog, Janvier watched as it pulled its upper lip back, seemingly in a sneer at her impotence, at her human stupidity. Another near-laugh and a relaxed bobbing of its head conveyed that it had outsmarted her, that it was in control, that it despised her and her fellow dogcatchers as well as all the humans who had yelled at it, thrown rocks at it, shot at it, and laid traps for it.

The brute laid its thick, heavy tongue on her face and rubbed it back and forth, smearing Janvier's makeup until black mascara filled her eye sockets, giving her the appearance of a dead person or an unusual raccoon.

Retracting its tongue, the monster snarled and slapped the left side of her face with its muzzle, turning her head and exposing an ear, which the dog bit hard enough to pop the earring off. Then the animal raised itself and raked her cheek with the hard nails of a front paw.

Growling a warning, the beast slowly stepped off Janvier but kept a close watch to make sure she didn't reach for a weapon on her utility belt. Satisfied that she wouldn't, the dog licked the blood off her ear and cheek, picked up the earring in his mouth, showed it resting on his tongue, growled another warning, and walked slowly, insolently away.

Terrified by the encounter, Janvier lay on the asphalt without moving, giving the dog time to disappear. Finally, she got up, crying and shaking, but also angry. Angry at the dog, at herself, at everything.

Now she was late for roll call at the station. She didn't bother to fix herself up.

When she walked into the room with her black eyes, smeared makeup, and blood seeping from her ear and cheek, the guys were shocked, but it didn't take long before they started in on her.

"You look like hell!"

"Don't you know how to put on makeup?"

"What happened, rookie? Did you get ambushed?"

"Sure she did because now she smells like a dog."

"Hey, you're supposed to be catching dogs, not making love to them."

Looking at her tormentors, listening to their inanities, Janvier had had enough.

"Yes, I got ambushed, you sorry sons of bitches," she snapped back, "but I'm going to get the dog that did this. I'm going to make him pay. And if any of you ever mess with me again, I'll make you pay."

Astonished that a rookie, especially a girl, would talk back to them, the guys sat in silence until Fred spoke up.

"Well, too bad you had a rough morning, but I want my doughnut," he grumped, standing up and waddling over to where she stood holding the box.

As Fred reached to take a chocolate-covered doughnut, Janvier grabbed it and punched it against his nose, then smeared the chocolate all over his face. She slapped on a couple more until it looked like he had a coating of dogshit.

Raising the box high and turning it upside-down, she dumped the rest of the sticky contents on Fred's head and yelled, "NO MORE DOUGHNUTS!"

From then on, Janvier wasn't "nice." She was mad as hell. In fact, she was more than mad. She seemed possessed. She drove her van in a fury, roaring from good spot to good spot, poaching the other dogcatchers' territories and breaking their blockades by shoving their vans out of the way with hers.

She brought in more and more dogs, gradually winning the guys' respect but rejecting their new offers of friendship. There was a time when Janvier had wanted to be one of them, but she didn't want that anymore. Now all she wanted was to be better than them, to shame them at being beaten by a woman—a woman who didn't try to cover up the scar on her cheek and who wore only one earring as a reminder of the day that marked her transformation.

She trashed the white shirts and beige slacks that she had worn for work and began dressing in black. She cut her long hair short and spiked it up. Around her neck, she affixed a black dog collar with silver spikes.

Janvier needed only one more thing to complete herself. She wanted the dog that had terrified her, that had humiliated her. In a sense, though, she owed it everything. It had changed her, made her powerful.

She didn't know what she would do when she found the dog, whether she would bring it in or break it to her will and make it her pet, but one thing was for sure.

I'll never relent in finding him.

4

HAPPY VALLEY

Day after day, the sun beat on Whiskers' butt like a rolled-up newspaper as he trudged over hills, shambled along dusty trails and sweated like a dog.

Sure, he could have continued to take it easy at the camp of the hobo dogs, but they just sat around and talked. Nobody got in danger, so there weren't any opportunities to save someone. A hero-in-waiting needed to move on.

After getting the traditional canine farewell from the hobos —"Watch out for the dogcatcher"—he decided to try his luck in a place they said to stay away from, Happy Valley.

They may be afraid of danger, but I'm not.

Arriving in the late evening, he moseyed over to an area that had a patchwork of flat rocks embedded in the ground. Plopping down on a large one, Whiskers rolled onto one side and stretched out his legs as far as he could, letting the tiredness flow out of them.

He was soon asleep on the warm rock.

WHISKERS OPENED HIS EYES. Refreshed, he soaked in the first rays of the sun.

This is the outdoor life that dogs were always meant to lead, not the life of a house dog who gets soft and wimpy, even though I was one and liked it. But I'm a real dog now, living a real dog's life, ready for a real dog's adventures.

Getting to his feet while squeezing the sleep out of his eyes, Whiskers began stretching his neck skyward. In mid-stretch, he opened his eyelids—and froze. Drawn during the night to the warmed-up rocks, hundreds of sleeping rattlesnakes surrounded him.

If Whiskers didn't tiptoe away soon, he would be twitching his way off to eternity, a furry sack bloated with poison. As he took a few soft steps, a head sprang up—big, ugly and triangular.

Staring at Whiskers, the viper swayed slowly, hissing and vibrating the hard segments of its tail in a death rattle.

Not waiting for the snake to finish sizing him up, Whiskers leaped forward and as high as he could, hoping to surprise the deadly reptile by sailing over it.

At the top of his arc, Whiskers glanced down, catching a glimpse of the surprised viper striking awkwardly upward and backward.

Yikes! What if he bites me in the ying-yang? Do I die or does just it die?

Then...

AAAAAAHHHHH! HE GOT ME!

Yes, the rattlesnake nailed him.

The bite, however, wasn't in the wang or on the stomach or even a leg. Instead, the snake had struck Whiskers with one fang that bounced off a back toenail.

He landed hard on a sleeping rattlesnake. Whiskers jumped off and bounded over another sleeper, followed by more bounds on top of and over stiff reptiles until he got clear of the wretched, legless, slithering abominations.

Gasping from fright and exertion, Whiskers collapsed at the knees as his surge of adrenaline dissipated. Struggling over to a fallen tree, he found it was hollow and crawled inside to hide until he could regain control of himself.

WHISKERS' legs flailed about, banging into the sides of the log. In his dream, he was trying to fight off waves of hissing snakes slithering toward him. He woke up panting and wild-eyed, but the hissing didn't stop. It became louder, turning into an angry buzzing.

Oww! Something stung him in the side. OWW! Another in the butt. Whiskers craned his neck to look back. Bees were flying from a nest deeper in the log and landing on him.

Oh, no! Are these killer bees?

That's when Mother Nature spoke directly to him: *"GET UP, FOOL! RUN!"*

Clawing wildly on the bottom of the log while banging his head on the top, Whiskers scrambled out with the bees trailing after him.

As he ran, a bee flew past his eyes, heading for his nose. Whiskers watched cross-eyed as the bee came in butt-first and, phfffft, zinged him in the shnozz, sparking a new shot of adrenaline that sent him flying until the bees were far behind.

Finally stopping, exhausted, Whiskers felt stinging pains on his back, sides, gut and butt. But altogether it didn't compare to the pain in his nose, which was swelling bigger and bigger and still bigger.

He had a new, devastating concern.

What if my nose explodes?

He wouldn't be able to sniff out danger or decipher the information in the aroma from other dogs' butts or find the spots of pee that dogs left as their calling cards.

Or what if it doesn't explode and stays swollen like a big pile of poop?

Then he would be a laughingstock. No matter how great a hero he was or how spectacular his deeds, his nose would always be the first topic of conversation, like it was for that French fry guy that Mr. Professor talked about, Seeanose de Birdbath.

A WOUNDED DOG HIDES. No point in giving malefactors an easy target.

So Whiskers had lain hidden in a tall patch of sunflowers until his nose recovered from the bee attack, shrinking back to its normal size and shape with no permanent damage to his olfactory sense.

He emerged on a beautiful, warm day, glancing around for any cowardly snakes or bees who fight in unfair numbers. Seeing none, Whiskers set off with a breeze blowing oh-so-soothingly on his appreciative butt.

After trotting for a while, he noticed that tall, thick bushes off to his right were being shaken by more than the wind. Suddenly, they exploded apart and a bear burst through. He locked eyes with Whiskers.

Whiskers' legs shook like the bushes.

Oh, catshit, what have I done?

Whiskers had violated the first rule of wildlife traveling—keep the wind blowing on your nose so that you can get the scent of other animals, especially the dangerous ones. There's no point in having the wind blow on your butt because it can't smell a thing.

"What's your name?" the bear asked with a big, phony smile.

"My name? Whiskers."

"Oh, really? You're such a cute dog, I think a better name would be Dogchop. Anyway, how nice to meet you. My name is Bonecruncher."

"Is that your stomach growling?" Whiskers asked nervously.

"No, of course not. That's just a little growl that we bears do without thinking. It's part of our nature, just like that little doggy toot is part of yours."

Whiskers had let go a real stinker bred from fear as he recalled what the hobo dogs said about a bear's fart, that it lets other animals know whom he had eaten.

Am I going to be a dog-flavored fart coming out of him?

"When we growl, we bears don't mean anything by it," Bonecruncher continued smoothly, almost apologetically. "Maybe that's what gives us such a poor reputation, which is so unfair when you think about it. Just because we're big doesn't mean we're bad. I'm a really sweet fellow when you get to know me. Why just this morning I was frolicking with the chipmunks and squirrels and rabbits and deer. We had lots of fun. You should join us."

"I still think that's your stomach growling."

"Look, I explained that," Bonecruncher said with a weary sigh. "Besides, you're all by yourself. There are lots of very bad animals around here. Coyotes, wolves, cougars, mountain lions, bobcats. They jump from behind rocks or drop on you out of trees. But I can protect you from all of them. After we've had a good time together and you are ready to leave, I'll lead you out of this place and send you on your merry way. Now, come on over here and let's be good friends."

Bonecruncher had a way with words. Charming and soothing, they exerted a hypnotic pull. Whiskers felt himself falling under that pull, wanting to believe that maybe this bear really was a nice guy, but he shook himself and came out of it.

"No way," he snapped. "Go eat some berries, and you'll feel better."

"Berries? I don't want no stinkin' berries," Bonecruncher grumped as his phony smile disappeared. "What I want is a nice, soft, city dog. That's the best-tasting kind. Come here, right now."

"No. Go suck on a pine cone."

Incensed by the smart remark, Bonecruncher stood up on two legs and glared down at the impertinent should-be meal. Reaching high with his forelegs, he roared and ripped his claws downward, upward and sideways in a fury.

Whiskers stood stock-still, paralyzed by Bonecruncher's size and ferocity.

Although Whisker's body was frozen, his mind cast about desperately for what to do.

To him, Bonecruncher was like a demon in those religious shows he had watched with Mr. Professor. There was a word people used to get rid of demons.

"Heal!" Whiskers commanded. "I said heal!"

The word had no power over the hungry, pissed-off bruin.

Bonecruncher walked upright toward Whiskers, eyes glistening, teeth grinding, saliva dripping.

Whiskers then recalled what Mr. Professor told him about the Survival Channel's advice: Play dead.

Play dead? Just fall over for no reason? Bears might not be as smart as dogs, but they can't be stupid enough to be fooled by that old trick. Besides, he knows I'm not a possum.

There also was: Don't run because a bear can run faster than a man.

But what about a dog? I've got more legs than a human. They never said if a bear was faster than a dog.

"You're thinking about running, aren't you?" Bonecruncher asked as he took another step forward. "Don't try it, you'll just make me madder. If you come here right now, I'll kill you quickly before I eat you. That will be much more pleasant for you. But if you run, I'll catch you and eat you very slowly while you're still alive, little piece by little piece, from your toenails through your entrails up to the tip of your cold, wet nose."

Whiskers considered both options. The first one was a guaranteed dead end, while the second at least gave him a chance, lousy though it was.

"You're too fat to catch me!" Whiskers jeered.

He turned around and took off. Bonecruncher roared, dropped to all fours and ran after him.

Heart hammering and adrenaline surging, Whiskers' paws barely touched the ground. Bonecruncher, however, was extremely fast. The thudding of his paws foretold doom and the sound was coming closer.

Whiskers spied an area full of tall boulders. He ran for it and sped between the rocks, twisting and turning on a zig-zag course, hoping the big bear would get stuck. But when Bonecruncher got there, he didn't bother working his way through the boulders. Instead, he leaped on top of the first rock and bounded across the tops of the others until jumping off the last one and landing with a loud whump.

Despair shot through Whiskers when he heard that sound because it signaled that his effort to lose Bonecruncher had failed. With his heart banging harder and harder to keep his legs going, he began to pray.

Oh, Mother Mary, Jesus, Joseph, Saint Peter, Peter Peter Pumpkin Eater and all the other saints, I really need you to send an angel to save me. Gabriel, Michael, Angeline or Tangerine, any one of them will do.

And behold, an angel did appear. Only its name was Huey. And Huey begat a barricade of trees that issued from the heavens, landing with an earth-shaking crash between the two runners. And lo, the barricade was good because Bonecruncher ran headlong into it and knocked himself out.

Thenceforth, the angel Huey flew away using rotors rather than wings, for it had lost its load of wired logs when the belly hook underneath the helicopter broke from metal fatigue and too much weight.

Whiskers lay spread-eagled, dirt plugging his nostrils from stumbling and then skidding face first through soft dirt when the logs shook the ground. Snorting out the dirt, he rose slowly, feeling heavy thuds in his chest from a still-pounding heart.

He stared at the pile of logs, amazed to see them but fearful that Bonecruncher would suddenly come leaping over the top.

Not hearing a sound, Whiskers walked cautiously to the log pile and peered around it. The big bear lay crumpled against the logs, a line of blood trickling down his face.

Is he playing possum? There's no way I'm getting any closer to find out.

Whiskers turned back around and ran, then trotted, followed by walking and repeating that pattern until he came to a stream and crossed and re-crossed it to hide his scent until he was miles away.

He did not know which angel to thank for saving him, since he had asked for anyone who was currently available. Surely he had a namesake up above.

St. Whiskifer, please pass my thanks along to whomever.

As Whiskers continued on his way out of Happy Valley, the fear of Bonecruncher gradually faded.

That bear needs to be in a zoo where he can get a regular meal.

After a while, something started to bother Whiskers. He had boasted to the hobo dogs, "I'm not afraid of a bear." But he had just met a bear, and he had been very much afraid. His braggadocio had taken a good kick in the rear from reality.

On the other paw, maybe I played it just right. In fact, most dogs would have turned tail and run the moment they saw Bonecruncher, peeing and pooping every step of the way. But I stayed and palavered with the bozo. Not only that, I told the big badass that he was fat and dared him to catch me.

The more he thought about the encounter with Bonecruncher, the better Whiskers felt about it.

Too bad the hobo dogs weren't there to see me stand up to a bear, just like I said I would.

5

DOGGALOOZA

E ven though he had survived Happy Valley, Whiskers
was anything but happy.

*This hero business is tough. Too much running, and the
only one I've saved is myself.*

Not only that, he had been wandering for days with no
opportunities.

The best thing to do was mope. Somehow, making oneself
feel really bad on purpose can feel pretty good.

Trudging along with his head down, Whiskers was doing an
excellent job of feeling crappy until...

"Hey, where are you going?"

Whiskers turned to look. It was an Airedale who had spotted
him poking along.

"Nowhere in particular. Just walking."

"I'll walk with you. What's your name?"

"Whiskers."

"Well, Whiskers, perk up. Come with me. I'm Joker, and I'm
going to make the scene at Doggalooza."

"Doggawhatta?"

"You never heard of Doggalooza? Where have you been? All

the cool dogs go there. Even uncool dogs go there to get a break from Dullsville. It's what's happening, and it doesn't happen long. Just a couple of days and then it moves on. But it's here now, not far away. Cats that don't go to Doggalooza are doggy losers."

"Cats go there?"

"No, Doggy-o, cats don't go there. Cats are not cool. Look, I say cats because that's the opposite of what I really mean. Normally, it's a put-down but I can say it to you because I think you'll stay cool. Hey, I'm not gonna say it to some German Shepherd that I don't know. I may be cool, but I am not a fool."

"I still don't understand what this get-together is."

"Hey, cat, it's a cornucopia of canine culture. Make the scene. Be there or be square. You dig?"

"Dig what? A hole?"

"No. I mean, do you understand?"

"Not really, but if you don't call me 'cat,' then okay, I'll go and take a look at this Doggotloose or whatever you call it."

"Now you're cookin'. Hey, that makes you a hot dog."

"So I'm hot, and you're cool?"

"Now you're gettin' hip, Doggy-o. Let's go."

They walked over two hills and then down into a field next to some woods. Throngs of dogs were at Doggalooza, strolling from one venue to the next.

Whiskers and Joker settled in at the nearest one. American Fido featured aspiring amateurs who barked, howled, yowled and bugled song after song:

"Like a Rolling Bone"

"I Did It My Doggy Way"

"Put a Collar on It"

"I Want to Hold Your Paw"

"Somewhere Over the Fence"

"Bitches Just Want to Have Fun"

"Pawloose"

"Who Let the Humans Out?"

"Trot This Way"

"Barking in the Rain"

"The Dog House of the Rising Sun"

"My Fart Will Go On"

The amateur singers were pretty good, but the best singer was at the next venue. Joker and Whiskers watched bug-eyed as the famous Dogalicious stood up on her hind legs and twisted salaciously while belting out "I Know What Sparky Wants."

"Forget about cool, that's more than hot," Joker said as his tongue fell out of his mouth.

Whiskers didn't say anything. He was staring too hard to talk.

Wow, if this is culture, I want more of it!

After Dogalicious finished tantalizing them, the boys moved on to DoggyMania where teams like the Dog Tags, the Tail Waggers and the Rabid Rascals engaged in a Dog Royal of rolling, tumbling, chasing and fake-biting that stirred the spectators into frenzies of crazed barking, yelping and foaming at the mouth. The championship bout saw good overcome evil when the Happy Ball Chasers beat the Bone Stealers.

Having barked themselves nearly hoarse, Whiskers and Joker were ready for a breather and walked over to a quieter area where dogs were declaiming in various forms of poetic verse. Their first stop was at Pooch's Corner, where they heard a number of poems.

"Pooping in Woods on Snowy Morn" by a Puli:
Whose woods are these
That I poop in?
I do not know
But I sure gotta go

"The Dinner Bell" by a Basenji:
Ask not for whom the dinner bell tolls
It tolls for me
So stay away from my bowl
It is full
But soon no longer will be

"The Garbage Can" by a Belgian Malinois:
January is the cruelest month
For rooting in a metal can
I will show you fear
In a mouthful of asparagus

"The Craver" by a Corgi:
Once upon a midnight dreary
As I wandered weak and weary
Barking from door to door
Quoth each human: "Get your ass out of here!"

"Hey, I liked those poems," Whiskers said as they trotted to the next performance area. "I mean they're not as good as Dogalicious or as exciting as DoggyMania, but they're still, like you say, cool."

"I knew you'd dig it," commented Joker. "Now, look at all these dogs lying so still on the ground. We're at Dogku, which is cooler than cool. It's ice level. So tight, so meaningful. And it was taught to us by a foreign dog, an Akita."

"One of those Jumponknees dogs?"

"Right, but close your mouth so we can hear this cat. Just tap your toenails together when I do," Joker said as a French Bulldog walked to the front of the crowd and emoted:

I pee upon a tree
A thirsty flower observes
Its roots quiver

Then followed a Retriever:
Tongue laps in big bowl
Sweet bouquet hints of mold
Human, no yell, try some

Next was a Springer Spaniel:
Walking through cactus
Jumping over porcupine
Ding-a-ling so scared

When that speaker finished, Joker got off his haunches.

"Whiskers, sorry, but this cat, meaning yours truly, has ku he got to do."

With that, Joker slouched to the front and spoke in a soft, oh-so-cool tone:

I mark my territory
Am I bad? Who is sad?
Are you a cat?

An insouciant, all-around, rub-clicking of toenails signaling subdued ecstasy hailed Joker's dogku, followed by slow and just barely audible too-cool half-howls.

Whiskers had heard enough at Dogku. Joker was in his element, though, and obviously wasn't going to leave. So, Whiskers walked over to Barkoff which, as the noisiest venue, promised to be more entertaining.

Dogs were competing to show the loudest bark, longest bark, highest note, lowest note, bellow style, bugle style, idiosyncratic freestyles, barks to call pups, barks about sirens, fear barks, happy barks, bored barks, barks to get in the house, barks to get out of the house, barks to get attention, barks to protect, barks to scare, and barks for no reason at all.

In addition to pure-noise barking, dogs barked odes to the joy of barking.

A Baltic Shitz:
We bark in the morning
We bark at night
We bark all day
Whether it's wrong or right

A Farffarandou:
If something's there
We'll bark away
If nothing's there
We'll bark anyway

A Wisenheimer:
There's nothing like barking
When there's nothing to do
So we'll keep on barking
Even though it irritates you

A French Bourgeois:
I barked so much
I barked off my head
But I kept on barking
Even though I was dead

Whiskers was thrilled to see so many dogs competing in barking and declaring their love of barking.

How could anyone get tired of great barking like this? It makes me so proud to be a dog.

Barkoff also re-emphasized to Whiskers how barking, keening, whimpering, yelping and growling are far more communicative, authoritative and emotional than the wimpy voices and lame "words" that people use. When contestants belted out spectacular full-throated howls, he was reminded of how pitiful human "singing" was for conveying passion and being heard over long distances.

Wow! Barkoff, and everything else at Doggalooza, demonstrates how absolutely superior our culture is.

"SHUT UP, YOU DAMN DOGS!"

Whiskers and all the other dogs whipped around to see humans stumbling out of the tree line. The organizers of Doggalooza had pulled a real boner by pitching their event near the Geezer Glen Continuing Care Until Dead Retirement Community.

"Where in the hell did all you dogs come from?"

"We moved here for peace and quiet!"

"You ruined the end of 'My Favorite Idiot,' and that's my favorite program, you idiots!"

"I'll cut your balls off unless they're already off!"

"Balls, hell, cut their vocal cords!"

These normally kind old folks were now mad as hell, and they weren't going to take it anymore. Stutter-stepping on spindly legs with bellies bouncing, fallen boobs flopping, bathrobes unwrapping, tallywhackers swinging, hair curlers falling, toupees sliding, comb-overs uncombing and false teeth ratcheting in and out, they were an ugly sight, something no young dog should see.

The sightseeing stopped when a geezer wearing a tattered army jacket raised his arm and fired a pistol while shouting, "I didn't fight in a war to put up with this shit at home!"

Hundreds of dogs began running in every direction that led away from the raging humans. Doggalooza was over.

Far up on a hill, a huge dog watched the frantic commotion. Somewhere in the fleeing mob was his nemesis, the upstart whom hobo dogs had ballyhooed on their travels as some kind of hero with no fear of anything, who had beaten lions, tigers and hippowhatevers and was itching to tear up the big dog with a special fighting system.

The large dog had sneered at what he heard, but he had to do something about this new fighting dog. If he didn't, all of Dogdom—the canine branch of the Animal Kingdom—would say he had become soft and was afraid, and then every other so-called tough dog would be emboldened to come and challenge him. He would never be left alone. He would never know peace. There was only one thing to do.

Scut was going to find Whiskers and put an end to him.

You're a dead dog running.

6

A BITE IN TIME

"There he is, Pops!"

"Got you now, you damn raccoon! You won't be killin' no more of my chickens."

Whiskers froze in the spotlight, caught in mid-sniff.

Moments before the light hit him, he had a suspicion that something wasn't right. Freshly roasted, steaming chicken was sitting on a plate in the middle of a backyard in the dark.

"Look, Pops. He's white! He's an albino!"

"Worst kind of coon, boy. Unnatural as hell and twice as mean."

"Shoot his ass off, Pops!"

Pops raised a .22 rifle while the teenager pushed his grandfather's wheelchair forward and adjusted the chair's spotlight to keep it on Whiskers.

Pwwsshh!!

The bullet went a little off-target, lightly skimming the hair on Whiskers' tail.

Whiskers unfroze himself. If he didn't get away quick, he was going to be a dog without a butt, and a dog without a butt is at a real disadvantage socially. Snatching a chicken leg, he whipped around.

"He's a'runnin', Pops!"

"Push the chair as fast as you can, boy, while I keep a'shootin'!"

Whiskers ran across the yard and headed into the woods. The wheelchair bounced after him, its spotlight veering crazily up to the sky, back down to the ground and then sideways from tree to tree.

Pwwsshh!!

The spotlight had found him.

Pwwsshh!!

Tree bark splintered beside Whiskers.

Pwwsshh!!

He ran faster, letting go of the chicken leg.

Keep it if you want it so bad!

Pwwsshh!!

Suddenly, the ground was gone.

Did he get me?

Whiskers floated in a dark void.

Is this what the end is like?

Time seemed to slow down.

Am I going to a good place? If I am, it's taking forever.

In reality, forever lasted only a few seconds.

Whiskers' unexpected leap into the dark had been off the end of a high dirt embankment overlooking a road. He landed with a whump on something that was both soft and hard. Sniffing quickly, he smelled blood. And death.

Wind blew his ears and whiskers back.

He was in the bed of a fast-moving pickup. Humans were talking.

"Bud, you sure know how to hit those rascals. Three new

dents fer the bumper. I guess you could say we got us a bumper crop, and I'm gonna make us a damn fine stew out of 'em."

The voice was that of an old woman of the backwoods.

"Ma, I can't wait fer some of your good stew and biscuits," said another backwoods voice, that of a youngish man.

The sky lightened, revealing Whiskers' lifeless companions —a turtle, a possum and an armadillo—slow creatures who didn't stand a chance against a truck that was going to hit them on purpose.

The pickup slowed, then turned off the asphalt onto a dirt road full of deep ruts that started the truck jouncing. Whiskers tried to jump out, but couldn't keep his footing with the rapid rocking and bouncing. Sliding in the truck bed, he managed to hook his toenails into a pile of ropes. Just as he pulled himself onto the top of the pile to jump from it and make an escape, the pickup slammed to a stop. Whiskers fell backward, banging his head on the truck's metal bed.

The doors of the pickup opened and slammed shut. Bud and Ma stepped around to the back to get their night's reward.

"Ma! Look. There's a dog in here. Where did he come from?"

"Gollybejiggers, don't that beat all! He must'a fell out'a the sky. Like I always say, heaven will provide."

"Ma, can we keep him fer a pet?"

"Oh, Bud, look at him. He's some kinda sissified dog. He ain't no country dog. He won't last no time 'roun here. Let's just eat him up with these other varmints."

"Ma, will you really eat a dog?"

"When hard times come, I'll eat anythin' that don't eat me first, even without my false teeth. And let me tell you, dog can taste pretty doggone good."

Recovering from the jolt to his head but playing possum with one eye barely open, Whiskers was alarmed at becoming dinner.

A dog is supposed to be a human's best friend, not a best meal.

Bud loomed over the side of the pickup. He looked strong but dumb. He reached into the bed toward Whiskers' neck.

I can't let him get hold of me.

As Bud's hand came close, Whiskers reared up and bit deep into it.

"Ma, he's bitin' the bejesus out'a me!" Bud screamed, jerking his arm up and back with Whiskers still attached.

Whiskers had to time everything just right. Wait too long and Bud would sling his arm forward and down, smashing Whiskers on the hard metal edge of the truck's side panel.

His timing was perfect. Just as Bud reached the apex of his backswing, Whiskers let go and sailed off into the woods, crashing through branches until slamming into a tree with a split trunk and sliding down into its rotted-out crook.

High above the ground, Whiskers scrunched down until only his ears showed, twitching and turning, listening to his would-be chefs.

"Ma, I'm a'bleedin' bad."

"Aw, shush up, Bud. You got enough blood fer two people. It won't hurt you to lose some."

"Well, maybe if you said he coulda been my pet instead of wanting to eat him, he wouldn't'a bit me."

"Boy, you know dogs don't unnerstan' whut people say," Ma scolded. "But I tell you this, if we find him, we'll be the ones doin' the bitin'. Now start lookin'. If he busted his head against a tree or fell in some briars, we can get him afore he runs off."

They traipsed over the ground, looking under bushes and around trees.

All Whiskers could do was wait them out, trying to be quiet while pawing at tree ants crawling around his eyes and nipping at the ones tickling his butthole.

Still searching, Ma and Bud moved farther away from

Whiskers' tree. When he could no longer hear Bud bellyaching and Ma telling him to shut up, Whiskers peered down from his refuge.

It's too far to jump. I'll belly-flop on branches so they can break my fall.

Down he went, landing on a branch with a whump, then letting gravity pull him off while desperately twisting his body to keep from cracking his back on the next branch.

I should have paid more attention to how cats do this.

The ground beneath that branch was sloped. When he landed he didn't hit full on but went down the slope like a roly-poly. Although bruised, he wasn't hurt. Standing up, Whiskers had to get moving quickly.

There was only one safe direction—deeper into the woods, away from Ma and Bud.

7

A FEARLESS GUARDIAN

Forcing his way through bushes, twisting his head to keep branches from scraping his eyes, Whiskers could see more daylight entering the woods, signaling a clearing.

Good. I've had enough of this stuff.

Relaxing, he smugly recalled his escape from Ma and Bud using the fighting, stealth and acrobatic skills of ancient Jumponknees warriors. Mr. Professor had demonstrated their techniques by attacking, hiding behind and rolling off the living room sofa while swigging from a bottle.

Maybe I should hire myself out to some futile lords as a salmononrye to vanquish their enemies. Now, where would I find...

Aahhh! What's that?

Whiskers ducked under a bush and flattened himself, heart pounding, sphincter tightening. Peering through the dense foliage, he caught glimpses of movement, but not enough for identification.

What if it's a lion or a tiger that escaped from the zoo or a television show? They're way bigger than dogs. I'm not saying Mother Nature screwed up, but it's not fair.

Turning around to head back in the direction of Ma and Bud was not an option.

I'd rather die an honorable canine death in deadly combat than be eaten by hillbillies.

Surprisingly, even though Whiskers was upwind, the other animal didn't give any indication of having picked up his scent. Nor did it act with the confidence and intense energy of a lion or tiger. It moved in a slow, haphazard fashion—stopping, turning, moving a few steps, then turning again.

Maybe it's pretending to act lame so I'll show myself. I'm not falling for that old trick. I'm going to hide and sneak up on it like a ninjacompoop.

Getting up off his belly, Whiskers stepped slowly and quietly forward in the brush as his adversary wandered ahead into the clearing.

But the closer Whiskers sneaked, and the more glimpses he got, the more the size of his foe seemed to diminish. It wasn't matching up to the huge adversaries that prowled through his imagination.

So what if it's not full-grown, it's still dangerous. Rather than take it on with my toenails versus its claws, I'll use surprise and speed to zoom past it and get away before it can react.

Then it will die... of embarrassment. Yes, fooled by a dog, proving that dogs are smarter than cats—any cats, even the vicious jungle types. Forget about size; it doesn't matter.

Nerves jangling, Whiskers crouched for a quick start. Pumped up with flatulence from his scared-as-shit intestines, he sprinted forward, crashed through the brush and burst into the clearing with gas shooting out his ass.

With his peripheral sight turned off by fear-induced tunnel vision, Whiskers whipped past the deadly menace without really seeing it while croaking out a few weak growls to keep it at bay.

Nearing the other side of the clearing, Whiskers angled his course for a quick glance back to see if the jungle beast was closing in on him.

What the...?

Whiskers skidded—front legs stiff, back legs collapsing, butt bouncing in the dirt, spinning half-around to stare across the clearing.

Staring back was his potential assailant.

A human toddler.

Are you kidding? All that stalking and power running and gas blasting had been for that?

Whiskers was wary of toddlers, knowing that their natural habit is to walk up to a dog with their mouths hanging open and emitting annoying yells while happily slamming their arms up and down Frankenstein-style on a dog's back.

But this one didn't seem like that. Dressed only in a diaper, it had tear tracks on its cheeks and dried snot from nostrils to lip.

"Dawg-dawg!" the tiny human exclaimed. "Dawg-dawg! Dawg-dawg!"

Oh, catshit! It's coming toward me, but I need to keep moving.

Whiskers took a few steps to continue his escape from Ma and Bud, then stopped.

Would Sassie walk away? No, she'd go look for people who could help, but the only ones around here are dog eaters. Maybe baby eaters too. Forget that.

Besides, who knows what's lurking in these woods? This lost lump needs a protector with the skill, brains and courage to take on any wild beast. Hadn't I just charged out of the forest ready to engage in a battle to the death with one of Mother Nature's monstrous creations? It doesn't matter that it turned out to be a tiny human. My willingness to confront a formidable foe without any hesitation, that's what counted.

Whiskers trotted over to the toddler and barked, "Fear not, I will protect you."

The child understood immediately and hugged him.

This one's not so bad. At least it's not trying to hit me on the back. Oh, no wonder, it's a girl child.

I've got to get her moving, but these things can't even walk in a straight line. How will we make any progress? Normally, I would train her to get down on all fours and trot like a dog, but there's no time for that with hungry hillbillies on the loose.

What about this road running through the clearing? Is it the one that Ma and Bud used? If so, and we go the wrong way, we might both wind up with them chewing on us.

Whiskers took a chance and went to the right. He had no idea how far away help was, and there was no point in asking a person who wore diapers.

As they walked, the little kid patted him gently on the back. Although the mite got the idea that Whiskers wasn't into dawdling, their trekking was slow-going of the slowest sort.

After several hours, daylight started to fade. The little nipper was now yawning. A tired child this young would quit walking and lie down without warning.

We need to get off this road and find a hiding place fast. Who knows if an owl might try to carry her away in the dark?

Whiskers barked softly at the toddler to let her know they were going into the woods. He led the way with the child holding his tail. There was no fear of losing her in the dark because this dirty kid would be easy to find by smell. The problem was that wild animals could smell her too.

Whiskers located a spot with a deep carpet of tree leaves. He pawed at the leaves and worked them around until he was satisfied with the bed he had made and lay down. The little girl lay next to him. Whiskers had no intention of sleeping. He would be awake and on the alert all night.

Snake, coyote or tiger, come and do your best; I'm ready for you.

The temperature began to plunge. Whiskers and the child huddled closer. Soon, the little girl and her fearless guardian were deep into sleep.

"I FOUND HER, I found her! About three miles down the old logging road! And she's got a dog with her!"

Whiskers woke up.

Is that Bud talking to Ma?

Shaking off the sleep, he realized this was a different voice.

"Yes, she's right here. I'll check her out while I wait for you."

Oh, catshit!

Whiskers had made a serious mistake by going for the first batch of leaves and not taking the toddler farther away from the road. A wide opening in the vegetation made him and the girl clearly visible. They had been easy targets for prowling animals and no-good humans.

The man walked toward their bed of leaves.

"Grrrrrr," Whiskers began, giving a low warning to stay away.

The man kept coming.

"GRRRR!!!"

Whiskers jumped up and curled back his upper lip to show his canines. Hair rose in a line down the center of his back as he placed himself between the sleeping child and the man.

"Easy, boy, easy," the man said in a gentle voice. "I'm not here to hurt her. We're going to take her home to her mommy and daddy."

As the man spoke, Whiskers analyzed his voice, attitude and smell.

He seems to be okay, not trying to hide bad intentions.

"Grr."

Whiskers turned down the volume and the menace, keeping just enough to let the man know who was still in charge and who would, if necessary, spring into devastating action at the slightest wrong move.

"That's a good boy," the man said, extending his arm, showing Whiskers the back of his hand, fingers pointing down in a non-threatening position.

Whiskers took a sniff.

Still okay.

He gave a tiny lick to the back of the man's hand to signify slight approval while retaining full rights to withdraw that approval.

"That's a good dog, that's a good dog," the man repeated in a soothing voice. "Now, just let me check our little friend here."

He gave the girl a gentle shake. The toddler moved slightly. The man took off his red-and-black-checked wool jacket and laid it on the girl. Then he turned to Whiskers.

"All she had was a diaper. You kept her from freezing to death. You're a hero."

Hero! I guess I am!

"I'll bet you kept all the wild animals away," the man added.

Yes, I did! The gorillas, bears, leopards, lions, cobras and hippowhatami knew I was on the job, so they were scared to take on Whiskers, Hero of the Perilous Woods.

His reverie was broken by cars roaring down the road, braking and throwing up dust. A dozen people piled out of sport utility vehicles, sheriff's cars and an ambulance. Paramedics quickly examined the girl.

"Considering she was only wearing a diaper on a freezing night, she's in good shape," one of the paramedics said.

"You can thank this dog," said the man who found Whiskers

and the toddler. "They were both huddled together. I'm sure his body heat did the trick."

"We'll take her to town to get her thoroughly checked out," the other paramedic said. "You can call the girl's parents and tell them to meet us there."

"You're going with me," the sheriff ordered, leaning down and picking up Whiskers.

As the sheriff walked up to his car, Whiskers spotted the steel cage barrier that separated the back seat from the front.

What? Where is he taking me? Should I jump out of this guy's arms and make a break for it?

The sheriff stopped by the front passenger door and opened it.

"Heroes ride in front," he said, grinning as he deposited Whiskers on the seat.

Whiskers relaxed—somewhat.

Surely he won't pull a fast one and put a hero in the dog pound. Or will he?

8

ON THE UPSWING

"I just want to say that this is uncomfortable for me."

Yes, it was uncomfortable, because Janvier was staring holes into burr-headed, pear-bodied Jimbo Barnes, Manager of Dog Catching Unit No. 9. He shifted uneasily in his office chair.

"I mean, your dad was a good friend and a great dogcatcher. I told him I would always look out for you."

"You did a lousy job of that, didn't you?"

Jimbo's eyebrows pulled together as he rubbed his chin.

"That's harsh. I think you've misjudged the guys."

"It's hard to misjudge people who take pride in acting like jerks."

"That was guy stuff when you were new. They just wanted to see if you fit in."

"Yeah? Well, I fit in just fine now. I grew my own set of balls so I could bust theirs."

Jimbo's face flushed.

"Anyway, I'm sorry to tell you this, but there's a list of charges against you."

"Like what?"

"Your clothing and your hairstyle are not regulation. Up until now, we've overlooked it because you've been like one of those protected government species."

"Species?"

"You know what I mean, a female. You're our distaff diversity, even though you don't look like one of the staff with those black clothes and the dog collar and that spiky hair."

"My appearance reflects who I am, a dogcatcher who will pursue any dog anywhere."

"Well, that brings up the next charge, which is that you're bringing in way more dogs than everyone else."

"Isn't that my job?"

"Yes, but you're embarrassing the guys, and they don't want to work that hard to keep up with you."

"So they prefer to be lazy, right?"

"Well, that's not really fair. You've got to understand that some slacking off is expected because they've been here a lot longer than you and they've earned it."

"How about this? Since I'm outproducing them by far, maybe I should earn more money and a step up in this organization."

"Oh, no, I can't do that," Jimbo said, shaking his head vigorously. "The guys wouldn't stand for it. I'd have a riot on my hands."

Janvier stared at Jimbo's face like she wanted to spit in his eyes.

"This place operates on the Peters Principle," she said with disdain.

"What's that?"

"The people with peters get the principal pay and the principal jobs."

Jimbo jerked back in his chair, his mouth open.

"Janvier, I... I... I don't know what to say, other than I'm sorry that you don't have one. But since we're talking dirty, I have to tell you that a general overall charge of sexual harassment has been made against you."

Janvier raised her hands palms up as if to say, "Are you kidding me?"

"No, I'm not kidding," Jimbo responded. "You're also charged under a specific sub-category called sex diminishment. As for the general charge, rather than trying to blend in and be inconspicuous, you've gone to the other extreme. You project yourself as such a strong female that it makes the boys very uncomfortable in your presence. Now here's where the diminishment part comes in. They don't feel masculine anymore. In fact, they're depressed about it. That's why they're having to buy that new pill called Upswing to keep their wives and girlfriends happy. But that doggone pill is so expensive it's eating up the budget for the medical plan, and top management is kicking my ass about it. They want that Upswing to go back down fast, and they sure as heck don't want to pay for any sex change operations if the guys can't take it anymore and they start thinking about switching over. Now, since this whole mess got started because of you..."

Jimbo stopped and sighed.

"You used to be such a nice girl. Look, if you tone down your appearance, start buying doughnuts again, and let the boys take credit for a certain percentage of the dogs you bring in, we'll forget everything."

"No, no and no."

"You sure?"

"Yes."

"Well then, what do you have to say to these charges."

"They're ridiculous, and this conversation has firmed up my decision."

"What decision?"

"I quit."

"Oh, no, no, no! You can't do that. Without you, we won't meet our unit goals for the Bring 'Em Back Alive Challenge. We won't get our bonuses."

"Tough. Once I walk out that door, I'll be going after the most wanted dogs in the nation."

"You don't mean...?"

"Yes, the FBDI. The Federal Bureau of Dog Investigation. They've accepted my application."

9

OUR'N, NOT YOUR'N

"There he is!"

"There she is!"

"YAAAAHHHHH!"

People were out of their minds—cheering, screaming, jumping up and down, clapping and waving at the flatbed trailer pulled by horses.

Sitting atop a hay bale on the trailer, Whiskers whipped his head back and forth, arfing non-stop at the spectators lining both sides of Main Street. The toddler, sitting beside Whiskers with an arm around his back, alternated looks of befuddlement and joy.

On separate hay bales were the man who found them, the little girl's parents, the sheriff and the paramedics.

"Whitey, Whitey!" the onlookers shouted.

Whiskers didn't care for that name, but he got stuck with it when the local newspaper reporter had asked the sheriff for one. "Let's just call him Whitey," the sheriff had replied. That's what got printed up on the front page of the Junction News: "Hero Dog Whitey Saves Lost Child."

After that, the sheriff rode Whiskers around town in the

patrol car, showing him off to pedestrians exclaiming, "There's Whitey!" Initially, Whiskers would bark at them to correct his name, but he soon gave up because people weren't intelligent enough to understand anything except English.

The townsfolk quickly decided that seeing Whitey in the patrol car wasn't good enough. They needed a parade—a parade fit for a dog, a hero dog.

Now, here they were, every man, woman, child and canine in Junction cheering and barking their guts out, because they'd never had a feel-good story like this.

However...

"He's our'n!"

"Whitey is our dog!"

Whiskers' ears perked up.

Oh, catshit!

Despite all the cheering and yelling by hundreds of people, his hearing could zero in on specific sounds. One familiar voice was shrill. The other was deep.

Ma and Bud.

As the trailer crawled along, the backwoods duo paralleled it, pushing their way through the crowd.

"Danggit, sheriff, give him to us!" Bud bellowed.

They certainly want their dog food.

"We own that there hero dog!" Ma screeched. "And we wants a reward on account'a him findin' that girl child."

If they get their hands on me, I'm a goner.

Whiskers had to get out of town fast, but there was a problem. The sheriff was such a glory hog that he had been determined to get his share of the public adulation by carrying the hero dog tucked under an arm everywhere he went. Not only that, the sheriff was in a hot race for re-election, and Whiskers' popularity was going to help him win.

He'd probably shoot it out with human criminals while holding me in his arms.

One possibility of getting away was to jump off the parade trailer and scoot through the crowd. That was dicey because there were too many people. Someone was sure to grab him.

What if it's Ma and Bud who get me?

As Whiskers continued to mull over escape possibilities, the trailer reached the far end of Main Street and turned right, leaving the crowd behind.

This is my chance. I'll jump into that cornfield next to the road. The corn is so tall they'll never find me.

Whiskers hopped off the hay bale and headed to that side of the trailer. Suddenly, he was lifted straight up.

"Whoa, hold on there, Whitey," the sheriff cautioned. "Don't get too frisky. We don't want a hero like you to go a'fallin' off this here trailer and a'hurtin' yourself."

The trailer stopped and the sheriff slid off on his big belly, holding Whiskers tightly. Then he settled Whiskers in the patrol car and drove slowly to the office while doing little blips of the siren to draw the attention of parade-goers walking back to their cars.

Once inside the office, the sheriff put some water in a soup bowl.

"Have a good drink. You earned it."

That's all I get? What about a collar with a hero tag?

BAM! BAM! BAM!

The front door shook in its frame.

"Well, open the damn fool thing," screeched a woman.

"I'm a'tryin', but it's stuck," a much-deeper voice said.

Oh, no! It's them.

Desperate to keep the sheriff from turning him over to Ma and Bud, Whiskers turned to prayer. To help his plea cut to the front of the prayer line, he led off with his best approximation of

Latin, *"Ima no domino,"* which was followed by *"Joy to the world and the home of the brave, when fools rush in, I pray me to save."*

Outside, Bud spit on his hands, grabbed the doorknob with both of them and jerked it up, down, sideways, forward and back.

Bam-a-bam-a-bam-a-BAM-BAM-BAM!

The knob came off in his hands and the door flew open, smacking the bowl and sending water across the floor. Eyes bulging, Whiskers churned his legs on the wet vinyl, scrambling, slipping and sliding until banging up against the sheriff's legs.

"Dadgummit, Bud, can't you open a door like a normal person without breakin' the fool thing to pieces? Now I'm gonna have to fill out one of those dadburnit TPS reports to get it fixed."

"We ain't got time fer social niceties," Ma yammered as she and Bud walked in. "We come here fer our dog."

"Now where would the likes of you get a dog like this?" the sheriff spat back. "He ain't a tick hound or some mangy junkyard mutt. This is the kind of dog that folks in the big cities have to pay lots of money for, and I know you wouldn't pay a dime for a dog. If he's really yours, show me your registration papers."

"People around here don't mess with no dog papers," Bud said. "Besides, we found him and took him in and give him a good home."

"Dadblameit, sheriff," Ma butted in, "he's our'n 'cause when you possess somethin' under one of those nine tents of the law —campin' tents, army tents, teepees and whatever other kind there is—it's your'n. That's why the first thing we did when we got Whitey was stick him under a teepee, makin' him bonafide and there's nothin' you can do about it. That's not all. He saved that girl child, so we're here to claim our reward. And it better be a big 'un."

"I don't believe this is your dog," the sheriff argued back, "and he ain't no ordinary dog anymore. He's a hero of the town. As the sheriff, I now deputize Whitey as the official K-9 patrol dog of Junction. Don't give me no more guff about him or a reward, or I'll have cause to lock you both up. So, you all might as well git."

Wow! The sheriff made me a K-9 dog!

"We'll be back!" Ma railed over her shoulder as she and Bud stomped out the door. "We're gonna get us a lawyer and sic the law on you, Mr. Lawman, and then we're gonna get our dog and our reward. And we're gonna vote you out in the election."

"You two never voted for nothin' in your lives," the sheriff said to their backs, "and you ain't gonna get nothin'."

Whiskers' head drooped.

He knew from watching shows with Mr. Professor that riled-up hillbillies don't know when to quit and that lawyers find ways to get people what they want even if they don't deserve it.

Rats! I was looking forward to patrolling this town as a K-9 hero, but it's now too dangerous for me to stay.

"Chester, I'm a'fixin' to get somethin' to eat," the sheriff said. "You take good care of Whitey while I'm gone."

Chester was the deputy. Dumb as a broomstick.

"Don't let nobody have him," the sheriff warned. "In fact, lock him up just in case those fools think they can rush in and grab him. I wouldn't put it past 'em for nothin'."

As the sheriff left, Chester shoved Whiskers into a cell and locked it.

Glum, Whiskers flopped on the floor, rested his chin on his front paws, and watched the deputy pick his nose while taking a comic book out of a locker.

He perked up when Chester blocked open the front door to let in fresh air. The deputy sat down at the sheriff's desk with the comic book and began air-mouthing the words.

Whiskers got up, walked to the cell bars, pushed his muzzle partway through and growled.

Chester looked up from the comic book.

"Whut you growlin' at me fer?"

Whiskers raised his upper lip to show his teeth and snarled in the kind of menacing tone that says, "I want to tear you up."

"Dawg, you done gone stupid," Chester said, scowling. "You must need a rabies shot."

Whiskers barked, stood up on his hind legs and threw punches at the air.

"Wh-wh-whut the..." Chester stammered. "Is you a dawg or is you one of them boxin' kangaroogoos?"

Whiskers barked louder and threw more punches aimed at the deputy.

"Dang, is you a'wantin' to fight me? Heck, I'll fight ya all day long and into the night. I don't care if ever'body in town thinks yore some kinda hero dawg, 'cause I don't like yore sassiness. So if ya wants to fight, and not bite, I'll take ya on, 'cause I knows some boxin' myself."

Barking enthusiastically, Whiskers nodded his head up and down.

"Well, I'll be, yore pretty dawg-gone smart. I guess I'll just hafta knock that smartness right out'a ya," Chester said with a smirk.

He unlocked the cell door, stutter-stepped his way inside like a boxer and put up his fists.

"Come on, ya sissy dawg, let's get it on. Fair fight. Show me what ya got."

Whiskers lowered his front paws.

"Hey, whut ya doin'?" Chester asked, frowning. "Quit droppin' yore dukes. Put 'em back up, dawg."

Instead of putting them up, Whiskers put his dukes on the ground, shot between the deputy's legs and ran out the front door.

"Run, ya little pecker!" Chester squawked. "I knowed ya wasn't no hero. Yore a coward!"

Whiskers had no time or concern for the bitter words of a fool as he tore down the sidewalk, weaving around the legs of pedestrians.

"Hey, there goes Whitey!"

"Look how fast he's runnin', like a wonder dog."

"I'll bet he's goin' to save someone."

Yes, me.

10

BOXCAR BADDIES

Sprinting down the sidewalk, Whiskers heard the chuffing sound of a locomotive.

Taking a left at the next intersection, he charged toward the train station. It didn't take long to get there because the town was small and he was fast, especially when someone might be after him.

The front door of the station was open and so was the back door. The train was leaving. No one was there to see his escape. Junction would never know where he had gone.

Whiskers shot through the front door and out the back. Luck was with him. The train was hauling empty boxcars, and their doors were open. He never broke stride. Nearing the edge of the platform, he leaped up, flew over the gap between platform and train, and sailed into a boxcar. Landing on all four paws, he skidded across the metal floor to the open door on the other side, stopping just before going over the edge.

Whoa, that was close, but a cat couldn't have done any better. Now, I'll...

"WHAT THE SHIT?"

"Where in the hell did that dog come from?"

"Son of a bitch if I know. He just flew in here like some goddamn white angel."

"That piece of shit almost fell out the other side. Go kick his ass out the rest of the way. We don't need no damn dog in here."

The speakers were two men. One was short and chunky. He was sitting against the wall at one end of the boxcar. The man beside him, tall and skinny, handed over a bottle and stood up.

Perched at the edge of the boxcar door, Whiskers turned around to see them. They were nasty-looking with scraggly, greasy hair and clothes spotted with dirt. Their language was foul and so was their body odor. Everything about them was wrong, menacing.

"Like I said, give his ass a good kick out the door so he can keep on flyin'. We got business with that gal over there," said Chunky, grinning and taking a swig from the bottle.

Whiskers smelled whiskey.

And something else.

More humans.

He twisted his head to look at the other end of the boxcar. A girl in her mid-teens was scrunched in the corner, her knees pulled up tight to her chest. She had a boy with her, probably about eight or nine years old. They looked terrified, and Whiskers could smell their fear.

"Hold steady, dog. I'm goin' to kick you like a football," Skinny said, laughing as he approached.

Whiskers knew all about footballs and how they got kicked. He had no intention of letting that happen. In reply, he growled to convey the message, "Don't come near me."

The man stopped, taken aback. He hadn't expected this average-size dog to give him a problem.

"Shit, I ain't scared of you," Skinny said after a pause to size up Whiskers. "Now you're really goin' to get it."

Whiskers knew this was his last opportunity to leave without chancing a hard kick to his face. All he had to do was jump out of the slow-moving boxcar, roll down the grass embankment and be on his way.

He took another look at the girl and boy. The smell of their fear was overpowering. If he left, something very bad would happen in this boxcar.

Whiskers leaped at Skinny and bit him hard on the closest ankle.

"Oh, my God, he's bitin' me!" Skinny screamed. "He's bitin' the hell out of me!"

Skinny shook his leg hard and fast, but Whiskers remained attached, going forward and back, side to side, up and down. Desperate, Skinny leaned over to grab him, but Whiskers let go and ran to the kids' end of the boxcar.

"Damn, I'm bleedin' like a pig!" Skinny wailed. "That dog bit the fool out of me."

Skinny limped back to his end of the boxcar, blood dripping from beneath his pants leg.

"That ain't no big-ass dog. Why did you let him bite you?" Chunky asked scornfully, taking another swig of whiskey.

"He surprised me. He's too fast. If you want that dog out of here, you get him out," Skinny said, sniffling and wiping a tear.

"All right, I'll take care of him. I'm goin' to bust this bottle on his head. And then I'm goin' to get what I want."

Chunky pushed himself up, wavered in place for a few moments, then began lurch-stepping across the boxcar. Whiskers ran to place himself in the man's path, barking non-stop.

Staring at Whiskers, Chunky hesitated, then turned back.

"Hell, she ain't pretty enough to make it worth gettin' bit," he said.

"Aww, we was goin' to have some fun," Skinny groaned, "but that damn dog has spoiled it."

As the train rocked on, Chunky and Skinny stayed at their end of the boxcar, while the girl and boy huddled with Whiskers, petting their newfound friend. Whiskers never stopped watching the two men. Occasionally, he would give a low growl to let them know that he never slept and he always had his eye on them.

After an hour, the train slowed down at a curve on a steep grade. The two bums slid out, keeping a wary watch on Whiskers in case he was tempted to give them a parting bite in the butt.

Until then, the girl and boy had been too scared to speak.

"Oh, thank you, doggy. That man said you are an angel from heaven, and you truly are," the girl said. "This had been our boxcar all to ourselves. Then they snuck in at the last stop."

"You're on the road just like us," the boy said.

They told him how they had lost their parents in a car crash. The state was either going to put them with an alcoholic aunt and uncle or split them up in foster homes.

"We knew our relatives didn't want us. If we went to foster homes, we would never see each other again. So, we ran away from the juvenile hall," the girl explained.

"Oh, gosh, we forgot to introduce ourselves," she said. "My name's Tracy, and this is my brother, Ricky. What's your name, doggy?"

Whiskers barked his name, but, of course, they didn't understand it.

"Look at his whiskers," Ricky said. "Let's call him Whiskers."

"I like that. You don't mind us calling you Whiskers, do you?" asked Tracy.

Whiskers couldn't believe it. Somebody finally got it right. He shook his head side to side to show that, no, he didn't mind, and then up and down to show, yes, he liked it.

11

CANINA NON GRATA

"Look, there's a circus," Tracy said.

"Let's go see it!" Ricky enthused.

"We don't have the money. Anyway, it doesn't look like it's open yet."

With their train stopped for the day at the town of Newberg, there was no point in sitting in a hot boxcar. Lowering themselves and Whiskers onto the ground, they walked away from the train yard and across an empty field toward the circus. Entering the grounds, they mingled among scores of workers hustling to arrange the living quarters and put up the tents, concession stands and sideshow.

"Go on, move out of the way!" ordered a sweating worker carrying two sledgehammers as he brushed by Ricky and aimed a foot at a backpedaling Whiskers. "You want to watch, come back later and buy a ticket."

"Wow," Ricky said, "he's sure grouchy. I thought circus people were nice."

"Honey, don't mind him. He's just got a hangover," came a voice from behind.

Everyone turned around. Standing before them was a woman with a beard. Whiskers' eyes went as wide as the kids'.

"What's the matter? Haven't you ever seen a bearded lady? That's my job, having people look at me. It beats working like him, and I make good money."

Nobody knew what to say.

"My name is Roxie and you all look tired. Where did you come from? Where are you going? What's your names? Where's your parents? Is that your dog?"

Tracy and Ricky answered with the story of why they had run away from the juvenile hall and how they had met Whiskers and what he had done for them.

"Well, my goodness, you're an honest-to-gosh hero," Roxie said, looking at Whiskers.

"Yes, I am," he barked.

"You kids and your dog are okay," Roxie said. "I'm going to talk with Mr. Jones. He's the owner of this circus. I have no doubt that he'll say you can stay with us."

Roxie was true to her word. She went over to Mr. Jones' trailer and banged on the door. The kids and Whiskers watched him come out and talk to her. Then they saw Mr. Jones wave at them and go back into the trailer.

"I told old Jonesy that if he didn't let you stay, I would shave off my beard. That scared the pee-wadding out of him. So, welcome to the circus!"

That very day, Tracy and Ricky were taken in by husband and wife trapeze artists with two children of their own.

As for Whiskers, he was given the run of the circus. He could go anywhere he wanted. People liked him and shared whatever treats they had.

One day, while making his rounds among the tents and trailers, he stopped short. Up ahead, a troupe of about twenty dogs scampered up and down ladders, crawled across narrow planks, jumped through hoops, and tumbled over and around each other.

This was quite different from the lions' and tigers' practice he had seen the day before. They had gone through their tricks grudgingly, moving as slow as possible while their tamer shouted, cursed, cracked his whip and fired a blank pistol. Whiskers had gotten close enough to hear the big cats' conversation:

"I hate this."

"Me too. I'd like to chew that guy up."

"But then they'd shoot you."

"Yeah, I know. What a life."

Whoa! Not everyone in the circus is happy.

Unlike the lions and tigers, the dogs were a different story. They were in heaven—running, jumping, rolling, dancing, somersaulting, fetching, pulling and hopping. They even barked a ditty as they cavorted:

> *We've all got our ups and downs*
> *Sometimes we're heroes*
> *And sometimes we're clowns*

They couldn't have been happier. One of those happy dogs was a gorgeous West Highland. Whiskers was entranced. He sat down to watch the dogs practice their routines.

"Hey, you. Are you the boxcar dog?"

The dog trainer was talking to him.

"You're the one called Whiskers, aren't you? You came here with the runaway kids, didn't you? You're the one who saved them from the bad guys, right?"

Whiskers barked, "Yes, I am."

"Well, you're obviously a brave dog. I'll bet you're also a smart one."

"Yes, I am," Whiskers barked again.

"Tell you what," said the dog trainer, "why don't we see if you can pick up some of the routines. Maybe we could work you into the show in one of the next towns down the road. Would you like that?"

"Oh, yes!" Whiskers barked, pulling back the corners of his mouth to do his best impression of a human smile.

He relished any chance to show off, to prove that he was smarter and better than all others. Besides, who wouldn't want to get closer to that cute West Highland?

"Okay, let's give it a shot," the trainer said.

He began by teaching Whiskers some of the simpler tricks and routines. Whiskers got them right away. Whenever other circus people walked by, the trainer would holler at them, "Hey, look at my new performer, Whiskers. He's a sharp cookie; he really latches on to this stuff."

Then came a dress rehearsal. The trainer and some helpers began putting costumes on the other dogs.

Why are they doing that? Dogs don't need clothes. We've got fur. It's a heck of a lot more comfortable.

Then they came for him.

First, a worker put a tiny, pointed yellow hat on his head.

"I don't want a costume!" he barked while jerking his head around, trying to make the hat fall off.

"Oh, come on, don't be so hard to deal with," said the helper. "All the dogs love to dress up."

She picked up his jerking front legs and forced them through holes in a yellow jacket that had red and blue circles on it. Because Whiskers was white, makeup would show well on him, so she put blue eye shadow above and below his eyes and hot-pink blush on his whiskers to give him rosy cheeks.

"You are darling!" she said.

He was mortified.

Whiskers clamped his teeth on the jacket.

I'm going to pull this thing off and then go find a nice pile of dried zebra doo to scrub this mess off my face.

"No, no, no! You can't be in the dog act if you pull that off."

Whiskers didn't want to get kicked out, so he stopped barking and wriggling and resigned himself to wearing his clown outfit.

In time, the dress rehearsals turned into the real thing—performing with the other dogs in front of hundreds of people. Everyone cheered and applauded the clever act because they enjoyed dogs who could actually do something besides sleeping all day.

Aside from dressing like a miniature clown, Whiskers loved being a part of the dog act. It let every bit of the ham in him come out.

Of course, the other benefit was being close to the West Highland. Her name was Cindy. She liked Whiskers, particularly because he wasn't really a circus dog. He was different—an adventurer, explorer, hero, a dog who had seen and done things that no circus dog had ever seen or done. His world was not tied to railroad tracks and canvas. His stories made the circus seem small and the world outside it big and exciting.

"Tell me more, Whiskers. Where else did you go? What else did you do?"

That's all Whiskers required to start another long-winded tale. After running out of real-life adventures—in which he was always the hero, no matter what had actually taken place—he felt the need to invent more to keep his admirer admiring him.

"Did I tell you about the time I fought the mighty hippowhatabigbottomus?"

"No, what is that?"

"It's a ferocious animal that has killed more people than all the bears and wolves combined. That's why human cities are so big; the hippos scared all the people out of the woods. You're lucky you don't have any of them in the circus because they are so big they would trample the giraffe and the elephant. They have to be kept in zoos, which are extremely dangerous places. Only the fearless, like myself, are allowed to enter to keep them under control."

"Oh, wow! If I ever left the circus, I'd want you to protect me."

"You don't have to worry about that. Nothing will bother you while I'm around."

Cindy was perfect for Whiskers. The more he talked and she listened without interrupting, the more he wanted to be around her.

With Cindy by his side, life in the circus was wonderful, except for one problem. It bothered Whiskers that he was lost in the crowd of the other dogs. There were so many that he didn't stand out in any way. He was just a rookie, taking part in the simpler tricks and routines. When it was time to execute complicated patterns learned through years of practice, he would sit on a bench while other dogs shone in the spotlight. They got the admiration he craved.

Whiskers knew there was one way to elevate his standing among the dogs. Like Mr. Professor, he could display his superior knowledge. Compared to him, these circus dogs were hillbillies. Sure, they could cross tightropes, walk upright on their front paws and ride galloping horses, but other than that they didn't know anything. It was time for Whiskers to let the others know what was what and who didn't know what from squat.

He took action one day after a long rehearsal. The circus dogs were idly licking themselves and each other prior to taking a good nap.

"I've been to school," Whiskers suddenly announced.

"School? What kind of school?" asked Mimi, a Pomeranian.

"I know where he went. He went to obedience school," smirked Odie, a Corgi.

That smart-aleck comment got all the dogs laughing.

"Obedience school is for babies," chimed in Rocky, a Rat Terrier.

"Yeah, obedience school is where they send losers," snorted Booboo, a Pug, who finished his statement by letting out a particularly musical doggy fart.

The other dogs howled. They all started squeezing out farts, trying to top the pugnacious Pug.

Whiskers was furious. This wasn't going the way he had planned.

"No," he retorted, "I didn't go to obedience school. I was too smart for it. I went straight to a university."

"What's a university?" asked Candy, a Poodle.

"It's a special school where only the smartest dogs and people are allowed to go," Whiskers said.

"You're a liar," Rocky snarled. "People don't let dogs inside their big buildings. The only school they go to together is obedience school, and that's to teach dummies like you the simplest tricks in the world—sit, stay, come. Real baby stuff."

"Oh, yeah?" Whiskers growled back. "You're the dummies who don't know anything except how to run and jump around in circles until your noses get stuck in each other's butts. I could learn all of your tricks if I wanted to take the time and then make up much better ones of my own."

"You're dumber than a cat," squeaked Pipsqueak, a Pekingese.

Uh-oh. That did it. The ultimate insult. And it came from a Pekingese, of all dogs.

"Oh, yeah?" sneered Whiskers. "Let's see who's dumb. I'll ask you the type of stuff I learned at the university. First question: Who's the smartest bear in the world?"

The circus dogs looked at each other quizzically.

"I don't hear any answers, so I guess I have to tell you. Yogi Berra, of course."

The dogs didn't feel too bad about not knowing, because that bear wasn't in their circus. Still, as the next questions rolled out, only silence would follow until Whiskers eagerly supplied the answers, becoming haughtier with each one.

"Who has claws, but no paws? Answer: Santa Claws."

"What would we have if cats took over the world? Answer: a cat-astrophe."

As the quiz went on and on, the circus dogs were no longer laughing or farting or snarling. Often, they didn't have a clue what Whiskers was talking about. Maybe he really did go to school with people. He seemed to be even smarter than the trainer.

"Okay, okay, okay! You made your point," Pipsqueak squeaked. "Just stop your yapping. You're hurting my ears, and we're missing our nap time."

"All right," Whiskers snapped, "but don't start with me again, or I'll recite the entire Bicyclopedia Titannica. Oh, by the way, I also have a good idea about where to find the Big Bone."

"If that's so, why are you hanging around here?" asked Luna, a Papillon.

"Well, this is just a rest stop on the way."

"Hah, you're not looking for anything," said Booboo. "You're just a big phony."

Shaking their heads, the circus dogs turned their tails to Whiskers and lay down to rest and forget the whole belittling episode. Simmering mad, Whiskers went off by himself to lie under some bleacher seats. Cindy trotted over to join him.

"Where did you learn all that, Whiskers?"

"I went to school where Mr. Professor taught—LBU."

"What does that mean?"

"Lame Brain University. He had a lot of other special names for it because it was such an important place. That's where I got my dogtorate degree."

"What's that?"

"It's a special piece of paper that's given only to dogs and people who are smarter than everybody else."

"Whiskers, could I go to LBU?"

"No," he answered, "you're a circus dog just like the rest of those dummies. Circus dogs stay in the circus because they aren't smart enough to do anything else."

Whiskers knew Cindy was trying to be nice to him, and he shouldn't have answered that way, but he was still fuming from the disrespect shown by the other dogs.

"In fact, you're lucky that I'm even talking with you. I really didn't want to let you and the other dogs know how much smarter I am, but there's only so much humility in me when the quality of my mercy is strained."

Cindy didn't say anything. She got up to walk away.

"Where are you going?"

"Away from you," Cindy replied sadly. "I thought I liked you, but I don't think I do anymore."

After that, Whiskers was pretty much canina non grata among the other dogs. Rather than spend his free time with them, he wandered around the circus taking in the sights, but they didn't excite him as they once had. Even the pungency seemed to have gone out of the smells. Now he knew what humans meant about being in the doghouse.

"Hey, you, dog. Come here."

The voice was grouchy and unpleasant.

Whiskers looked around. He saw the elephant staring at him.

"Who, me?"

"Yes, you. You are a dog, aren't you?" the elephant asked crossly.

Hmm, what's rubbing his big butt the wrong way? Maybe he's got a giant hemorrhoid.

Being curious, Whiskers started to trot around to the elephant's backside to see if anything was sticking out. It might cheer him up to know that someone else had a bigger problem than he did.

"Where are you going?" snapped the elephant. "Get back around here where I can see you. It won't be my fault if you get stepped on."

Whiskers was disappointed that he didn't get to take a look, but it seemed wiser to stay on the elephant's good side rather than trying to sightsee on his backside.

"What do you want?" Whiskers asked.

"You look as bad as I feel. What's with that hang-dog expression?"

"The other dogs don't like me. Not even Cindy, and she used to be with me all the time. Now she won't even look at me, much less let me get close enough to nuzzle her."

"Why do you think that is?"

"I don't know."

"News travels fast in the circus," the elephant said. "I heard how you smarted off with the other dogs and how you hurt Cindy's feelings. Maybe you didn't know it, but a lot of the dogs used to say you were okay. Not anymore. Now, everyone thinks you're a jerk, and you walk around looking so sad and feeling so sorry for yourself."

The elephant lowered his head and waved his trunk hard for emphasis.

"You know what your problem is? You think you're something special, so you inflate yourself with self-importance. What's so special about you? Just the fact that you exist? You can't come close to doing what real circus dogs can do. And what's with all that bragging about something called a university? What did you learn that's of any real use? Not much, I'll bet. Did it make you a better animal? I don't think so."

The elephant wasn't through. He had plenty more to say.

"You're unhappy? Give me a break. You could've had it made. Dogs in the circus get to do what they love: chasing balls, running in circles and jumping over each other. It's all brainless and stupid stuff, but it's in your dog nature to love it.

"Not only that, you're walking around free. You've got the run of the circus. In fact, you can leave the circus anytime you want and go anywhere you want. Look at me and the tigers and the lions and the giraffe. We're either chained up or caged up. We've barely got space to turn around, and we don't like doing stupid tricks. You're unhappy? I should hope to die and come back as a dog."

There was a silence. Whiskers cocked his head from side to side and screwed up his face as if pondering the points in the elephant's scolding.

Dogs love doing tricks. He hates tricks. So why does he want to be a dog?

Noting Whiskers' concerned expression, the elephant softened his tone.

"I didn't mean to take my frustrations out on you. Forget that. Just let me give you some advice. Go back to the other dogs and apologize. Be sincere about it. You've got a good life here. Enjoy it. Quit messing things up by trying to be a big shot. It only makes you smaller."

Maybe the elephant's right.

"Could you talk to the dogs for me and tell them I'm sorry for letting them know they aren't intelligent?"

"No, you have to do it, and don't say it that way," the elephant replied, shaking his head in exasperation. "Now go."

Whiskers took a few steps to leave, then stopped.

"May I ask you a question?"

"What?"

"Do you have a hemorrhoid?"

"Why, you little..." was all the elephant said before letting out an ear-splitting trumpet blast.

I think it's time to go. Rats, I really wanted to know. Good thing he's chained up. What a temper.

When he got back to the other dogs, Whiskers tried to apologize.

"I'm sorry you're not as intelligent as I am. If anyone wants to go to the university so they can be like me, I'll help you with your application. And more than that, someday when I find the Big Bone, I'll bring back a piece of gristle to share with all of you."

The other dogs, Cindy included, turned away.

As the days went by, Whiskers' performance under the big top started to drop off. He was dogging it because his heart wasn't in it. Eventually, the trainer gave up on him and took him out of the show.

Aimlessly trotting around the circus grounds soon lost its appeal. Whiskers would see Tracy and Ricky from time to time. They would wave and say hi, but they were caught up in their new life practicing their acts and spending their spare time with the other circus kids. Everyone else in the circus assumed he was happy being a roaming dog, so no one offered to take him in.

Why did I mess things up? This was the best life I could have found. All I had to do was keep my mouth shut.

Then he had another thought.

Maybe it wasn't me, maybe it was them. The other dogs were probably jealous that someday I would have learned all the tricks and created my own and been the star of the whole circus, way above them and the lions and tigers and that wiseguy elephant.

The more he thought about everything, the harder it was for Whiskers to stay. The circus hadn't exactly matched its image. Not all the animals were thrilled to do tricks and perform to applause and cheers. Others were just envious and petty.

He got up early one morning in the dark, hoping to steal away while everyone was asleep. The elephant, however, was awake and saw him leaving.

"Where are you going? Didn't you listen to a thing I said? The answer is not down the road."

Whiskers heard the elephant's words, but he just kept walking, never turned around, and disappeared into the dark.

12

SEEKING FORECLOSURE

P anting hard after reaching the top of a steep hill, Whiskers sat down to behold a beautiful sight stretched out below—rows of houses.

The neighborhood looked clean, orderly and welcoming, a place of respite after days of ambling beside railroad tracks, dashing across highways, traversing creeks, skirting around industrial buildings, and scooting away from shady-looking humans with fake smiles and grabby hands.

I'll bet the folks living in such a nice place have some really tasty handouts. And there must be some decent dogs down there instead of the cliquish, stuck-up kind back in the circus.

Padding down the hill through brush took a while, but Whiskers finally made it into the neighborhood. Skirting around the side of a house, he trotted across the front lawn to the sidewalk.

Strolling along, he noticed that some yards had signs in them. Although Mr. Professor had suspended block letters above his doggy cushion and played Blarney Stone video lessons for him, Whiskers couldn't read human words. They were blobs. Still, some blobs conveyed recognizable meanings in certain contexts. He knew that a sign in a yard usually meant some people would be leaving and new people would be arriving.

The signs in this neighborhood, however, didn't have the usual two short blobs in big letters. Instead, they had one long blob. Also, their front yards weren't as neat as those of other homes. Pocked with brown dead spots, the grass was starving while the weeds were doing just fine.

What's going on? Something's not right.

"Help! Help! Brother dog, help us!"

The sound was muffled, but Whiskers' ears had no problem picking it up. Twisting his head from side to side, he scanned the sidewalks and yards but saw no one.

Then a knocking, a rapping, came from a house to his right.

Staring back at him through a window, half-crazed, banging his head against the glass, a dog yelped, "Help, help, help!"

Whiskers ran to the house. The window had a brick sill about a foot off the ground. He propped his front paws on it and raised himself to see better.

"Thank you for coming," said the inside dog, a heavily panting Weimaraner. "We are desperate."

Whiskers looked past the gray dog into the living room. Furniture had been ripped open and the stuffing thrown about. Walls full of holes were splattered with paint, ketchup and mustard.

Dog and cat food cans were strewn everywhere. The cans were empty, but it was obvious that the food had been purposely thrown all over the beige carpet, leaving it streaked and mottled with brown stains.

To top off the scene, yellow spots of dried piss and piles of dog crap were everywhere.

"Please, brother dog, don't leave us," begged the Weimaraner. "We're out of food, and we drank all the water from the big bowls in the little rooms where people go to hide themselves when they poop and pee. We're burning up in here, and if we don't get out soon we're going to die."

"Who are you, and where are your humans?"

"I'm Bixby, and we don't know. The man and the woman were so nice and kind for a long time, but something must have happened. Instead of leaving in the morning and coming home in the evening, they just stayed home all the time. They became more and more worried. After a while, they were yelling constantly into that ringing thing and ripping up all the stuff they got out of that thing that stands by the side of the street. Every day was tense like that until they tore this whole place up, told us to 'stay,' and left, closing us inside."

"But I saw those things that humans put in their yards to tell other people to come inside. Hasn't anyone come by?"

"Some did, but when they opened the door and saw what it was like in here they slammed the door shut in our screaming faces and never came back."

Looking toward the door, Whiskers saw a Boxer lying on his side on the filthy carpet, not moving.

"Is he dead?"

"No. We tried to turn that thing on the door with our paws, but we couldn't do it. So, we've been running at the door with our heads to see if we can bust it open. Sometimes, though, we knock ourselves out. That's what happened to poor Brutus."

Whiskers slowly shook his head, disbelieving. Mr. Professor would never have done this to him.

"Before we got left in here," Bixby continued, "we used to hear about dogs who died after they sliced their guts open going through windows. We were getting close to the point that one of us would have to sacrifice himself."

"WAAAAH!"

A screaming blob flew from an overturned chair.

"BWAHMM!"

The blob smacked hard against the window.

Startled, Whiskers pulled back.

What the...? Oh, it's just a stupid cat.

A yellow and white, scrawny, rib-showing cat. Rather than being grateful for Whiskers' appearance, it slid down the window to stand on the inside sill, arching its back, showing its pointy teeth and hissing at him.

"Okay, I'll get you dogs out, but not that idiot."

"But Cuddles is our friend. We can't leave her behind."

The Weimaraner licked the cat on its head.

Oh, no. This is worse than I thought. They've gone stir-crazy. It's bad enough that humans with no sense make dogs and cats live together, but it's nuts that a dog would actually want to be with a cat.

"All right, hang on. I'm going to look around to see what I can do to get you out of there. And stop running into the door."

Whiskers backed off the windowsill.

What a bunch of knuckleheads. When their humans tore up the place and told them to 'stay,' they should have run through their legs and out the door. I guess they didn't want to believe that this could happen to them.

Every dog in Dogdom had heard about such situations. Now, Whiskers was seeing such a scene for real, how ugly it could be.

Even though I like people a lot, there's always some who could use a good bite in the ass to make them do right.

Now, it's up to a hero to undo this wrong. But in this case the heroics don't call for barking, biting, chasing or even tracking. This is a job for brains, of which I have plenty because Mr. Professor said that I am the smartest dog in the world.

Whiskers examined the front of the house and both sides, looking for a way in, but there wasn't any.

The backyard, though, had a possibility. The yard ran flat for a short way to a low brick wall. The wall was backgrounded by a slope. A decorative rock garden was partway up the slope.

Taking a running leap, Whiskers landed on the wall, trotted up the slope to the rock garden and got to work. Starting near the base of one of the largest decorative stones, he began digging a trench several inches deep and several inches wide down the slope.

While he dug and moved small rocks out of the way, Bixby, Cuddles and a revived Brutus went to the den at the back of the house. Looking through the locked sliding glass door, they were perplexed by Whiskers' industrious activity.

"What's he doing? Digging for a bone?" Brutus asked.

"I hope not. Surely he hasn't forgotten about us," Bixby said.

"Maybe he's going to poop a lot and is getting ready to bury it like a civilized animal," commented Cuddles.

After a while, Whiskers felt he had made the trench long enough and sat down to take a break. Glancing around, he was high enough on the slope to see past the side of the house and out to the sidewalk where a Scottie was ambling along. Barking loudly, Whiskers told him to pass the word that something exciting was about to happen. The Scottie got right on it, barking non-stop while running up and down the sidewalk, dipping into yards, and crossing the street back and forth.

Good dog. If you want something done right, call a terrier.

Eager for something to break up their humdrum day, barking dogs blasted through doggy doors, scrunched under fences, and ran to get the best spots for viewing. Uninvited cats also showed up, zipping into the backyard too fast to be stopped from climbing into a tree, causing even wilder barking.

After the last spectators arrived, Whiskers sauntered down the incline and jumped off to give instructions to the imprisoned animals.

"Get away from this giant window. I'm going to roll that huge rock at it."

Bixby and Brutus started backing away, but Cuddles jumped

at the glass, extending her claws and yowling. She clearly hated Whiskers for no reason other than being a dog, one that she was not raised with.

"Fine with me, you fish-eating fool," Whiskers growled. "Get ready to eat a big rock."

Alarmed, Bixby grabbed the crabby tabby by the scruff of the neck and lugged her spewing and spitting to the far end of the room. Whiskers turned away, trotted to the low wall and jumped onto it.

Forget the stupid cat, it's showtime!

Making the most of his role, Whiskers walked slowly up the slope to increase his time in the spotlight. Stopping partway, he turned around, lifted a paw to just above his right eye, and tilted his chin up to adopt a heroic pose for the yapping, woofing crowd. Resuming his walk, he arrived at the big stone, turned to face the baying canines and coughed for silence.

All great deeds must be preceded by a great speech. Whiskers was prepared because he had listened to the greatest speeches in human history as Mr. Professor declaimed them while staring with one eye into a bottle.

"Four sore ears ago, Humping and Dumping sat on a wall. He lived in an eggs-is-sensual world. To pee or not to pee, that was his dilemma before all the king's hearses took him away. But I digest. Today, we are gathered on a great field of daydreams because I built it and you did come. You are here to see the undoing of a great wrong. Two of our Dogdom brothers and one lunatic are trapped inside this house without food and water, abandoned by their humans. That leaves us to ponder this question: Do we suffer the swings and sparrows of outrageous fortune cookies or take up arms and legs and put pantyhose on them? Read my quips: You have nothing to fear but getting bathed. Hark, I see a shining outhouse on a hill, from which comes the sweet smell of mess. And now we have the moment I have waited for: Never have so few like the poor Boxer, the Weimaraner and the ignoramus owed so much to just one—namely, me."

Finishing his speech, Whiskers looked over the multitude and saw they were spellbound, wondering what they had just heard.

Pleased with his splendiferous eloquence, Whiskers gave the assembled pooches a grin as wide as he could make it, then bounced jauntily to the rear of the large rock.

He stood up and leaned against it with his front paws, but it didn't budge. He got on all fours and pushed with his head, but it still wouldn't move. Growling at the rock for its obstinacy, Whiskers whipped around to the front, bowed his head to the spectators and dug rapidly under the stone, throwing dirt as far as possible to make everyone think that all the scurrying around was a planned, comical part of the show.

Panting from the exertion, he hurried once again to the other side, desperate to avoid being humiliated. Whiskers backed up to the rock, scrunched down and jammed the nails of his paws into the dirt. Suddenly, he straightened his legs and jerked backward, pushing against the rock until every muscle in his body trembled and his legs wobbled. Straining more than he had ever done, even when constipated, Whiskers felt the stone begin to shift until it reached the tipping point. The ponderous rock dropped into the guide trench, rolled slowly forward for one revolution, then another and another and another, picking up speed each time until it thundered down the hill.

The spectating dogs went wild, hopping about and barking madly at the onrushing stone as it hurtled onto the wall, shot off it and flew over their heads.

WHAAA-BOOM!

The sliding glass door exploded in hundreds of flying shards. All the dogs in the yard flattened on the ground to avoid being cut. Inside, the cannonballing stone smashed the tiles in the floor of the den as it bounded across the room straight at the frightened trio of animals who skittered frantically to get away from it.

When the noise and destruction stopped, Bixby and Brutus emerged unhurt from the house. The canine spectators were so astounded by the successful rescue that they ignored Cuddles as she zipped past them to climb the tree and join the other felines.

While some of the spectator dogs eagerly licked the ears and sniffed the butts of the freed captives, the others began a tremendous delirium of barking, woofing and howling. Not only had they been entertained, they had been amazed. They had seen a dog use his brain to do something that none of them would have ever thought to do. His rescue of their canine brothers was a story that would be passed from dog to dog, whenever two or more gathered at fire hydrants and garbage cans, in boarding kennels and dog parks.

As time went on and word of the rescue spread throughout Dogdom, the story became bigger and more elaborate. Each retelling was loaded with new embellishments. Thousands of dogs swore that everything they said was true because each claimed that he or she had been there on the scene and witnessed it firsthand.

—*"Those poor dogs were dying. We could see them gasp their last breaths and fall over. Whiskers ran and jumped off a hill so fast that he flew through the air like a bird, breaking the giant window with his head. Then he dragged those dogs out and jumped up and down on their ribs to get them breathing again. He even pulled out a cat and bit it in the butt to wake it up."*

—*"The house was on fire. The Dalmatian that came with those humans in the strange clothes was too scared to do his job, so Whiskers grabbed the water shooter from him and ran inside to save the dogs and their stupid cat friend. When he brought them out, his own whiskers were burned off and his back was on fire, but he just rolled around on the ground to put it out and then all the humans cheered and put him up on their giant car and threw the Dalmatian off it."*

—*"The dogs were being held prisoner by a bad human who was probably a cat lover. The people who were supposed to go in and get the bad guy were hiding behind their cars doing nothing, but Whiskers wasn't afraid. He climbed a tree while knocking cats out of the way, sprang from a branch onto the roof and jumped down inside that thing people make fires in. Then we heard ferocious growling and awful screaming, and the human ran out of the house with Whiskers attached to his rear-end, chewing on a butt burger."*

One listener, however, was not impressed by the recounting of such marvelous feats. More than anything, Scut was irritated by the gullibility and irrational exuberance of dogs who wanted to believe them.

Dumbasses all. But they are useful idiots.

Ever since the chaos that ended Doggalooza, Whiskers' trail had been more than obscured. He seemed to have disappeared. But with his rescue at the foreclosure house as the new talk of Dogdom, he was no longer just another average dog. He was being noticed, pointed out and fawned over everywhere he went.

To pick up the trail of the cocky terrier, Scut went to the now-infamous House From Dog Hell. Once he learned which direction Whiskers had gone from there, he trekked from one starry-eyed dog to another, listened to their excited recitations of having met Whiskers in person, and sniffed out specific repeating molecules to construct a scent profile of his prey.

After leaving his latest unwitting informant, Scut mused about the irony of Whiskers' celebrated deed.

By saving some dogs and a cat from death, he's ensured his own.

13

MOST WANTED

"Aarf, aarf, aarf!"

"Woof, woof, woof!"

"Bow, wow, wow!"

Canine greetings were sounding everywhere, but dogs weren't making the racket. Human beings were good-naturedly saying hello to one another in Chugalot, Nevada, as they strolled on the sidewalk leading to the massive facility formerly known simply and fondly as Domezilla. They ignored the irony that the city had sold the naming rights to a cat products company and that the National Dogcatchers Convention was being held in Mandy's Hairball-Free Domezilla.

"Ruff, ruff, ruff!" happily barked an enthusiastic greeter at the entrance to the mammoth building.

"Grrrr," Janvier snarled back as she stepped through the doorway.

It was the new agent's first time at the convention and her reward for being the top student in her basic training class. She had graduated with honors, earning the highest academic distinction granted by the Federal Bureau of Dog Investigation —Summa Cum Dogged.

Inside the convention hall, the atmosphere was of one big party. Dogcatchers let out howls as they tried on baseball caps that had plastic dog faces and plastic dog ears sewed onto them.

Other attendees wore T-shirts they had bought and pulled over their regular shirts to display canine-oriented humor:

"The best dog is a hot dog."

"I love dogs, so why do they run from me?"

"I catch dogs for a living, and then I go home to one."

Janvier scowled as she passed the Good Licking booth where guys were getting their cheeks licked by hot brunettes and blondes for a dollar. Two dollars got an ear licked.

Farther into the hall, she came across a stage with a singing group called the Dog Treats bellowing out "It's Hard To Be a Dogcatcher":

It's hard to be a dogcatcher
When the sun is burning hot
Or the wind is freezing cold
And my nose is dripping snot

It's hard to be a dogcatcher
When people get out their guns
Or they sic a Doberman on me
So he can bite me on my buns

It's hard to be a dogcatcher
When no one understands
Although we enforce the law
We love our animal friends

It's hard to be a dogcatcher
When I start to scream and shout
Running from a Mastiff
Because my pepper spray ran out

It's hard to be a dogcatcher
Watching doggies get away
While men and women chase me
Yelling how they'll make me pay

.... and after each stanza would come the chorus:

I coulda been a doctor
I coulda been a chef
I coulda been a quarterback
Or maybe even a ref

But this is what I chose
The hard life of a fetcher
I serve and I protect
I'm just a... proud... dog... catcher!

Janvier kept walking, even though it meant she would miss the next group, the Pooper Scoopers singing "Oops, I Stepped in It Again."

She did pause by the booth for World Canine Tours. The salesman latched on to her.

"Ma'am, I can tell by your spiked collar that you are a canineisseur, pun intended. A person of your obvious astuteness and sophistication in all things canine simply must take one of our worldwide photo tours. You will see wild dogs of every description in their natural habitats. Sorry, no catching is allowed, so you'll have to restrain your natural impulse to go get 'em. But believe me when I say you'll come home with the most marvelous photographs for your scrapbook. And, for an extra special treat, try one of our Asian tours that feature restaurants where you can sink your teeth into the dog breed of your choice. Now that's what I call payback for all the bites you've taken, don't you?"

Janvier started to respond but stepped aside when a group of loud-mouthed, fat-gutted men with binoculars, cameras and safari vests suddenly swarmed the booth, grabbing trip brochures and pointing at pictures in canine identification books. Their vests were plastered with patches showing the exotic types of dogs they'd spotted in the wild.

Janvier left the bellowing blowhards and headed to the splashiest exhibitor—Dog Pro Shops—to look over the latest gear, including radar for detecting roving dogs by their microchips, drones that drop nets, bitch-in-heat dog calls, and multi-barrel paintball guns with color-coded ammo for marking running dogs as either being extra sneaky in evading capture or so menacing as to require backup. Dogs with lots of paint on them brought big bragging rights when they were finally captured.

Walking some more, Janvier came upon the Dog Bowl Java Bar where dogcatchers were exchanging stories and advice about everything canine—dangerous dogs, high-value dogs, smart breeds, dumb and dumber breeds, unusual hiding places and the best catching strategies.

While sipping coffee, she overheard one group debating whether time was better spent scooping up lots of mutts in rough neighborhoods that didn't care about leash laws or riding through ritzy subdivisions on the off-chance of scoring a rare, imported dog like the Nosferatu from Transylvania, the Louis

XIV Chevalier Limited Edition Sun Dog from France, or the Shaved Face from Burma.

Guys who tried to gain glory with tales about bringing in friendly breeds like Beagles and Labradors were serenaded by the other dogcatchers lifting their chins up, letting their tongues hang out, and starting a mocking chorus of the "whimper"—a high-pitched, so-sad, so-pitiful-me keening sound. The whimpering was especially soulful when one dogcatcher tried to explain why he had such a difficult time trying to corral a particularly grouchy Dachshund.

Other dogcatchers told frightening stories of barely escaping from livid dog owners and even whole families who came charging after them with clubs, knives and baseball bats, cussing and banging on the dogcatchers' vans and firing guns in the air.

Of course, just like in big-game trophy hunting, there were tales about very big dogs—the bigger and scarier the better. As Janvier heard one man say, "When I saw him, I said to myself: You're gonna need a bigger net."

Tired of hearing the braggarts go on and on about their adventures, she finished her coffee and left the java bar. But she did learn something from listening to all the tales, whether true or not: The way to gain real respect was to bring in a dog that was either very special or very intimidating.

The best place to bone up on a likely candidate was at the "Most Wanted" section run by the CIA—the Canine Intelligence Agency. That organization's job wasn't to capture dogs but to maintain a central database for the processing and dissemination of information about canines who had come to the attention of dogcatching units across the nation.

Under a banner with the words "Watch for These," three video screens rotated pictures of ill-tempered dogs who wouldn't be taken without a fight, wily dogs who had eluded all attempts to capture them, and particularly vile dogs who refused to take a bath.

Janvier stopped to check out the display board of "Known Con Dogs" who used good looks and charm to work their way with people who took them in. These canines rejected dog beds and dog food, sleeping only in the humans' beds and eating only the best human food. Afterward, they would pee, poop and throw up at will anywhere in the house while feigning clueless-ness about going outside to take care of their business. At first, people would put up with it because "she thinks she's human." But once the bad habits got really old and the cuteness no longer compensated and people started rolling up a newspaper, the con dogs would pretend to make a stab at doing their busi-ness outside while taking the opportunity to sneak away in the dark and move on to a new victim.

Moving on herself, Janvier noticed that many dogcatchers were winding their way through rows of easels that displayed wanted posters.

She made her way over to a knot of men in the "Up and Comers" area. They were studying a poster about a terrier who had been responsible for damaging a house and causing three pets to run away and be lost. Janvier scanned it briefly, noting the terrier's photo that authorities had obtained from the cell phone of a person in that neighborhood. Average-size dogs, however, didn't especially interest her.

She joined a large crowd gathered around a poster with a somewhat fuzzy photo taken from a restaurant's alleyway secu-rity camera. In relation to a trash can in the picture, the animal beside it was obviously much larger than other dogs. Janvier knew that a huge dog like this could make her reputation, because in this business size always matters.

"What is he?" she asked.

"Who the hell knows," mused a guy. "We can't figure it out. He just looks like a whole bunch of breeds all stuck together."

"What's his crime?"

That brought forth a slew of responses from the group:

"Nothing's been pinned on him yet, other than being too damn big."

"I know anything that big has got to have done something wrong."

"And probably not just one thing. A whole lot of things. And that's a fact."

"Anybody who gets him has bragging rights for a lifetime."

"That's because he's like a lake's biggest fish that no one can catch. Or like that whale, Mopey Dick, the baddest of all."

"I'm glad I don't have a mopey dick," snurked a guy who looked Janvier up and down several times with wide eyes and a big grin.

Janvier narrowed her eyelids and said, "Shut up, Dickless."

Taken aback, Dickless stopped grinning, dropped his chin down to his chest and eased away.

When the crowd thinned, Janvier moved closer to the easel. Since no crimes were listed on the wanted poster, there wasn't much intelligence about the dog other than a few sightings in locations separated by great distances. Obviously, whatever drove this frightening specimen kept it on the move and away from the nets of local dogcatchers. She studied the poster photo intently, using her knowledge of canine morphology to get an idea of the breeds that may have gone into the dog's makeup, which would help her form a profile to gauge its cunning and potential threat level.

"Uunnhh."

A strange feeling, a weakness, enveloped Janvier. She closed her eyes and tried to rub the center of her forehead with her right hand, but her arm fell back. Her entire body was sluggish.

She wasn't in pain, but she felt trapped within herself. The old panic from that day had come back. Breathing in and out slowly, she willed it away.

Looking at the photo again, she knew, deep within her gut, that this was the dog.

They can't catch you, but I will. You'll face justice—either society's or my own.

14

KEEP THE CHANGE

"You need a ride?"

"Rowf!"

The passenger door of the car opened slowly as the driver, a man with a thin black mustache and thick black glasses leaned across the passenger seat, straining with his right arm and fingertips to push the door a little farther out.

"Hurry up, hop in. The name's Jasper and I haven't got all day."

Whiskers eagerly jumped through the opening and onto the seat. Getting rides beat walking along roadways in his search for someone new to save after his glorious triumph at the House From Dog Hell.

Of course, an inoffensive-looking dog like himself had no trouble getting lifts from humans bored on long drives.

They liked to complain about their nagging spouses and spoiled kids or gripe about bosses who were complete idiots or rattle on about how high school was either the best time or the worst time of their lives. As a freeloading rider, Whiskers would contribute a woof now and then to pretend that he was interested in what they had to say.

Jasper showed off by tromping the accelerator to spin the rear wheels. Rocks and dirt shot into the air as the car fishtailed, then roared back onto the highway. Barking with excitement, Whiskers stood up on the passenger seat and propped his front paws on top of the dashboard. Wide-eyed at the scenery flashing by, he panted non-stop, filling the car with hot, stinky doggy breath and causing Jasper to lower the windows.

After twenty miles, Jasper took an exit ramp and beelined to a fast-food restaurant. Pulling into the drive-thru lane, he eased the car up to a microphone embedded in the mouth of a grinning plastic cow head.

"Welcome to Grease Burger, where we recycle grease collected from the grease traps of the town's finest restaurants. May I take your order?"

The smell of grease was heavenly. Panting loudly, Whiskers pivoted to land his front feet hard on Jasper's lap, his cheek scrubbing against the man's nose in an attempt to get closer to the aroma coming through the car window. Grimacing, Jasper strained to push Whiskers back so he could order.

"I'd like two Lardburgers with extra grease and a Big Guzzle."

"That's sixty-four ounces, but for another fifty cents, you can super-duper your drink to one hundred and twenty-eight ounces. That's a full gallon, enough to last you at least half a day. Whaddaya say?"

"Uh, yeah, okay. That sounds good."

"What flavor would you like?"

"Strawberry."

"Sorry, we're all out of the usual flavors that taste good. But you can try our new healthy line of government-approved flavors called Taste Buds Sensations: kale, quinoa, arugula or tofu. Plus, we can add a spritz of chipotle, soy sauce or wasabi to tickle your tongue."

"Are you kidding me?"

"No, sir."

"What the... son of a... oh, all right, I'll try plain quinoa just to wash the burgers down."

"Thank you, sir, and drive to the second window."

As the car rolled past the first window, Whiskers watched in puzzlement as a male employee and a female employee stuck French fries in each other's nostrils.

They missed their mouths.

Holding out the bag of food at window number two, the cashier said, "That will be twelve dollars and nineteen cents, please."

Jasper took the bag of burgers and set the gallon-size drink in the ultra-large cup holder. He handed two fives, two ones and a quarter to the cashier.

As she turned to put the money in the register, Jasper scooped up Whiskers and shoved him through the cashier's window, saying, "Keep the change and this stinking animal!"

Laughing wildly, Jasper stuck his head out the car window and panted like a dog at Whiskers, then gunned the engine and sped away.

After staring for a moment at Whiskers, the cashier gently pushed his butt into a sitting position on the counter, slid him to the side and gave him a bag of fries. Later, when a car came through that had open windows, the cashier grabbed Whiskers and pitched him in the back seat as the car rolled away.

Hearing a whump behind him, the elderly driver pulled the car into a parking space, turned off the engine and twisted around to see Whiskers standing on the back seat, staring at him.

"Hey, fella, looks like nobody wants you. I know the feeling. You can stay with me if you like. I'm Jimmy. I'm going to the Big Apple. That's where I live."

The old gent fished a chocolate chip cookie from his bag of food and held it out.

Scarfing down the cookie, Whiskers was thrilled. He recalled that Mr. Professor had called the Big Apple the Big Craphole.

With a name like that, it must be a swell place to live.

So he thought.

15

YOU WALKIN' YOUR MOP?

"Fella, have you been a good boy?"

Whiskers wagged his tail, flopped his mouth open and panted to say, in effect, "Yes, I have."

Of course, he hadn't done anything noticeably good since arriving at Jimmy's apartment the night before, but he certainly hadn't done anything bad like peeing on the carpet the way some dogs do when entering a new place.

"Well, my friend, your reward is going to be a nice walk so we can work off the ham and eggs we had for breakfast. After we come back, we'll pick out a good name for you."

Whiskers spun around and raced back and forth to the door. Not only was he excited to go for a walk in a new place, but he was happy that this man with the sagging, fleshy face and the slow way of talking had taken him in, especially if hot human food was going to be the common fare.

After rummaging through several desk drawers, Jimmy pulled out a worn leather leash.

He doesn't need one of those. I'll never leave his side.

"I used to have a dog. Poor guy, he got real sick and... well, that was a long time ago. I haven't walked a dog in quite a while, but let's give it a try. Please don't pull me. My hands hurt a little bit, and I might lose my grip."

With the leash on, they went out of the apartment and into the street.

Sensing that Jimmy was old, Whiskers walked calmly beside him, taking in the constant flow of people on the sidewalk and the road noise of passing cars, taxis and trucks. Unlike the walks with Mr. Professor during which several passers-by would have something heated to say and Mr. Professor would have something even more vociferous to say back, Whiskers and Jimmy walked in silence, ignored by all the people streaming past them.

That is, until they rounded a corner.

"HEY, OLD FOOL! WATCH WHAT YOU DOIN'!"

Jimmy stopped and sucked his breath in hard as his head jerked back in surprise.

Whiskers' new friend had almost collided with a man in his early twenties walking a gray, muscular, crop-eared dog. Diagonally opposite from Whiskers and a head taller, the intimidating animal locked eyes, growled, and strained forward on its leash, eager to tear him up.

Although physically outmatched, Whiskers growled back. He had an obligation to Jimmy.

This doesn't look good, but maybe everybody growls a little bit and then we all go our separate ways.

"What up? Is that your badass dog? Looks more like somethin' an old fool like you would use to mop the floor. So you walkin' your mop, old man?"

"Please, I don't want any trouble. We're just going for a walk."

"Yeah, you just about walked into us. I need an apology."

"Okay, I'm very sorry that I almost bumped into you."

"That's what you say, old man, but what about him?"

"What do you mean?"

"You apologized, but your dog hasn't."

"He's just a dog. He doesn't understand."

"Understand or not, old man, we goin' to settle this."

"I don't know what you mean. I just want to go home. I don't feel well."

"Feel well or feel like hell, you ain't goin' nowhere, 'ceptin' into that alley right over there, 'cause that's where your dog is goin' to fight my dog. Loser pays winner fifty dollars. You do have fifty dollars, don't you?"

"No, I don't have that much money. Please, just let us go."

"Not 'til Glock kicks your dog's ass and I take whatever you got. Now let's get goin'!"

The man grabbed Jimmy's left arm and pulled hard.

"AAIIEEE!" Jimmy screamed, grabbing at his chest with his right hand.

What the...?

Whiskers snarled, lunged at the man and bit him on the right leg.

"OWW! YOU LITTLE BASTARD!"

The man tried to kick Whiskers with his left leg just as Glock leaped at his canine opponent.

But the man's leg crossed into Glock's path, and the dog's mouth clamped automatically around the first thing it contacted —the calf of that leg, halting it in mid-kick. Totally out of his mind, Glock held on while Whiskers continued to bite the shin of the right leg.

SH-I-I-I-I-I-T! SH-I-I-I-I-I-T! SH-I-I-I-I-I- T!"

Over the man's yelling, Whiskers heard a moan as something heavy fell across his back, causing him to let go of the man's right leg. He scampered a few steps away and turned around.

Jimmy lay face down on the ground, an arm stretched out where Whiskers had been.

"WHAT THE HELL'S GOING ON OVER THERE?"

Shouting and blowing his whistle, a police officer on the other side of the street was holding out an arm to slow down traffic so he could weave his way through it. Before the officer arrived, Glock's owner punched him several times in the nose to break the hold on his left leg.

Running up and seeing Jimmy prone on the sidewalk, the cop spoke into his transmitter to call for an ambulance.

"What happened here?" the officer asked as he knelt and rolled Jimmy over to begin CPR.

"That dog of his attacked us for no reason. When he jumped at me, he pulled the old guy off balance, so the dude falls down and hits his head on the sidewalk. But officer, look at this, I'm bleedin' real bad."

The cop glanced as the man pulled up his right pant leg to show blood seeping through an athletic sock. He did not show the bite his own dog had made.

While an ambulance blared its siren in the distance, pedestrians crowded around the officer to watch his desperate effort to save the old man's life.

Whiskers' canine senses, however, had already told him the condition of Jimmy's heart.

I don't know what the human is doing, but it won't help.

He barked at the officer to tell him that. The cop looked up, scowling.

"Somebody grab that dog."

For several moments, no one did anything. Finally, one woman approached Whiskers. Bending down, fearful that he might bite her, she slowly snaked her hand toward his leash.

Having seen the anger in the cop's face, Whiskers wanted to tell what really happened, but it wasn't possible. He knew he was going to be punished for biting the younger man, maybe even for Jimmy's death.

I said I'd never leave his side, but...

Just as the woman picked up his leash, Whiskers spun and ran, pulling it out of her hand.

16

GOT IT GOIN' ON

Upon returning from lunch to her FBDI office in Ringworm, Pennsylvania, Field Agent Janvier turned on her computer to scroll through the latest news clippings about dogs, looking for anything out of the ordinary.

There wasn't much:

"Dog Inherits Owner's Pension"

"Picking Up Doggy Doo New Path to Riches"

"Hairless Dogs Need the Most Grooming"

"Dog Treat Beats Martha's Cookies in Taste-off"

Except:

"Dog Walking Tragedy Prompts Jimmy's Law"

That seemed promising. Janvier clicked the link.

The news release that appeared gave background on how a despicable terrier caused the death of an elderly New Yorker, horrifying a Good Samaritan and his timid companion dog. A time was listed for a televised outdoor celebration of the hastily passed new law. Curious, Janvier waited an hour, then brought up the broadcast on her office television.

The mayor of New York City had yet to arrive, so the telecast's cameras swarmed around a police officer confronting a

New Jerseyan who had dared to bring a Big Guzzle into the Big Apple. Grabbing the guy in a headlock, the cop plunged the man's head up and down, forcing him to spit out the soda and spill the rest.

Attention switched when the mayor's limo pulled up. Out popped sandy-haired, charm-oozing, slick Bill Dumberg who scampered up the steps of the outdoor stage and began working the people on it—pumping hands, slapping backs and slow-stroking the hot backup singers while smiling and laughing beneath a large banner bearing his campaign's re-election slogan: "Who's Your Nanny!"

Suddenly noticing all the broadcast cameras swinging around and moving toward him, the mayor had a moment of panic as he mouthed "Are we live?" to his public relations person who frantically nodded and mouthed back "Yes!" Like a chameleon, Dumberg immediately assumed a painfully sad expression of deepest mourning, hung his head on his chest, drooped his shoulders and slowly turned to face the live audience and the millions viewing the telecast.

"I, my political donors and other outraged citizens have gathered here to honor Jimmy Ornstein, a man who exemplified the best of New York. Before the advent of computers made him obsolete, Jimmy was a distinguished typewriter repair person, one of many who have long faded away but who in their day performed the vital work of keeping hundreds of thousands of typewriters clicking, clacking and ring-a-ding-dinging to churn out the millions upon millions of legal documents with carbon copies in triplicate that made New York the great city that we enjoy today. Bless you, Jimmy. You truly were a man for all seasons."

With zombie-leaden footsteps to demonstrate profound grief, Dumberg paced his way to an old Royal on a small table. He slowly pushed down keys one by one until the typewriter's bell signaled the end of the line. The mayor stepped back as the telecast's cameras zoomed in tight on the message:

"This last ding tolls for thee, Jimmy. We hardly knew ye, but thanks for the memories."

"There is no return of the carriage because Jimmy is gone," Dumberg said to get the cameras back on himself, "but our lives will be better thanks to his death. We can't always curb a bad dog's behavior, but we can mitigate it with Jimmy's Law, which will require all dog owners over the age of sixty to wear a helmet and display a license hanging from their neck to show they passed a safety course on how to properly walk their animal.

"And now, I turn the program over to Mr. Randy Ghote, an honor student and aspiring rapper who witnessed the tragedy up close and personal and who has been selected with his trust-worthy dog Glock to appear on posters and in commercials promoting Jimmy's Law."

Stepping forward, Randy took a selfie with the mayor while the backup singers chorused over and over, "You know you wanna type it, yay, yay, yay! But you got your keys stuck, oh, no, no, no! And you got those smeared lines, boo, hoo, hoo!"

Head bobbing to the beat, Randy slow-stepped with Glock to the front of the stage, finishing with a short moonwalk. For this solemn occasion, he sported his best gold grill, gold chains, gold watches, gold rings, sequined sunglasses, baseball cap, hip-hop pants, hockey shirt and laser-shooting sneakers.

"Like yo, Jimmy was a good dude with a bad dog, not like Glock who is obedient, respectful, kind, and goes to church. Listen up, mofos. Don't get you no punkass small terrier. They got that Napoleon thing. Makes 'em sneaky and lookin' to take you down. You feel me?"

Randy looked around at the audience and began to clap his hands above his head, getting the crowd to do the same.

"Now, let's get down with my new rap called 'Jimmy Gone, But He Got It Goin' On.'"

Heart-stoppingly loud, thumping music blasted from huge speakers as Randy pranced about the stage with Glock pitter-pattering excitedly beside him.

Jimmy, Jimmy,
You was the man
One who I called
My best frien'

But that punkass dog
Trip you down
Make you smack you
Head on the groun'

Blood squirtin' out
It would not stop
I tried the CPR
I even called a cop

Ambulance come
And take you away
Stick you somewhere
In a pauper's grave

Now that's all wrong
But it be okay
My man the mayor
Got a new law today

Gonna make old folks
Put a helmet on the head
Learn to walk their dogs
So they don't be dead

Finishing his rap, Randy crossed his arms across his chest as the audience screamed in rapture.

The program concluded with Mayor Dumberg and Randy chest-bumping and shouting, "Yo, peace out, Jimmy!" followed by two hard fist-smacks on their chests in tribute.

Appalled, Janvier swiveled her chair away from the television screen. Jimmy Ornstein had become something in death that he never was in life—a prop to serve the ambitions of others.

Swiveling back, she watched as the telecast ended with a bystander's photo from the tragedy growing larger and larger until it filled the screen. Jimmy lay on the sidewalk in the background while in the foreground a white terrier with a wild look ran away.

The dog resembled the culprit Janvier had seen on a poster at the National Dogcatchers Convention—a poster that told about property destruction and illegally freed pets at a house in foreclosure.

She studied the televised photo closely, planning to have it matched against the poster's picture. Just then, computer-generated words crawled across the bottom of the screen: "Fugitive Dog Still at Large."

17

AN UNEXPECTED PLEASURE

After his dream of living in the Big Craphole had turned to catshit, Whiskers pawed off Jimmy's leash and skulked his way out of the city, avoiding all humans in uniforms.

Reaching open country, he wandered without care for days, happy to relax through peaceful communion with nature.

This day in particular started wonderfully, not too cool and not too warm, but just right. It was so perfect that Whiskers sat down, lifted his chin and began a combination of crooning and dog yodeling to let the world know how good he felt, the kind of noise that goes on and on and on and used to make Mr. Professor's neighbors yell something in appreciation like, "Shut that damn dog up, we can't stand it anymore." Mr. Professor would thank them by waving his middle finger and yelling back, "Kiss my ass while I take a dump on your grass."

Today's sweet crooning was drawing its own attention, but not a verbalized kind. Rather, it was acting as a homing beacon.

Oblivious, Whiskers gazed at the sky through half-closed eyes, pouring out his feelings in soulful singing. That is, until rapid, thudding footsteps added an unexpected bass line to the melody.

Lowering his head, Whiskers' eyes widened. A large, dark figure was racing toward him, its face full of anger. Breaking off his dreamy vocalization in mid-yodel, Whiskers yelped and ran in the opposite direction.

Am I going to be killed by a music critic?

After a half-mile of running, Whiskers skidded into the soft, squishy mud at the edge of a lake. Trembling all over as the adrenaline in his body receded, he stared at the water.

I'm too worn out to swim. Where's a duck when you need a ride?

The heavy thudding of his pursuer stopped.

Right behind him.

The only thing I can do is see what this character wants. Either he didn't like my singing or I woke him up from a nap and he's pissed about it.

Whiskers pulled his feet from the muck and slowly turned to face the music. But instead of another face looking back at him, only the powerful forelegs of the beast were in his vision. Fearfully, Whiskers' eyes scrolled upward along the legs and then traced the outward curve of a great bowed chest. Tilting his head to follow the length of the thick neck, he found himself looking straight up at a massive head that stared straight down.

Whiskers had never been afraid of lions or tigers. In fact, he had faced them down many times in his imagination and dominated them until they begged for his gracious mercy. This creature, though, was real.

There was no need to ask the brute's name. Whiskers grasped immediately who it had to be.

But what is he?

No one really knew.

He was tall like an Irish Wolfhound or a Great Dane, but he didn't look like them. Not only tall, he was massive, but not bulky like a Mastiff. Overly thickened muscles were sculpted onto a long, rangy frame built not only for strength but also for endurance. His fur was black, short and coarse. It had a spikiness and was marked with occasional streaks of brown and gray.

He seemed to have elements of Wolf and German Shepherd in his makeup. The face and muzzle, though, were somewhat widened as if they had touches of Pitbull and Boxer. Still, nothing about him could be definitively pinned down, leaving plenty of other canine genes that could have gone into his makeup, from Rottweiler to Doberman to Chow to huge mountain breeds known for fearlessness.

Whatever he is, it's obvious that his parents were up to no good when they had him. And why did I have to say all that crap about him? Stupid mouth, you always get me in trouble.

Scut opened his own mouth and let saliva drip insultingly from his huge tongue onto Whiskers' upturned nose, filling his nostrils. Whiskers snorted out the slime only to have it fall back onto his face.

"You're an elusive runt," Scut snarled, "but all I had to do was follow your bragging trail. It seems you had to tell every dog you met that you were something called a salmononrye who goes around saving dogs and people. And everywhere I went to find you, I was warned that you're not afraid of anything and you would beat me up with some special fighting system. But look at you. You're just a punk Schnauzer. Then I remembered how terriers are so stupidly full of themselves that they can't stop running their mouths even when they know they're full of catshit."

Scut pulled his top lip up, revealing much longer than normal fangs. Freaked, Whiskers backstepped until lake water lapped against his feet.

I'm trapped. Even though I'm getting my breath back, there's no way I can outswim this monster.

"That big mouth of yours has put me in a very bad spot," Scut continued, "and I haven't known any peace because of it. Dogs have either been sniggering behind my tail or trying to make their reputations by testing me to see if I was slipping. I've had enough of it. So now we're going to settle things. Your so-called system better be good for your sake because I'm ready to snap your neck."

What's he complaining about? I've had to run for my life from bees, snakes and a bear, not to mention having humans wanting to cook me and eat me. But this time I'm a goner for sure unless I can bamboozle the big oaf.

After coughing a few times and snorting out more saliva, Whiskers began what he hoped would not be his farewell address.

"B-b-b-beat you up? A-a-ah, m-my g-g-good f-f-fellow, I-I-I-I, ay-yi-yi-yi-yi..."

Stop it! He'll think you're afraid. Act confident. Remember, terriers, especially me, are smarter than all other dogs, especially this one. He's all body and no brain. So, breathe slowly. Calm down. Relax. That's it. Okay, brain, try again.

"Gosh, pardon me, my esteemed colleague, but I seem to have momentarily tripped over my tongue because of the unexpected pleasure of finally meeting you in person and having this opportunity to set the record straight about how those other dogs misled you. They either garbled my words or misquoted me or were maliciously trying to stir up a false controversy. Believe me, in no way did I say that I would beat you up. In fact, I said that I would be happy to build you up. That's right, build you up, not beat you up. You see, I once was a fighting dog who took on all comers. But those days are long gone because I retired from active combat to become a fighting instructor, teaching the techniques handed down from the greatest masters of an ancient art called carrot-rotty. It's so deadly that I can only show it to students who promise never to use it except in the direst of situations. I would be most happy to teach it to you since you came all this way to meet me. All you have to do is take the Oath of Timid Deadliness, which I will dumb down to your level since you don't understand Jumponknees. But wait, don't thank me yet, because there's more. For you and you alone, as a courtesy from one professional to another, and on this day only because it's a limited offer, I will throw in the secrets of the renegade skunk masters who taught me how to expel extra-gassy fighting farts, which smell horribly bad. As you know, nobody messes with a skunk, and once you learn this nasty technique, you can put an entire pack of dogs on the run with just one blast. And since your butt is so big, you can probably knock out several packs at the same time. As to when we can begin your instruction, you must understand that everyone wants to tap into my fighting knowledge, and not just dogs, but turtles and ducks and lizards and squirrels and hippos and high-enemas. You're in luck, though, because I do have an opening. Come back in as many days as you have toes on all four paws. That's when I can squeeze you in."

"How about I squeeze your ribs between my jaws right now, no waiting required?" Scut growled.

Disappointed that his linguistic legerdemain hadn't lessened Scut's preoccupation with mayhem, Whiskers closed his mouth, cocked his head to one side and stared at the ground as if he was seriously considering the proposition Scut had put to him. Cocking his head to the other side, Whiskers rubbed his chin with a paw as if in deep thought. Actually, he was having a religious moment.

Hey Jude, patron saint of the lost and found, this is me, Whiskers. I am desperate. Please save me from this big lummox.

What he didn't expect happened next.

He screamed.

Loud, piercing, wailing, heartbreaking.

Oh, no! It just jumped out of my mouth. I've lost control of myself. Showing fear like that to Scut is the worst thing I could do. He'll pounce on me for sure now.

Frozen in such terror that he was already entering rigor mortis, Whiskers waited for the noisy crunching of his bones, the squishy popping of his eyeballs, and the ultimate disgrace—his tail being ripped off.

But Scut didn't pounce. Instead, he whirled around and ran.

What? Maybe I scared him away with my screaming. Perhaps he thought it was the opening prelude to my system.

Then Whiskers realized the screams couldn't have come from himself. His mouth had been closed. In fact, it was still clamped tighter than a clam's ass.

He watched as Scut plunged into a wide swath of brush, heading toward the source of the screaming.

This is my chance to get away. All I have to do is run in the opposite direction.

But Whiskers had a problem. His curiosity wouldn't let him flee to safety. Instead, he ran after Scut.

Charging into the brush, dodging around bushes and breaking through tall grass, Whiskers came to the edge of a clearing and stopped. Off to the left, he saw the source of the screams—a woman. She was running toward the lake. Looking off to the right, Whiskers saw a child, about two years old, laughing as he toddled up to the water.

Midway between them, Scut was standing still, eyeing the woman, then the child. He sniffed the air and stood up on his hind legs, facing the lake. Dropping down, he sped toward the water.

"My baby! My baby! That dog is going to kill my baby!"

Focused at first on the danger of drowning, but now on the frightening dog, the running woman failed to see a huge head gliding silently through the water toward the easy prey at the lake's edge.

Still laughing, the child stepped into the water and leaned over to splash the surface, unaware of Scut running at him and of the fifteen-foot anaconda coming fast just yards away. As the snake raised its head and opened its mouth to strike, Scut leaped over the boy. Landing his paws on the serpent's head, Scut drove it underwater.

Writhing violently, the surprised snake slipped its head from under Scut. Whipping its thick, powerful body against Scut's legs, the snake knocked him off his feet, then maneuvered for position so it could coil itself around the big dog and squeeze the life out of him.

Lying on his side, Scut kicked all four legs at the heavy body, thrusting it back. The snake closed in again, but Scut had enough space to regain his feet. Jumping at the anaconda, he ripped chunks from its body.

Terrified at the sight of the huge, snarling dog thrashing the water, the mother ran up to the toddler, grabbed him and ran back, yelling, "Help me! Help me!"

Thwarted in its attempt to fight back against Scut, the anaconda twisted around to head for deeper water. Scut bit into the body once more and held on, but let go when his feet could no longer feel the lake bottom. The wounded serpent continued toward the other side of the lake, trailing blood in the water.

Having heard the mother's screams, two dozen men came running. They wore softball uniforms and carried bats.

"What happened?" asked the screamer's husband.

"I saved our baby from that vicious dog!" she screeched.

"Pumpkin, what was Peanut doing down here in the first place? Why weren't you watching him better? He could have drowned."

"Don't you blame me. I only took a minute to freshen my makeup, and when I looked around he was gone."

While listening to his wife's excuse, the man spotted movement on the opposite side of the lake. The anaconda emerged from the water with a bleeding body.

"You know, sugar meat, I don't think that dog was after our baby. I think he saved Peanut's life."

"Are you crazy? I know what I saw, and I didn't see anything except that dog jumping at our baby to attack him. But he missed, and it was thanks to me, not you and your stupid softball game, that I got there in time."

"But honey booger, look at that snake on the other side of the lake. It's bleeding bad. I think that dog drove it off. I think he's a hero. Maybe we ought to think about keeping him. Every boy needs a dog. He could be Peanut's big protector."

The woman turned around to look but was too late to see the anaconda disappear into the grass on the opposite side.

Watching the couple and listening to the kindness in the voice of the man who was beckoning to him, Scut came out of the water.

Really? Some humans actually want me? Maybe I should smile.

He tried smiling while taking tentative steps toward the family.

The problem, though, was that Scut had spent most of his life scowling and growling and snarling. His smile muscles had been out of action so long they had trouble arranging themselves properly. The result was a cheesy, lopsided grin. He looked deranged.

Still focused on the other side of the lake with one hand shading her eyes, the woman said, "I don't see any snake over there, and I sure didn't see any snake over here. All I saw was that dog and... oh my God, he's coming at us! Look at him. He's out of his mind. He must be rabid. Get him out of here before he tries to attack my baby again!"

The husband sighed and looked around at his ball-playing buddies, who just shrugged their shoulders. Knowing his wife was mistaken, but not wanting to hear about this incident any more than was necessary for the rest of his life, he said, "Okay, boys, help me run him off."

The ballplayers shook their bats and advanced toward Scut. He tore down the lakeside with the men yelling and running after him to put on a good show for the upset woman.

Still at the edge of the clearing, Whiskers had watched everything.

I'm no fan of Scut, but right is right and wrong is wrong.

He charged after the softballers, barking, "Leave him alone! He saved that baby!"

After a brisk but short chase, the weekend warriors couldn't take the heavy bouncing of their beer bellies anymore. Stopping to lean with hands on knees to catch their breath, they were too exhausted to pay attention to the dog yapping at them.

They're pretending to be tired in order to save face, not wanting to acknowledge they were wrong. They know I barked sense into them and prevented a great injustice.

Trotting smugly away, Whiskers thought over everything that had taken place.

My prayer worked. Even though they didn't know it, the mom and baby did their part to get Scut away from me.

Scut, for his part, saved the baby. So, is he both bad and good, or just a bad dog who loves a good fight?

As for myself, a dog of only noble intentions, I flung my body at an angry mob to save the very scoundrel who meant to do me harm.

Scut, I am your hero.

18

FIRE EATERS

Following the day he had both escaped from and felt he had saved Scut, Whiskers traveled as much as possible through creeks and streams to keep the brute from picking up his scent.

Fed up with being waterlogged, he was thrilled to receive the happiest of messages in a brain flash.

It's on. Go. Follow your instinct.

Yes! It was that time, a time for hijinks, frivolity and comradeship that came around once in every so many dog years thanks to Mother Nature's gentle reminders.

Woo-hoo! I'll finally be able to lick this off my dog bowl list.

Energized, he trotted eagerly for miles until he came to the base of a ridge and worked his way to the top.

Far below on the other side was a flowing river, a great tide, a molten sea, a frothing ocean of dogs of every shape, size, color, pattern, breed, mixed breed and no breed.

Whiskers flew down the ridge, ecstatic to journey with so many canine brothers and sisters. Day after day, they filled their traveling time by swapping tales about famous dogs, fantasizing about the Big Bone, smelling butts non-stop, and bragging about their adventures. Oftentimes, it was hard for the listeners to know if they were hearing the truth or one of those Paw Bunion tales.

"That's nothing," Whiskers interjected upon becoming bored listening to Chippy, a Pomeranian who was telling about his duel to the death with a Norwegian rat.

"What you really need to watch out for is javelinas," Whiskers warned, looking quickly from side to side as if the danger was at hand, ready to spring forth.

"What's a javelina?" asked Lottie, a Bearded Collie.

"They're wild pigs."

"Wild pigs? I'm not scared of any pig," scoffed Skippy, a Blue Heeler. "All they do is grunt and waddle."

"You're thinking of farm pigs that are kept in pens," Whiskers said. "But if a pig escapes, he goes what humans call 'hog wild.'"

"What's that?" asked a Sealyham called Figaro.

"When a farm pig gets loose, his instincts take over. They drive him to start looking for the most horrible thing to eat."

"Like what? Cat litter? Especially after the cat has done it?" inquired Bruno the Briard.

"No, that's just nasty stuff. This is something worse. Something that drives the pig crazy—hottalottapainyos."

Whiskers' listeners looked puzzled.

"They're poopers, really hot things. When you eat one, your mouth gets on fire, your stomach gets on fire, your butt gets on fire, and you feel like you're going to die. In fact, it's so bad you may even want to die."

"Oh, Whiskers, you're full of it," said Flapjack, a slobbering French Mastiff. "I never heard of food putting your mouth on fire."

"Whiskers is not lying," affirmed Sadie, a Scottish Deerhound. "He's telling the truth. I got hold of one of those hottalottapainyos. It happened when I knocked over a garbage can. I was eating some real good stuff—meat, cheese, rice, beans, chips and then this large green thing that was mixed in with them. That's when a human comes out of her house and starts yelling, 'Stop eating that Mexinacan food. It's not for dogs'. Oh, she was so right. Suddenly my mouth was on fire, and I did feel like I was going to die."

"It's a sad time," commented Oscar, an Old English Sheepdog. "The wonderful days when a dog could trust the local garbage can and gobble anything in it like crazy are long gone, thanks to humans. That's because of how they are. They always have to find something to mess themselves up, and now they've gotten hooked on this Mexinacan stuff. They can't get enough. They're addicted. They're spreading it everywhere. So you've got to be very careful in a garbage can or you can really hurt yourself."

"He's right," chimed in Nitro, a Cairn Terrier. "You have to be extra cautious because it really does tear up your guts. Every time my human ate those hottalottapainyos in that Mexinacan food, she would run into that tiny room in the house. You want to talk about noise and stink? Even I found it offensive. And then she would come out rubbing her rear end like it hurt real bad. That's why people call them poopers."

Those comments were all the verification Whiskers needed.

"So, now you know, I'm not making up any of this. Those hottalottapainyo poopers are powerful. And for some reason, their worst effect is on pigs. I don't know why, but when pigs eat hottalottapainyos, they change into monsters, like what Mr. Professor called Dr. Jackal and Mr. Cowhide.

"Hard hair sprouts all over their bodies," Whiskers continued. "They grow very sharp teeth and two long, curved tusks. All the fat they had gained from being lazy and pigging out on the farm melts away. Their chests get extra big while their rear ends get smaller so they can run faster. Fire belches from their mouths and smoke blasts out of their butts. When they get to that point, they have turned into javelinas. They have lost their minds, and they are afraid of nothing."

All the dogs opened their eyes wide.

"Have you ever seen one, Whiskers?" asked Zelda, a Whippet.

"Oh, yes. In fact, I tangled with a whole passel of them in a deep forest. Maybe someday I will tell you how I showed them who's the boss. But right now, it's late and I'm tired. Let's go to sleep."

And so it went for several more days with happy dogs sharing happy times and Whiskers gaining renown for his self-promoted feats of derring-do as they drew nearer to the venue of derriere-doo.

19

POOPARAMA

Woofing with delight, the horde of dogs converged on a forest. Locating an obscure trail, they followed it deep inside until they came to an enormous open area.

This was the Bonehemian Grove, the gathering place for Pooparama.

In the middle of the grove, the trail-weary dogs lapped up water from a large pond backgrounded by a cliff. When the sun filtered through the trees and hit the cliff, shadowing brought into relief an outline, a shape, a figure. The dogs filling the grove howled in ecstasy as they gazed up at what resembled the frontal view of the head, neck, shoulders and legs of a sixty-foot-tall dog.

Some viewers claimed that it depicted their breed, while others disagreed, saying it was not any modern dog but rather a representation of the first dog in the world, the ancestor of all dogs. Heated debates commenced about how the figure came to be. Some argued that Mother Nature created it to show that she favored dogs over all other animals. Others retorted that it had been carved by the lickings and gnawings of huge but now extinct dogs, claiming "there were giants in those days."

No matter how the carved dog came to be, these live dogs were here for contests and fun. They split up into small groups to camp together according to their personalities, mutual interests or chance attraction, followed by howling and barking in harmony and dis-harmony throughout the night.

The next day, Pooparama officially began. One of its champions from yesteryear, Winston, an English Bulldog, stood on a rise in the ground to recite El Barko, the declaration known throughout Dogdom.

"What is poop? It is a dog's ultimate calling card. Unlike pee, it is visible to all. Glorious as it comes out hot, moist and steamy, rich in aroma that perfumes the air, poop sits brilliantly in the grass, basking in the sunshine, slowly and steadily changing until it enters a state of complete dryness. As dogs, we accept poop in all of its stages. It cloaks us in nature's most primeval scent, one that says: 'I smell, therefore I am.'"

Winston paused, surveyed the crowd with a stern visage, then growled out the stirring climax.

"After we are forced into a bath and scrubbed with the abomination called soap, do we bear the shame? No! We run to dry poop and roll in it to reclaim our dignity. No matter how much we are subjugated, we will not stop. We shall roll on the beaches, we shall roll in the fields, we shall roll in the hills. We will never quit. Never! Never! NEVER!"

The thrilling words of El Barko drove the audience into a frenzy of barking. Thousands of dogs responded in voices of every distinction—guttural, shrill, strong, weak, bass, soprano—all shouting, "VIVA POOP! VIVA POOPARAMA!"

After the conclusion of the opening ceremony, dogs hotfooted it throughout the grove to the various contest venues.

The ever-popular Rolling In Poop attracted the most contestants because it was something every dog could do and loved to engage in when humans were not around or were too slow of foot to stop them. There were two divisions: wet and dry. Dry attracted the majority because it was more normal. Also, it lacked the disadvantages of wet, which only appealed to dogs who wanted a reputation as wild and crazy canines. The big problem in the wet division was putting up with the hordes of green flies that swarmed all over the sticky, matted, smelly fur of each contestant.

Losers in the wet division and their flies often headed straight to the Most Decorated contest where their sticky coats gave them an advantage for rolling in forest floor detritus and having dirt, grass, leaves, twigs, pine needles, worms, bugs, spiders and cockroaches adhere to them.

Gourmands, epicures and the simply curious were drawn to Poopalicious, also known as the Great Poop Chowdown. "You'll never go hungry when you learn to eat poop" was a common saying. Most dogs, though, didn't partake unless they were desperate. Others, however, considered poop a delicacy, not only enhanced by whatever a particular dog had been eating but also by the subtle flavor differences endemic to different breeds. The fun for the spectators came from watching the contestants mouthing the dry turds that rolled in and out of their jaw flaps, looking very much like humans chewing on stogies. "He looks just like my human" was a common observation.

Of particular interest were the events that could be measured, such as the Longest Poop competition. Shoulders hunched, rear ends lowered to just above ground level, the participants did a stiff-legged slow walk, laying lines of caca as straight as possible. Giggles greeted contestants who splatted out puddles instead of firmly packed logs, but the greatest laughter was for the poor saps who managed nothing more than gas accompanied by sound.

Another measured event was for the Tallest Pile. Obviously, there was no point in pitting a Miniature Pinscher against an Alaskan Malamute, so there were many divisions according to the sizes of the entrants. But no matter how small or large, each winner of a division received the prestigious honorific of Ph.D. —Piled Higher and Deeper.

As much as he enjoyed watching the various contests, Whiskers had to shake a leg and move on because one of the big events—Poop Surprise—was coming up, and he had entered.

Size didn't matter in Poop Surprise. All contestants competed equally. Poop Surprise was all about what unexpected poop a dog could plop, no matter how big or small or firm or watery.

Feeling the fullness in his rear end, Whiskers ran onto the designated field and scooted from side to side to find a great spot for displaying what would fly out the back door when he opened it.

I can't wait until they see what I've got!

"On your marks," barked Albert, a Beauceron acting as the starter.

Dogs in an array of breeds and sizes nervously circled their spots a few last times.

"Get set."

Total silence. The dogs hunched over. The only movement was the nervous trembling of legs as the entrants willed their intestines to perform and not hold back. Spectators danced about, bumping into each other, giddy with great expectation for what these canine crappers would produce.

"POOP!"

First came the pent-up gaseous explosions of what sounded like a canine air force revving for takeoff.

Brrrrrp! Brrrraaaapppp! PwoooopPwoooopPwoooop! Booowapawapwapwapa! Pooowooowooowooowaaahhh! Vrrrii-

ihhhpipipipipVvrrrriiiihhhpipipip! PaaahpPaahpPaaahpPaaaph!
FwweeeoooohFwweeeoooohFweeeoooh!   Pooooooshhhh!
Fwooooosh! SsssseeeeeShhhheeeeShhhhwwwooooosssssshhhh!

Then it was bombs away.

Poop plopped everywhere as hundreds of dogs grunted, grimaced and groaned in bringing forth what they had purposely held back for a day or more. The most desperate were those who had become constipated from retarding their natural function while waiting for Poop Surprise to begin. The rest gave moans of relief as the agonizing pressure buildup was finally released.

Some, however, gave startled yips of dismay when they realized their blast effect was so powerful that it had blown their special surprise to smithereens and that jillions of particles were wafting through the air and coming in for a landing on the fur of contestants and spectators. For them, the contest was over.

Those who were not plugged up did a quick about-face to see if their advance preparations had come to mellifluous fruition. Many whipped their tails rapidly from side to side in ecstasy while others drooped theirs in the agony of sure defeat.

To signal they were done, the contestants began to lie down beside their entries. When everyone was flat on the ground, the judges started their inspection.

They snorted with exasperation upon encountering piles that showed their preparers lacked imagination or, worse, had added the one element that gave them no chance of winning—grass.

In the earliest Pooparamas, dogs could win at Poop Surprise by eating grass and having it come out either in impressive quantities, artistic configurations or a multiplicity of different types of grass. But those days were gone. Grass was passé. The judges had seen it too many times in all of its possible forms, and it was no longer interesting. Forward-thinking dogs realized that something else was needed to impress the judges.

So, dogs had begun raiding garbage cans, trash piles and campgrounds for special treasures to carry in their mouths on the way to Pooparama while calculating the best moment for ingesting them. Anything dogs could swallow would later emerge from rear ends—buttons, paper clips, beads, bugs, strips of plastic.

Of course, a lot depended on luck. If a particular object of potential victory was totally encased inside a big zeppelin of poop, then it was all for naught because touching the brown package was forbidden and no amount of pleading to break it open ever worked with the judges. They would simply give a quick look at what seemed to be a lack of effort and move on to contestants who did have surprises to show—a race car missing from a board game, a candy bar wrapper, undigested kernels of corn punctuating a turd's surface, and even gravel from those who couldn't find anything more interesting.

Now, walking among the current contestants, the judges seemed most intrigued by the work of Zsa Zsa, an attractive Golden Retriever. She had eaten a box of crayons and her effort came out peppered with a variety of chunky wax pieces. Unfortunately, the vividness of the different colors was for the most part lost on the judges' canine vision.

Whiskers was next.

He lay still but stared up at the judges with his eyes widened and mouth fully open in an extra-big grin.

Hello, I love you. You are my new best friends.

The judges, however, didn't notice his attempt at manufactured camaraderie. Instead, they stood frozen in place—flabbergasted, stunned, astonished, amazed and totally barkless. The entry that rested beside Whiskers was unlike anything they had ever seen.

Circular and piled five logs high, vapor steamed from it. Obviously, Whiskers would get brownie points for architecture and moistness. But that wasn't what astounded the experienced observers of gastrointestinal finished products.

The poop surprise blinked at them, winked at them and sometimes blinded them with flashes of light.

Fascinated, the judges stared at it, smelled it and even tried listening to it in an effort to decipher this feceological marvel. Careful observation revealed that many tiny bits sprinkled throughout the poop had the ability to suddenly turn bright while other bits just as suddenly went dark. In fact, one judge could see a bit turned on and shining brilliantly while another judge viewing it simultaneously from a different angle would see it turned off and so dark as to be almost invisible. Stupefied, the judges looked back and forth from the pile to the insanely grinning Whiskers; but he lay absolutely still, not doing anything to manipulate what they were seeing.

Hurry up, guys. My jaw muscles are starting to hurt.

While the judges twisted their heads in puzzlement, trying to understand what animated the ever-changing luminosity, the crowd went berserk—hopping, yipping and nipping one another in the excitement of witnessing something so unexpected.

No doubt about it. Whiskers had produced a masterpiece, a disco pile of outright fabulousness.

After much discussion with her colleagues, the chief judge, Mixie, a Samoyed, turned to Whiskers, shrugged and said, "We give up. How did you do this?"

Still lying prone, Whiskers responded, "With the greatest of respect, I would love to tell you, but if I did then any dog would know how to do it, and a good buttician never tells his or her secrets. The only clue I can give is that I think lots of happy thoughts. The sparkle they put in your life touches everything you do, as you can see."

Basically, the contest was over. Whiskers' poop surprise was off the scale for originality, not only physically but also intellectually in that it came wrapped within a philosophy. The judges made a perfunctory effort to review the remaining entries, but compared to what Whiskers had done everything else seemed pedestrian.

After the officials made a show of conferring among themselves, the chief judge faced the spectators to announce the winner.

"What a wonderful competition this has been," Mixie declared. "We have had more entries this time than ever before. Many were excellent, once again showing there is more that can be done with poop than just taking a dump. The process can be carried out with intelligence aforethought for manufacturing something special that all your friends can admire and all your enemies can envy. Now, I call upon the winner of Poop Surprise to come forward. Whiskers, you are our new champion."

Whiskers jumped up.

Look out, plebeians!

He sped through the field of contestants, racing around most while hurdling some and stepping on others in his eagerness to wallow in glory. Skidding to a halt in front of the panel of judges, he spun around and around in a tight circle, then stopped and kicked up a flurry of grass and dirt with his back legs.

"That's what we like to see," said Mixie, "an excited winner. You certainly must be thinking those happy thoughts. But please calm down for the honors."

Except for some slight trembling following his exertion, Whiskers stood still as the judges commenced a single-file march past his rear end. Coming abreast of Whiskers' derriere, each judge executed a snappy nose-right and smelled his butt.

Every sniff and bark of approval brought cheers from the onlookers.

When the officials completed their marche du odeur, they made two lines to form a path for the entrance of the festival's ceremonial royalty—King Pooparamus, a Newfoundland, and Queen Pooparella, a Leonberger. The queen gave Whiskers an approving lick on each cheek, and the king gave him a command.

"Canine, kneel."

Which he did, forelegs on the ground, muzzle upon them, butt up in the air.

"Whiskers, you have thrilled all those in attendance with your marvelous performance. I am told that the decision in your favor was unanimous."

The king dropped a massive paw heavily onto Whiskers' right shoulder and then his left, saying, "I hereby dub thee, Whiskers, PSC, Poop Surprise Champion."

Stepping back, the king said, "Rise, Whiskers, PSC. Go forth among all dogs, knowing that you are one of the best of the best at Pooparama."

Talk about fame!

Dogs hurried throughout the Bonehemian Grove, regaling others about what they had missed by not attending Poop Surprise. As word of Whiskers' feces feat traveled from muzzle to muzzle, the creation he wrought became even more magical:

"I saw it levitate."

"I heard it bark."

"It broke into pieces that ran around and then reassembled themselves."

"He did it with happy thoughts."

"No, he said sappy thoughts."

"Wrong, he used crappy thoughts."

Whiskers overheard quite a few of those exaggerated claims,

but neither confirmed nor denied them. No matter how much any dog begged, he refused to tell the secret—that he had found a cellophane packet of glitter in a trash pile, hid it until the right moment, chewed it open and swallowed the contents.

As hard as it was to get those dry, pointy things down, suffering for my art was worth it.

Like the sun that reflected off the glitter, the glory of Whiskers' win would eventually reflect throughout all of Dogdom.

All good things come to an end though, even the good things that for dogs come out of their ends. So it was at Pooparama. The contests wound down until none were left. The next day everyone would leave the Bonehemian Grove.

Knowing this was their last chance, dogs began a frenzied running throughout the grove, furiously smelling the posteriors they still had on their buttit lists.

This also was their last opportunity for serious tree and bush marking. Each male, having husbanded his pee and stretched his bladder as much as possible, doled the precious liquid out parsimoniously in the hope that he would gain bragging rights for having marked more trees and bushes than any other dog. The activity in yellow rain grew frenetic. Dogs ran and peed as fast as possible, even executing the difficult and crash-prone Flying Leg Maneuver that consisted of three-legged running with one of the rear legs held up horizontally so that Mr. You Know Who could do a rapid-fire flyby on stands of bushes and trees.

When all was squirted and night came on, it was time for a last singing of the "Hop 'n Poop" song around the pond in the center of the grove.

As cute little pups
We were misunderstood
We chewed up things
Because we thought it was good
Baark, baark, baark

We pooped and peed
And barked endlessly
But they didn't understand
Because they don't think like we
Baark, baark, baark

That's why we ran away
And made ourselves free
May the dogcatcher
Have mercy on such as we
Baark, baark, baark

We're poor little pups
Who lost our way
Little black doggies
Who've gone astray
Baark, baark, bark

While singing, each dog hopped on its back legs and held its front legs up with paws bent, hoping while hopping that he or she could squeeze out some poop, which would bring cheers all around and encourage more singing, more hopping and more pooping until all the dogs were out of ammo and couldn't stay upright anymore.

All pooped out from the frolicking, Whiskers lay panting on the ground among the other dogs, his mind drifting off toward sleep.

If life could be like this every day, just full of good, clean, doggy fun, I wouldn't have to be so... so... so...

With the sunrise, the dogs arose.

After yawning and stretching, old friends and newly made ones licked out each other's ears followed by a ubiquitous sniffing of butts, twats and you-know-whats. Many rolled vigorously in the grassy areas where the various contests had been held so they could wear a souvenir smell home.

When all were ready, they gathered into a huge traveling band, leaving behind the Bonehemian Grove and one of the best times of their lives, having bonded through hijinks, silliness and friendly competition.

Moving along in their great canine flood, still feeling the marvelous experience of Pooparama within themselves, the dogs broke into cries of "Poop Power," "Feces Forever," and the new favorite, "I've Gone Crap Crazy."

But among all the happiness of spirit, Whiskers could hear Miser the cranky Cattle Dog grumping: "It's not like the old days. Modern dogs wouldn't have stood a chance back then. When I came to Pooparama in the Time of the Dead Passenger Pigeon, or was it the Time of the Lightning-Fried Woodchuck, or perhaps the Time of the Ingrown Porcupine... anyway, back then we came here in the worst of winter, and it was so cold that when we peed on a tree our pee froze all the way up deep inside us and then we had to go over to the giant cliff dog which belched fire back in those days and we ran back and forth in the flames until the peecicle inside us was all melted. And that's not all. When each Pooparama contest was over, the contestants had to clean the fields of competition by eating their frozen entries, and the spectators had to help. In fact, we were so glad to help that we ran from pile to pile trying to outdo each other by eating the mostest the fastest. We kept it all inside of us and walked back to our homes with our stomachs so full of shit that they were dragging on the ground and all the fur rubbed off our bellies and then all of our hide scraped away and then we were dragging our intestines through mud and over rocks and into sharp sticks until we got back to our humans' homes and then we pooped it out all over their floors just to show them who's the real boss. But these girlie-dogs of today just walk away from the contest poop and let poor old Mother Nature do all the work of cleaning up. It's just pitiful. In fact, I'm so disgusted I don't think I'll ever come back. And that's not all…"

On and on he went, and so did the canine caravan until it began breaking up bit by bit as dogs peeled off to cross fields, swim across streams or plunge into woods on the way back to the place each called home. Day after day, the farther the column went, the smaller it became until every dog had said goodbye and left, except for Whiskers, who just kept walking alone and wondering where in the world he was and why all the others had places where they belonged and when and where and even *if* he would ever again have a place where he belonged.

Maybe someday.

20

DADDY'S HOME

"Ook, ook!"

"What is it?"

"Oh my God!"

Whiskers opened his eyes.

He had been wonderfully asleep with his back snug up against the wall of a house, hidden behind an oleander bush but unknowingly thrashing his legs against the leaves while making muffled yips. Now, his happy dream of chasing a herd of rabbits was ruined. Opening his eyes and looking past the base of the bush, he saw little shoes, which meant little feet, which meant young children, which could be good or bad.

I hope they've been trained.

"Mom! Come quick!"

"What's going on? Is it a snake?"

"No, Mom! Look! It's a dog, and he's got long whiskers! He's so cute! We want to keep him."

Yes, Whiskers was cute, and this was a moment for being even cuter.

If I can't get some rabbits, maybe I can at least get some good food.

He crawled out to face the mother and three kids—a little

girl with light-green snot running from one nostril, an elementary-age boy crowned by a blue mohawk, and a teenage brunette who had dyed her ponytail bright pink.

"Ook! Oggy sit up!"

"He's holding his paws out in front of him! All by himself! And nobody told him to do it!"

"Mom, can we please, please, please keep him? I'll fix him up real nice and start a new blog called 'Got Dog?' Then I'll take a million pictures of how cool we look together and put them all on MyFace and then we'll do something stupid in a video for YouFlub so we can get on that show called 'Americans Who Got No Talent' because we obviously qualify and then we'll be famous and get to hang out on the red carpet with other no-talents like Coco Siliconoli. And here's the best part, we'll all be rich!"

"Well, he is cute, and he does seem nice," Mom answered. "I know you kids have wanted a dog for so long. Bring him in the house, and we'll give him last night's leftovers. But I'm not making any promises. We'll have to ask your father when he gets home."

"Hear that?" asked the boy. "Dad is really nice, and I know he's going to like you. You're going to be our dog for sure."

But Whiskers wasn't listening.

Sparked by the magic word "leftovers," he ran to the front door, stood up with his front paws against it, ran halfway back to the mother and kids, and then to the front door again.

Come on, hurry up!

Inside, Mom placed a plate of hot roast beef with red-eye gravy and mashed potatoes covered in brown gravy on the kitchen floor. Burying his face in the plate, Whiskers gobbled up the food non-stop, then slowly dragged his tongue over every speck of gravy grease until the plate sparkled.

Best leftovers ever. I'm glad they woke me up.

Sated, he went to the living room and lay on a rug, rubbing his front feet against his gravy-soaked whiskers, then licking the gravy off his paws.

He spent the rest of the morning and afternoon being the center of attention for Snotty, Mohawk and Pinkie until the big girl took him into the bathroom, grabbed a bottle of hair dye and began applying it to his whiskers and tail.

Whiskers didn't know what she was doing, but...

At least it's not a bath.

"You're going to be so cute and famous," she said.

Whatever.

As they came out of the bathroom, the springs on the front screen door creaked.

Uh-oh, it must be the dad, probably home from that thing humans gripe about called work. I'm not looking forward to this.

He knew from the tales of other dogs that it was never a good idea to be a surprise for a dad.

"What the hell is this? Who told you that you could get a dog?"

Whiskers sat up on his hindquarters and held out his paws, looking friendly and cute.

Mom, on the other hand, stood up and looked concerned.

Nice Dad had gone to work, but he hadn't come home; instead, it was Mad Dad. He'd had a real shitty day starting with confronting the bitch in the next cubicle because he was tired of her sniping at everything he did to make him look bad and then the big boss had jumped on him for not doing something the assistant boss claimed he had told him to do but which the assistant had actually forgotten to tell him to do and then the company cafeteria refused his debit card for lack of funds and he had no cash and nobody who knew him had any money to loan him so he'd gone hungry all day and his gasoline card was expired so he couldn't get any gas on the way home so he'd been driving on fumes all tensed up wondering if he was going to be stranded on the freeway.

The kids began their pitch for adding a new member to the family.

"Ah wike oggy."

"We found him under the oleander," Mohawk said. "He's lost, and he's really nice and really smart. Please, Dad. We'll walk him and feed him and bathe him and teach him tricks and..."

"I don't want a damn dog," Dad interrupted. "It'll just be pooping and pissing everywhere and chewing up the furniture. Then he'll get sick and need to go to the vet, and the vet's going to charge me money I don't have."

"Please, Dad, please let us keep him. He won't do anything bad," Pinkie pleaded.

"You want a dog? Fine, you can get yourself a dog after you're all grown up and out of my house and on your own, which can't come soon enough for me. All I do is work my ass off for you people, and then I come home to find something like this!"

With that, Dad lifted up a foot and swung it against Whiskers' right side, knocking him over. His head smacked against the leg of a wooden chair, and he slumped onto the floor.

Stunned, Whiskers looked up at the man's contorted face.

"You're lucky I didn't kick your ass out the window."

This dad is out of control. What if he finds out I ate all his leftovers?

Whiskers scrambled up on all fours, faced Dad and growled.

"Oh, what's this? Growling at me in my own house? Take this, you damn dog!"

Dad leaned down and drew back his right hand to slap Whiskers in the head.

Whiskers didn't wait for the blow. Spotting the left hand

hanging low, he sprang forward and grabbed it in his mouth, crunching into tendons and bones.

"SON OF A BITCH! THE BASTARD'S BITING ME!"

Dad ripped his hand out of Whiskers' mouth, leaving strips of skin behind. For several moments, he stared at the back of his hand, watching curiously as blood filled in the holes and grooves until...

"OWW! OH MY GOD IT HURTS!"

Shaking his throbbing hand in the air, Dad threw a fit like a child, pumping his legs up and down while turning in circles.

"GET HIM OUT OF HERE! Dump him on the highway or take him to animal control. Just get him out of here before I get a gun and shoot him!"

"Hurry, kids, hurry!" Mom said. "Put him in my car, and we'll take him somewhere."

Somewhere turned out to be a gas station on the edge of town. Mom cradled her arms around Whiskers and lifted him out of the car.

"Sorry, doggy, but it seems we got you on a bad day. Maybe somebody else will pick you up and give you a place to live."

Mom placed Whiskers on one of the gas pump islands and got back in the car. Leaning their heads out the back windows, tears on their faces, the kids waved as the car started up and slowly rolled away.

"Oggy, oggy!"

"Find yourself a good home."

"We were going to be so rich and famous."

Watching them leave, Whiskers sat for a while, pondering.

Why does everything that starts out so good have to go so bad?

Not getting an answer, he got up and wandered to the rear of the station where he found a pothole with some water. After a good drink, he moseyed to the front.

A car had arrived, and the driver's door was open. No one

was in the car. Whiskers jumped inside and scooted over to the passenger seat.

After several minutes, a string bean of a man walked out of the station and climbed in on the driver's side.

Stringbean did a double take.

"Whoa, who are you? Where did you come from?"

"Woof, woof, woof."

I know he doesn't understand, but that's okay. Humans are happy to make up their own stories about us.

Stringbean glanced about, but there were no other cars and no one was inside the building except the cashier.

"Well, I guess you're mine for a while," Stringbean said. "Do you want to take a ride?"

"Ride" was a magic word for Whiskers. He stared at the man with widened eyes and shook with excitement.

"I take that as a 'yes,' so let's get going. Stick your head out the window if you want."

For Whiskers, the ride wasn't long enough. After only a couple of miles, his new friend turned off the road and parked the car in front of a one-story, gray building.

Stringbean got out, walked around to the car's passenger side, opened the door, secured Whiskers under his right arm, and carried him like a football through the front door of the building while saying loudly, "Hey, looky here, I brought you a present!"

The comment got a head shake from a slight-of-frame man with blond bangs brushing the top of his wire-rimmed glasses. A mullet draped the back of his neck.

"Oh no, we don't need any more dogs," Mullet said. "We can't get rid of the ones we have."

"Come on," countered Stringbean. "Look at him. He's so damn cute. He jumped into my car at the Hexxon station. Who knows how long he was there? If you ask me, he's lucky he didn't get run over or die from drinking antifreeze off the pavement. Anyway, while driving I called the radio station on my cell phone and said that if anybody is looking for a dog like him, he'll be right here. So, it looks to me like you're stuck with him."

"Aw, okay. But until somebody picks him up, you're going to pay for his dog food."

"Hah! He's so cute, he'll be gone in no time."

"All right. Keep a good hold on him, and follow me into the back."

Stringbean and Whiskers trailed the guy through the door and into dog noise hell.

Dogs of all sizes, colors and dispositions were sizing up Whiskers, barking at him, spinning in circles and lunging against wire doors to bare and snap their teeth. The timid and dispirited cowered in corners.

No matter where Whiskers looked, he saw the bane of every canine—cages with very little room to move.

The men stopped by an empty cage.

"I need a terrier in here like I need another hole in my butt," Mullet muttered. "They're always trying to outthink you and take over."

He opened the cage door, and Stringbean gave Whiskers a gentle toss inside.

After closing the door, Mullet looked quizzically at Stringbean.

"Well, that's done. But tell me something, why does he have pink whiskers and a pink tail?"

21

JAILBREAK

The black FBDI van stopped in the dirt parking lot of the gray building.

A sign on the building featured the cartoon-style artwork of a bug-eyed, long-tongued dog leaning away from a disembodied hand.

Stepping out of the van, Janvier surveyed the woods that backgrounded the building. Not a dog in sight.

Newly promoted after outstanding work, she was now Inspector Janvier, assigned to investigate the report of a massive jailbreak at Slap Happy Pets. It wasn't a typical escape. Apparently, some dog had learned a new trick. The fear was that he would teach it to others.

Her boots kicking up puffs of dust, Janvier walked to the building's door and stepped inside, drawing a lopsided grin from the mullet-headed man behind the counter.

"Hey, lady, what's with the dog collar? Did you escape from somewhere? Should I put you in a cage?"

Walking up to the jokester, Janvier tilted her head slightly forward, furrowing her brow and showing only the bottom half of her ice-blue eyes from their hooded position.

She placed her business card on the counter. It wasn't regulation. In the middle was the picture of a chess queen. Running across the card were the words: "Have Net Gun, Will Travel."

Mullet picked up the card and stared at it through his wire-rimmed glasses, moving his lips while slowly reading each word.

"'Inspector Janvier,' it says. Hey, you must be the cop they sent to find out about the jailbreak."

"I'm not a cop. I'm with the Federal Bureau of Dog Investigation."

"Oh, yeah, that's on the card, too. Sorry, I didn't mean any offense. What would you like to know?"

"Why do you call this place Slap Happy Pets?"

"Because they're happy to be here."

"You don't slap them around?"

"No, they're just so happy, they're slap happy."

"I don't think so."

"Why not?"

"The initial report says they all ran away."

"Yeah, every last one of them."

"So how did they get out?"

"Uh, well, I, uh, they, uh, well, they..."

"You're not so funny now, are you?"

Mullet's mouth opened, then shut without a word.

Janvier pointed to the ceiling.

"You've got surveillance cameras. I want to see the tape of the incident."

"Yeah, sure, but, uh, maybe you could keep what you see to yourself, because I'm not too..."

"Just put the tape in the machine."

When the tape was ready in the office, Janvier sat in Mullet's chair to watch. The black and white tape was a little grainy, but it was easy to tell what was taking place.

She could see Mullet walking by the cages in the back of the building. He stopped to look in one of them. A white dog with darkened whiskers and a darkened tail lay on its side at the rear of the cage near a food bowl and some dried poop. The dog had vomited and was jerking in convulsions. Mullet opened the cage, walked inside and squatted by the dog.

The tape's audio quality wasn't the best, but good enough for Janvier to hear what Mullet was saying.

"Hey, fella, what's the matter? Food didn't agree with you? Are you sick? Want me to call the vet?"

He reached out to touch the dog. Instantly, the dog jumped up and barked in his face. Surprised, Mullet flopped back on his butt while the dog quickly grabbed one end of a stick of dried poop in its mouth.

"Hey, what are you going to do with that?"

Instead of answering, the dog made lunging motions with the poop stick. Mullet scooted back from each lunge until stopped by one side of the cage.

"Okay, nice doggy, take it easy. Watch where you're pointing that thing."

Rather than taking it easy, the dog growled and moved closer to Mullet, leveling the poop stick directly at his eyes.

"No, no, anything but that! Just tell me what you want!"

In response, the dog jerked his head to one side. Complying, Mullet butt-scooted to the rear of the cage. The dog backed toward the open door of the cage, growling and waving the poop stick as a warning for Mullet not to move.

Reaching the opening, the dog stepped out and rammed the cage door shut with the top of his head.

Spitting out the poop stick, the dog began barking and running through the corridors, stirring all the other dogs into frantic jumping against their cages. At the rear of the kennel, the dog leaped onto a table set against the back wall. The table was next to the cage of a Great Dane who watched the dog prop his front paws against the wall, twist his head to grab the knob of the cage's slide lock in his teeth, and pull it sideways. Apparently in on the caper, the Great Dane butted its cage door open, ran out and began opening all the other cages.

After being freed, a German Shepherd and a Golden Retriever followed the white dog to the back door of the building. They stood shoulder to shoulder against the door. The white dog jumped onto their backs, grabbed the oblong knob of the deadlock in his teeth and twisted his head one way. Getting no result, he twisted the other way and the bolt released, letting the off-balance door move open a crack. The dog barked an order to the Retriever and Shepherd. They started sidestepping with the white dog balanced on their backs, gripping the deadlock knob in his teeth.

With the door open, all three of the dogs barked at the other escapees who had been running mindlessly up and down the corridors. The mob rushed toward the open door and out to freedom in the woods. Instead of fleeing with them, the white dog ran back past all the cages and through a doorway into the office area. Stopping, he looked around, smelled the air and looked up. He seemed to smile.

The tape stopped.

Janvier sat still, unbelieving.

It was all planned. And it was him!

No doubt about it. It was the same Schnauzer whose televised image at the end of the festivities for Jimmy's Law had been positively matched with that on the wanted poster at the National Dogcatchers Convention by using POOP, the Pooch Optical Optimization Program.

One thing was very clear. This fugitive terrier on the FBDI's Most Wanted list had graduated from involvement in individual crimes to organizing mass institutional escapes. What happened at Slap Happy Pets had serious implications for dog pounds, humane shelters, private kennels, animal control facilities, pet shops, veterinarians and dog shows.

"Do you have more tape?"

"No."

"What happened next?"

"Well, I was scared."

"And?"

"I started biting my fingernails."

"Just the facts, man."

"Oh, sorry. I stayed in the cage."

"For how long?"

"Until he ran past me again and went out the back door."

"Why do you think he entered your office?"

"I know why. He had it in his mouth when he ran by."

"What?"

"My sandwich. Peanut butter and jelly. I was really looking forward to eating it. My mom made it."

"I'll include that in my report. Theft of sentimental personal property."

Mullet smacked a fist against the side of his head.

"I am so stupid! I never should have let that terrier in here. Geez, Inspector Janvier, do you think you'll catch him?"

"I'll pursue him to the ends of the earth to make him pay."

"For my sandwich?"

"For the crimes he's already committed and any future ones he's planning. Anyway, I've learned all I can here. I'm leaving, but there's one last thing."

"What?"

"Don't count on getting your sandwich back."

PART II

SWAMPED

22

___

AN ACE IN THE HOLE

Sauntering down the sidewalk of a strange city, Whiskers no longer sported a two-tone look. The pink detailing on his whiskers and tail had worn off while thrashing through brush and splashing across creeks to get far away from Slap Happy Pets.

After fleeing out the back door of the kennel, his fellow ex-prisoners had romped around in the woods barking with joy, then scattered without even one thanking him for gaining their freedom.

At least they could have said I was their hero, especially the ladies, but of course they went trailing after the biggest dogs.

Oh, well, I'm hungry. Where's a garbage can when you need one?

Nose up high, sniffing, he got a whiff of something disgusting.

Not rotten food.

A rotten attitude.

Whiskers twisted to look behind him. About two blocks back, a large, non-human shape had its head down, smelling the sidewalk. The head raised up and stared straight at him.

Oh, no! Not again!

The glory that Whiskers won at Pooparama was about to bite him in the ass.

Using the same detective technique that had kept him on Whiskers' trail from the foreclosure house to the run-in with the anaconda, Scut had let dog after dog regale him with the thrill of having run across the charmingly verbose Poop Surprise champion. None saw any harm in pointing out Whiskers' last known direction of travel to "an old friend."

Eventually, Scut met some Slap Happy escapees who were delighted to guide him to the spot where Whiskers had bid farewell to their disappearing butts by calling them "ingrates," which they assumed was a compliment. From there, with the help of more unwitting dupes and using a sense of smell far superior to that of the average canine, Scut followed the trail and the scent of the cocky dog to this city and sidewalk.

Now, while Whiskers' brain desperately searched for words of beast-calming brilliance to funnel through the madly clicking teeth of a mouth terrified of having its jaw ripped off, his entire body heaved from side to side as the skeleton attempted to dislocate its bones so they could crawl out of the ass, reassemble and run away, leaving behind a floppy bag with a brain whose questionable faith in eloquence was scaring the shit out of every other body part.

But all internal commotion ceased in puzzlement when Scut sat on his haunches and tilted his head skyward.

What is that numbskull doing?

Opening his mouth wide, Scut howled a banshee-like scream that rolled down the street, echoing off glass and brick. Finished, he lowered his head, stared intently at Whiskers, then once again looked upward.

Maybe the idiot got religion and he's trying to pray. I could show him how since what he just did was a total botch. We could even be prayer buddies. I'll teach him about mercy and forgiveness and turning the other butt cheek.

This time, though, Scut didn't howl. Instead, his deep, booming voice bugled out the musical notes of the "Dogüello," the feared canine call signaling that no quarter would be given to his foe, that they would fight to the death.

When the last note faded, Scut got off his haunches. Growling and barking at Whiskers, he worked himself into a frenzy, lowered into sprinting position and charged down the sidewalk.

With death hurtling toward them, Whiskers' brain and bones rejoined in common cause, whipping him around in an adrenaline-fueled panic. Peeing nonstop, he sprinted along the edge of the sidewalk while his churning intestines did their part by bubbling up gas that gave him an extra boost when it whooshed out his ass.

It wasn't enough.

An incredible roaring accelerated toward him. The excruciating sound overwhelmed Whiskers' ears, their drums banging so hard they were about to beat themselves to pieces.

Too scared to look as the enormous noise roared up close enough to smell his butt, Whiskers ran straight at a telephone pole a few yards ahead.

I'll dodge at the last moment so he can smash into it and knock himself out and...

OH, CATSHIT! HE'S GOT ME!

Whiskers rose in the air, a death grip clamped around his neck, the prelude to a ferocious shaking that would snap the connection holding his head to his spine.

Please, make it quick, but be gentle.

He wasn't shaken. Instead, he was flying horizontally, legs splayed out like a super-dog, traversing city blocks faster than any dog can run.

After a couple of miles, he flew around a corner, his legs dropping as he slowed down. The man gripping Whiskers' neck brought the motorcycle to an easy stop and set him on the curb.

Whiskers trembled uncontrollably as the adrenaline left his overstressed muscles.

"Relax, dude, you're safe. Man, that sure was one big, badass dog chasing you. He had a hell of a mad-on. I must have been on a mission from God. Either that or it's just your lucky day."

The noise that had terrified him was now a soothing "potato-potato-potato" sound that reminded him of the time he had been in the basket of Mr. Professor's bicycle at a stoplight and they had become surrounded by a number of such noisemakers whose riders laughed and hooted instead of beating up Mr. Professor while he railed at them in funny-sounding ancient foreign languages.

From that experience, Whiskers expected to see a full-bearded man with long hair, jeans, boots and a studded leather jacket. Instead, this rider was clean-shaven and short-haired, wearing flip-flops, khaki shorts and a brightly decorated Hawaiian shirt. A chin strap secured a beanie to his head. A little propeller was spinning on top of the beanie.

"Who do you belong to? Hmm, no tag. I guess you belong to me now. I need a riding buddy."

The man leaned over, scooped Whiskers up and plopped him onto the seat.

"My name is Ace. I call a spade a spade. If you don't like it, I'll club you. And I shower the ladies with diamonds before I break their hearts."

Ace guffawed at his own humor.

I don't get it. I guess it's what humans call jokes.

Ace removed his belt to rework it through the shorts' front loops and around Whiskers. He gunned the motor and took off at a hell-bent speed.

The motorcycle roared down street after street until Ace drove into an old neighborhood and parked in the driveway of a small house, revving the bike's engine to shatter the residential silence.

That night, Ace motioned to Whiskers to jump on a chair beside the small kitchen table. Sitting in another chair, Ace opened a large can of stew and gave Whiskers a spoonful, then himself. They alternated eating from the spoon until the can was empty.

"We're going to be good buddies," Ace said as he wiped brown stew juice off Whiskers' whiskers. "I go where I want when I want and I do what I want. I want fun, fun, fun all the time. Get with it or get out of the way is what I say."

Wow! This human is like me, a fun guy. And he's kind of a hero since he saved Scut from getting his butt chewed up by me.

The next morning, Ace shook him awake.

"Come on, traveling buddy, get up. You thought riding a motorcycle was fun? You're going to have the best time of all today. And when we're done, I'll get you a big bone."

Whiskers shook his still drowsy head.

What did he say? He couldn't have been talking about the Big Bone, could he? Is that where we're going? But how could a human know?

Soon they were on the motorcycle, zipping through traffic, rushing toward the outskirts of the city and into the countryside. After several miles, Ace turned the bike down a side road and headed toward a small airfield.

Ace parked next to a hangar where a group of men in brightly colored outfits were standing around.

"Hurry up, Ace," one shouted. "Get your chute on. We were getting ready to leave without you."

"I'll catch the wing and ride on it if I have to," Ace yelled back as he pulled a woman's large shoulder tote bag out of one of the bike's saddlebags.

Picking up Whiskers, Ace carried him to the hangar's side door. Inside, Whiskers cocked his head from side to side as he watched Ace suit up, get his parachute on, and loop the wide strap of the tote bag over his head and down onto the back of his neck.

"Come on, boy. Follow me," Ace said, flinging open the door and hustling over to the group starting to enter the plane.

Whoa, this guy is going to jump out of a flying thing like what Mr. Professor and I used to watch on the boob tube.

"Where did you get that dog?" one of the jumpers asked.

"He dropped out of the sky and into my lap while I was riding my bike," Ace joked. "And now I'm going to take him back up where he came from."

What's he talking about? I'm not a bird dog.

"You can't jump with an animal," another jumper said.

He's right. Listen to him!

"If you can jump with some lard-ass bozo of a customer strapped onto you, I can jump with my dog," Ace retorted.

He picked up Whiskers and scrunched him in the bag.

"Make yourself useful," Ace told the doubter. "Take this cord and tie it to the strap's buckle on this side, run it around us a couple of times and tie it to the buckle on the other side."

"Aw, hell, Ace, this is crazy," another jumper chimed in. "He'll fall out. And where did you get that huge bag?"

"No, he won't," Ace said. "I know what I'm doing. And this bag was left by one of my old ladies. Having her around got mighty old, and it turned out she wasn't no lady."

Ace whooped and laughed at his witticism as he entered the plane, settled in and patted Whiskers on the head. The pilot started the craft rolling down the runway, increasing the speed until it lifted off.

"What's his name?" a jumper yelled at Ace over the roar of the engine as the plane climbed.

"He hasn't told me yet, so for now I think I'll call him Speedy because he likes going fast on my motorcycle."

Right now, I'd rather be in a bed and called Sleepy.

Reaching jump altitude, the plane leveled off. As the craft approached the drop zone, the jumpers stood up, shuffled toward the open door and went out one by one.

Now, it was their turn. Ace braced himself in the doorway. Staring at the ground far, far below, Whiskers' mouth fell open in shock. His butt blasted out a procession of beef-stew-flavored farts.

"Good Lord!" Ace whooped. "Was that me or you? Man, the air up here smells so good I can taste it. But it's time to go."

Jumping out, Ace splayed his arms and legs horizontally to slow their descent. He bent his head close to Whiskers' ear to be heard above the rushing air.

"See that dark area below us? It's the Great Abysmal Swamp. You don't want to get in there. Gators and snakes are everywhere. If one of them don't eat you, quicksand will suck you down. But don't worry, we're going to steer far away."

A few moments later, Ace opened the parachute, putting them vertical. He patted Whiskers on the head, grabbed the steering toggles and started to turn while yelling, "Yee-haw! Yee-haw!"

BWAMMM!

BWAMMM!

BWAMMM!

BWAMMM!

BWAMMM!

Blows like punches from a boxer hammered Whiskers and Ace.

When the barrage ended, Whiskers' nose was touching the beak of a duck. The bird looked just as confused as he did.

The flock of blindsiding ducks flew on, leaving behind those held against Ace and Whiskers by air pressure. Slowly, the birds fell away, some going straight down while others flailed about to get their wings working.

One last, large duck slid off Ace's helmet and past Whiskers. Ace was quiet, no longer guiding their flight as they headed into the Great Abysmal Swamp.

Trees that had seemed soft and fluffy when far below now rushed up at them like spearpoints.

Whiskers barked, "Ace, wake up! Wake up!"

No response.

Catshit! Catshit! Catshit!

Scrunching his head inside the leather bag, Whiskers watched his life pass in front of him, but just as he was getting to a really good part...

WHAM!

Slamming into the top of a tree, Ace's body plunged through, breaking branches and bouncing off others until a thick branch caught him under the chin, snapping his head back.

Slipping off, he crashed through more branches until the canopy of the parachute snagged above him. His body swung out on its lines. They pulled him back and bashed him against the trunk of the tree.

When all movement ceased, Whiskers poked his head out of the bag. He was unhurt, protected from the branches by the leather bag and cushioned by Ace's body.

He twisted to look up at Ace, whose head was pitched forward.

Maybe he's just knocked out.

Whiskers licked Ace on the chin.

No response.

He barked.

Still no response.

He licked harder and barked louder.

Ace never moved.

Whiskers turned around in the bag, whimpering for his brother from a human mother.

Why is it that when I find a good home, the human has to die on me? First, Mr. Professor. Then, Jimmy. And now, Ace. Maybe I've got what humans call bad luck.

When he could whimper no more, Whiskers looked down. He wasn't far off the ground, but not close either. He spotted a duck lying half on dirt and half in water.

I'll bet it's one of those that hit us.

Something hidden beneath a mass of algae flashed forward, snatched the duck and dragged it under the water.

Yikes! That could have been me.

He waited a while, but the thing didn't reappear.

I do not want to go down there, but I can't stay here.

Whiskers wriggled until more than halfway out of the bag, leaned over, pushed with his back legs and fell out.

Streaking past an astonished squirrel, he hit the ground—and disappeared.

23

I DON'T LIKE YOUR ATTITUDE

W hiskers gently moved his legs, then his back, then
his neck, checking for broken bones.

There were none.

Instead of breaking his fall by breaking his bones on hard
ground, he had plunged into a hole full of soft, cushioning tree
moss that completely covered him, cutting off all light.

Particles of the moss clogged his nose, irritated his eyes and
filled his mouth. Snorting, blinking and coughing, Whiskers
rolled onto his stomach, got to his feet and poked his head out of
the hole. Wearing a cap of tree moss, its tendrils draped down
the sides of his face and neck like a grayish-white wig, he
surveyed the environment.

Some trees grew on patches of land, others grew out of the
dark water. Floating plants concealed what swam below. No matter
where Whiskers looked, all directions appeared equally gloomy.

Whiskers stood up on his hind legs and flopped his front
legs out of the hole. Jamming his back toenails into the wall of
the hole, he pushed up while pawing madly at the dirt in front
of him and rocking side to side. Inch by inch, he wriggled

forward on his chest and then his stomach until finally freeing himself.

Standing up, he glanced toward the water.

What the...?

A head with an unseen body was moving swiftly through the murk toward the patch of land he stood on. It came out of the water about ten yards away, walking on four legs.

As big as some terriers, it had longish brown fur, beady eyes, tiny ears, a little mouth with two large reddish-orange buckteeth, a humped-up rear end, webbed hind feet and a long, round, hairless tail. A slim ring of white fur encircled its flattened gray-black nostrils. More of that white fur ran down to its mouth and chin. Starting just below each nostril, about two dozen overly long, stiff white hairs spiked out perpendicular to its face.

I know what that is!

Whiskers had seen its ilk with Mr. Professor while watching the Human Planet Channel, which had the tagline "Surprisingly Animalistic."

It's a nutria. An overblown, waterlogged, disgusting swamp rat.

"Hey, you, nutria!" Whiskers barked with an insolent tone. "Tell me how to get out of here."

Scrunching up its face, the nutria looked Whiskers up and down.

"What are you?"

"I'm a dog. Whiskers by name, if you must know."

"A dog? Oh, yes, I can see that now. You're really full of yourself, aren't you? And what are you doing here? Looking for that stupid Big Bone that dogs yap about?"

"Oh, is it here?" Whiskers asked, slapping on a cheesy, friendly smile.

"Don't be ridiculous."

"In that case, just tell me how to get out of this swamp," Whiskers snapped.

"Why would you want to do that?"

"Because it's dark and creepy, not my kind of place."

"That's too bad, because I think it's very nice here," sniffed the nutria. "It's my home, and I like it."

"Yeah, fine for a big rat, but not for me. I want to get back to pretty skies and sunshine. Now show me a way out of here!"

"I think not. I don't like your attitude. You'll just have to find your own way out. Good luck, you're going to need it."

With that, the nutria stepped into the water and began to swim.

What a jerk, refusing to help a fellow animal in need. I ought to jump in the water right now, bite his butt and... Yikes! He's really leaving me!

"Please, come back! I'm sorry. I don't know what came over me. I didn't mean to act like that. It must have been the stress of being in distress."

The nutria turned around, paddled leisurely back, walked onto the land and cocked its head to eyeball Whiskers.

"Are you really sorry?"

"Yes."

"Kiss-a-cat sorry?"

Ugh.

"Well... uh... yeah."

"Then you must say, 'I am very sorry for my insolence, and if I lie, I hope to die because I'm a stupid dog.'"

No-good, rotten piece of swamp shit! First the gross cat thing and now this insult. But I'll pretend to play along so I can get out of here.

The nutria stood on its hind legs and held out its front paws, soundlessly signaling that it was waiting for Whiskers to humiliate himself.

"Okay," Whiskers said while crossing his back legs. "I am very sorry, and if I lie, I hope to die, because I'm a stupid dog."

"That's better," the nutria smirked. "Now here's what you need to do. Turn around and start walking. You'll soon come to a little bridge of land that goes off to the right. Walk over it to a big piece of land that has a stand of trees. On the other side of the trees you'll find more water that you'll need to cross, but don't worry because there are plenty of fallen trees in the water to walk on and lots of spots of dry land. Going by your earlier bluster, you're obviously energetic, so you'll be able to hop from one thing to another without getting in the water. Don't worry if everything looks the same. Just keep going and it won't be long before you're out. That's because you're already very close to the edge of the swamp."

Whiskers' ears perked up at that news.

"In that case, I shall forgive you for having been so insufferable," he said. "But now I must be off, because a hero's work is never done, not that you'd know anything about that."

Whiskers kicked back some dirt and trotted away, smugly glorifying at getting in the last jab.

He came to the land bridge sooner than expected. It was very narrow and broken up with its pieces separated by deep swamp water.

As he put a paw on the first narrow strip of dirt, Whiskers looked sideways to his right. The nutria was still back at the spot where they had talked.

"Are you sure this is the right way?"

The nutria didn't answer but made a waving motion for Whiskers to go on across.

With a sense of unease in his gut, Whiskers took tentative steps followed by little hops and bigger jumps, sometimes with a back leg slipping into the water and a quick scramble to pull it out before something awful could latch on to it.

As Whiskers neared the bigger piece of land, the nutria slid into the water with a self-satisfied smile and swam away.

What the nutria hadn't told Whiskers was that he could have gone a little farther up the swamp and taken a different land bridge, one that went to the left. At the end of it, there was a well-defined, hard-packed trail that would have led him out of the swamp very quickly.

Instead, Whiskers was heading into the hidden heart of the Great Abysmal Swamp.

24

DID YOUR WINGS COME OFF?

With one last jump, Whiskers cleared several feet of water, plopping down on the piece of land to which the nutria had pointed him.

That wasn't so bad. Let's see, just keep going straight ahead and I'll soon be out of this creepy place.

He made his way through the stand of trees mentioned by the nutria. Coming out of them, he stopped and stared. Everywhere lay dark, still, swampy water. The whole atmosphere was gloomier than on the side he had left.

Some fallen trees lay partly on the bank and partly in the water. Others floated on the surface or just below. Patches of earth in the swamp were few. Nothing was as close together as the nutria had indicated.

Whiskers jumped up onto the dry portion of a fallen tree. Taking tiny steps, he moved carefully toward the submerged part until all four of his feet were in several inches of water. He hesitated, then moved cautiously to the end of the tree where a longer, wider one floated a few inches away.

I don't want to do this, but I've got no choice.

Gingerly, he put a paw on the floating tree, then another.

With the front paws on, he carefully brought up a back foot, then the other. The tree started a slow roll. Whiskers shifted weight slightly in the opposite direction and the tree stabilized.

Gradually, he developed a feel for how to walk on the floating tree. He also found that the gas built up in his intestines from fear of the water could be used to counteract any roll by the tree when he pointed his butthole in the appropriate direction and jetted out a blast of air pressure—similar to the way astronauts jetted around when doing home makeovers on the Flip My Space Channel that he and Mr. Professor had watched.

This makes me an ass-tronaut!

When he neared the end of the floating tree, however, there were no other trees to step on. A piece of land beckoned, but it was too far for jumping. He had to get in the water, which was bubbling ominously in some spots.

I do not want to do this.

What if a water snake gives me a zing in the ding-a-ling?

What if a snapping turtle bites off a paw?

What if an alligator needs a snack?

Stop! This is not the way a hero thinks. I'll just have to outswim, outmaneuver and outfight whatever comes at me.

He jumped in, heart thumping, legs pumping, dog paddling faster and faster until he pulled himself onto the land.

Nothing got me! I can do this! I am dog! Hear me bark!

But he didn't bark out loud.

Only in my mind. I'm not dumb enough to give away my location to the rotten wretches in this place.

Confidence renewed, Whiskers walked toward the other side of the land. But his stride stopped when he stepped in something gooshy.

Uh-oh. Could this be alligator poop?

He looked down. His feet were not in anyone's poop. They

were in squishy, wet dirt. As he stared at his feet, they started to vanish.

What kind of dirt is this? It wants to move up my legs.

Oh, no! It's not moving. I'm sinking!

He had watched a show with Mr. Professor about this stuff.

I'm in quicksand!

Then he remembered how the person in the show had lain on his back and made wide swimming motions with his arms and legs until he slowly got to solid ground.

Lying on my back won't help. I'm a dog. My legs will just point straight up. I'll be paddling in the air.

Instead, Whiskers flopped over onto his right side. That stopped the sinking. Forcing his four legs forward and then pulling them back, Whiskers made agonizingly slow progress against the suction. After a while, something touched his ear. He rolled his eyes to look up at a root jutting out from solid earth. Whiskers twisted his head and clamped his mouth on it. He pulled with his teeth while continuing to move his legs, but the more he worked at it the more exhausted he became. Finally, he stopped, closed his eyes, and just lay there.

What a way to go. The hero dog who saves everyone else can't save himself. I'm done. I'm a goner.

"Well, look at you," said a female voice.

Startled, Whiskers opened his eyes, but couldn't see who it was. He tried to lift his head to see behind him but was too weak to free it from the quicksand's suction.

"You must be stupid. Don't you know quicksand when you see it? That's one of the first things all baby swamp animals learn."

"I'm not a swamp animal. I'm a dog," Whiskers responded to the unseen visitor.

"Well, that explains it. Anyway, you better get out of there. If you don't, the ants are going to eat you alive."

"What ants?"

"Why, swamp ants, of course. They're smart. They'll get bits of leaves and moss and whatever else and place them end to end so they can walk across the quicksand. They'll get in your ears, your eyes, your nose, your mouth and those other holes you have, but which I am too polite to mention."

"That sounds horrible. Please help me get out of here. I'm not sinking anymore, but I'm stuck and so tired that I can't move."

"You really are in a predicament, but I have lots of things to do today, and they won't get done if I spend any more time with you."

"But I'll die if you don't help me."

"You should have thought of that before you came into the swamp."

"I didn't have a choice. I fell out of the sky."

"You fell out of the sky? I don't see any wings on you. Or did they come off? Is that why you fell out of the sky? Anyway, I need to be going. Maybe somebody else can help you before you die."

This must be the most callous or the most stupid animal I have ever met. And I don't even know what kind it is.

"Can't you stay just a little bit longer?" Whiskers beseeched.

"I don't think so. In fact, I never should have said a word to you. I should have just gone on by without you knowing I was here. So, goodbye. Have a nice day."

Oh, no! I can't let this thing get away. I've got to outsmart it.

"Wait, don't go just yet," Whiskers said urgently. "I have something important to tell you."

"To tell me?"

"Yes."

"But how could you have something important to tell me? I don't even know you."

"Let me introduce myself. My name is Whiskers."

"So?"

"Well, now you know me."

"Hmm, I guess that's true. Okay, Whiskers, hurry up. What is the important message?"

"You'll have to help me out of the quicksand. I have to write the message in the dirt because it cannot be spoken aloud."

"Why?"

"Because it is for your eyes only."

"Oh, then it must be really important. Let's get you out of there quickly so I can be on my way."

Suddenly, Whiskers felt something hard jabbing him repeatedly in the back.

"Oww, stop, what are you doing? That hurts. That's not helping."

"I can help."

It was a different voice. A silky-smooth voice coming from the water.

"How can you help?" the first animal asked.

"I can bite him and put him out of his misery."

Whiskers' eyes widened.

Bite me?

"No, because he has something for me to see. But stop by later just in case I wasn't able to get him out. If the ants have been chewing on him all day, he'll probably appreciate your services."

"Okay, I'll do that. Bye for now."

"Toodle-oo."

"Who was that?" Whiskers croaked.

"Oh, him? He's just the local cottonmouth. Not really a bad guy when you get to know him."

Good grief, you've got to be kidding.

"Oh, look at who's dropping in now."

Whiskers couldn't look but could hear the sound of flapping wings coming close. When that sound stopped, there was a moment of silence, then a male voice—sharp and demanding.

"What's going on? Who's that in the quicksand?"

"This silly dog fell out of the sky right into it. I'm trying to help him out even though I shouldn't because I have so much to do, but he has an important message for me."

"A dog? That explains it. I've dealt with them before. You sit in a tree, and they run around in circles barking up at you like they're really doing something. They are so stupid. No wonder he fell in the quicksand."

What a jerk! But as long as I'm stuck in this muck, I'm not going to tell anyone off.

"I tried to push him out," the first animal said, "but it didn't work."

"I've got a better way," said the newcomer. "I'll drill some holes in him, and all his body fluids will run out. Then he'll be much lighter for us to pull out of the quicksand."

"But he'll die with no body fluids."

"No problem. After we get him out of the quicksand, we can float him in the swamp. The water will go in through the holes I made and fill him back up. Then he'll be as good as new."

"Well, it might be worth a try."

I'm not believing what I'm hearing.

"Please, no holes," Whiskers implored.

"Well, you heard him, he doesn't want any holes," the first animal said. "So, I guess I'll try something else."

"Okay, go ahead," said the newcomer. "But I'll stand by ready to drill holes if whatever you do doesn't work."

Silence.

Then splashing noises. After a short wait, sloppy wet material was dropped beside Whiskers. Suddenly, something hard gripped each side of his neck and yanked his head and shoulders up and down, again and again.

"What are you doing? Stop!" Whiskers yelped.

The animal relaxed its grip.

"Whiskers, you can't just lie there. You've got to help too. When I say 'go,' kick your legs loose and twist your body as hard as you can to the other side."

"GO!"

Whiskers wrenched himself leftward. At the same moment, the animal jerked his neck hard, flipping him onto a pile of slippery swamp slime and sliding him onto dry earth.

Panting and bruised, Whiskers looked up to see his rescuer. Staring back was the strangest animal he had ever seen.

25

DON'T GO THAT WAY

"What are you?" Whiskers asked.

"What am I? I'm the prettiest thing in the swamp. I'm not always here though, because I do travel around to other places. You're lucky I happened by. Just imagine if you had asked an alligator for help. Well, hello, can you say 'mealtime'?"

"You still haven't told me what you are."

"You're so silly. I'm a spoonbill, of course. Everyone knows that, except, I suppose, a dummy like you. So, I'll make it simple. I'm a bird."

A huge bird—three feet tall with a wide body supported by red, stork-like legs.

She spoke through a huge, gray beak about nine inches long. It was unlike any beak Whiskers had ever seen. It started out very thick at the face but became more narrow and started to flatten as it approached the middle. From the middle onward, not only was the beak completely flat, both top and bottom, but it flared out, becoming wider and wider until the end of it was the widest part of all, and circular in shape.

Good Lord! Looks like Mother Nature stomped on the last part of that thing.

"Oh, dear," she said, "I forgot to introduce myself. Whiskers, I bet you can't guess my name. Here's a clue. It's Rosie."

The name fit.

Although her neck, chest and upper back were white, the rest of Rosie's body was covered in pink feathers. Each pink wing had a thick band of red feathers running along its forward edge.

After getting an eyeful of Rosie, Whiskers turned his head to see the other would-be rescuer.

So that's what a real idiot looks like.

It was a woodpecker, and he seemed half-mad.

"We could have gotten you out a lot easier if we had drilled holes in you. That's my specialty. It's not a problem, no big deal. Wham, bam, you're out of your jam. Instead, you made poor Rosie work so hard to get you out even though she told you that she had a lot to do. You are so selfish, dog."

The woodpecker practically spat out the word "dog."

"Oh, fiddle, please don't get your feathers ruffled," Rosie said. "The important thing now is my message. I can't wait to find out what it is."

She turned to the woodpecker.

"I'm sorry, Woodrow, but you have to go because it's for my eyes only."

"Okay," he said, obviously miffed at being excluded from the message. "I'll go, but here's something for you, dog."

With those words, the woodpecker quick-stepped over to Whiskers and gave him an extra-hard rat-a-tat-tat in the side.

"Ow, ow, ow!" yelped Whiskers. "Get away from me, you lunatic!"

"So long, doo-doo head," Woodrow cackled as he took a hop, lifted up in the air and flew away.

Whiskers eyeballed his side. No holes there, just a lot of pain.

"Are all woodpeckers crazy?"

"Oh, forget about him," Rosie said. "Come on, what is the message? I need to get going, so hurry up."

"Oh, yes," Whiskers said. "The message. I almost forgot."

This bird is strong. I don't want her to whack me with that thing, so I better give her something good.

Whiskers shakily stood up on his tired limbs. Lifting his right paw, he started drawing in the soft dirt.

"What is it? What does it say?"

"Shh, I'm not finished."

After making some crude symbols plus some random squiggly lines, he stopped and said, "There it is. There's your message."

Rosie stared at the sandy hieroglyphics, cocking her head from side to side. She turned around, bent over and looked between her legs.

"No matter how I look at it, I don't know what it says," she wailed.

"That's because it's a secret message. It's written in a special code."

"Then you tell me what it says."

"I can't."

"Why not?"

"Because it's for your eyes only."

"But you wrote it."

"Yes, but I kept my eyes closed while I did it. And I still haven't looked at it."

"Well, in that case I give you permission to look at it and read it to me."

"Okay, but don't tell anybody that I saw it. I don't want to get in trouble."

"I promise I won't tell."

"Very well, the secret message is: 'True love is coming your way. You will meet a tall, dark and handsome stranger who will fly away with you to Whenever Land. There, you will have many baby birdy bambinos.'"

Rosie stiffened. She looked Whiskers up, down and all around as if seeing him for the first time: not tall, not dark, maybe handsome for a dog, but no wings left for flying. Obviously, he wasn't the one.

But it didn't seem to matter. She was ecstatic.

"Oh, I'm so glad I saved you. From now on, I'm going to save everyone from the quicksand, or at least I'll save any dogs that fall from the sky, especially if it's you again, Whiskers, so I can get another secret message."

Rosie made Whiskers read the message three more times.

"Thank you, thank you, thank you. And now, I really must go. Bye-bye, Whiskers. I love you."

Rosie flapped her wings and flew gently up into the sky, displaying a gorgeous spread of pink and red feathers. She was beautiful.

She said she loves me. Now I feel like a dirty rat. Sure, at first she was going to leave me to die, but she can't help it if she's a birdbrain. Anyway, maybe what I told her will come true.

After sitting for a while to get his strength back, Whiskers resumed his journey of walking on floating trees, swimming to low rises of land and gingerly testing patches of earth for quicksand.

The more progress he made, however, the less he seemed to be getting anywhere. The swamp didn't seem to have an end. On a stretch of land, Whiskers sat down for a break.

I miss Rosie. Even though she was so dumb that she was dangerous, she was nice. And how I wish Ace had made it. I'll bet he would know how to get out of here.

Hey, wait a Nude Pork minute. Mr. Professor and I saw lots of shows about people in places like this. The big thing is that no one ever gave up, like that guy Barbecue Grills.

He got up and resumed walking.

"Don't go that way."

Startled, Whiskers looked behind him. An animal was swimming in his direction. Whiskers stood up to see better, jiggled on his back legs a bit, then dropped down and spun around while his tail wagged feverishly. The swimming animal was a dog, a brown Labrador.

"Hey, come out of the water and join me!" Whiskers woofed. "I'm so glad to see you. I'm a dog too."

"Dog or frog or stick on a log, it doesn't matter," the Labrador said as it stayed on its watery course.

"Please come over here," Whiskers begged as the Lab drew near.

"Come over here, come over there, what does it matter, do you really care?"

"You're not making any sense."

"Scents and non-scents. In the end, they all smell the same."

The Lab swam past Whiskers.

"Come back. The alligators will get you."

"Gators in, gators out, gators here and all about, so why worry? I'm a water dog, you know, or I think I am because here I am."

"At least tell me how to get out of this swamp."

"I'm sorry, I can't. I've been in here forever," the Lab replied with a tone of despair. "All I can do is keep swimming. Oh, yes, there is something I can tell you that I've already told you but that I need to tell you again."

"What?" Whiskers asked in exasperation.

"Don't go that way."

"Which way?"

"The way you've been going. My parting advice is to be extra nice or you'll never find your way."

With that, the Lab continued swimming down the swamp. Whiskers watched until he disappeared from sight.

That dog is out of his mind. I'm better off without him.

Shortly though, a creepy, weird sensation generated by Mother Nature's GFS—the Gut Feelings System—told Whiskers that something was wrong, that he needed to be on alert.

He looked to each side, then behind and up, but nothing threatening was in view. Twitching his ears brought only the usual, constant noises of insect buzzings and far-off bird calls. Sniffing the air detected only the normal miasma of dank, fetid swamp odors.

Standing here isn't going to get me anywhere.

He found a floating tree that was the first in a long line of floaters. Hopping aboard, he stepped toward the end.

That is, until he stopped and looked down.

What's going on?

Something had bumped the bottom. The bumping came again—faster, harder, insistent.

As his GFS ratcheted from Alert status to Possible Danger, Whiskers' intestines went into queasy mode and his breathing came harder.

Well, uh, I think, uh, I better get off this thing.

He took three steps backward when...

BAMMMM!

The forward end of the tree shot out of the water, taking Whiskers several feet up in the air. Crashing down, the tree rolled and dumped him under the water.

Paddling madly, he got to the surface, but couldn't see. Thick, nasty algae was wrapped across his eyes. He thrashed about blindly, desperate to get back on the tree.

Oww!

His nose banged against something hard. Clawing at it with his front toenails and kicking with his back legs, he scrambled up on it.

If I ever get out of this miserable place, I should just find a nice home and never leave it.

Although still unable to see, he realized this was not the same tree, because it wasn't trying to roll under his weight. It was very stable.

Flattening down on his belly, Whiskers wiped his paws across his face to get the stinking algae off. But something was poking him in the belly. As he stood up, the fur along the ridge of his back, even though wet, also stood up.

26

TAKEN FOR A RIDE

W *hat kind of a tree is this?*
Whiskers' paws were perched on spiky lumps arranged in long lines.

The bark on this tree is so rough and weird-looking. And those spikes remind me of something in a movie. Oh, yeah—what Mr. Professor said was the Naughty Us in All Dizzy's 20,000 Leaks Filled Up the Sea.

Suddenly, the tree began to move.

On its own.

Oh, no! This isn't a weird tree. It's an alligator!

Whiskers braced himself, sure that any moment the alligator would whip around, latch on to him and drag him underwater to drown him in a death roll.

But it didn't happen. Instead, the alligator swam into deeper water and headed down the swamp.

He has to know I'm on his back. So what is he doing? Giving me a tour of the swamp? Taking me home to meet his family? Feed his family? Maybe a little conversation will get this beast to see me as something more than supper.

"Hello, my name is Whiskers. What's yours?"

No reply.

"I'm a dog. I guess you don't see many of us in this swamp, or do you?"

No answer.

"Excuse me, this is a very nice ride, but where are we going?"

Still nothing.

This isn't working. Maybe a new approach—one showing that I'm a friend, an ally, a sympathizer.

"As I've always told everyone, alligators are the most maligned of all creatures. Oh, how my heart has broken when I've seen humans carrying those bags and wearing those protectors on their feet made from the hides of you poor, misunderstood beings. Every time I saw such a crime, I barked at those horrid wretches, saying, 'That is so wrong' and 'Shame on you.'"

The alligator gave no reaction to this declaration of compassion and outrage.

Hmm, maybe I can connect on a more personal level and find common ground.

"Do you all sniff butts? We do."

No answer.

"Do you pee on bushes? If so, how do you do it? I'm only asking because it doesn't seem like alligators are built for lifting a back leg."

Again, no response.

"What about cats? Don't they just piss you off? So cynical, stuck-up and sneaky. Hey, I haven't seen any in this place. Now that's a real selling point for somebody who's considering moving here, in addition to having good neighbors like yourself."

That didn't work, so...

"Well, I think I've seen enough, and I thank you very kindly. You could drop me off anywhere, but there's a patch of land over to your right that looks perfect."

The alligator ignored the patch of land. And so it went, with Whiskers trying to get the beast to talk, but it never said a word.

I've had enough of this. I'm going to slowly step off into the water and quietly float away.

He gently moved each of his four feet until they faced the right side of the alligator. Just as he began to step off, the gator turned its head.

Whiskers shivered.

The gator's eyes were changing color. From brown to green to yellow to blood red.

That's not normal.

Without any prompting, Whiskers readjusted his feet to once again face forward. The gator resumed its silent swim, taking Whiskers deeper into the swamp, eventually coming to a line of tall trees growing tightly together, forming a barrier.

This dope is going to crash into them!

But as they approached, a gap opened in the middle, and the gator swam through.

On this side, vapor floated across the surface, the water was blacker, and some spots were bubbling.

As the gator plowed on, Whiskers jerked in surprise when a brightly colored parrot flew past his face. His whole body shook when a twenty-foot-long python emerged from floating vegetation to stare at him.

Where did they come from? Are we still in the same swamp that I fell into?

Farther along, a horrible howling started. Whiskers looked up. A monkey sat on a tree branch, gesticulating and yowling in anger at him.

This place is getting weirder.

Whiskers nearly fell off the alligator in shock when a huge monitor lizard on a slice of land flicked its forked tongue at him as if to say, "I want you."

Eyes wide, mouth hanging open, Whiskers looked down at the gator for some kind of reaction, but the creature continued swimming at the same pace, seemingly unperturbed by these animals so out of place.

Where are we? Has the alligator swum the entire Pedantic Ocean? Did he cross the Tropic of Popcorn? Are we in the Dead Whores Platitudes?

There were no answers to his questions, only a continual, silent journey through the gloom of the day into the darkest of nights.

Exhausted from nervous tension, Whiskers lay down on the alligator and fell into a fitful sleep. Awakening at dawn, he shook his head in wonderment as they floated by an iguana using its face to push a coconut up a large mound of earth. Just as the iguana made the last push to get the coconut on top, the coconut moved the tiniest bit off-center and rolled back down to the bottom of the mound. Each time this happened, the iguana made his way down the mound to start the laborious process all over.

Why is he doing that? For exercise? Because he's stupid? Or is that some kind of punishment?

Leaving the iguana behind, a new sight astonished Whiskers —on a bank of land, a rabbit was walking upright on its hind legs. The rabbit spotted Whiskers and waved cheerfully.

"Hello there. I've heard so much about you. Honestly, I thought you would be a mean-looking cur but you're not. In fact, you're quite cute. But I wouldn't want to be you. Oh, no, not at all."

He's heard about me? Uh-oh, it sounds like he heard something bad.

Shaken, Whiskers simply lifted a paw and did a half-hearted wave back.

The rabbit next addressed the alligator.

"Forgive my manners. It's so nice to see you again. How have you been?"

The gator ignored the rabbit. It paddled on by without slowing down.

"My goodness, you certainly take your duty seriously," the rabbit said. "As much as I would have liked to exchange pleasantries, I am in no position to blame your constancy, because I must confess that I am most shamefully guilty of lollygagging. Therefore, I shall be off or you'll get there before I do. I need to hurry, hurry, hurry, and scurry, scurry, scurry."

Rather than hopping away like most rabbits, this one dropped to all fours and ran through the vegetation like a cat.

27

YOUR CRIMES ARE NUMEROUS

"Charon's here!"

"She brought the dog!"

"You knew she would," someone said. "Nobody refuses Charon. I wonder if she had to beat him with her tail."

A girl? I was captured by a girl?

Whiskers and his reptilian escort had glided into a natural amphitheater. The water dead-ended at a semicircular swath of earth on which the vegetation had been trampled down. Tall trees overhung with long strands of thick moss framed the back of the gathering place. Mounds of dirt were scattered about the eerie setting.

This place is freaky, like the one I saw in that movie Mr. Professor called Allpuckerlips Now.

On and around the mounds of earth were scores of animals, including birds, possums, raccoons, a porcupine, chipmunks, rats, foxes, squirrels, snakes, monkeys, skunks and toads. The water was full of fish, eels, frogs, water snakes and turtles, some resting on floating trees.

Seeing Whiskers, the animals went wild. On land, they erupted with screeches, buzzing, caws, clicks, cheeps, squeaks, grunts, howls, yowls, growls and mindless chattering, all of which was accompanied by a fervent mad-as-hell-at-you shaking and pointing of paws and claws.

In the water, hundreds of fish, including piranhas, jumped and splashed. The waves they created rocked the alligator. Whiskers gripped hard with his nails to keep from falling into the water.

I'll bet those piranhas are already calling dibs on the best parts of my body.

Charon floated sideways to the edge of the land, rolled to her right and dumped Whiskers in the dirt. He lay still for a few moments, then stood up.

Casting about, he spotted the same rabbit who had hailed him during his journey down the swamp. The rabbit was sitting atop the tallest mound.

"The defendant is here," the rabbit said. "We may proceed."

Did he say "defendant"?

"The prosecutor, Mr. Scratchy, will step forward."

Prosecutor? Where am I? What's going on?

The howling multitude parted and the same nutria who had misled Whiskers emerged to wild cheers.

Seeing the nutria, anger swirled through Whiskers' veins.

If I wasn't outnumbered, I'd run over to that lying rodent and bite his butt so hard it would fall off.

WHAM BAM BAM!

WHAM BAM BAM!

WHAMMA BAMMA BOOMA BAMMA de BIPPITY BOP de BING BONG!

A beaver was slamming his tail on a reverberating piece of sheet metal propped at an angle against a log. When he had the attention of all present, the beaver intoned:

"Order in the court! Order in the court! Silence be unto you as we convene this proceeding with the Honorable Judge Sylvilagus. Be not ye bespeaking or beseeching or beguiled into doing so unless ye be spoken to by officers of the court or thee will suffer a great besmirching that will proceed in due course following the presiding of this proceeding which precedes, succeeds and supersedes all others that may come before or after it now or in the present or in the hereafter after everything else has been done or not done forthwith and forevermore in a world without end or middle or beginning, so it hath been written and stamped and purveyed and purloined and witnessed by those here present and not present whether they bring presents or be presentless in their presence or be prescient and omniscient whether through omission, commission, nocturnal emission or... uh... uh..."

The beaver appeared stymied, his memory blank. Some animals mouthed the next words, but he obviously was no good at reading lips or beaks.

"Bailiff, please finish the opening oration," remonstrated Sylvilagus.

"Uh, Your Honor, that's all I've memorized so far," said the beaver. "I'm sorry."

"Well, you are doing better, Bucky," the rabbit soothed. "Please continue practicing, because there's still a lot more to it."

He turned his attention to Whiskers.

"Defendant Whiskers," queried Sylvilagus, "how do you plead? Guilty a little or guilty a lot?"

"Guilty? What are you talking about?"

"You heard him, Your Honor," snapped Scratchy. "He just said the word 'guilty.' The rest of what he said was an attempt to mislead the court. As the prosecutor, I request that you proceed to sentencing."

"I didn't say I was guilty," Whiskers squeaked, his voice breaking from surprise and fright. "I don't even know what this is."

"It's a trial, Mr. Whiskers," Sylvilagus said. "Your trial. You come before this court presumed guilty as charged because otherwise there's really not much point in you being here, is there?"

"But I wouldn't even be here if it wasn't for that nutria you call a prosecutor. I asked him how to get out of this swamp, and he told me the wrong way on purpose."

The judge looked sternly at Scratchy.

"Is that true?"

"You should have heard him. He was arrogant, rude and disrespectful to me personally. Even worse, after I told him there was no Big Bone here, he insulted our beloved swamp in the most brutal terms. So, I sent him in the direction he deserved. Besides, what difference does it make?" Scratchy said, shrugging and screwing up his face, looking at Whiskers with contempt.

"At this point, not much I suppose," said the rabbit, "since the defendant still has to answer for the offenses he committed upon entering the Great Abysmal Swamp."

Turning his attention back to Whiskers, Sylvilagus said pleasantly, "By the way, there is the jury that will convict you."

The rabbit pointed to his left where a fearsome group of animals lounged on a collection of earth mounds.

Oh, catshit, what have I stepped into?

Leering, sneering and jeering at him were a snapping turtle, rattlesnake, wolverine, javelina, badger, python, bobcat, monitor lizard, cougar, copperhead, vulture and vampire bat. It was a true rogues' gallery, vicious and bad-tempered, flashing teeth, baring fangs and flapping ugly wings at Whiskers. A burnt smell seemed to waft from their direction.

"Mr. Whiskers," Sylvilagus said, "as a matter of convenience for you, we're just going to go ahead and plead you guilty. Is there anything you would like to say before you are sentenced?"

"Yes, I don't know what I'm accused of!"

"Your Honor, I object," Scratchy said. "It doesn't matter if he knows as long as the prosecutor, yours truly, knows the charges."

"Quite right," agreed the judge. "Mr. Whiskers, since justice is blind, I should turn a blind eye to your request, but I would like to know what the charges are so that I can pass an appropriate sentence according to the guidelines of the Swamp School of Jurisimprudence."

The rabbit looked toward the beaver.

"Bailiff, please reveal the charges against Mr. Whiskers."

The beaver held up a piece of bark and read it aloud.

"The charges against Mr. Whiskers, also more properly known as the Impertinent, Conceited, Mangy, Flea-Bitten, Tick-Filled, Hair-Shedding, Poop-Rolling, Nose-Running, Eye-Mucusing, Jaw-Slobbering, Stinking-Breath, Good-for-Nothing Dog are, to wit: illegal entry into the swamp; destroying swamp property, specifically, tree limbs; sunbathing without a permit; failing to rake smooth the sand after getting out of the trap; deceiving a swamp inhabitant; and whatever else the court's officers, participants or attendees might remember or make up as we go along since even though the defendant may not actually have done anything else, it is totally within his character to have done so, which is as good as actually doing it, and is therefore deserving of punishment in the extreme."

"Mr. Whiskers, as cute as you are, it is my sad but glorious duty to pass judgment on you," said Sylvilagus. "Your crimes are numerous, and I'm afraid your punishment will be harsh."

"But I need a chance to defend myself. It is my right to have a lawyer."

"A lawyer! He wants a lawyer?" Scratchy yelled. "Your Honor, why does a guilty defendant need a lawyer?"

"That's an excellent point," remarked the rabbit. "Mr. Whiskers, a lawyer is pointless when you are guilty."

"But I'm not guilty!"

The nutria stamped his feet in disgust.

"Judge, remember that when the trial started he said, and I quote, 'guilty.' He said that word without remorse or shame, but now he claims he's 'not guilty.' Your Honor, he's playing games and making a mockery of our judicial system."

Rubbing his chin, Sylvilagus turned toward Whiskers.

"I'm warning you, you're irritating the prosecutor. When Mr. Scratchy gets worked up, he's a real demon. There's no telling what punishment he may want for you."

By now, though, Whiskers also was fired up.

"I don't care. I know my rights from the boob tube. I want a puppet defender!"

28

TWO DOO-DOO HEADS

Sylvilagus shook his head in exasperation.

"Oh, my goodness. This is so unnecessary. But if you insist on exercising useless rights, let's get on with it."

He pointed a paw at the nutria.

"Mr. Scratchy, whom do we have available to represent the defendant?"

The nutria smirked and called out, "Will the unfathomable, hapless and woeful Mr. Loser please come forward."

From the crowd of spectators stepped the Labrador that had swum past Whiskers in the swamp.

"An excellent choice!" exclaimed Sylvilagus. "You heard that list of accolades, Mr. Whiskers. Plus, he's a dog, just like you. That should make you very happy."

Jeers and boos from the other animals dogged the Labrador's every step until he reached Whiskers' side.

"You're in big trouble," Loser whispered.

"Why?"

"Because you're going to die, or even worse."

"Why do you say that?"

"Because I'm your attorney. I always lose court cases. That's why they call me Loser."

Oh, no!

"But surely your real name is something much better, like 'Winner' or 'Stud' or 'Tiger.'"

"I don't know it anymore. One day I made the mistake of wandering into the swamp, and Scratchy had me punished. I had to roll a coconut up a mound over and over until I lost my mind. Now I just swim around looking for it."

Yikes! With him as my lawyer, I could be stuck here forever and go just as crazy as he is. I've got to take charge.

"I'm glad you're with me," Whiskers whispered. "In fact, I've got a plan."

Loser listened and nodded.

Whiskers looked up at the judge.

"Your Honor, Mr. Loser is having a problem talking, that's why we've been whispering."

"Is that true?" asked the rabbit.

"Ye…" was all that Loser got out before going into a coughing fit that buckled his front legs. Dropping to the ground, he rolled from side to side on his back, all the while choking and hacking, "Hahhch, hahhch, caaahcaaah, caaahcaaah…" He drooled foam for good effect.

That's a great acting job. He hasn't lost his mind. He's only lost his confidence. That fat rat stole it from him.

"Oooooh, poor animal, even if he is a dog," said Sylvilagus.

"Your Honor, may Mr. Loser simply be my consulting attorney? If I'm not sure what to do, he can whisper to me."

"Any objection, Mr. Prosecutor?"

The nutria looked at the dogs with disdain.

"No, Your Honor," scoffed Scratchy. "Two doo-doo heads just double the stupidity and make my job even easier."

"Very well," affirmed the judge. "And now, on with the show. Mr. Scratchy, please commence your prosecution."

"With great delight, your honor," Scratchy said.

He gave a slight nod to the bailiff.

"Ms. Rosie to the witness spot," boomed out Bucky the beaver.

As the spoonbill flounced her way to the mound beside that of the judge, she waggled her long beak at Whiskers.

"Oh, hello! I'm so happy to see you. Did you fall out of the sky again?"

Before Whiskers could reply, Scratchy intervened.

"Ms. Rosie, do you really believe that Mr. Whiskers fell out of the sky?"

"Well, yes, that's what he told me. I assume it's because his wings fell off. And where's my tall, dark and handsome stranger?"

"What stranger?" asked Scratchy.

"He said a stranger would fly away with me to Whenever Land and I would have lots of baby birdy bambinos."

"And did it happen?"

"No, it did not."

"Obviously, because 'whenever' really means it's never going to happen. He tricked you."

Rosie darted a pained glance at the sheepish defendant.

"Oh, Whiskers, how could you? I saved your life because I believed in you, but now I find out you're nothing but a liar."

Scratchy turned toward Whiskers with a sneer.

"Do you have anything to say to that?"

Whiskers gulped.

Mind be nimble, mind be quick. Help me outsmart this tricky dick.

"Rosie, I gave you hope, and it can still come true. Whenever Land is called that because you can have babies whenever you want, and they'll never grow up because whenever never ever really comes, and that means they'll always be your babies forever. Not only that, because you'll never grow old there you can keep popping out baby after baby. In fact, I'll put in a good word to Peter Pancake who's the tall, dark and handsome leader of the lost toys there. I think the two of you will really hit it off."

"Oh, that sounds so nice. Your Honor, that's what I want."

"Mr. Whiskers," queried the judge, "is this true? Do you really know this Peter Cupcake?"

"Your Honor, like George Who's Washing Tons of Clothes, I cannot tell a lie. I don't know Peter Clambake up close and real personal, but I do know where humans keep what they call books. One has his name in it and a map to Whenever Land. All I have to do is leave the swamp and go on a long, dangerous journey to get the book. So, the sooner I get out of here, the sooner Rosie can raise her muchachos on seed-covered nachos."

"Oh, judge, I didn't know about the book!" Rosie exclaimed. "No wonder I haven't met the handsome stranger yet. It's not Whiskers' fault. He hasn't had time to get it because he had to come here. He's not a liar. He's my hero."

Scratchy hung his head and shook it slowly from side to side. "Please, just step down from the witness spot."

When Scratchy raised his head, his face radiated anger, but he quickly assumed an ingratiating smile.

"Dear, kind jurors, fairest be ye of all in the Great Abysmal Swamp, you may disregard Ms. Rosie's well-intentioned but addlebrained testimony. Of course, you may ask 'Why?' This is why: She believes Whiskers fell out of the sky because that's what he told her. But take a look at those chicken-wing legs of his. How could anyone believe that he was happily dog-paddling his way through the air with those puny things while making such small talk with the birds as 'Hello, Mr. Hawk, Hello, Mrs. Robin, isn't this a lovely day for a little fly-around?' Don't you believe it. He's a dog like Mr. Loser over there. Take a good look at both of them. As you can see, dogs don't have wings. They don't even have feathers. Therefore, he lied to Ms. Rosie, but she's too caught up in a wishful fantasy to see the truth. Please note that whenever he speaks in court, he will be lying to you just like he lied to her. In fact, only a few moments ago, he openly lied about some place that doesn't exist. Therefore, do not believe anything that prevaricator says. He is as shameless a scoundrel as has ever come before this honorable court. It pains me to even look at him."

With that, Scratchy dramatically draped a foreleg over his eyes and turned his head away from the repugnant sight of the despicable, conniving, no-account defendant. The audience and jurors screeched in delight at the prosecutor's theatrics.

"Oh, that was so good," Sylvilagus said, waving his paws about and fairly hopping in his seat. "Mr. Prosecutor, keep it up."

"Yes, Your Honor," Scratchy said while bowing slightly.

He signaled to Bucky, who rattled the tin sheet and called out, "The rotten, no-good, sure-to-perjure-himself dog known as Mr. Whiskers is called to the witness spot."

When the beaver finished, Loser whispered, "Watch out, Scratchy pulls surprises, and he counts on you being flustered by them. Keep thinking and fight back. I couldn't do it, but I know you can."

"Thanks," Whiskers said, "I'll do my best."

He walked to the witness spot and settled on it as the audience and jurors rained boos upon him.

Scratchy stared hard at the insolent dog who had the gall to challenge him by demanding legal rights.

"Mr. Whiskers, and I only call you that because court etiquette requires it, we have checked up on you. Not only have you committed dastardly depredations in the Great Abysmal Swamp but we also have hearsay affidavits about awful deeds in which you engaged outside the swamp."

"Such as?"

How can any of these boneheaded, babbling buffoons in this backward backwater know anything that happens in the real world? This bozo must be bluffing.

"Such as in the circus," Scratchy replied, smiling hugely.

At the word "circus," Whiskers' head jerked as fear rippled through his body.

29

YOU'RE OUT OF CONTROL

Whiskers sat on the witness spot transfixed, his lower jaw flopped open so low that a mosquito flew in, took its sweet time sucking blood from the tongue, then flew out.

All the while, the swamp animals screamed with delight at seeing the shock on Whiskers' face, knowing that Scratchy had rattled the detestable canine with the word "circus."

I don't know of one thing wrong that I did there, but who knows what some of those low-intelligence ingrates might have said.

"Oh, yes, Mr. Whiskers," Scratchy said, "we have checked up on you. It was so easy to do. When one animal speaks, many others hear because they are all around, starting with the lowest of insects. Information spreads instantly with a buzz, a click and..."

Scratchy suddenly broke into a high-falsetto singsong:

A croak here
A caw there
A cheep, a screech
A hoot and howl
A-N-Y-W-H-E-R-E!

Finished with drawing out his little ditty, Scratchy held up both front paws to signal "No applause, please," which really meant: Hoot, cheer and howl your asses off, which all the animals gleefully did. Then he got back to business.

"Yes, we broadcasted inquiries about you and received many juicy messages back via Flapper Express, the bird messenger service. For example, we know all about your vile reputation among the circus dogs."

Oh, no! Any animal in the circus but them!

"C-c-circus d-d-dogs a-are d-d-dumb d-dogs," Whiskers stuttered.

Pausing, he breathed deeply several times until calm.

"They can't be believed. They are jealous and envious. They are so stupid that they do the same tricks over and over for the crummiest of treats. They are in the circus because dogs in the real world won't have anything to do with them."

"That's for the court to decide," Sylvilagus said. "Who here can testify about the character of circus dogs?"

"I can," piped up a monkey in the crowd. "I escaped from a circus. What a rotten place that was. But while I was there, I saw the circus dogs many times, and I gained a great respect for them. They are not jealous or envious or stupid. They are kind and gentle and happy. Their tricks are extremely complicated. Only highly intelligent dogs are chosen for their act. To hear this Whiskers dog insult them is pure jealousy and envy on his part. He is the lowest and meanest of dogs compared to them. He is not even fit to wallow in their poop. I would happily throw my own poop on him if the court would allow it."

"Perhaps another time, but we'll remember your kind offer, you cute, swinging thing," said Sylvilagus. "And now, back to you, Mr. Prosecutor. Take it away."

"Thank you, Your Honor," Scratchy said while accepting a piece of bark from the bailiff. "What powerful testimony the monkey gave. It was most convincing. In fact, it makes you look like a fool, Mr. Whiskers."

Scratchy whirled and faced the jury, waving the piece of bark at them.

"Let's list a few more of Mr. Whiskers' vainglorious, deceitful, ego-filled and self-gratifying actions in the circus. We have sworn affidavits that:

"He made no effort to be a real friend to any animal.

"He held himself to be superior to his own kind.

"He smarted off to an elephant."

The court spectators and jurors were aghast at the last comment, saying among themselves:

"Smarting off to an elephant?"

"What animal in his right mind would smart off to an elephant?"

"Who does that jerk think he is?"

"In fact," Scratchy continued, "the elephant reported that he was so mad at this dog that he felt like stomping on him. Mr. Whiskers, it appears that, thanks to the birds of the Flapper Express, your sins are coming home to roost."

Loser was right. This fat rat is full of surprises.

At that moment, a large crow flew in, circled overhead a few times, then flapped to a landing beside Scratchy. The bird had a thin piece of bark in its beak. Scratchy took the bark and studied it intently.

"Your Honor, I have just been apprised via the Flapper Express of something most awful about this defendant."

Oh, no, what now?

"We have it on good authority from unnamed and confidential sources that Mr. Whiskers, a dog, therefore a member of the Animal Kingdom, enjoys consorting with humans. He actually seeks out their company."

With that news, exclamations of disgust erupted among all the animals.

"Eeww!"

"Ugh!"

"Awful!"

"Outrageous!"

On land, the loudest cries came from those who had escaped from circuses, pet shops and research laboratories.

In the roiling water, the fish were screaming:

"He probably likes to go fishing just to ride in their boats!"

"He probably warms their worms in his mouth!"

"He probably baits their hooks for them!"

The judge stared at Whiskers, slowly shaking his head while digesting the shocking information.

"Oh, Mr. Whiskers," said Sylvilagus, "if this is true, I am so disappointed because I was hoping you might be different. This goes to the heart of why dogs are so despised by other animals. Yes, there are times when animals have to be around humans because they have no other choice, either being trapped by them or born into their service. But to actually want to be with them? Don't you know that humans are bad for you? That they are bad for all animals? That even when they are nice to you and give you things, such as a warm home in the winter and a cool house in the summer and easy-to-chew, boneless food in a bowl, that they are actually degrading you? Wouldn't you prefer to run free as a wild animal of nature rather than being walked in humiliation on a leash?"

The judge's remarks brought Whiskers up short.

I never thought that being with humans was wrong. There's no law or code against it in Dogdom. Humans and dogs have been working and living together forever, helping one another, protecting one another and being happy in each other's company. But maybe the rabbit has it right, that dogs did go wrong somewhere. I hate to say it, but maybe cats are on to something, taking food and an easy life from humans while scorning them at the same time and refusing to do tricks for them.

Wait a moment. When that big-ass bear Bonecruncher chased me in Happy Valley, it wasn't done in fun. And those rattlesnakes, my so-called "fellow" animals, would have gladly pumped me full of poison. And the bees? They showed no mercy when they almost ruined my nose.

Running free? Really? More like running for your life. What's so great about that? Besides, what's wrong with a house that knows when you need warm air and cool air? It beats freezing or broiling to death. It definitely beats being stuck in quicksand with ants gnawing on your brain.

That's it. I'm done messing around with these morons. The judge is full of catshit. And so is that water-soaked rodent that has him wrapped around his claws.

"Mr. Whiskers," Sylvilagus asked, "what do you have to say for yourself?"

Whiskers burst out, "Jacuzzi!"

"Whatever do you mean by that?"

"It's French, from the land where people make French fries. 'Jacuzzi' means I accuse you of falsely putting me in hot water."

Two spots bulged and throbbed on opposite sides of Scratchy's forehead. Hissing air past his reddish-orange buck teeth, he advanced toward Whiskers and thrust a paw at him.

"You put yourself in hot water! We didn't do anything to bring you here. You brought yourself here. And your putrid life has been revealed to be one of shameful, empty, sorry actions in service to your overblown, ridiculous, lying ego. So now you're being judged for it. That's the real truth, isn't it?"

"No, it isn't!" Whiskers stormed back. "And you know what else?"

All the animals who had ears perked them up. Others shook their heads and murmured to one another:

"Who does that dog think he is?"

"No one has ever stood up to Scratchy."

"That dog is too stupid to know who he's dealing with."

Hunching his shoulders and pushing his face forward, Scratchy stared hard at Whiskers.

"What is it that you want to tell me?"

"You can't handle the vermouth!"

Taken aback, Scratchy raised both front paws and gave a puzzled glance at the judge. Sylvilagus frowned in thought, shrugged his shoulders and leaned toward Whiskers.

"Dear me, whatever does that mean?"

"It means being drunk and out of control, like birds who eat rotting berries or cows who fill up on loco weed."

Whiskers whirled and yelled at Scratchy.

"You, Mr. Prosecutor, are drunk with power and out of control!"

He spun and aimed a paw at the rabbit.

"You, Mr. Judge, are presiding over a farce with a jury that is out of control—it belongs in a cage! And all of these leering, jeering, jabbering spectators are out of control! This whole court is out of control!"

30

I FEEL YOUR PAIN

S tunned by Whiskers' tirade, Sylvilagus and Scratchy waved their paws frantically at the beaver.

BAM de BAM BAM!

BAM de WHAMMA BAM BAM!

BAM de OOMPA LOOPA ALLEY OOPA de WHAMMA BAM BAM!

The eager beaver beat the bejesus out of the sheet metal with his tail until Whiskers stopped ranting.

"Mr. Whiskers, I am surprised by your behavior," Sylvilagus admonished. "Even though this is a criminal court, it is still a civil court. We observe rules of decorum."

Panting hard from his tirade, Whiskers looked from the jury to the prosecutor to the judge.

That felt so good. I blistered the fool out of these idiots. But I know it didn't help me. If I want to get out of this hellhole, I better take a softer approach.

"Your Honor, I apologize. I would never disrespect this court on purpose. I have a condition called appleplexy, which over-comes me with theatrics."

"Oh, really?" Sylvilagus said, replacing his frown with a

smile. "I must say that you certainly put on a show. In fact, it was excellent. What a way to liven up this proceeding."

Looking from the jurors to the audience, Sylvilagus began to clap, saying, "Let's have a round of applause for Mr. Whiskers and his bravura entertainment."

Incredulous that they were being asked to applaud a defendant, those animals who could clap did so, but half-heartedly.

I've got the judge softened up. Now to seize the moment.

"Your Honor, Mr. Scratchy is a most formidable opponent. He has obviously made his case. May I now say a few humble words on my own behalf?"

Putting a paw to his chin, the rabbit studied Whiskers for several moments.

"I suppose so. Mr. Prosecutor, any objection?"

Scratchy turned his back to Whiskers, bent over and released a tremendous blast of odoriferous gas accompanied by tiny, dried-out brown flakes that wafted delicately on micro-currents of warm air before gently settling on the ground.

Whiskers' nose went on high alert, nasalizing the gaseous molecules that came his way.

Good Lord! What do they feed on in this swamp?

"Well, Mr. Whiskers," said the judge, "in his own magnificent way our esteemed prosecutor has expressed total contempt for your ability to sway this court. In other words, you may state your case."

Thank goodness for all the lawyer shows that Mr. Professor and I watched. May their antics be with me.

Whiskers stepped away from the witness spot. He paced back and forth solemnly before the judge and jury until all was quiet. Gravely, he hung his head for a few pensive moments, then raised it slowly toward the jurors.

"Hath a dog not eyes like you?"

The jurors glanced from one to another, puzzled. Normally,

defendants were so frightened they peed on themselves and pleaded for mercy. Instead, this dog was batting his eyes at them.

"Hath he not ears like you?"

Whiskers wiggled his ears as fast as possible. The jurors who had ears tried to wiggle their own.

"Hath he not a nose like you?"

The jurors nodded agreement and flared their nostrils as Whiskers pointed his own up in the air, inhaling deeply and exhaling noisily.

"Doth a dog not poop in the wild like you?"

There were big nods to that one, even without a demonstration.

"Bite me, and do I not bleed like you?"

With that, Whiskers bit the skin of his left foreleg just enough to bring a trickle of red blood. Impressed, the jurors bobbed their heads in recognition of their common bond.

"Dear kind, misunderstood jurors, what I have shown you is that we are all brothers and sisters under the hide. As such, do I speak only for myself? No. I stand here today for all animals who have been vilified and maligned beyond all reason, which leads me to ask: Have you ever been unjustly accused?"

A number of the jurors mouthed the word "yes."

As Whiskers' elocution drew the jurors in, they began to sway in a slow, easy, rhythmic, rocking motion. He was killing them softly with his words, offering a tonic for their tortured souls.

"I feel the pain you have felt because here I am unjustly accused of insignificant, teensy-weensy things. These things are so tiny that they are smaller than an ant's eyeball, smaller than a flea's whisker, smaller than a gnat's hiney hole.

"Oh, my sweet and most fair jurors, shall we examine these pitiful, trumped-up charges? The prosecutor says I entered the swamp illegally. I came by air. How can that be illegal? Have we forgotten that birds enter the swamp by air? Why can't a dog? What's the harm? Oh, wait, there is no harm to the air. The air is perfectly fine.

"As for the few dead, dangling, barely-hanging-on tree limbs that I broke, they were a danger to all animals below. Who knows when poor, harried Mother Nature would have had the time to remove them? I ask you, what's wrong with giving her a little help? Is that not our civic duty?

"Did I leave the quicksand a little messy? Yes, but I had no choice. If it had been watered properly, it would have been easy to smooth out. It's not my fault that the groundskeeper here wasn't doing his or her duty. As for sunbathing without a permit, one cannot bathe in something so sticky."

The jurors were buying it. They nodded emphatically each time Whiskers made a point.

"And what is all that blather about things that supposedly happened in a circus? Just take a moment to imagine the horror of yourself being trapped in a cage there, trotted out only for exhibition. How could any decent animal maintain civility in an environment that stresses one to the absolute breaking point?"

The jurors shuddered. All through childhood, their parents had threatened to send them to the circus if they continued to misbehave.

At that moment, Loser coughed to get Whiskers' attention. After conferring in whispers, Whiskers faced the jurors with a notable air of confidence.

"Do any of you really believe that the bird from the Flapper Express—the one called Phelonius—made any effort to get the real truth about my time in the circus? Or, more likely, was this just another one of his sudden, overly dramatic appearances—a gimmick, a fraud, a sham that was staged to prejudice you?"

Loser's advice paid off. The jurors glared hatefully at Phelonius. They had all been burned by his flying entrances with a list of supposed misdeeds in his beak.

"I also am accused of deceiving a swamp inhabitant. That means Rosie. But did I bring joy into Rosie's life? Did I give her hope? Does she still have hope?"

Nods all around. Yes, he was right. He had brought her joy, and she still had hope.

"I ask you, how can my offering of hope be called deceit? Instead, I accuse the prosecutor, Mr. Scratchy, of being the true deceiver. I was hopeful of leaving the swamp, but he misled me with false directions just so he could torment me the same way he has tormented all of you for his own malicious pleasure."

During Whiskers' ongoing monologue, Scratchy had become more and more agitated, scrunching up his face and shaking his paws as the too-clever dog ingratiated himself with the jury. Now, the despicable canine was questioning his true motivation.

"This is outrageous! The defendant is on trial, not me. Your Honor, this dog has besmirched my honor. I am the attacker, not the attackee."

"Oh, yes, you're right," Sylvilagus responded, "but this is so much fun and far more interesting than the usual show trial that I am going to allow it. I just love a feisty fellow. Please continue, Mr. Whiskers."

Whiskers still had one serious issue to deal with.

"I know that many of you were shocked to hear that I seek out the company of humans. I must admit that it's true."

The spectators' jaws dropped open. Rather than trying to pooh-pooh away a charge, Whiskers had openly confessed to a heinous activity. Smiling now, Scratchy pumped a triumphant "gotcha" paw in the air.

"But there is a reason. And it is this: I am a spy."

All the animals looked from one to another, shaking their heads as if not sure they had heard correctly.

"Yes, you heard right. I am a spy, a spy for the Animal Kingdom. By telling you this, I'm breaking my cupboard. My secret code name is DoubleOhSevenUp. I'm one of the last surviving members of the Free Animal Reconnaissance Team. My job is to steal the secrets of humans. How? By pretending to be the dumbest dog in the world. That's so they won't see the harm in letting me watch their shows like 'Don't Leave It to Beaver,' 'Not Born Free,' 'Snoopy Don't Come Home,' and 'Keep Willy Locked Up.' That's how I learn what they are planning to do to animals. I tell you, it's a dangerous life. If I get caught passing on this top-secret information, I face death at the hands of animal control."

"NO, NO, NO!" screamed everyone. "NOT THAT!"

"But I do it anyway, without a care for myself," Whiskers said, tilting his head skyward in his best heroic pose. "I regret that I have only one life to lose for the Animal Kingdom. Yea, even if I were so unfortunate as to be a cat, I would gladly give all nine of my lives."

The audience erupted.

"Bravo!"

"We forgive you!"

"Free Whiskers!"

"Scratchy stinks!"

"Rotten, no-good nutria!"

31

DEATH UNTIL DEAD

S cratchy's head ratcheted back and forth like a weed whipped about in a gale. Everywhere he looked, animals on land and in the water were making angry faces.

At him.

For the first time ever, he had been outmaneuvered in his own court of retribution.

Standing tall, Scratchy moved toward Whiskers while pumping his paws as if to give the impertinent dog a right good whacking, but he stopped. Attacking the public's newfound "hero" could backfire and cause a runaway jury. A different, calmer approach was needed.

"Wow! A spy! I didn't know. I must say that I am most impressed. How about you, jurors?"

Enthralled with Whiskers' disclosure, every one of the black-hearted ne'er-do-wells nodded vigorously, stirred by a vestige of patriotism for the Animal Kingdom.

"Yes, indeed, most amazing. What a totally unexpected development," Scratchy said, cocking his head and tapping his reddish-orange buck teeth with a paw.

He leaned forward slightly, furrowed his brow, stared at the ground and stuck out his lower lip while turning his head slowly from side to side as if trying very hard to figure out something.

Watching Scratchy's facial contortions caused the jurors to also adopt puzzled looks. What was befuddling the seemingly all-knowing prosecutor?

"As much as I enjoyed that dramatic performance by the defendant, there's something that perplexes me. Therefore, Your Honor, based upon this new information, may I reopen my questioning of Mr. Whiskers?"

"Please do," said Sylvilagus. "We are all most intrigued by his spying revelation."

Whiskers returned to the witness spot. Scratchy approached in an offhand, easygoing manner.

"Mr. Whiskers, are you visiting old friends in our swamp?"

What? Why is he asking me that?

"Uh, no," Whiskers responded.

The spectators snickered because no dog has any friends in any swamp.

"You have family here?"

What is he getting at?

"No, I don't," was greeted with laughter by all the animals, including the jurors and the judge.

Scratchy paced around, one paw held across his chest and the other slowly tapping his cheek as he pondered Whiskers' answers.

"So, if you're not visiting old friends and you have no family in our swamp, then you must be here on a spy mission, right?"

I don't have a good feeling about these questions, but I've got to play along.

"Yes, I am."

"And you were given this specific mission by what you call the Free Animal Reconnaissance Team, correct?"

"Yes."

"Let's see, the acronym for that would be FART, which means you're a dog fart, right?"

Whiskers sighed and nodded, "Yes."

The judge, jury and spectators whooped, howled and screeched with laughter until Scratchy signaled for quiet.

"Now, let's clear up a point," he said unctuously. "You claim that you are doing this spying for the good of the Animal Kingdom, correct?"

"Yes."

"And to do that, you spy on humans, right?"

"Yes, of course."

"Then tell me, Mr. Whiskers, who are you spying on in our swamp?"

It's time to put a stop to this.

"I cannot tell. It's top secret, confidential and classified," he answered firmly.

"In that case, Mr. Whiskers," Scratchy said, "I have a surprise for you."

Oh, catshit. What now?

"There are no humans in the Great Abysmal Swamp for you to spy on."

Whiskers sat there blinking, his mouth open.

"Therefore, you must be a double agent. As such, I demand that you tell this court which one of us you are spying on..."

Scratchy leaned forward until his nose almost touched Whiskers' nose, opened his mouth wide and yelled, "...FOR THE HUMANS!"

Dumbfounded, Whiskers opened and closed his mouth over and over, but no sound came out because his brain couldn't come up with any believable response to Scratchy's attack.

Comments like "traitor," "double-crosser" and "why wait for a verdict?" were being muttered in the audience. Some animals started walking toward Whiskers while others slithered forward.

The rabbit waved his forelegs frantically at Scratchy.

"Mr. Prosecutor, we need to finish this trial, not start a riot. Do something."

Scratchy bowed to Sylvilagus. Holding up his forepaws to stop the encroaching animals, he motioned them back to their places.

"Animals of the swamp, I share your feelings about this loathsome dog. Either he is a traitorous double agent on the side of the humans or he made up that heroic spy story to save his pitiful hide. Therefore, let's add suspected high treason and shameless perjury to his other misdeeds."

Scratchy turned his head to look away from Whiskers' odious presence while waving him dismissively off the witness spot.

Walking slowly with his head down, Whiskers rejoined Loser who whispered, "Are you really a spy?"

"No, I just made that up. I was trying anything to get out of here, but it backfired."

"Mr. Whiskers, do you have anything else to say in your defense?" the judge asked.

Dejected, Whiskers answered, "No, Your Honor."

"May I say something, Your Honor?"

It was Loser.

"Well, you are the consulting attorney, and it seems you've recovered your voice, so proceed."

Loser looked at Whiskers.

"That is, if it's okay with you."

"You can't hurt me any more than I've hurt myself," Whiskers said.

Loser smiled.

"I appreciate that," he said, then walked to the center of the court.

"Your Honor, Mr. Prosecutor, jurors, and everyone else, I saw

Mr. Whiskers in another part of the swamp before this trial began. He looked lost and begged me to tell him how to get out, but I couldn't because I don't know how. And we heard earlier that he also asked Mr. Scratchy for help in leaving the swamp. Those aren't the actions of a spy. Mr. Whiskers made up that story out of desperation when he saw that he was trapped in a much bigger lie—that this is a fair trial. As for those other things he's accused of, I think they're either small matters or exaggerations by the prosecutor, or should I say persecutor, because Mr. Scratchy is just plain mean, and that's all I have to say."

Loser resumed his place beside Whiskers.

"Thanks," Whiskers whispered, "you're better than you think."

"Rebuttal, Mr. Prosecutor?" asked the judge.

Angered at being called to account by a known loser like Loser, Scratchy replied with scorn.

"Well, wasn't that just too precious? Two dogs sticking together. What else would you expect?"

"Now that's sophisticated contemptuousness, expertly done," commented Sylvilagus. "May I take it that the prosecution rests?"

"Yes, Your Honor, the animals of the Great Abysmal Swamp rest their case and ask for the ultimate penalty: death until dead."

Whiskers and Loser exchanged sad looks. One was close to losing a new friend, and the other was close to losing his life.

This whole stupid thing started because I asked for directions. I'll never do that again.

"It's now up to the jurors to confer," Sylvilagus said, "but I must point out that, unlike all other trials, Mr. Whiskers made this one a real contest. Therefore, jurors, you have a weighty task, so consider carefully what you have heard."

Instead of coming back with the usual quick verdict, the

jurors took their time. Putting their variously shaped heads together, they conferred viciously among themselves with low growls, hisses and screeches, considering justice versus the law, prosecution versus persecution, whether a wrong can still be right, whether something right can be all wrong, and which of the arguments were the most entertaining.

Finally, the snapping turtle signaled to the judge that they had come to a decision.

"What is your verdict?"

"Guilty."

"And the punishment?"

"Death until dead."

Whiskers' head drooped. Either Scratchy's artful impugning of his spy story had trumped his own brilliant theatrics or the jurors knew that only one verdict was acceptable.

"Mr. Scratchy," intoned Sylvilagus, "as the prosecutor, do you have any recommendations for how the delightful Mr. Whiskers' life should be terminated?"

"Your Honor, why should I have all the fun? I think it's time for some special input."

32

DON'T FORGET THE EARS

Smiling at the compliant jurors and the ecstatic spectators, Scratchy paced jauntily back and forth, rubbing his forepaws together.

"Termination. What a beautiful word. Fortunately, we have a wonderful variety of methods to carry it out. But let's throw it open to the public to make their suggestions so they can really feel like they are a part of this."

With that, he did a half-twirl to face the audience. Holding his forelegs outstretched, he asked, "What say you? How shall we dispatch this detestable dog?"

"I would be happy to bite him," volunteered the civic-minded cottonmouth.

"I could squeeze the shit out of him," said a python, its coils moving suggestively. "He's obviously full of it."

"Throw him to the piranhas!" shouted someone in the audience.

Then everyone joined in, jumping about and screeching what each would be most happy to do to Whiskers.

BAM de WHAM BAM! BAM de WHAM BAM!

"Silence, order in the court!" yelled Bucky, slamming his tail over and over on the sheet metal until the mayhem subsided.

"Mr. Whiskers, you have heard a variety of demises put forth by the virtuous citizens of the Great Abysmal Swamp," Sylvilagus said. "They are all equally excellent or awful depending on one's point of view. So, guess what? It's your lucky day. You get to choose the punishment you want and have it administered to you by the enthusiastic audience member who suggested it. What a special way for you to shuffle off this mortal coil."

Whiskers rubbed a paw against his jaw as if carefully mulling over each horrible punishment screamed out by the blabbering multitude. Each time he rubbed, he displayed a new facial expression, from pensive to wistful to mournful to disturbed to horrified.

"Your Honor, I choose death by that animal over there, the cotton mou..."

All heads whipped around to gaze enviously at the lucky snake.

"You have chosen the cottonmouth," remarked Sylvilagus. "An excellent choice. He's a fine, upstanding public serpent."

"...se."

"Please slither forward to do your duty," the rabbit said to the snake, who began to uncoil.

"No, Your Honor," interjected Whiskers, "I did not choose the cottonmouth."

"What? But we all heard you say that."

Whiskers pointed at a cute brown mouse.

"I chose that cotton mouse. Him, over there, standing near the cottonmouth."

"Mr. Whiskers, are you fooling around with me? In a legal way, I mean."

"No, Your Honor. The cotton mouse was hollering and jumping about more than anyone, saying he was going to bite me into tiny little pieces. He seemed so vicious and energetic that I figured he could get the job done quicker than anybody, and I wouldn't have to suffer for so long."

The judge looked askance, first at Whiskers and then at the mouse.

"Hercules, what were you thinking? Were you proposing to palpate, pulp, pound, pummel, pulverize and pirahnacize this dog who is so much larger than you?"

The cotton mouse looked abashed as the animals around him whispered insults, particularly the cottonmouth who was hissing, "You idiot!"

"I'm really sorry," squeaked Hercules. "Mr. Scratchy asked us what we wanted to do to the defendant, and I just got carried away."

Hearing his name, Scratchy began yelling.

"Judge! I demand that you negate any thought of rolling over for this dog and acceding to his request for death by mouse. It would be insane, ridiculous and just downright stupid of you to even consider it."

The rabbit grimaced at the nutria's lack of respect.

"Your most gracious honor," Whiskers countered in a smooth, polite tone, "you said I could choose from all the punishments proposed by the public, and death by cotton mouse was one of those offered up."

Sylvilagus sighed.

"Although I have been amused, bemused and just now abused, I will not have my honor as an honorable honor dishonored by me dishonoring my honor, and therefore I must uphold my honor and the honor of this court by honoring my word of honor. Death by cotton mouse it shall be."

Scratchy twitched, jerked and spasmed with the shock of the judge's pronouncement. His eyes rolled and steam puffed from his nose. "No! No! No!" was all he could say in a conniption fit.

"Okay, Hercules," Sylvilagus said, "even though you're really up against it, give it all you've got, you little nipper."

The mouse, both proud and scared to be in the spotlight, tiptoed over to what, for him, was a very large animal. Never in his right mind could he have taken on a dog, unless it was one of those teacup types.

But duty called, and Hercules answered by flinging himself at Whiskers. Acting as sideline coaches, the other animals screeched, hollered and screamed advice on how to dispatch the canine.

Watching the mouse intently, Scratchy wrung his paws. He almost started to put them together as if to pray for a miracle, but stopped and apparently limited himself to fervently hoping for one.

Hercules did his best. He tried to munch, crunch and have lunch on Whiskers' legs, sides, back, tail and head, but his tiny teeth and nails couldn't get far into the fur. In fact, Whiskers was enjoying the little fellow's tickling ministrations, saying "a little more to my right," "oh, that feels good on the neck" and "don't forget behind the ears."

Exhausted, Hercules gave up when the hometown rooters stopped cheering for him and began laughing at his sad, puny, comical effort.

The judge stepped in.

"That's enough, Hercules," said Sylvilagus. "Please stop. This may be a travesty of justice, but it's something I will always remember when I need a good laugh. As for you, Mr. Whiskers, you certainly know how to take advantage of a situation."

With that, the rabbit began to rummage through a pile of bark slabs with scribbling on them.

"Ah, yes, here it is. By swamp law, an animal cannot be condemned to suffer the mental anguish of undergoing a second execution attempt, although I doubt you suffered much anguish from feeling our little friend trying to gnaw you to death. There-fore, you are freed from the punishment of being terminated with extreme prejudice until extinct. However, you are still guilty and must be punished in some way.

"And I see, according to Arcane Section No. 543, Obscure Subsection 84, Explanatory Adjunct 29, Buried Clause 41 and Non-stated Condition 37 of the Great Abysmal Swamp Law Guide, that I, as the judge in such situations, have the latitude to levy punishment per my discretion.

"Mr. Whiskers, despite your illegal entry from above, frol-icking in the quicksand to deface it, and wanton trickery of a swamp denizen, the court finds that you were endeavoring in all good faith to leave our swamp. If Mr. Scratchy had aided you in your effort, rather than wishing to inflict vindictiveness upon you for a perceived slight, this trial would not have been neces-sary because you would have been out of our jurisdiction. Addi-tionally, because of his prior contact with you, Mr. Scratchy should have recused himself as the prosecutor for your trial. Considering all of the above, the court rules that it is only fitting and proper that you may leave the Great Abysmal Swamp rather than be inflicted with the customary harsh punishments."

It's finally over! I'm getting out of here!

The rabbit fixed Whiskers with a solemn gaze.

"I can read the look on your face: eyes wide open, tongue hanging out and excited panting. You think you're going free, right? Hmm, not quite. Defendant Whiskers, you are banished to the Isle of Elbone."

What the...? I thought this rabbit liked me.

"Sorry about that," Sylvilagus added.

"Sorry, my furry ass!" screamed Scratchy. "Banishment! That's a joke! What do you want to do, sneak over there to hold paws with him? He needs to suffer. He needs pain. Send somebody along to beat the dog crap out of him every day. How about the beaver? He could do a bang-up job of it."

The judge ignored Scratchy's tantrum.

"Any last words, Mr. Whiskers?"

I've got plenty of them, but I'm not stupid enough to tell these idiots what I really feel and make it worse. Hmm, maybe...

"Your Honor, I have a request."

"Yes?"

"May I take Mr. Loser with me?"

"What a curious request, since he was of no significant help to you. Normally, a companion would not be allowed, but since you made this such an entertaining trial and you are so cute, I'll make an exception. Permission granted, if the prosecutor agrees."

Scratchy threw his front paws up and then let them drop in disgust, saying, "The Mr. Loser that we could always count on for a pitiful defense has now learned too many tricks from this arrogant interloper. Because of that, I don't want him to give any future defendants an unfair advantage. So, goodbye and good riddance."

"Mr. Whiskers, your request is granted," said Sylvilagus. "Before we conclude, though, I do have a personal postscript. I really wish I could have ordered you to stay. Although you put on airs, you are most interesting, unlike so many of the locals. We would have had such great fun educating one another. But now, off with you."

He motioned to Charon, who swam to the point nearest the dogs.

After both stepped aboard, the alligator began swimming leisurely away while Whiskers and Loser turned to look back.

Most of the animals were leaving the scene of the trial with grumpy expressions, convinced that Whiskers had escaped the judgment he truly deserved, thereby depriving them of the gladiatorial entertainment they deserved. They so much had wanted to feel so good about him getting it so bad.

Sylvilagus, however, was still on top of his judge's mound, waving a wistful goodbye.

Scratchy, though, was wading on two legs partway into the water and pointing at Whiskers.

"Hey, Jerkface!"

"What?"

"Remember when you asked me if the Big Bone was here? Guess what, I found it."

"You did?"

"Yeah. In fact, I'm looking at it right now. It's you. You're the Big Bonehead for thinking you could get the better of me. Ha, ha, ha!"

Sneering gleefully, Scratchy raised his forelegs and stretched them out diagonally in a victory pose.

Whiskers looked at Loser and said, "Let's have some fun with that rat."

He stood up on his hind legs and began shaking and twisting and wiggling all over.

"Hey, Scratchy, you're too stiff. You need to loosen up and move like this. Let's all do the Doggy Twist."

Excited, Loser stood up on his hind legs and joined in the mockery.

Scratchy jerked his paws down, punched the water and yelled something made unintelligible by the foam that frothed in his mouth and flew out in a white spray.

Laughing, the two dogs turned away from the furious nutria and settled down on the swimming alligator's back. They spent the rest of the day watching the scenery change until the day itself changed into night.

At the end of a deep sleep, Whiskers awoke and it was daylight again.

"Look over there," said Charon, gesturing with her head to the left at an opening in thick vegetation. "If the judge had let you go free, that would have been your path out of the swamp. They are so hard to find, and that one is starting to close."

"Charon, I know you like me. Please, please, please give me a break and let me off here. I'll even give you a big, slurpy doggy kiss with extra slobber. It's really good. I guarantee you'll like it. Then you can go back to that pesthole and tell the judge and the overgrown rat that you took me to Elbone. They won't know the difference."

"I can't do that. Look around you. See all those birds in the trees? Spies are everywhere. Scratchy knows everything that goes on here."

SPLASH!

Startled, Whiskers looked behind him. Loser was in the water, swimming away from them.

"What are you doing?" Whiskers called out.

"I know it's somewhere in here. I just have to keep looking."

Whiskers barked louder, "Come back!"

Loser paused.

"I'd like to go on with you, but I can't leave until I find my mind. I'm no good without it."

"Your mind is where it always was," Whiskers said. "It's in your head. Besides, you don't need it anyway. Hardly anyone actually uses theirs. I can do the thinking for both of us."

"You can't leave," Charon interrupted, "but he can. His punishment for wandering in here was up long ago, but he won't leave without his mind."

Whiskers looked back at the opening in the vegetation. It was disappearing as sudden new growth began to cover it. Soon it would be gone.

"Loser, I saw your mind. It went through that opening."

"Really?"

"Yes. It went right through there. Hurry up before it closes."

Loser swam rapidly, clawed his way onto the earth and ran to the opening, barely squeezing through as the rough brush poked, scratched and stabbed at his sides and butt. Then it closed up, and Loser was gone.

As the alligator continued to swim, Whiskers sat on its back quietly. Losing Loser meant losing a friend, one who had been beaten down and maligned but still had courage.

He stood up for me when all were against me.

Whiskers started to whimper but stopped.

I don't want that rotten rat's spies to tell him I broke down. Besides, I should be happy that at least one dog has escaped from this horrible place.

33

WE'VE BEEN EXPECTING YOU

Banished to the Isle of Elbone, Whiskers passed day after monotonous day with nothing better to do than sleep.

Until the day all hell broke loose.

As he slept on his side at the beach, his legs pawed furiously against the sand. A pissed-off, giant alley cat was chasing him. No matter how hard he ran, Whiskers wasn't fast enough. The beast caught him and bit him in the ass. His butt bones cracked and blood spurted.

After finishing the butt, the giant cat started chewing on ribs and legs. Blood flowed and bones broke until Whiskers woke up in drenching rain with lightning bolts cracking into the island's trees. Stumbling and crawling, bombarded in the eyes by wind-driven raindrops, he forced his way across the beach to a small hole in the base of a cliff.

When the wind and rain stopped after three days, he came out to find plants and pieces of trees strewn over the beach with hundreds of objects floating by the island.

Maybe I can get on top of something and escape from this place.

Whiskers trotted into the rough water. As he paddled out,

the water broke over his head in waves, causing him to gulp the nasty murk and struggle to breathe. Debris rushed by at high speed. A wooden board came straight at him. He ducked under the water before it smashed him in the head.

I've got to get out of here before I get killed.

He paddled back to the beach and ran up a slope toward the edge of the cliff.

Maybe something big will float by so I can jump and land on it.

Reaching the edge, he looked down and off to his left. His eyes widened and his jaw dropped open. A house was rocking from side to side in the fast-moving floodwater and coming on a line that would bring it next to the cliff.

I wanted something big, and that is really big. I can't miss it. But if I jump on it from so high up and hit it hard, I could break a bone or even knock myself out, roll off and drown.

The other option was jumping in the water close to where the house was rocking and dipping the eaves of its roof. He might be able to crawl up on the roof during one of the dips into the water. But if he missed his timing he could be pinned beneath the roof's overhang and dunked up and down until he was almost senseless like that time when Mr. Professor took him to a backyard hot dog party at the Farleys' house and the neighborhood mean kid threw him in the pool and jumped on top of him and tried to ride him like a bucking bronco until a drowning Whiskers turned and nipped him on the leg very close to Hot Dog City and then was yelled at by all the adults for being a bad dog and maybe even a rabid dog instead of giving him a nice treat for teaching the stupid brat a lesson. The good thing, though, is that all the boys in the neighborhood spread the word that you better treat Whiskers nicely or you could lose your wiener.

As for now, the house was coming alongside the cliff. Whiskers had a quick choice to make: roof or water.

Broken bones or drowning? Not good. But I don't want to be stuck on this island forever.

He went for the roof.

Ears blown back, tongue flapping wildly against his face, legs flailing uselessly, falling headfirst faster and faster like the cliff divers of Cacapulco, Whiskers twisted his body and... WHUMP!... hit the roof on his right side, knocking the breath out of him and leaving him stunned and scared to move. However, he was moving. He was sliding down the roof.

Whiskers tried to dig his toenails into the wet shingles, but the shingles were too slick and too hard. He flailed at a ventilation pipe with his forelegs, but they bounced off. With nothing else to stop him, he slid to the roof's edge and flopped off into the foaming river.

As the house rolled to its right, the eave of the roof crashed down and pushed him under the water.

It's drowning me!

Before his air ran out, the house rolled back up. The sudden suction of water jerked Whiskers to the surface, gasping, eyes wild.

He churned his legs furiously to get away from the house, but he couldn't make any headway. Instead, he went backward as water pouring through a broken window sucked him inside butt-first.

The interior was nearly full of water and almost pitch black. After paddling in place for a while, Whiskers' eyes adjusted and he spotted a wall cabinet. He swam toward it and scooched himself on top near the ceiling. There he stayed in the dark as the house continued heaving down the waterway until ramming itself into a bend of the river. As the sky became less overcast, light began to come through broken windows.

Items were floating around the room—magazines, papers, playing cards, whiskey bottles.

Whoa! What's that?

In the middle of the room, a patch of hair floated on top of the water but stayed fixed in one spot. The water level began to recede inch by inch until the hair slowly settled back in place on the crown of a human head.

Yikes! I've been in here with a dead person? I'm getting out of here.

He jumped from the cabinet onto a floating cushion. It flipped over on top of him. Upside-down and sinking to the bottom of the dark water, Whiskers thrashed about to right himself. Swimming blindly under the water, he smacked into a hard object. Trying to surface, a front leg became stuck between the hard object and something clammy.

The dead man's got me!

Panicked, Whiskers twisted and jerked until his leg came free. Breaking the surface, he paddled slowly in place, breathing heavily. To his right, he saw nothing.

To his left, bubbles were popping in the water. A long bulge formed under the bubbles. The bulge rose higher, the water covering it fell away, and the dead man broke onto the surface, floating on his back in the roiling water.

In freeing his leg, Whiskers had kicked one of the man's arms loose from where it had been hooked on a chair.

The water calmed around the slim body, which had a large knife protruding from the chest.

The head rolled to one side so it could look around. Its eyes widened as they stared into Whiskers' eyes. The mouth opened and the tongue moved. Under the water, one of the man's hands touched Whiskers' belly.

AAAAAAAAHHHH!

"Go away! Leave me alone!"

Whiskers spun in the water, swam toward a doorway and went through it. Inside that room, he stopped paddling.

AAAAAAAAHHHH!

A hefty man was floating on his back, his face turned to one side.

He's got a hole between his eyes!

The body floated toward Whiskers.

Do I know him? Yeeks, I remember both of them.

Chunky was coming closer. The floating body in the first room was Skinny. The two bums from the railroad boxcar. The ones he had kept from harming Tracy and Ricky.

Have they been following me? For revenge? Even if they're dead?

Then he remembered how something fun in the past had really been a life lesson.

Mr. Professor had put him and a bottle of booze in the basket of the bicycle and pedaled to a drive-in movie where they watched an awful show while horns honked at Mr. Professor to shut up because he was loudly explaining the science behind how people can come back to life—in a dead sort of way.

The main thing was that these semi-dead people move really slowly and they want to kill you by eating you.

These guys are moving real slow.

Whiskers paddled away from Chunky, who now had an arm outstretched and the middle finger on the hand pointing at him.

Whiskers swam into another room where the top of a desk was visible below a busted-out window. He paddled over to it, put his front paws on the desktop, pulled hard to get his forelegs on it and kicked water with his back legs. Straining madly, he made it.

As Whiskers stood up on the desk, Chunky floated into the room with his traveling buddy. The knife sticking out of Skinny's chest looked like a mast without a sail.

They are after me. The floating dead.

But Whiskers was on deska firma with a clear way out. His confidence and bravado were coming back.

I'm not afraid of them. A hero dog doesn't run from anyone.

"That's all, dead people. Whiskers is out of here. Pasta la pizza. Seeyanomora."

Pointing his rear end at them and shaking it, he added, "You can't touch this."

One of Chunky's hands lifted out of the water. As his body slowly rocked on the surface, the hand curved closed, then opened, closed, opened, closed, beckoning to the cocky dog.

Whiskers yelped and jumped out the window.

PART III

A GREAT IDEA

34

GO COUNSEL YOURSELF

"Five... four... three... two... one."

On cue, the voice-over announcer said, "Welcome to the Dr. Sid Show, hosted by the creator of the 'How to Get Better Without Even Trying' line of products, including the books 'Don't Blame Yourself, Blame Your Parents'; 'Laziness Is Just a Different Way of Getting Things Done'; and 'The Tapeworm Diet: Eating for Two.'"

The applause sign lit up, and the audience happily clapped along as the announcer intoned, "And now, h-e-e-e-r-r-e he comes, Dr. Sid!"

The mostly female audience stood and cheered as an elegantly dressed, balding man in a black blazer, gray slacks, maroon shirt, yellow club tie and pinkie rings stepped from a door at the back of the studio and made his way down the center aisle, smiling and touching hands with his fans.

They adored him, and he adored being adored.

Only a year ago he had been a proctologist appearing on the book club segment of Poperah's show to promote "A Million Little Farts: What Your Butt Is Trying to Tell You." During his interactions with her audience, he discovered that poking around in the minds of people was no different from poking around in their butts. He was a hit, and when television executives called, he gladly accepted their offer to have his own show on CTN—the Celebrity Talk Network.

Now, after sliding a palm off the last hand, Dr. Sid jauntily waved to the entire audience, took his seat and faced the camera.

"We've had some strange folks on this show, but you might say that today's guest, if I may make a pun, is one of the doggonedest ever. In fact, I think she could use some counseling, but let's find out what she has to say. Please welcome Inspector Janvier of the FBDI—the Federal Bureau of Dog Investigation."

Loud boos echoed throughout the studio.

To drown out the boos, a number of women jumped up to cheer, shout and clap as the long-legged, black-suited, spiky-haired, spike-collared, utility-belted woman strode out from the wings to take the chair opposite Dr. Sid. A thin, pink, jagged highlight now graced each side of her jet-black hair.

"You certainly are most striking," her host commented. "What do you say to people about your prickly appearance with that dog collar and spiky hair?"

Janvier looked at the audience and then at Dr. Sid.

"It's better than having no hair, baldy."

Whistles, cheers and laughter greeted that comment, provoking one enraged audience member to begin arguing with another one.

"Whoa now!" Dr. Sid cautioned as cameras zeroed in on the combatants. "Try to maintain some control, ladies."

He pointed at one of them.

"Our guest seems to bring forth strong emotions in people. How do you feel about what she's doing?"

"I'm an animal-lover and I think she's disgusting," the

woman answered. "I heard that she roams around the country snatching pets out of people's yards for no reason. Who knows what their fate is after that? She's on some kind of psycho warpath for bragging rights or body counts or something. Sure we need some control, but she's out of control. Just look at her."

Dr. Sid pointed at the other woman.

"And I take it that you like our guest?"

"I think she's wonderful. Janvier's a strong woman who's beating men at their own rigged game. I read how they treated her when she started. The way she dresses now lets men know that she isn't going to take any crap from them. I'd dress that way too if I could get away with it at work. I only hope that someday I'll have the guts she has."

Dr. Sid turned back to Janvier.

"Well, the audience certainly seems divided. And so does America based on its reaction to this article about you."

With that, he held up Peephole magazine with a headline that asked "Obsession or Duty?" next to a head-and-shoulders shot of Janvier. Over her left shoulder was the cutout photo of a white dog. Next to that photo was the black silhouette of a larger dog with a question mark superimposed in the middle.

"This cover article hints at the allegation made by that upset lady in the audience. Let me ask you directly. Is it true that you snatch dogs from pet owners' fenced-in yards? Let's be clear, we're talking about dogs that no one called animal control about."

"I never locked up a dog that didn't need locking up," Janvier replied. "If a dog is registered, has a collar with a non-expired rabies tag on it, isn't running loose or exhibiting out-of-control threatening behavior, and has no warrants, then that dog has nothing to fear. Otherwise, that dog is in violation of the law, and I am sworn to uphold the law."

"And how far will you go to get a dog?"

"As far as I have to go, wherever it may take me."

"I hate to make another pun," said Dr. Sid, smiling, "but I will. Do you like to hound dogs?"

Prepared in advance by his writers, that line got the expected laughs from the audience, but Janvier didn't take the bait.

"My job is to bring dogs to justice," she said flatly.

"Okay, let's talk about the dogs on the cover of this magazine," Dr. Sid said, holding it up again. "I don't know about the big fellow, but we've heard some good things about the other one. The magazine was able to identify him as Whiskers, the former pet of a university professor who was so highly educated that his rectum gave his farewell speech. As an ex-proctologist, I can definitely appreciate that."

Dr. Sid put on a big smile because he had a surprise for Janvier.

"We were able to contact people who have met Whiskers and who said they will testify on his behalf anytime. In fact, they are in our studio audience now."

Excited murmurs broke out as a cameraman zoomed in on Tracy and Ricky. Dr. Sid encouraged them to stand up and relate how Whiskers had saved them from the dastardly intentions of the drunken hobos in the railroad boxcar.

"I was so scared," Tracy said after telling her harrowing story. "There's no telling what those awful men would have done. Whiskers was wonderful. He saved us, and then he watched over us until we found a new life as circus performers. We owe him everything."

Next, one of the adults from the neighborhood of the foreclosure house told how Whiskers had taken action to save the lives of two dogs and a cat while all the humans had been paralyzed into inaction over the fear of lawsuits.

"It took a courageous dog to shame us all," the man said. "He wasn't thinking about lawsuits. He was just thinking about doing the right thing. And the way he freed those animals, why it's the smartest thing I ever heard of. Heck, I wish my kids were half that smart."

Lastly, an older woman in a faded, flowered dress stood up with a younger man wearing overalls. They seemed very out of place in the studio.

"I'm Ma, and this be my son, Bud. We jus' simple country folk. That Whiskers dog, he's our'n. That perfesser feller you talked about give him to us outta grattytude when his car broke down by our place and Bud fixed it. We was so glad to get that dog 'cause he was a good 'un, always helpin' out aroun' the house, sweepin' the dirt wif his tail and everythin'. Why he even saved my boy from a near-drownin' when Bud were a li'l tyke and fell in the well. That Whiskers dog just grab aholt o' that crank handle wif his teef and start spinnin' hisself in a circle through the air jus' like one o' them Ferris wheels at the county fair. He was a'goin' all up and down 'til he cranked up that rope wif my sweet li'l Bud in the bucket. I'm a'tellin' you, that's how much that dog love us. But some blame fool went and stole him from us, 'cause he wouldn't ne'er run away on his own. And we ain't ne'er be the same since. Now, we jus' mope aroun' all day. All we wants is our poor li'l dog back to the home he love and the home-folk he love. We wants anyone who find him to bring him back to us in our holler. Or you jus' holler and we'll come git him. We jus' wants to smother him wif love."

Ma exchanged a glance and a smile with Bud. They surely did want to smother Whiskers—with wild onions, salt, pepper, garlic, potatoes, tomatoes and plenty of lard, followed by coffee and wild peach cobbler.

"Wow," said Dr. Sid. "We have just heard powerful testimony

from people who actually met Whiskers. And yet, Inspector Janvier, you want to chase him to the ends of the earth so you can lock him up. How do you respond to what these folks said about him being a hero? In fact, not just a hero, but three times a hero."

"How do I respond?" she said, incredulously. "This is how I respond: Not only did he damage a house in foreclosure, he thwarted animal rescuers who had a court order providing a new home and psychiatric care for the two dogs and the cat. Now, they run from all attempts to aid them. Even worse—and what you haven't told your audience—is that, intentionally or unintentionally, he was directly involved in the death of an elderly dog walker who tried to give him a home."

Dr. Sid didn't know what to say to that, so he just sat blank-faced as Janvier continued.

"His latest act of outlawry was a massive jailbreak. I went to the kennel where he freed all the dogs that had been legally captured—some with expired rabies tags, many with no tags, and others who had been intimidating entire neighborhoods. If a dog is locked up, it's because he or she deserves to be locked up. We can't have them running loose, out of control. I've experienced firsthand what it's like when a dog is out of control. That's why we need to stop this Whiskers. Chaos is what he thrives on. We can't have him ranging across the country, breaking the law. You heard how smart he is. What if he starts teaching other dogs how to free themselves? As for those stories of heroism that some people told in this studio, to me they're just fanciful tales, not reported facts."

A woman in the audience jumped up and screamed, "You bitch! He's a lifesaver. He's a hero dog, just like Lassie and Rin Tin Tin and Spuds MacKenzie."

Janvier glared at the woman.

"Your hero is a zero, and I'm zeroing in on him. It's just a matter of time until I get him."

"Ladies," broke in Dr. Sid, "let's stay civil. Everybody take a deep breath and calm down because what I'd like to do now is talk about this other dog."

With that, he again held up Peephole magazine and pointed to the black silhouette with the question mark.

"Inspector Janvier, who is this mystery dog? What does he mean to you? I'm asking because you mentioned just a moment ago that you experienced what it's like when a dog is out of control. Did he give you that scar on your cheek? Why do you only wear one earring? You were pretty close-mouthed about all of this in the magazine article. You never really opened up."

Janvier stared at Dr. Sid. She didn't want to tell baldy anything of significance. It wasn't any of his damn business. Still, she had agreed to come on the show because his producers wouldn't stop trying to land her as their latest B-list celebrity so they could scoop the other talk shows.

"This is not a small, cute, friendly dog. It is an undetermined mix of breeds, very large and very dangerous. If you met him, you would be terrified. He gave me this scar when I was a rookie, new to the job and not well-trained. Every time I look in a mirror, I see the reminders of that day. I'll replace the earring when I bring him to justice."

Dr. Sid leaned toward Janvier.

"I see some real issues here. A young girl—excuse me, woman —faces social survival issues in a hostile work environment and then survives an actual physical confrontation in a hostile real-world environment, with the result that she carries not only a physical scar but also mental scars, and yet rather than succumbing to them develops her own über hostility as a coping mechanism."

Dr. Sid paused to suck in some air, then soldiered on.

"Now, that was doc speak. But to put it in plain English, work has consequences, and one of those is that people can take a job too seriously. This dog-catching business seems to have taken over your life, Inspector Janvier. As I mentioned at the beginning of the show, I think you really could benefit from some help, and I'll be happy to personally work with you at a discounted rate to develop a healthier mental perspective. So, would you be willing to get some counseling?"

That word set Janvier off.

"Counseling? I don't need your stinking counseling."

With that, she stood up, reached into a pouch on her utility belt and pulled out a gun. She aimed it at Dr. Sid's head. He shrank back in his chair, paralyzed with fear.

Janvier snapped, "Go counsel yourself!" and pulled the trigger.

Dr. Sid's head rocketed back and his arms splayed out. Listening to the screams in the audience, Dr. Sid saw his TV life flash before his eyes and knew in an instant that it was all over.

Yes, it was all over him.

Janvier had fired a net gun, launching a net that spread out as it shot through the air and splatted on top of Dr. Sid, trapping him in his chair.

When they realized that Dr. Sid was not dead, Janvier's fans in the audience began to laugh and whoop, thrilled that their role model for female assertiveness had scared the shit out of television's top-rated guidance counselor. Their laughter turned to screams when the pissed-off fans of Dr. Sid grabbed them by the hair and jerked their heads viciously up and down.

As for the good doctor, he lay in the chair with the net still on him, marveling that he was actually alive. But he realized something even better: This confrontation would lead to a ratings bonanza.

With subtle hand motions, Dr. Sid signaled to the security

guards who had grabbed Janvier not to drag her away but to hold her in place. He wanted this television tableau to last as long as possible for the viewers while the screen credits rolled.

Also, by keeping much of the viewers' attention on Janvier, there wouldn't be as many eyes to notice him trying to free his hands from the net so he could cover the dark wet spot in the middle of his natty gray pants.

35

IT'S JUST IDIOTS TALKING

"Janvier, you're doing a swell job, but..."

"But what?"

"You're kind of a liability, and we need to do something else with you."

"What are you talking about?"

FBDI Field Supervisor Emil Preshrunk of the Ringworm, Pennsylvania, office stroked his chin with the fingers of one hand while tapping his desk with the fingers of the other.

"Look at this," he finally said, swiveling his chair to the right, picking up a remote control and pointing it at a digital video recorder.

The monitor attached to the recorder lit up with the image of four women sitting on a semicircular sofa. They were the talking heads for the "Where Are They Now" segment of the "Celebrity Ratings" show on CCN, the Constant Chatter Network.

"Lotus, where is that dogcatcher? Did they put a muzzle on her? Is she in a cage?"

The questions were posed by the host, Serena Macarena.

"We're all puzzled, Serena," said co-host Lotus Flower. "After that delicious net gun episode on the Dr. Sid Show where he wet his pants, FBDI Inspector Janvier broke onto our celebrity list with a B-minus rating, rose quickly to an A-plus and then suddenly fell to a boring C-minus."

"Sheila, what do you think caused that?" Serena asked.

"My dear, it was bad timing," cultural critic Sheila Shoat commented. "Sassy Britches knocked her down the list by appearing buck-naked at the Gimmee Awards with her back to the audience. Everyone was absolutely shocked but also very disappointed when she didn't turn around. I'm like: Don't tease, if you can't please. All bets now are on Kilometry Virus to break the next shock barrier. She claims the First Amendment of the U.S. Constitution protects freedom of exposure on television, so she's going full frontal on the next awards show."

"I can't wait to see what she uses for a microphone," chimed in comedian Lulu LaLoca.

"Oh, Lulu, you're awful," giggled Lotus.

"Girls, that's what it takes to keep up," Lulu said. "The days when an aging Belladonna could top the celebrity list by bending over and shooting a middle finger between her legs at the nearest cathedral are long gone."

"I hear you, Lulu, but I wonder if she does," Serena said, turning her head to look directly into the camera. "Dear dogcatcher Janvier, are you listening? You have to step it up to keep up, sweetie, or you're going to be a one-hit wonder."

"Ladies, that's a wrap on the wild and sexy but missing-in-action dogcatcher," chirped Lotus. "After the commercial, we'll dissect the see-through thong that Susie Wrong wore to a black tie affair."

Preshrunk paused the video recorder and swiveled back to face Janvier.

"So what?" she said, shrugging her shoulders. "It's just idiots talking."

"True, but every now and then those idiots send their camera crews over here hoping they'll catch you doing something outrageous, and I have to run them off."

"I'll make sure to stay out of their sight," Janvier offered.

"Unfortunately, that's not all," Preshrunk said, frowning.

He picked up the remote, did some fast forwarding and hit the play button to show the recording of a different program.

A slim woman in an elegant, fuchsia pantsuit was sitting in an overstuffed chair on one side of a coffee table while on the opposite side sat an overstuffed man in a charcoal-gray, pinstriped suit.

"Hello, I'm Jane Crank, business analyst and host of 'Who Do You Sue?' Our guest today is Brick Houser, attorney at the firm of Ambeu, Lanse, Chace and Sehrs."

"Thanks for inviting me, Jane. I appreciate the free publicity."

"Brick, we've heard that you are seeking an actionable suit involving an agent of the FBDI. Fill us in on the particulars."

"Jane, my position is that Inspector Janvier is a stressed-out victim of the system, and I would be happy to represent her and all the other women of working age in the United States of God Bless America who applied to work at the FBDI or, even worse by government inaction, were never informed that they could apply to work at the FBDI. At a moment's notice, I can file a one hundred million dollar class action suit on their behalf. I just need Inspector Janvier to contact me so we can get started."

"Hold on, Brick. At a forty percent lawyer's take, that would be forty million dollars for you, and... let me get out my pocket calculator. Hmm, there's roughly seventy million women of working age and... oh, my goodness... they would each get about eighty-five cents. Do you think that's fair?"

"Jane, you ignorant slut, it's not my fault there's so many of them that they split the pie into microscopic slivers. Like I said:

Women are victims of the system. Someday it will be fairer, but until then we will just have to suffer with the system we have."

Preshrunk pushed a button to stop the video.

"That guy is persistent. His firm won't stop calling, texting, tweeting and emailing. Several times we've caught his assistants rummaging through the trash in our dumpster. And the other day he tried to hold a news conference on our front steps.

"Run them off too."

"It's not just them. The receptionist and the file clerk are complaining that they're tired of confrontations with tourists who say they have a right as taxpayers to take a selfie with you and get your autograph."

"This is why I'm a liability? Because of what other people are doing?"

"Janvier, we're just a small field office. We're not staffed to deal with disruptions by nosy media, money-hungry lawyers and pushy tourists. But at our national headquarters near Washington, D.C.—where you're going—none of these clowns can get on the grounds. Then all of this craziness can die down, and you'll be a nobody again."

"Headquarters? I didn't join the FBDI to be a paper-pusher."

"You won't be pushing paper. You'll be a trainer."

"A trainer? No way. I need real action in the field. I'll even take some isolated post—Maine, North Dakota, Alaska, wherever."

"Sorry, Janvier, but there's something else."

"What?"

"Headquarters has its own problem."

"So?"

"You're the solution."

36

DID I HIT A NERVE?

"I hate dogs!"

"Me too."

"They are so stupid!"

"Yes, they are."

"Especially this one!"

Rather than agreeing with Scratchy's last comment, Phelonius kept his beak shut. He did not dare remind the nutria-on-a-tirade that this so-called stupid dog had outfoxed him in court and become the talk of the Great Abysmal Swamp. On top of that, this same stupid dog had escaped from banishment on the Isle of Elbone.

The escape had put the sentinel birds of the Flapper Express in a swivet. No one wanted to tell Scratchy that Whiskers got away, especially since they had taken an unauthorized break to visit lady birds on another island. So, they did Pebbles, Twigs and Leaves. Phelonius lost.

The reaction was just what the crow expected. Scratchy had screamed and ripped his claws through the air. Phelonius had to turn his head when steam began wisping from the nutria's ears, nose and mouth. It just wasn't natural.

"I wish I could tear the hide off him! That's what he deserves! Damn dumb dimwitted dopey dumbass dickshit dog!"

"He couldn't have planned it," ventured Phelonius. "It had to be luck, don't you think?"

"Whatever! It's done. How he got away doesn't matter now. What concerns me is that this is going to get out. All the animals in the swamp will know. They'll think I'm slipping, that he outsmarted me. I'll lose respect. I can't have that!"

"So what do you want to do?"

"He's out of my jurisdiction. We need to recruit someone on the outside. Check around."

FAR BELOW, Phelonius saw his prey—a dog.

He didn't like dogs, because they were idiots. But duty called. He needed to turn this dog into a useful idiot.

The crow flew down to a low brick wall. At its base, the dog was pawing at a wrapper on a half-eaten, supersized hamburger that someone had thrown away.

"Hey, you."

Scut looked up and growled.

Startled by Scut's fierce expression, Phelonius took a step back. This dog had obviously done a lot of walking on the ugly side of life.

Phelonius needed to stay alert. Fresh, raw, hot meat with a still-beating heart would beat a cold hamburger any day, even one that had lettuce, pickles and special sauce on a sesame seed bun. If the dog made a leap for him, he had to be ready to helicopter straight up.

"What do you want?"

"I have an offer for you from someone you don't know, but who has heard good things about you."

"What are you talking about, turd bird?"

"Oh, dear. What hostility. Well, it's understandable since I violated proper etiquette by not first introducing myself. I am Phelonius, the famous flier from the Flapper Express. We gather and dispense information. I'm sure you've heard of our current motto: 'Our wings are never still.' But I am thinking of instituting a new one: 'Overflight for oversight.' Catchy rhyme, don't you think? And it gives a better idea of what we're all about. Anyway, I'm here to do you right, brother, with something that I know will interest you."

"Cut the phony 'brother' crap, and nothing coming out of that beak could interest me unless you say you're going to come down here and get between these pieces of bread."

"My goodness, you certainly don't mince words, but I have no intention of becoming your mincemeat. Get it? Funny, right? No? Never mind, I'll get to the point, which is that we can point you toward someone in whom, might I say, you have a pointed interest."

"Who are you talking about?"

"The one, the only, the famous Whiskers."

Scut's eyelids narrowed and his nostrils flared.

"Did I hit a nerve?" Phelonius asked. "Looks like I did. Oops, sorry about that, but everyone is talking about this Whiskers. He's supposed to be bonafide, a real up-and-comer thanks to a secret fighting system that negates the natural advantage of large individuals like yourself. It seems that he stole it from the humans."

That surprised Scut.

"Stole it from humans? When I caught up to him beside a lake, he blabbered on and on about how great the system is, but he never said it's a human one. Fortunately for him, something drew me away as I was about to put him and his system to the test. It had a stupid name, but I don't recall it."

"No one's really sure what it's called," Phelonius said. "Carrot-rotty, carrot tee, carrot pee, crotch pee—depends on whom you're talking with after it has gone in and out of so many ears."

"You know anything else about it?"

"The scuttlebutt is that it comes from another part of the world called Aphasia. There, instead of speaking, humans yowl like cats and make awkward, stilted movements with their arms and legs until their inner cheese reaches critical mass and knocks you on your ass."

"Sounds stupid. Bite 'em in the neck and shake it until you break it is what works for me."

"Well, think what you want, but I hear that Whiskers is on a rampage, peeing on trees, bushes and big rocks, marking more and more territory as his."

He paused after giving that false information. Scut's lips were pulling up and back, revealing more of his gums and large teeth. But Phelonius continued.

"Do you know what else they say he does?"

"What?"

"When he shoots a stream of pee on a new marker, he says, 'Smell that, Scut, you big dummy.'"

Scut leaped at the wall, got his forelegs on top, pulled upward and slashed viciously with his teeth at the crow.

Doing a remarkable imitation of a hummingbird and with heart beating just as fast, Phelonius shot up and landed on a tree limb. He barely escaped taking the place of the hamburger.

What a dumbass. You're supposed to listen to the messenger, not eat the messenger.

Now perched on the wall, Scut stared upward and snarled, "Why are you telling me all this?"

"Well," said Phelonius, breathing heavily, "my client, a nutria by the name of Scratchy, has something in common with you. He doesn't like this Whiskers dog either and wants him to get his comeuppance with... how shall I phrase this delicately... extreme prejudice."

"I'll do more than that when I get him. Where is he?"

"That's where we can be of service. You see, I and the other birds of the Flapper Express can track Whiskers and give you his location. We would be your personal Guided Pooch Surveillance, or GPS for short."

"What I trust is what I see, hear, smell and track right here on the ground. From up in the air, I don't think you can tell one type of terrier from another, much less a specific individual, but you can give it a try. If it helps me get the jerk, fine."

"So, we're agreed. We'll be your eye in the sky. As for now, go back to your lovely lunch, dumpster doggy."

With that smart remark, Phelonius flapped his wings and flew off.

That should take care of the Whiskers problem for Scratchy, proving once again how indispensable I am.

37

COME OUT YOU FOOLS

"I tell you. Eet ees heem."

"You are full of it, Jacques," said Puffy, an Affenpinscher. "That is not him. A famous dog like that would not be walking alone. He would be surrounded by admirers. Lady dogs would be all over him."

"I know what I am talking about. Eet ees heem. I will prove eet," Jacques said and took off running.

Some distance away, Whiskers watched as the wild-eyed dog ran toward him at full speed.

It's a French Poodle. Those things are insufferable, always putting on that phony accent.

Now, fur standing up along his spine, Whiskers braced himself for a head-on confrontation.

It didn't happen.

The Poodle dashed past his head, made a skidding turn, stuck his nose in Whiskers' butt and began sniffing furiously.

"What do you think you're doing?" Whiskers growled menacingly.

But the Poodle had already smelled enough. He took off running, exclaiming with great joy, "Quelle odeur! Magnifique!

You never forget a smelly butt like that. Eet ees the same butt I smelled at Pooparama in the meet-and-greet. There ees no doubt. Eet ees the great Wheeskers!"

That did it.

As soon as other dogs heard the news, they came running from yards, houses and fields to smell Whiskers' butt. A few dogs ran off to spread the word even farther: The great Whiskers, the champion of Pooparama, is here!

That brought more dogs. As they showed up, Whiskers did not stop for the new arrivals but kept walking. Even so, he was constantly jostled by dogs squeezing their way into the growing pack so they could get a quick smell of his seemingly magical butt.

His masterpiece at Pooparama had become known throughout Dogdom as the Fabulous Turd Pile with stories of its fantastical properties passed from one star-struck dog to another:

"It twinkled and sparkled more than the stars."

"It gave off a smell so wonderful that one whiff and you would pass out in ecstasy."

"It could even do its own toots, from a high-and-tight squeaker to a low-and-slow blap-blap-blapper."

"It could fly so fast that it beat a bird in a race."

Overhearing the other dogs, Whiskers marveled at how a little bit of glitter dressing up a pile of shit could shoot someone to stardom.

Wow, they like me! They really like me!

Of course they liked him—he was famous. But there was more to it. Every dog who heard these stories about Whiskers' unique turd pile swelled up with pride. It was simply more proof that dogs truly were the best creatures in the world, because only a dog could have created something so special.

Naturally, every dog wanted to be associated with the best of the best. At the moment, that was Whiskers, and if he wasn't going to stop walking, then they would go with him, marching across the countryside from one town to the next.

As they went on and weeks of marching turned into months, they attracted more dogs with the pack growing by tens, then twenties, fifties and hundreds, thanks to the overly exuberant Jacques always running ahead and calling, "Come out you fools, you knaves, you blackguards. Kneel down you curs. Wheemper in subservience. Thees ees the opportunity of your meeserable lives. Join the Grand Armee led by the Great Wheeskers, Champion of Pooparama, Conqueror of All Dogs and therefore Conqueror of All Animals. We march toward Destinee!"

Once the new recruits had fallen in, Jacques would nip Scrappy the Beagle to start bugling out the marching song: "Allons en bone de la poo pee-ee-er..."

Each time he heard Jacques sound the invitation and Scrappy begin to blare, Whiskers reflected on how he had muddled around the countryside after leaving the flooded house, traveling to random places until finally being recognized for his personal greatness.

After all, I've saved dogs and people, won at Pooparama, and outsmarted the evil Scratchy.

Now that he was followed by dogs woofing, howling and yowling his praises as their leader, Whiskers realized he had a purpose to fulfill.

He just had to figure out what it was.

Jacques had a suggestion.

"You must take over the world."

Whiskers' mouth flopped open. He cocked his head and stared at Jacques as if to say, "Are you kidding?"

"Leesten. Eef penguins can have emperors, why not dogs? So, you declare yourself the emperor of Dogdom. We will spread a blanket over your back and crown you weeth a shiny dog bowl.

Fait accompli. Then you conquer all the outlying breeds who will not submit to your rule—the German Shepherds, the English Setters, the Belgian Sheepdogs, the Russian Wolfhounds. After them, we go for total domination and wage war against the cats."

"That sounds like a lot of work," Whiskers objected. "How about something simpler?"

"But a great champion and a great leader like yourself must have a great goal. If not that, then what?" spluttered Jacques, almost apoplectic at Whiskers' hesitation.

Whiskers pursed his lips and shrugged, conveying that he had no idea what it would be or even if he would have a say in it.

38

KISS MY DERRIERE

"You are wrong!" snapped the Cairn Terrier.

"I am wrong? Au contraire, you can kiss my derriere, Gruffy. You are the one who ees wrong."

"The gall! Just because you are an arrogant French Poodle doesn't mean you are right. Can't you get that through your fuzzy head?"

"Fuzzy head! I would rather have this fuzzy head than your wormy brain!"

Jacques was steamed.

He wasn't the only one.

The problem came every night when the army made camp. At first, everything had been congenial, but close quarters soon led to irritations which in turn led to small arguments and finally to one very big argument that wouldn't go away.

"Top Dog has to be the biggest dog, the meanest dog, the scariest dog," yapped Buddy, a Bull Terrier. "Otherwise, why have one?"

"That's right," agreed Charley, a Golden Retriever. "How can an average-size, inoffensive-looking dog be the Top Dog? It doesn't make any sense. I know that Whiskers is smart, and he is a born leader. You can tell that by how magnificently he is leading us here and there and everywhere. We are seeing and smelling new things all the time. But he is not large enough to be a real warrior, a fierce fighter. That's why Scut is Top Dog. He is huge and not afraid of anything."

"You're both fools. We've all been fools," grumped Max, a Spaniel. "What's wrong with us? We've been mindlessly glorifying that brute. Why? Just because he terrifies us? Top Dog should be about the best of us, not the worst of us."

"Exactly," chimed in Dixie, a Saluki. "Why shouldn't the smartest dog be the Top Dog? Or the friendliest dog? Or the cutest dog? In other words, a dog who is more like the rest of us. A dog like Whiskers. Now there's a dog who is interested in helping, not hurting."

"Absolutely correct!" exclaimed Jacques. "I ask you: What has Scut ever actually accomplished? Ees he an official champion of anything? No. Has he even attended Pooparama? No. Why not? What ees he scared of? That he might lose in a contest to a smaller dog? Wheeskers was not afraid to compete. He ees a tested and true champion. He ees one of us, not a freak of nature. We are tired of Scut. Who made Scut the Top Dog? You? Me? Anyone? No!"

"Well," said Gigi, a Kerry Blue, "everyone just assumed..."

"It's time to stop assuming," interrupted Otto, an Otterhound. "It is time for a change. Why else do you think we are following Whiskers?"

"You're full of catshit," harrumphed Buddy. "I still say that Scut is the Top Dog because he can beat up any dog in Dogdom."

That's the way it would go, on and on and on, night after night, until one evening Bo, a normally quiet Great Dane, had had all the bickering he could stand. So, he stood up.

"That's enough! There's only one way to settle this. Let's

make the title official. Let's have a competition. Whiskers versus Scut. Whoever wins is the official Top Dog. Then you all can just shut up and talk about something else."

The other dogs were dumbstruck. Obviously, it was a great idea.

Because it came from a Great Dane.

39

STOP DROOLING AND TELL US

"I'm telling you we've got to come up with a name," asserted Heinz, an officious German Pointer. "If we're going to have an official competition, then our committee has to have an official name. Otherwise, how can anything we do be considered official?"

"All right, let's keep going until we settle on something," said an exasperated Bo, the Great Dane who had agreed to head the competition committee.

"Everybody listen to me," said Spitzella, a Finnish Spitz. "In order to come up with a name, we need to be dogactive by leashing everyone into the same yard, circling our tails and thinking outside the doghouse so we can bring to the dog bowl the best of breed of the low-hanging toots using scentergy and all the barkwidth we have starting at tree-top level and digging down into the dirt for a hole-istic solution that satisfies all the stickholders."

"Oh, go chase a stick," smarted back Scrappy, a Fox Terrier.

"You two can stop chewing on each other, because I just thought up a great name," said Cowboy the Border Collie. "Let's call ourselves The Committee to Figure Out What Type of

Competition Should Be Held to Determine Whether Scut or Whiskers Will Win and From Then On Will Be Accorded Without Objection the Official Undisputed Title of Top Dog and Will Therefore Then Be Recognized by All in Dogdom as Such Until He Either Dies or Just Can't Cut It Anymore."

"Don't you think that's a muzzleful?" Swifty the Whippet asked. "I mean, I can't remember anything of what you just said, and you probably can't either."

"Then why don't you come up with something better?" Cowboy snapped back. "Oh, I know why, because your brain is even smaller than a lizard's."

It was another spiteful comment in what had been a very long day. The dogs on the committee were irritated, annoyed and frazzled because once again they had been getting nowhere. While canines throughout all of Dogdom had quivered with excitement and anticipation ever since the idea of a competition had been broached, the committee had bogged down in feckless bickering.

Part of the problem was that the committee had been set up to be fair to both contestants. As such, it was carefully chosen to be evenly divided between Whiskers supporters and Scut supporters. Surprisingly, finding Scut backers hadn't been difficult. Even though they loved Whiskers' playful personality and had no love for Scut, many dogs truly believed that only a large dog should be the Top Dog. Since Scut was so big and famous, he was the logical choice.

The other part of the problem was that every member of the committee had an opinion. Because each dog considered itself to be extremely intelligent, its opinion therefore had to be equivalent to established fact. The result was that each dog would bark its opinion louder and louder and louder so the other committee members with opposing views could get it through their furry skulls of lesser intelligence that their opinions were absolutely, totally and irredeemably wrong. Of course, those in opposition would respond with snarls, growls and flashing of teeth until the whole committee devolved time and again into a carnival of excruciatingly loud barking in which nothing could be understood.

Such divisiveness and bias were reflected in suggestions that had been made earlier for the name of the panel:

The Committee in Favor of a Different Kind of Top Dog

The Committee Who Thinks It's Time That Smaller Dogs Get Their Due

The Committee Who Knows That Only a Large Dog Can Be Top Dog

The Committee to Crown Scut as Top Dog

The Committee to Scuttle Scut's Butt

"Come on," Bo, said, "we need something neutral."

"How about Canines Advocating Toughness?" Fidelita the Havanese posited.

"That's still slanted, but I think we can work on that idea," Bo responded. "Let's try."

They started coming up with names like Canines Actuating Tranquility, which was rejected as too wimpy, and Canines Advising Togetherness, which was turned down as getting off-topic. But they doggedly stuck with it, adding more words until they hit a winner.

"So there we have it," said Bo. "We are officially the Canine Action Team Looking Over Very Excellent Righteous Solutions. All agreed?"

Every dog nodded approval. They had finally learned to work together and were proud of themselves.

"It's a wonderful official name, but it's kind of long for normal conversation," pointed out Punchy, a Boxer. "For short, can we just put the first sound of each word together?"

"Another fine idea," said Bo. "Let's all sound it out."

And they did, with every dog barking in glorious harmony to work out the sounds:

"C-c-c-c-c-c-a-a-a-a-a-t-t-t-t-l-l-l-l-l-o-o-o-o-o-o-v-v-v-v-v-e-e-e-r-r-r-r-s-s-s-s."

"Excellent!" exclaimed Bo. "Now, everyone speed it up and bark, howl, yowl, growl, yip or woof, whatever, just do it all together, loud and proud of what we are on this committee."

Which they did.

"WE ARE... CATLOVERS!"

Silence.

Double silence.

Triple silence.

Then...

"AAAAAAHHHHHH!!!"

"OOOHHHHHNNNOOOOO!!!"

"WHAT HAVE WE DONE?!?!?!"

There followed a long round of paw pointing, blame dodging and passing the duck, after which the abashed committee members took a vow to never reveal what had transpired. Otherwise, they might as well go live in a hole with the prairie dogs.

Zena, a Kuvasz, proposed that they simply call themselves the Top Dog Committee, to which everyone quickly barked, "Yes."

After the naming fiasco, they got down to the business of determining what type of competition to have.

"It's obvious. Let them fight to the death," Crusher the Komondor said.

"That's not fair to Whiskers. He's much smaller," objected Daisy, a Dandie Dinmont Terrier.

"Well, what about that carrot-rotty that he's supposed to know?" asked an Irish Wolfhound named Shillelagh. "A friend of a friend's uncle knew someone who said that Whiskers eats lots of rotten carrots before a fight and then pees carrot juice that burns his opponent. He could whip Scut with that."

"I heard he's only supposed to use it in real emergencies. This is a contest, not an emergency," explained Dollie the Sheepdog.

"Let's not forget that dogs can smell better than any other animal," noted Violet, a Golden Labrador. "So why not make the competition about who has the best nose?"

"If it's just about who's got the best nose, then the Bloodhound, Old Smeller, should be in the competition," observed Digger, a Tennessee Brindle.

Everyone liked Old Smeller, but no one could see him as Top Dog. He was competent, but too boring—not enough charisma or personality.

"What about a race?" piped up Sophia, a Basset Hound. "I love a good race. It really gets me fired up."

"Yes!"

"Wow!"

"Of course!"

"Line 'em up, and let the fastest dog win!"

Everyone on the panel was excited about having a race until Shorty the Dachshund said, "Whiskers is fast, but he won't have a chance against Scut's long legs."

"Maybe a different kind of race would work," conjectured Belle, a Blue Heeler. "What if we hide a bunch of things and give them clues? Whoever finds them all and gets them back the fastest wins."

Scut's supporters were not enthusiastic about that idea.

"That may not be fair," said Booger the Coonhound. "We all know that Whiskers is very smart because sometimes he says things we don't understand and we don't think he does either. On the other paw, we don't know anything about Scut's brainpower. What if he's just a big dummy? The whole contest will become a joke if he can't figure out any of the clues."

Bo saw that guidance was needed.

"We need a competition that's fair to both and demands more of them than just one skill—something that calls on many attributes like speed, cunning, strength, agility, intelligence, smelling, resourcefulness and courage. Scut will be better in some while Whiskers will be better in others, so it should all balance out. Then we'll have a true Top Dog."

"Ooh, ooh, ooh! I've got an idea!" exclaimed Squirt, a Lowchen.

"Well, it better be good, not something stupid," warned Pisser, a Keeshond.

"Ooh, it's good. It's really good," Squirt responded.

"Well, stop drooling and tell us," prompted Sandy, a Lundehund.

"It's a contest to bring back the Big Bone."

Whoa!

This would be big.

Very, very big.

It would be something that every dog everywhere had talked about, but no dog had ever done even though many had tried. That caused doubt as to whether the Big Bone really existed. Still, there were dogs who swore they knew a dog who knew another dog who had a friend who had actually seen it but for some reason couldn't get to it. It always seemed to be just out of reach.

"What an idea! I can't think of anything that would be more spectacular and more of a test," Bo commented. "If either competitor brought it back, then he truly would be the Top Dog."

"But what if neither one of them can bring it back?" asked Shellie, a Vizsla.

"That's not going to happen. Nothing can stop Scut. He can do anything," harrumphed Cranky, a Chow.

"Not when Whiskers outsmarts him," snickered Ladybug, the Welsh Terrier.

That settled it. All were agreed. Big Bone it was.

Naming the contest was easy: The Race for the Big Bone and the Title of Top Dog.

But the panelists disagreed over how to promote the participants.

Scut's supporters pushed for: "Scut—the Strongest Dog in the World versus Whiskers, the Weakest Dog in the World."

Whiskers' backers countered with: "Whiskers—the Smartest Dog in the World versus Scut, the Dumbest Dog in the World."

Not wanting another imbroglio, Bo said, "Let's keep it neutral. Just simply tell other dogs it's 'Whiskers versus Scut' or 'Scut versus Whiskers,' whichever you prefer."

After settling on where to begin the race, Bo adjourned the meeting saying, "Because it will take many long days for dogs from all parts to make the journey, go forth now and spread word about the competition. I'll visit with Whiskers and tell him that he's been entered in a race. Then we'll get word to Scut, wherever he is."

THEY'LL SAY YOU'RE AFRAID

The only dog not excited about having a race was Scut.

He ran off every dog messenger who tried to give him the details, saying they could stick the race up their butts.

In desperation, the Top Dog Committee gave up on that approach and, gritting teeth all around, agreed to go the humiliating route of asking a bird for help. The thinking was to enlist the leader of the Flapper Express as an impartial party who could not be run off thanks to his enviable ability to perch himself out of biting range.

When he met with the committee, Phelonius assured them he wanted nothing in return, but was only too happy to help as a gesture of goodwill for improving relations between canines and avians. Of course, he didn't reveal his true motive.

Leaving the meeting, Phelonius couldn't stop chuckling to himself.

What a bunch of dopes.

~

FROM UP ABOVE, flying from one reported sighting of the big dog to another, Phelonius finally spotted him.

There he is, Mr. Bad Attitude himself.

As he glided down, Phelonius did not repeat the mistake of his first meeting with Scut. Settling on a tree branch that was definitely out of reach, the crow called out, "Hey, there, handsome. How are you? How's your day going?"

Scut looked up and glared.

"What now, you fool?"

"Oh, come on. Why do you talk to an old friend like that? We're partners. We help one another."

"All I've gotten is wrong information. Those birdbrains of yours have had me running from one place to another. And for what? For one lousy excuse after another like, 'Oh, so sorry, I thought that Bichon Frise was Whiskers.' Or, 'Whoops, sorry, we did it again, but it's so hard to tell dogs apart from the air.'"

"Aw, Scut, come on, give us a break. Anybody can make a mistake."

"Oh, really? Forget about dogs. Your flapping morons can't even tell one animal from another. Remember when they had me chasing after that 'sure thing'? It turned out to be a cat named Snowball. Flapper, my ass. Crapper is more like it. As for you, why don't you go fly into a porcupine?"

"Oh, that really hurts," Phelonius said facetiously. "Hey, I'm sorry for all the missteps, but that's old news now. Everything has changed."

"Do tell. Wait, don't tell, let me guess. You've figured out the difference between a black-and-white Boston Terrier and a skunk. One bites you in the ass while the other squirts you with his ass. And that's why you stink. Am I right?"

Phelonius sidestepped the continuing sarcasm.

"Listen. The news is that you've lost your chance to catch

Whiskers alone. He's surrounded by an army of dogs. And instead of chasing him, you're going to race him."

Scut pulled back his upper lip in a half-sneer.

"A while back some overly excited idiots came around here yapping at me about that crap, but I ran their butts off. And now, here's a feathered flunky bringing up the same stupid thing."

"I will ignore that insult because you need to understand why you should race Whiskers."

"Race him for what? The privilege of eating you?"

"No. For the title of Top Dog. Think of how proud you'll be."

"I've whipped every dog I've ever faced. I don't need a useless title. But I am intrigued by the other thing you mentioned. Why does he have an army?"

"We don't know for sure. It just seemed to happen. Some dogs took up with him and those dogs attracted more dogs, and it just kept growing until it got so big they called it an army. Then they started arguing about Top Dog, whether it's you or whether it should be Whiskers. I hear that all of Dogdom has gotten stirred up about it. That's where the race comes in, to settle the argument and make the title official."

"I don't entertain fools," Scut snarled, "and nobody tells me what to do. Not you and not your scuzzy boss. I'm done with you and your flying clowns. I'll get Whiskers on my own."

Scut turned his tail to Phelonius and began walking away.

"They'll say you're afraid."

Scut stopped and looked back.

"Your reputation is taking a beating," Phelonius said. "Dogs are saying that Whiskers has outsmarted you every time you tried to find him. They're also saying that maybe you really aren't trying to find him, that you're only pretending to try. The question they keep asking is 'Why?' More and more the answer one hears is that maybe the mighty Scut actually is afraid of a smaller dog. If you don't show up for that race, you'll be branded a coward. I don't believe it, but mistaken or not, their perception is becoming your reality, my friend. Unless you do something about it, every dog, big or small, is going to start laughing at you and disrespecting you. That's what you'll face for the rest of your life. You know it's true. Is that what you want?"

"And what's it to you?"

"I don't make any bones about it—pardon the pun since you're a dog—that I'm here acting on behalf of my boss. But let's set that aside because during the time I've come to know you, I have gained a true appreciation for the esteemed position you've held until now among your fellow canines. So, even though I'm a bird, it saddens me to see how one's compatriots could turn away from him so quickly to embrace a devious newcomer who has no real accomplishments that I am aware of except running his mouth in order to mislead, fool and take advantage of others. I tell you most sincerely, it's an absolute shame."

Scut looked at the ground and shook his head in disgust. He was being manipulated, not only by this phony bird and his shadowy boss but also by the expectations of the clamoring losers who stayed safely on the sidelines of the dog world. And it was all on account of one attention-seeking jerk.

"This is your best chance to get him," Phelonius continued. "You can do it during the race when you're both out of sight. Later, when you show up at the finish line but he doesn't, just say that the last time you saw Whiskers he was so far behind that he probably quit and snuck off from embarrassment. Yeah, that's the story we'll push: The smart-aleck dog who shot his muzzle off about how great he was turned out to be a great big nothing, a fraud, a joke."

Scut thought about the crow's words. It was a good plan. He wouldn't have to hunt for Whiskers anymore. His nemesis would come right to him.

"All right, I'll do it."

"Oh, I forgot to mention that there's a twist to this race. It's not about outrunning your opponent."

"What do you mean?"

"The winner is the dog who returns with something called the Big Bone."

"The Big Bone? Are you serious?"

"Yeah. What's the problem?"

"That's an old puppy dog tale."

41

WHOSE STUPID IDEA WAS THAT?

"Things have changed."

"What do you mean, 'things have changed'?" Scratchy asked, squinching his eyes and leaning forward.

"Well, uh," Phelonius said, "you know how Scut was supposed to take care of..."

"Of course I know, you idiot. Don't tell me what I already know. But I'm getting the idea you're here to tell me something has gone wrong."

"Well, it seems he's been entered in a race with Whiskers."

"A race! Whose stupid idea was that? Yours? His? Can't I count on anyone to do things right anymore?"

"Look, it wasn't Scut's fault. He got trapped into it. They've got something called Top Dog, and all the mangy mutts in Dogdom began clamoring for a race between him and Whiskers to find out who should be the official Top Dog. You see, up until now the title was actually unofficial, but that was okay because everyone always assumed that Scut was the Top Dog. Then Whiskers came along using his smarts and that caused a lot of dogs to start questioning whether..."

"Stop!" Scratchy commanded. "I have never heard anything so idiotic as that. Top Dog? What's the point? That's like being on top of a shit pile. Unbelievable! What a pathetic ambition for pathetic losers living pathetic lives. If I didn't hate dogs so much, I could possibly, almost, tentatively, slightly, minimally conjure up a nearly nil feeling of sympathy for them."

When Scratchy's diatribe was over, Phelonius told the fuming nutria how Scut would use the race as a convenient way to dispatch Whiskers.

"Hmm, that's not a bad plan, as long as it works. But that Whiskers, for some reason, keeps landing on his feet like a damn cat with too many lives."

Scratchy paused, then cut a quick glance at the crow.

"Phelonius, I know this sounds strange, but do you think Mother Nature believes he's a cat because of that dumb name he has?"

Phelonius drew in his breath and looked off to one side, amazed that Scratchy would even think of something so ridiculous. Apparently, he was desperate to blame someone else for his own failure.

Looking once more at Scratchy, the crow saw the nutria staring hard at him, waiting for an answer. Phelonius had to be careful, because disagreeing with Scratchy was never a good idea.

"Knowing how conceited he is, he probably thinks he has Mother Nature fooled, and he's probably going around bragging about it."

"Ooh, that sounds just like him," Scratchy said, rubbing his paws together. "If a little birdie can put that in her ear, then maybe she can stop cutting him some slack, just in case she's been doing it by mistake."

He smiled and gave a paws-up to Phelonius who awkwardly raised a foot but missed contact.

Scratchy's smile didn't last long.

"Now, let's get back to this so-called race," he said, frowning. "I better not hear that Whiskers won the stupid thing. He needs to come in last."

Scratchy leaned closer, eyes hooded, his hot breath enveloping Phelonius.

"Dead last."

42

THERE'S A LOT OF STUPID GOING ON

"Stand your ground, you pussy! Take the charge!"

But as soon as the Doberman ran at him, the trainee shrieked, turned tail and hotfooted away in terror.

Janvier spat in disgust. It was another frustrating day of dealing with the chickenshit recruits who were hoping to become agents in the Federal Bureau of Dog Investigation. She was especially pissed that she had been pulled from the field for this duty because a congresswoman taking a tour had raised hell when she saw only men conducting the training.

"Dammit, Bob, where do these weenies come from?"

The older agent with white hair and a white mustache sighed, "Every batch we get is like this. It makes me feel like old school versus new fool, especially with their parents tagging along through all their training."

Just as he said that, the Doberman caught the rookie's butt protector in its teeth and pulled the squealing FBDI wannabe to the ground.

"That's okay, sweetie," yelled the father to his son. "Everyone knows you're wonderful."

"Wonderful, my ass," Janvier said, gritting her teeth and reaching for her whistle.

"A hard bite in the ass through a thin uniform used to teach trainees real quick to face the problem head-on," Bob remarked. "But everything changed after your class graduated. Now, we're turning out wimps thanks to that new federal agency, OSHA, the Occupational Serenity and Happiness Administration."

"Tweeeeeeeeet!"

Hearing Janvier's whistle, the Doberman let go of the crying trainee and ran back to its cage.

"You were so brave!" shouted the downed recruit's mom as he recovered his feet and ran to her for a hug.

"Listen up, you gutless wonders," Janvier snapped at the trainees.

"You shouldn't talk to them that way," rebuked a mother who was well over six feet tall and tottering on platform shoes. "You'll lower their self-esteem."

Looking sharply at the woman, Janvier motioned to a security guard and said, "Get the giraffe out of here!"

While the woman scuffled with the guard, whacking him with a feedbag of a designer purse, Janvier jogged into the middle of the training field.

"Look, she's not wearing any padding," oohed a female trainee.

"Ms. Janvier, do you want to use my hiney protector?" asked a male recruit.

Janvier ignored the offer.

"When I say take the charge, I mean take it. You've got to man up, you wimps. Grow a pair that your mother would be proud to see."

As she spoke, one of the assistant trainers prepared to open a cage about thirty yards away.

"Release Kraken," Janvier commanded.

The cage door went up and a large Rottweiler stepped out, growling and snarling. Locking eyes on Janvier, it charged straight at her. She stood still, hands on hips. The dog closed in and leaped. Janvier dropped and rolled onto her back, bent her left leg tight against her chest, then kicked it up, contacting the airborne dog in the stomach and propelling it onward past her head, causing the Rottweiler to flip upside down and land on its back with a whump.

Janvier used the momentum of her leg flip to go into a backward somersault that brought her standing up. Spinning around, she raced toward the Rottweiler that was still down from having the air knocked out of it, whipped a muzzle off her utility belt, slapped it on, and finished the demonstration by winding a cord rapidly around the dog's legs to immobilize them.

Moms, dads and recruits stood with their mouths open.

"That's how you do it," Janvier scolded. "You don't need padding for your fat asses. You need technique and the guts to use it. Study your videos again tonight on your iPaps, because tomorrow I'm going to hogtie any rookie who even thinks about running."

That brought protests from the parents.

"Isn't running away just a different way of catching a dog?"

"Can't they practice with something less threatening, like stuffed animals?"

"Instead of saying 'fat asses,' can you say, 'the large thing you sit on'?"

Janvier was raising her hand to show them what they could sit on when a golf cart rolled onto the field and stopped beside her.

"The director wants to see you," said the driver. "Now."

He drove her to the headquarters building. On the fifth floor, she entered the office of J. Egbert Hooter, who was patting the top of his head, trying to force down hair that persistently stuck out in odd directions.

As she sat, he said, "We're going to put you back in the field. Three reasons. Number one: We're getting too many complaints from the parents. Number two: You're hurting the egos of the trainees."

"They need to be hurt," Janvier retorted. "In fact, their egos need a damn good ass-kicking."

"I'm with you on that," Hooter chuckled, "but we've got to follow federal policy. Feeling good about themselves is primary. Actual accomplishments are important, but secondary."

"Screw them, screw their parents, and screw the policy. What's the third reason?"

"I'm not putting you in the field to punish you. We need you there badly. We're getting reports of very unusual dog activity."

"Like what?"

"Rather than lazily lying around for most of the day indoors, dogs now want to be outdoors all day long, barking constantly over their fences, like they're communicating something significant. As for dogs on the loose, instead of wandering around haphazardly like they normally do, one will make a beeline to another. But instead of hanging around together and goofing off, the second one will take off to another dog, like the old Pony Express.

"It's obvious that something unusual is going on," Hooter continued, "but we just don't know what it is. We've got cryptologists trying to decipher what they are saying, but they haven't come up with anything. We asked the Navy's best dolphins to see if they could crack it since they're also animals and really smart, but they gave up. Then we tried the Dog Tickler. When we asked him to translate, instead of speaking English he started barking at us, grabbed his consulting fee in his mouth, dropped to all fours and ran away."

Hooter paused, messed up his hair to start over, smoothed it back down, and leaned forward.

"The only thing we know for sure is that dogs are really excited, like they're anticipating something big, something important."

"What about other types of animals?" Janvier asked.

"They aren't affected. I guess they don't give a shit about dog stuff."

"So, let me get this straight. Dogs bark a lot and get each other wound up. Big deal," Janvier scoffed.

"It is a big deal if you're a dog owner. Here, just listen to a couple of messages on our hotline."

—*"I don't know what's wrong with my dog. He seems unusually happy. Can you do something about that?"*

—*"My old dog used to lie around like he was dead. Wouldn't move for nothin'. Now every day he's up and perky and rarin' to get outside. I don't know what's come over him. It's downright spooky."*

—*"I saw my dog talking with the neighbor's dog, and every now and then she would turn and look at me like she was laughing at me, and at other times she would kinda squint like she was giving me the evil eye. I'm scared."*

"We've gotten thousands of messages like those," Hooter emphasized.

"People always overreact," Janvier said.

"That's exactly the problem," Hooter said excitedly while vigorously running both hands through his hair. "There's a wild rumor that aliens from outer space are behind this, that they are controlling the dogs' minds as part of their plan to take over the earth."

"How stupid," Janvier said, smiling.

"Stupid is as stupid does, and there's a lot of stupid going on, so we've got to do something about it," Hooter said, frowning. "I'm telling you that people are frightened. They're scared of dogs in the street. They see a dog and they start running, which makes the dog's prey instinct kick in and it bites them in the ass. Butt pads are selling like hotcakes on the Cheap Shopping Channel. It's even worse for people who own dogs. They're scared to go to sleep at night, afraid that formerly sweet little Sushi is going to chew them into tofu."

"It's really that bad?"

"It's even worse than that. Another rumor gaining speed is that once a person is bitten, they'll become something like a zombie under the control of the dogs and the space aliens. People are running in terror from lazy persons and geezers with walkers. I know it all sounds crazy, but we've got to get a handle on this situation before it explodes into a national panic.

"As for us at the FBDI," Hooter continued, "we don't believe the rumors, but we're very concerned that dogs are learning how to become organized, and that's dangerous because we don't know where it could lead."

"That is a concern," Janvier said, folding her arms and tapping a finger on her chin.

"You're the best agent we've got," Hooter said. "You're being wasted here. Your nation needs you. I want you to get out there and put a stop to this. You'll have full authority, because you're also getting a promotion."

He stood up, rubbed his hair with his right hand and held out his left to shake. Realizing he goofed, he brought down his right hand to hold it out while slapping his left on top of his head.

Janvier stood and shook his hand.

"I'll track down what's causing this situation and put an end to it. Nothing will stop me."

"That's my girl."

"I'm not your girl. I'm an FBDI agent," Janvier chided as she strolled over to the window.

Looking out toward the training field, she watched the recruits eagerly jumping up and down while reaching to get a participation trophy from the white-haired agent.

"What about Bob?" she asked. "He deserves better than this."

"I know, it's a shame," agreed Hooter, "but the parents insist that a full-fledged agent hand out the trophies, not an assistant. And as we in administration say, 'A trophy a day keeps the parents at bay.'"

"I am so glad I'm leaving," Janvier said as she opened the office door.

Hooter followed her.

"You're walking out with me?"

"Actually, I'm going to make my rounds."

"Of what?"

"It's time to give my staffers their daily hug. It makes them feel better about having to do work."

43

SCOOP DU JOUR

The buildup to "The Race for the Big Bone and the Title of Top Dog" was exhilarating.

Dogs everywhere had heard about the contest. Thousands had gone absent without leave to travel long distances and many days from their homes to the historic event.

The mystery that befuddled all dogs was why the Big Bone hadn't been smelled out long ago by canine ancestors, with dogs still enjoying it today if indeed it was self-replenishing. The fact that it had not been found gave credence to the ideas that the Big Bone had either been hidden by ancient giant cats out of sheer meanness or for some unknown reason was itself hiding out. Because it was so elusive, the most likely place for it to be was in the strange region called Offland.

The jumping-off place for entering was here at the Meadow of No Return, so named because no dog going into Offland with the goal of bringing back the Big Bone had ever returned. Obviously, it would take a very special dog to find and bring back the Big Bone.

Of course, everyone in the growing crowd wanted to look and smell special for the grand occasion. The biggest lickfest

Dogdom had ever known was under way in the meadow with each arriving pooch licking every spot it could reach on its fur and then being a good neighbor by licking out an adjoining dog's ears. When each dog had taken a darn good licking, it scouted around for just the right sun-dried poop to roll in for a dusty patina that would draw envious inquiries of where it had found such a marvelous odeur de resistance.

When their own ablutions were done, the members of the Top Dog Committee made a great show of reconnoitering the path the contestants would follow from the meadow into Offland. After much disagreement and overly loud arguing purposely designed to draw the admiration of the canine throng, the committee members settled on a spot for the starting line, not too close and not too far away, but just right. To show solidarity in their choice, all the committee members took part in kicking up the dirt and then ceremoniously lining up nose to tail. On the third bark from Bo the Great Dane, the committee began peeing in unison to officially mark the location.

Some dogs, however, were too busy to get themselves cleaned up or to admire the committee's handiwork.

These were the newshounds—small, scruffy, yapping dogs. As they saw it, their job was to run from one participant's camp to the other, hoping to stir up a controversy that they could convey to the multitude with an excess of frantic barking.

One asked, "Whiskers, what do you have to say about your opponent?"

Whiskers looked off to the side. His self-appointed advisers for public relations, hoping to preserve his life as well as his chances, nodded at him. He was supposed to reply with one of the barking points they had created, whether it actually answered the question or purposely deflected it:

— I am glad you asked that, because I am pleased to be here.
— I look forward to a spirited but clean competition.

— I am confident of victory, but for reasons which I am sure you can appreciate I cannot reveal my strategy before the race.

— I respect my opponent but I am not in awe of him.

— Occasionally, size does matter, but the ability of the performer matters more.

— I do not regard my opponent as a freak of nature. I see him as one of Mother Nature's unfortunate, overgrown stepdogs.

— His reputation does not concern me. I am certain that it has been overblown and that he is in truth kindly and misunderstood and probably has performed many good deeds in the service of his fellow dogs but which for personal reasons he has kept to himself.

— I would be pleased to answer your questions but at another time as I must now focus on preparations for the upcoming contest, and I ask that you respect my wish for privacy.

Those were the approved answers.

Whiskers, however, had discovered something in other sessions with the newshounds. Whenever he went off message and said something outrageous, they became very excited, so:

"Scut rhymes with butt."

Oh, no!

His public relations advisers dropped their heads. Why couldn't he have said something nice, pleasant and meaningless? Why make an angry dog even angrier? Especially when the angry dog is so damn big? What if Scut came to the starting line so enraged that he bit off one of Whiskers' legs or two or three or even all four? Whiskers sure wouldn't have much of a chance hopping and rolling along like a drunk rabbit.

The nattering news barkers couldn't have cared less as to whether Whiskers had damaged his chances or himself. The goal of each little yipster was to get to Scut first with this provocation.

They scurried off with their tails wagging so hard in anticipation that their hind ends practically helicoptered off the ground, causing them to weave, stumble, slip and slide as they sped along the twists of a trail to Scut's camp. Rounding the last turn, they spied the shade tree where he lay, surrounded by panting females drawn to the nonchalant confidence and charisma of The Bad Dog.

Arriving too fast and stopping too quickly, the newshounds piled into one another but quickly jumped up and began their screechingly annoying yippity-yip-yaps.

"Whiskers just said that Scut rhymes with butt!"

"How does that make you feel?"

"Do you think it's fair that Whiskers is smaller and you are so big?"

"Does that difference make you feel bad?"

"If you get way ahead of Whiskers and he gets tired, will you stop and wait for him?"

"Do you feel that's the fair thing to do?"

"We heard that Whiskers said your size hurts your ability to think because your brain is so far away from the rest of your body that it's basically useless."

"How do you feel about that?"

"Do you feel an answer coming on?"

"Should we give you more time for your answers?"

"What does Whiskers rhyme with?"

Scut fixed his eyes on the feverishly yipping Chihuahuas, Pomeranians, Maltese, Pekingese and Pugs mixed in with yapping designer dog Chimeranians, Pupoms, Malugs, Pekhuas and one Chipomalpekpu.

He had never seen a more brainless bunch.

Scut despised little dogs. They couldn't hunt, they couldn't fight, and their running was pathetic. With little bitty faces and little bitty teeth and little bitty barks, they were as useless as cats.

Now, he had to respond to this besieging mob of canine pretenders. The only way to make the yipping yappers go away was to give them what they wanted.

"Whiskers rhymes with catshit. I feel like you're idiots. As for the rest of your questions, go crap on yourselves."

They didn't have time to do that.

They were already running and bumping into one another, each desperate to be the first to tell Whiskers that he rhymes with catshit.

44

YEAH, BABY!

S tanding backstage before his primetime news conference, J. Egbert Hooter, Director of the Federal Bureau of Dog Investigation, was desperate.

He was under siege from critics and Congress for failing to stop the growing panic among the public.

Every day, people were reporting dogs to local authorities and the FBDI for overexcited, weird behavior. Neighbors came to blows after reporting each other's dogs. People suspicious of their own dogs were dumping them surreptitiously in veterinarians' parking lots and over animal control fences.

Hooter had appealed for calm, saying that not all dogs were dangerous or under space aliens' control.

That didn't work.

The President tried to help, saying that if he had a dog he wouldn't throw it over the White House fence.

That didn't work either.

Close to losing his job, Hooter had hired a consultant from Broadway who told him that his only hope was to put on a show.

Now, seated in the auditorium at the FBDI's headquarters, members of the news media thought they were going to hear

Hooter announce his resignation. Instead, he marched onstage rubbing his hair vigorously in time to the music of the "Battle Hymn of the Republic" as a giant American flag unfurled on one side of the room.

Hooter saluted the flag, stepped to the lectern at the center of the stage and said, "For too long, people on both sides of the Atlantic have believed that the British have the world's best special agent in James Bone at Scottie Yard. I'm here to tell you that America has an even better agent, and at this very moment, she is out in the field tracking down clues to crack the case of American dogs gone wild.

"Ladies and gentlemen," Hooter whooped, sweeping his left arm up and backward to point behind himself while smoothing his hair with his right hand, "I give you Special Agent Janvier!"

Fireworks exploded at the corners of the stage as an enormous curtain rose to reveal a thirty-foot-tall photo blowup of a fiercely determined Janvier dressed all in black with a pearl-handled stun gun on each hip.

Flames shot up beside four two-hundred-inch monitors arrayed across the front of the stage. Over and over the monitors looped the training video of Janvier going womano a dogo, fearlessly and easily subduing the beastly Kraken to "Who's Afraid of the Big Bad Wolf?" played with heavy metal power chords at ear-splitting volume.

The press fell in love.

Instead of a chair-bound, hair-rubbing Hooter to fight for America, they had a spike-haired, spike-collared vixen of an Amazon with the balls to take on any menace.

And the best thing is that she was hot.

"Yeah, baby!" yelled TV pundit Crib Mattress, feeling a tingle go down his leg as well as somewhere else.

"Space aliens and their dog lackeys, look out!" Hooter bellowed. "Special Agent Janvier is on the side of Uncle Sam, and she's coming for you. No quarter will be asked, and no quarter will be given. Not one damn dime's worth!"

Reporters stood and cheered because they too were scared shitless of their own dogs. Forgotten was Janvier's appearance on the Dr. Sid Show and the ensuing scorn they had heaped on her for rounding up God's helpless creatures. Now, the reporters giddily busied themselves turning her into a national hero and, even better, an A-list celebrity.

45

WAG YOUR TAILS

"I'm telling you that Whiskers doesn't have a chance!"

"Oh, yeah? You seem to forget that he was a champion at Pooparama!"

"That doesn't mean anything. Any dog can take a dump!"

"Hah! Not any dog can take a dump that sparkles, flies through the air, buzzes like a bumblebee and drops shit on morons like you!"

"Then he better hop on board one of his flying poop piles, because there's no way he can outrun Scut!"

"He doesn't need to outrun him. The big lummox will get so lost and confused that his brain will explode!"

That conversation was just one of many similar ones taking place among the thousands of overexcited fans on the morning of the great competition.

Most dogs wanted Whiskers to win, but they also felt he was truly the underdog of underdogs. Smarts could only take you so far in what many perceived to be a contest that most likely would favor brute physicality.

Aside from who actually would win, the other big draw of the race was the knowledge that the attendees would finally see what all dogs had dreamed of—the Big Bone itself. There was great concern, however, that it might be so big and so heavy with juice-filled, fat-marbled meat that even Scut might not have enough strength to carry or drag it back.

Maybe that's why dogs who set off on a quest for the Big Bone didn't return. It was easy to imagine them collapsing from extreme exhaustion, lying in the dirt with the Big Bone beside them, staring at it helplessly, their panting becoming slower and slower until it ceased, their eyes closed, and they died. Another possibility is that some may have been so dazzled by it they lost their minds and tried to eat it all at once and ate so much that they ate themselves to death because everyone knows that many a dog has no self-control when red meat is involved.

Even so, if death awaited Scut or Whiskers, it still had to wait. First, the race had to be run.

Suddenly, thousands of spectators jumped to their feet, yipping and howling as Whiskers led his army of camp followers into the meadow. Leaving them to mingle with the other spectators, he pranced ostentatiously to the starting line. After making sure that all attention was on him, he spun around in circles and kicked up grass and dirt with his back legs to show his spunk.

But the attention didn't last long.

Scut loomed into sight on the trail. The spectators seemed to lose their minds, erupting in wild, crazed barking as the deliciously fearsome bad dog sauntered through the crowd, followed by his coterie of gaga ladies.

As Scut neared the starting line and his opponent, viewers gasped at their physical differences. Very tall with exceptionally strong shoulder and leg muscles developed over years of non-stop hard traveling, Scut exuded power.

On the other hand, Whiskers, well, he was just a regular dog —not large, not small, just in-between. In other words, nothing special physically. Unspoken, but undoubtedly racing through the spectators' minds was the question: How in the world could Whiskers compete? Not only that, there was Scut's reputation to consider. Why would the brute even bother to play fair once they were alone on the other side of the dark woods bounding the meadow?

But what was this?

Standing up on his hind legs, Whiskers was twisting jerkily from side to side and making weird sounds.

"Yes! It's really real! It's carrot-rotty!" one dog yelped.

Dogs stopped barking like lunatics and surged forward, shouldering each other aside to get a look. As they watched Whiskers' gyrations, the thought began to spread that perhaps his size wasn't such a disadvantage. Maybe he could doghandle Scut with this fighting technique they had heard about but never seen.

With the attention back on him, Whiskers worked the crowd, amazing them by throwing paw punches in the air while dancing around Scut. He even did an air kick standing on one leg.

"Whiskers! What are you doing? Are you crazy? Stop that," hissed one of his advisers.

Whiskers didn't pay any attention. He was making his opponent an unwilling participant in his pantomime, and having a good time doing it.

Scut's face contorted with anger. Taking a step toward his foe and showing his fangs, it appeared that he was about to snap Whiskers' neck in front of everybody.

But he stopped. This giant gathering had come for a race. To not have it after all the buildup would be the greatest disappointment in the history of Dogdom, and he would be blamed for it forever. Instead of being known as Top Dog, he would be known as Top Piece of Catshit. He stepped back, stayed in place, and did nothing but snarl at the cheeky performer.

"That's enough, boys. Please settle down," said Bo the Great Dane, shaking his head at Whiskers, whose vanity seemed to have overcome his sanity. "Before the race begins, we will have a few words to mark this great occasion. Brother Biscuit will give the appeal to Mother Nature."

All the dogs hushed as a Parson Jack Russell walked to the front. Facing the throng, he solemnly said, "Mother Nature, watch over these two dogs as they race through your countryside. They are your favored children, as are all dogs. Protect them from slimy snakes, creepy cougars, big-butted bears and all the other rotten wretches you created. You must have had a good reason, but we sure can't figure it out."

"Woof to that," said Bo, and the thousands of other dogs responded with one great "WOOF!"

The Great Dane turned to the contestants.

"Before you embark on this historic endeavor, do either of you have any words you wish to say?"

Whiskers perked up.

Are you kidding? I've got to say something for my fans.

"Yes, I do," he answered, surmounting a rise so everyone could see him better.

"Purebreds, inbreds, mongrels and runts, I come not to bury my opponent, but to outsmart and outrace him. Which is more glorious, to lose with honor or to win by any means possible? Cry not for me, Dogdom, for I go on to a far greater reward, that of Top Dog. As for my competitor, what can you say about a big oaf who loves the smell of blood in the morning, who never had a friend in his fiendish life, who repels all who meet him? I'll tell you what you can say: Your day is over. We are now embarked on a kinder, gentler way to a beautiful doghouse on the hill. I say to the garbage chef, tear down the fence that divides one dog from another. There has been too much fighting, too much biting. We need more licking, more lazing in the grass, more hump..."

"Oh, shut up!" growled Scut. "Let's get on with it. You're trying to put off getting whupped, afraid of being shown that you're a loser, a fraud, a deceiver."

Those words jarred Whiskers' followers, breaking their reverie. Was he stalling, afraid to go dogo a dogo with Scut?

"My friends," said Whiskers a little shakily, but then recovering, "you have just heard the voice of ignorance interrupting my magnus opus soliloquious monologus speechifius. When I return as Top Dog with the Big Bone, I will make the longest speech you ever heard for your listening pleasure. As for now, though, my tail is up, and I am ready. Let's do it."

With all the racket and commotion that the thousands of jumping and rollicking canines were making, no one noticed a pack of large dogs stepping away and slinking off into the woods.

"Whiskers and Scut, take your positions," Bo ordered.

They placed their front paws just behind the starting line that sparkled in the sun thanks to a last-moment freshening-up by the Top Dog Committee.

"If you are ready, wag your tails."

Both tails wagged—Scut's furiously, Whiskers' not so much.

"For the Big Bone and the title of Top Dog..."

Scut and Whiskers lowered their necks, staring straight ahead.

"...I command you to..."

The two foes positioned their legs for springing forward.

"RUN!"

Scut leaped through the air, landing in front of Whiskers to block his path, ensuring that the lighter dog could not get off to a quicker start.

Looking back with a sneer, Scut churned his rear legs. The

onlookers howled as pebbles pelted Whiskers. Dirt flew into his eyes, and a cloud of dust covered him. Finished with his dirty work, Scut hurtled down the path leading into the woods.

As the spectators lining the path admired Scut's powerful stride, they expected to see Whiskers flash past them in an effort to catch up, but it didn't happen. Turning their heads, they saw that he hadn't gotten very far from the starting line.

Although his eyes had recovered, Whiskers was ambling along, pretending that he was having difficulty seeing as he made his way to the edge of the woods.

That's when he pulled a surprise for all the spectators who were muttering that he was too scared to race.

Standing up, he threw some paw punches and said, "I guess that's a good enough lead for the big dummy so he'll have a chance, if he hasn't run into a tree by now. Here's a promise: I'll see you soon, and everybody will get a bite of the Big Bone."

Cheers exploded from the crowd. Whiskers wasn't out of the race! He must know something—a trick, a secret or a shortcut.

Actually, the only thing Whiskers knew was that he couldn't match Scut stride for stride, and he wasn't going to take any chance on running blindly into an ambush by his angry opponent.

So, he had stalled. But he also had another reason. He did not want Scut to know where he was going.

I'm on my way to see the most interesting dog in the world.

46

IL BALONIONI

O nce inside the woods, Whiskers plunged into the trees on his right. He fought his way through underbrush until he found an animal trail.

Somewhere down the trail was supposed to live a Spinone Italiano who, according to himself, had traveled farther and seen more strange and wonderful sights than any dog who had ever lived.

He told so many fantastic tales that many listeners mockingly called him Il Balonioni. Others, however, enjoyed his stories and called him the most interesting dog in the world. It was said that:

When he howled, wolves whimpered.

Each time he scratched, fleas jumped off other dogs.

His bones dug their own holes.

And he always won at dog shows that he did not enter.

Whiskers was determined to see this dog. If only half of his tales were true, he might have an idea of where to find the Big Bone.

After several miles, Whiskers saw a beige and white dog,

taller than himself and with a longish fur coat. He was puttering around, sniffing at and rearranging a collection of old bones. As Whiskers approached, Barco Poocho looked up and smiled broadly.

"Ah, so nice to have a visitor. Come, friend, I welcome you as I was welcomed upon my own journeys. If you are tired, sit as long as you wish so that we may exchange tales to pass the time most pleasantly."

I've heard that Barco can talk all day, but I don't have the time to see who can tell the biggest whopper. Even so, I can't be rude to him. I need to know what he knows.

Whiskers sat.

"Barco, I have heard that you were a great traveler and have seen many amazing things."

"Oh, indeed! During my long journey deep into Offland, I saw things that were marvelous, incredible, fabulous."

"Like what?"

"Imagine dogs with tongues blacker than night, dogs with skin so wrinkled you would think they were wearing three hides, dogs with six toes, dogs climbing trees, dogs who had no hair at all except for some tufts on their head, and dogs with butts emitting aromas like you've never smelled before. Of course, that last was probably because of the food. However, that's not all. I could tell you many tales of lady dogs who were exquisitely charming and accommodating in the most pleasing fashion."

"That's very interesting," Whiskers said, "but I..."

"Wait! That's not all. You should know that I, Barco Poocho, traveler extraordinaire, became friends with the greatest of leaders, one in a long line of dogs that began with the feared fighter Genghis Khanine, who was succeeded by Tamayto Khan who begat Kukla Kahn who was followed by Humungus Khan—the

Great Dong himself—wisest of all rulers and one whom I served faithfully as an assessor of all that his empire contained."

Barco paused for breath and began to scratch himself. While the garrulous Spinone Italiano rat-a-tat-tatted on his left side with his hind leg, Whiskers watched as a flea fell off his own left side and jumped quickly away on the ground to save its life. Whiskers looked at Barco in amazement.

"You are most welcome," Barco said. "Now, my new friend, of all that I have told you, which interests you the most so that I may elaborate on it?"

"Actually, I was hoping that you could tell me something about the Big Bone."

"The Big Bone? Yes, we passed by its vicinity once on a tour of the Great Dong's empire. It was pointed out to me."

Whiskers jumped up on all fours.

"What did it look like? How big was it? Is it as wonderful as everybody says?"

"I wish I had the words to describe it to you, but it was far off in the distance. The late afternoon sun was so low in the sky that it was blinding me, and I could barely make out anything. Nor could I smell it, because we were upwind. Knowing that it was there, I wanted to run to it and bring a piece of it back, but the Great Dong forbade it. He said fools are always in a rush for what they don't need, and I was too valuable to lose. I didn't understand what he meant, but rather than displease him, I let it go."

What? Are you kidding me? How could any dog let it go? I wanted to hear that at least he got to lick it.

Barco could see the disappointment in Whiskers' face, but he continued with his tale.

"Eventually, the Great Dong gave me permission to return home. After many days on my long journey back, messengers brought sad news. The Great Dong had fallen in battle against the Great Wang and couldn't get up anymore. He lost face, and his empire collapsed."

Barco paused to draw in the dirt.

"Look, this was the mark of the Great Dong."

"Wow," Whiskers marveled, "no wonder he was called the Great Dong."

"He gave me a most valuable gift with that mark on it, a flat bone with many other markings that detailed the glories of his empire.

"Where is it? Can I see it?"

"Unfortunately, my traveling companions and I were attacked by a pack of wild beasts. I alone survived but lost the flat bone while running for my life. Alas, I came back with no proof of my journey, only to be disbelieved and laughed at."

I can't let him get started on another tale. I need hard information.

"Barco, I'm in a race for the Big Bone. Can you tell me where it is?"

The Spinone Italiano looked down as if in thought, then back up.

"Unfortunately, my travels took place so long ago that I can't remember all the details of how to make one's way through so many different landscapes."

"Then there is no way you can help me?"

"I wish I could. What I do know is that what I went through will not be what you go through. The trails in Offland crisscross, uncross and re-cross like a jumble of snakes. So, although the end of the journey is the same, it is different for everyone who takes it. But why rush off? Stay for a while. I have many other stories to tell you."

"Sorry, but I need to be going. As I said, it's a race."

Whiskers walked away, shaking his head.

Maybe other dogs are right. Perhaps Barco is a liar, telling stories that can't be proved or disproved. It's even possible he didn't go anywhere.

Maybe he just makes up stories to make himself the center of attention.

47

IS THIS WHAT YOU WANTED?

Scut came to a fork. He was stymied. There was no clue as to which way to go.

For days, he had faced the same frustrating situation —trails crisscrossing one another and fork after fork followed by dead-ends.

The race had gone haywire for him from the beginning. After humiliating Whiskers at the starting line, Scut charged deep into the woods until stepping off the path to set an ambush.

While waiting for his victim to arrive, he had begun to daydream.

What if I grab the jerk by the scruff of the neck, carry him back to the starting line like a helpless puppy, pitch him on the ground, and pee on him while saying to all the gawking fools, Is this what you wanted for Top Dog?

However, this was a race followed fervently by all of Dogdom, so Scut intended to play along—his way.

After I grab him, I'll break the twerp's neck and drop his body in some deep, bushy ravine where it won't be found. When I get back, I'll say I saw Whiskers once but never again, that he must have "dropped out" of the race. He'll be remembered as a quitter, a fraud who was all bark and no bite. And nobody will bug me about him anymore.

As for the Big Bone, if it exists, I'm not going to look for it just to please all those gutless cowards. Instead, I'll dig up some cruddy piece of old bone and roll myself around in a lot of mud and dust to look like I traveled far away. I'll say, Sorry, but it seems the Big Bone was chewed to bits long ago, and spit the cruddy piece of bone in their faces as evidence.

Then I'll be done with all of them:

That infuriating little braggart.

That manipulating bird.

And all the asinine expectations from all the fools in Dogdom.

But there was a problem.

The longer Scut had waited, the more he realized Whiskers wasn't coming, that he had sneaked off the path and taken a different route. So, giving up on ambushing his foe, Scut had ventured deeper into Offland in the hope of catching a whiff of Whiskers' scent.

As the days progressed, however, the trail Scut took eventually stopped going straight and began twisting and merging with other trails until it didn't exist anymore.

Now, here he stood, staring at another lousy fork in another rotten offshoot of another dumbass trail. The only thing he could do was pick one side of the fork and see where it would take him.

But Whiskers wasn't the only dog on Scut's mind. For several days, he had been catching occasional glimpses of other dogs.

Large dogs.

Always staying obscured in tree lines, they paralleled him wherever he went.

48

THE ONE THAT GOT AWAY

The introduction of Janvier at J. Egbert Hooter's primetime news conference helped to restrain the growing national panic.

Now that a real champion had been sent forth to combat the unnatural alliance of pet dogs and space aliens, Americans felt new hope. As patriots, they wanted to do their part on the home front while Janvier sought the enemy in the field.

So they pitched in by flooding the Federal Bureau of Dog Investigation with millions of useless and misleading tips in calls, texts, tweets, faxes, emails and telegrams from all over the nation:

—"A dog is following me in the parking lot of Big Ass Burgers. He's drooling. I think he wants to bite my ass and make me into one of those zombies. You better come quick."

—"There's a pile of poop in my front yard. It looks weird like it's from outer space and, oh Lord, does it stink. If your laboratory wants it for DNA, I can mail it to you."

—"A dog in my neighborhood is spying for those space aliens. He keeps looking at the sky and barking the same thing over and over. It sounds like *ah-oo-ah-oo-wuffa-wuffa-uck-ah-uck. I'm pretty damn sure it's some kind of Morse code, Martian-style."*

To stop the onslaught of inane messages, the FBDI turned to outside help. Normally, for a friendly communication, the agency would use the public relations firm of Hooey, Trype, Twaddle & Balderdash. For a misleading communication, the FBDI had Dodge, Hyde, Skeem & Weezel on retainer. This time, though, Director Hooter felt that a blatant in-your-face approach was needed to make the public pay attention, so he hired an edgy advertising company of former punk rockers: Screem, Yehl, Pyuk & Vahmit.

Soon, television viewers and movie theater patrons were watching a public service announcement showing a montaged film clip of Mommie Weirdest and Uncle Sam hitting smartphones, computers and a telegram delivery boy with wire coat hangers while screeching, "No More Messages!"

But the nation's patriots would not be deterred. Janvier needed their help, and she was going to get it.

Eventually, the millions of messages pouring into the FBDI turned into hundreds of millions, causing all electronic systems at the headquarters and the branches to crash repeatedly.

Out in the field, Janvier ditched her useless agency computer and went old-school detective, using shoe leather and the tire rubber of her black FBDI van. She had customized the van on each side with a pink lightning bolt and the word "Dogster" in gold with red flames leaping off each letter.

Driving long distances into different regions, Janvier observed dogs in yards, parks and on the street, always looking for increasing degrees of canine excitement as an indicator that she was on a potentially good heading. She stopped often to ask people if they had noticed groups of dogs on the move and in what direction they were going.

Even while carrying out her official FBDI mission to track

down the cause of nationwide abnormal canine behavior, Janvier never forgot about the pair on her personal most-wanted list.

At every opportunity since hitting the road, she had shown people the photos of the two very different dogs—one average-size and brainy, one very large and a mystery—but both very dangerous.

Taking a wild shot, she also contacted the Canine Intelligence Agency, sending it a photo of the mystery dog's poster that had garnered so much attention at her first dogcatchers convention. The CIA ran the photo of the poster through the Canine Recognition Aging Program—CRAP, for short. The software regressed the face on the poster backward through the younger stages of canine life. A hit was made when the face at the puppy life stage matched a photo in files that had been seized from a renegade dog breeder.

Shortly thereafter, a CIA drone located the Dogster and delivered a large envelope to Janvier. Inside, she found a copy of that puppy photo plus a number of documents. It seems the breeder was a mad scientist type who had been under surveillance for trying to develop a canine strain forbidden by law. When the feds raided his operation, the man ran from cage to cage to free his dogs, who ran off into the woods. They were recaptured in traps baited with steak from a nearby Australian Outhouse restaurant.

There was a second photo in the packet. As a double-check, CRAP had age-progressed the breeder's original puppy photo forward into what the creature would look like as a mature dog. Except for not having extra-spikiness in the fur, the progression looked very much like the dog on Janvier's poster.

Also in the packet was a chart that detailed the genealogy of the puppy's ancestors. It showed a volatile combination of very large and aggressive breeds. Forensic investigators deduced that the breeder was trying to re-create the monstrous war dogs of antiquity that had gone into battle running alongside chariots and helmeted men carrying spears.

Janvier next read a letter of apology that a supply company had sent to the breeder. It stated that a number of ampules of dog semen had been mislabeled and mixed in with the ampules of another breed, so some customers who expected to receive Scandinavian Berserker jizz may have received Saint Bernard whiz instead.

The large word "NO!" was scribbled across the top of the letter three times in red ink followed by, "I was so close! Have these idiots ruined my experiment?"

Finally, there was a note from the CIA to Janvier, stating, "In a recheck of our original files, there is no record of the recapture of the puppy in the enclosed photograph."

Taking another look at the photo, she noticed some handwriting in one corner, evidently the breeder's, with his name for the puppy.

"Scut."

The experiment that got away.

49

HERMIT SO HAPPY

"Hey, dog! Where you goin'?"

Whiskers stopped and looked to his left. A bush was in the way, but it was scraggly and he could see through it. Wearing a loin cloth, a bare-chested and bony man with scraggly hair and a scraggly beard was sitting in the dirt in front of a cave.

"Come on over here. It's rare that I get to see a dog, so let's hang out for a while. Hey, you look thirsty. I got some water."

He looks harmless.

Whiskers sauntered over as the guy pushed a gourd full of water forward.

Warm, but good.

"You ain't going to tell nobody where I am, are you?"

Whiskers shook his head "no."

"Good, 'cause I hates people. They're all mean. No good. Nothing but trouble."

I could disagree, but the guy gave me water, so I'll let it go.

"On the other hand, animals are great. I love talking to them and listening to them. I'll admit that it took me a while to catch on to what they say, but now we have some real gabfests.

"I'm so happy here," the hermit continued. "Just me and the trees and the beautiful wildflowers and the sweetest wildlife like butterflies and rabbits and squirrels and deer. Of course, it's not always so great 'cause I got to share it with flies and mosquitoes and gnats and spiders and centipedes and wasps and poisonous snakes and rabid bats and skunks, not to mention stinging nettles and poison ivy and a few other things like lightning and hard rains and high winds and whiteout blizzards and blistering heat that, pardon the expression in mixed company, makes me sweat like a dog.

"Other than all that," the man prattled on, "I'm telling you it's a great life 'cause it's so much better than listening to people piss and moan about what they don't have and trying to get what the other one's got and feeling oh-so-crappy for their oh-so-sorry selves when they can't get it. And then they go boo-hoo-hoo, waaah-waaah-waaah.

"Forget all that, don't go back to it. Just look at me. I'm living the good life. All I have to do is stay on guard against all the unpleasant things I mentioned earlier, which kind of ticks me off because they do use up quite a bit of the happy time that I'm supposed to be enjoying here."

As the hermit rambled on, Whiskers watched the guy go through continuous rounds of vigorously scratching insect bites on his legs followed by running fingers through his hair and then examining the tiny squirming things that he pulled out, after which he would lift up one arm and then the other so his long fingernails could dig deep and hard for who-knows-what in his hairy pits, the smell of which grossed out even Whiskers.

"Now, I'll just bet that the question you're asking yourself is how a handsome dude like me wound up living in a cave."

Whiskers gave a noncommittal shrug. That was all the encouragement the hermit needed.

"My hippie parents, who lived in Philadelphia, changed their last name to Cheese. When I was born they must have been really high on something 'cause they gave me Philadelphia as my first name and Cream as my middle name. If they had been rich celebrities, it would have been okay. But they weren't, and it wasn't. I was laughed out of schools and jobs.

"I tried to change my name legally to just one word, Philly, which I think is kind of cool, but the judge and the bailiff and the stenographer and even my lawyer were pointing at me and laughing so hard about my situation that they went into spasms that turned into deep coughing fits and then they all started throwing up, so I ran out of the courtroom and away from everything. That's why I'm here. Thanks a lot, Feta and Gruyere! Some parents you were! Ruined my life is what you did!

"You're lucky you're a dog. Dogs don't do stupid stuff like people do. By the way, when I talk to myself, I call myself Philly. I don't care if it's not legal. But enough about me. What about you?"

Whiskers barked and barked and barked, giving a condensed version of who he was and where he'd been.

"Sorry, but I didn't quite catch some parts of that," Philly said. "I think you understand me better than I understand you. I'm not that well versed in dog talk compared to that of other animals, but I'm sure it was all really interesting, so I thank you for sharing. Now let me ask you, are you looking for something?"

Whiskers nodded his head.

"I thought so. Maybe I can help you find it. You seem to be very smart, so how about trying to tell me in human talk? I'll bet you can do it."

Whiskers looked off to the side, recalling how Mr. Professor had tried to get him to talk like dogs on YouFlub who could say "maaaahmaaah" and "ah wohv oo."

That always took too much effort, but what the heck, I'll give it a try.

"B-b-b-b-..."

"Ooh, that's really good doggy, keep going," Philly encouraged.

"Be-bu-ba-bo-bi-bi-bi-bi..."

Philly jumped up, raised his arms above his head, touched his fingertips together to create a large circle and yelled, "BIG! Is that it? Is the word 'big'?"

Whiskers nodded vigorously.

"Yes! I love charades," Philly chortled. "That was my favorite game. I even used to play it by myself. Sometimes I gave myself a word so tough even I couldn't get it. But let's keep going, second word coming up."

"B-bu-be-bo-bu-bu-bu..."

"BUTT! It's 'butt', right?" Philly asked excitedly, turning halfway around and slapping his scrawny rear end.

Whiskers shook his head.

"That's okay, go again!"

Philly was jumping from side to side with excitement.

"B-b-bi-be-boo-boo-boo..."

"GHOST? Because a ghost says 'boo.'"

Whiskers gave another head shake.

"Wait, I think I got it. Boo, boo, boo... it's BOOBS! BIG BOOBS! That's it, isn't it?"

Philly pushed the flesh from both sides of his skinny chest together and did a shimmy-shake.

"Oh boy, if that's what you're looking for, can I go with you?"

Whiskers hung his head and shook it vigorously from side to side.

"Rats, I was so hoping it was 'boobs.' I haven't seen any in such a long time, but that's what I get for living in a cave. Thanks again, Mom and Dad! Anyway, let's give it another go.

I'll guess the word this time. Like they say, third time's a charm bracelet."

I'm getting tired of this, but the poor guy's so excited that I'll try again.

"Bi-bo-ba-bi-boh-bu-boh-bu-bwo-buh-buh-buh..."

"BUNDT! BIG BUNDT CAKE! Not as good as big boobs, but doggone... oops, sorry... but darn good in its own way. In fact, I love a good Bundt cake. Wish I had some right now. Am I right?"

Whiskers hung his head, not even bothering to shake it.

"Rats, double rats and rats again. I thought that was it because I had just got a memory flash from that movie. What was it called? Oh yeah, My Big Fat Bundt Wedding Cake or My Big Fat Butt's Wedding or something like that."

That's all. I'm not doing this anymore.

Whiskers took a few steps to pantomime that he was going to leave, then extended his paw in farewell.

Philly leaned over and shook it.

"Sorry I couldn't help you."

While shaking, though, Whiskers spotted a small bone under a bush off to the side. He ran over to it, picked it up in his mouth, ran back to Philly and moved his head quickly up and down.

"That's just an old, dirty, dried-up bone. Why would you want that? Wait! 'Big' and 'bone'. You're looking for a... BIG BONE?"

Whiskers dropped the small bone, stood up on his hind legs and spun around, then dropped back to all fours and looked expectantly at Philly.

"Wow, you must be after a really special bone the way you're carrying on. Hey, I got something you should see."

Philly went inside his cave, rummaged around in the detritus at the back and returned with a good-sized, flat bone.

"I found this years ago when I did a lot of adventure

exploring in the valleys and mountains around here. I thought this bone was kind of cool because of all the markings on it, like they were put there on purpose, but I couldn't make any sense out of them."

Whiskers looked closely at the bone.

"I haven't done anything with it. In fact, I had forgotten about it. I know it's not what you're looking for, but you're like a friend, so you can have it if you want it."

Whiskers nodded his head excitedly, took the flat bone between his teeth and shook once more with Philly.

"Say, whether you find your big bone or not, you're welcome to come back here and share my cave with me. I suppose boobs are too much to ask for, but if you find some Bundt cake, bring it with you. Then we can play all the charades you want. I'll even tell you the one word that nobody ever guesses, not even me. Give up? It's 'charades.'"

Whiskers cocked his head to one side and gave it a slow shake.

"Hey, no problem, I get it, you got to find your own cave. As you can see, I found mine, and that's why I'm so happy. Those other clowns out there haven't found theirs. You're smart, though, and I know you'll find yours."

Whiskers was only half-listening.

The markings on this bone don't make any sense to me, except for one. It's exactly the same as what Barco Poocho drew in the dirt.

The mark of the Great Dong.

50

WE WILL MOURN YOU

After he got the flat bone from the hermit, Whiskers dogtrotted for miles, looking for anyone who might be able to decipher the strange markings.

Going around a bend, he stopped dead still, his mouth fell open and the bone fell out.

Five large, black-feathered buzzards blocked the trail. Their scrawny heads had no feathers, only rough, wrinkled, ugly red skin. Off to one side was a pile of the disjointed, expertly cleaned bones of some unknown animal.

The buzzards had been conversing with one another, but they stopped to eyeball Whiskers.

"Well, looky here. We're just minding our own business, and a dog pops around the corner."

"Looks like he's all alone."

"Hey, Noggs, see if he's on the list."

One of the buzzards unfolded a large wing and stuck his beak inside.

"Okay, let's take a little look-see. Hmm. Nope. Nope. Nope. Oh, wait, here we go. There's some others ahead of him, but he's definitely on the list."

Taken aback, Whiskers cocked his head to one side in puzzlement.

"What kind of list are you talking about?"

"The Grim Beaker's list, of course."

Whiskers scrunched up his face.

They've got me outnumbered, but I know they don't kill anything on their own.

"Hah, you're just trying to scare me, but it's not working."

"Well, let me take another look at the description here. White dog, terrier-type, average size, last seen in this vicinity. Yep, that's you."

"You're a liar," Whiskers bristled. "You're just making that up."

"Oh, you don't believe old Noggsy? How about it, Smike, do you see his name on the list?"

A buzzard stumped over and looked inside Noggs' wing.

"Ah, yes, there it is."

"Hah. If my name is really there, tell me what it is."

"Your name is Whiskers," Smike said, grinning wickedly.

Whiskers' legs wobbled. His heart began to bang a death knell against his ribs.

"How did my name get there?" he asked in a weak, whispery voice.

"How? Everything is foreordained," Noggs answered. "You've got a time to appear and a time to go bye-bye. The Grim Beaker is clued in on who goes when. He draws up the list for us. Otherwise, how would we know where to go to clean things up? You wouldn't expect us to just fly around blindly hoping to luck into something, would you? Heck no, that's too inefficient. We've got a schedule to maintain. Right now, we're just taking a break between jobs. But this chance meeting with you is very nice because normally our work is so impersonal that we're always cleaning up someone we never knew. I'd say this calls for formal introductions. You heard that I'm Noggs and he's Smike. Our co-workers are Wegg, Squeers and Squod."

"Consider yourself most fortunate," piped up Squod. "Now that you know in advance your time is almost up, you can make goodbye arrangements with your family."

"I don't have any family," Whiskers said softly. "I'm going to die alone, and everyone I've ever known, animal and human, will never know that I died, and so they will never know how bad they're supposed to feel about living in a world without me."

"Aw, that's a downright shame," Wegg said. "In fact, I feel so bad about your plight that I'm going to speak for everyone here in saying that we would be most pleased to have you consider us as your honorary, temporary, surviving family members. We will mourn you with each bite we take."

"Thank... you... that's... nice... of..."

Whiskers gasped as his pulse skyrocketed and his breath started hammer-tripping in rapid, shallow bursts. His mouth moved silently as if he was trying to say more, but his stomach lurched and he threw up.

"Ugh," Squeers said. "How gross. Anyway, our break is over. See ya, dog, sooner than later."

With that, the five buzzards lifted off and swiftly flew up out of earshot, then glided around in a circle, laughing at their joke.

"Can you believe it, Squod? He fell for it! What an idiot!"

"Of course, Noggs, he's just a stupid dog."

"Wow, when Smike said his name, he looked like he was going to drop dead on the spot," Wegg said.

"Too bad he didn't. That would have made our day," chortled Squeers. "Hey, Smike, how did you know his name?"

"Judging by his whiskers, I just took a lucky guess and... kapow!"

"That was great! One of our best practical jokes ever!" exclaimed Wegg. "And what do we say every day?"

"We're just some wild and crazy guys!"

"Ah, look," Noggs said. "He's still sitting down there in the same spot. The poor sap hasn't moved at all. I kinda feel sorry for him, even if he is a dog. Smike, fly down and tell him it was just a joke."

WHISKERS HAD BEEN WATCHING the buzzards circling above him, wondering when his time would come. Then he saw one coming down.

Oh, no! I thought I would have a few more days. I guess I'm taking too long. They probably want me to hurry it up.

The buzzard landed beside him. The bird stank of death. It wrapped a wing around his back. Whiskers was too petrified to move away.

"Hey, pal, don't be sad. We were just jerking you around. Call it sanitation humor, death humor or whatever you want, it helps us get through work like ours. Otherwise, we couldn't do it. Now don't tell her I said so, but Mother Nature gave us the shittiest job in the whole Animal Kingdom. All guts and no glory. You, on the other hand, get to go through life as a dopey dog. Consider yourself lucky."

"You mean..."

"Relax, it's not your time. At least, not as far as I know. Of course, you could drop dead tomorrow, but so could any of us, because anything is possible at any time. As for me and the other guys, we don't have any schedules to follow or anything like that."

"So, there's no list?"

"Naw, of course not. Buck up. Get back to whatever you were doing. By the way, what are you doing out here?"

Whiskers took deep breaths. His racing heart began to slow down.

"I'm trying to find someone who can read the markings on this bone that I've been carrying around," he said, motioning toward it in the dirt.

The buzzard eyed it quizzically.

"Sheesh, it would take a really smart animal to figure out that mess. Say, I know we scared you out of some dog years, and I do feel bad about that, so I'm going to do you a favor and point you in the right direction. Look over there. You see that mountain, kind of far but not too far?"

"Yeah."

"Well, that's Shady Mountain, and the wisest animal in these parts lives there. That's where you ought to go to get that thing looked at."

"Really?"

"You bet, on the level, no joke. Trust me."

"Okay, I'll do that."

"Great. See you around," Smike said as he spread out his wings, took a few steps and lifted into the air. "Don't worry," he called back, "I'm sure it will be later when we see you, not sooner."

THE BUZZARDS FLEW AWAY, still cackling about the great joke they had played.

"I even helped the knucklehead with his problem," Smike said. "Told him to go to Shady Mountain."

"Hey, that's good," laughed Squeers. "Maybe he'll fall off it, and then we can clean him up. Anyway, let's call it a day. Hey, Squod, what are we doing tomorrow?"

"I don't know. Who's got the list?"

51

YOU ARE VERY TURNED AROUND

Whiskers approached Shady Mountain. Strangely, it didn't have anything of its own for shade. No trees. Not even a bush. Just rocks jutting out with a path between them. But there was one little cloud up near the peak. It didn't seem to be in any hurry to move on; it just hovered in the same place.

Whiskers started walking up the path, ascending higher and higher until reaching a level spot in the shade under the cloud.

"Welcome to the Hoalin Temple," said a Lhasa Apso, who began to howl.

"Aaaaoooo! Aaaaoooo! A stranger comes to see the master. Proceed stranger with eyes closed and crawling on your belly."

As instructed, Whiskers closed his eyes, got down on his belly and crawled until one paw felt nothing and he heard a creaky voice.

"You have gone far enough. You may open your eyes and see where ignorance ends and knowledge begins."

Whiskers opened his eyes. He was at the edge of the mountain. If the voice had not stopped him, he would have plunged to his death.

"Your first lesson, Asshopper: Seeing makes you blind, but blind you can see, while crawling takes you farther than running ever will. With the coming of wisdom, you will not need my voice; you will feel the edge of life's ledge. Now, you may rotate on your belly toward my ancient self and look up."

Whiskers did so.

Wow, that dog is really old. He's so dried up all his fur fell off. His body looks like it came apart in pieces and got stuck back together, and his head is tiny compared to his body. That's the weirdest dog I have ever seen.

Then it struck Whiskers that it wasn't a dog.

Oh, my goodness, it's an amordildo!

Whiskers' mouth flopped open. The flat bone that he had carried dropped into the dirt.

"Your surprise betrays you, Asshopper. So conceited and so typical of dogs, assuming that a canine must be the wisest of all. Anyway, I suppose you have come for the meaning of life. Very well, here it is: A wet dog doesn't smell at night."

"Begging your pardon," said Whiskers from his prone position, "but that's not true. I've smelled plenty of stinking wet dogs at night after a good rain."

"Oh, you mean that's not the meaning of life? I thought it was. The last time the Lhasa Apso over there got caught in the rain I couldn't smell him. I must be so old that I've lost my sense of smell. Well, let me come up with another meaning of life. You can go play footsie with the Lhasa Apso while I ponder up one."

"I'm not looking for the meaning of life."

"Do not give up so easily. You've been looking for answers in all the wrong places, listening to crap from too many faces."

"Also, I don't have much time for waiting around."

"Patience, Asshopper. The greater your hurry, the slower you go."

"Just let me tell you why I came here."

"When you talk, you do not hear. When you do not hear, you do not learn. I will tell you why you came here. Show me your paw so I can read your lifeline."

Rolling onto his left side, Whiskers managed to lift his right paw enough for the armadillo to see the bottom of it.

"Oh dear, this is not good."

"What's wrong?"

"Looks like you stepped in something. Oh well, that didn't work."

"Please, may we now discuss why I came here?"

"Well, perhaps, Asshopper. I'm always hesitant about situations where I cannot use my stock phrases."

"I've got a problem."

"Girlfriend trouble?"

Instead of answering, Whiskers picked up the flat bone with his mouth, crawled forward a little bit and placed it in front of the armadillo.

"I need to find out what this says. Can you read it?"

The armadillo took the bone in his tiny paws and studied it carefully.

"Yes, I can read it. It takes me back to glorious days when I held a position of importance as a scribe. In fact, I wrote this at the behest of Humungus Khan, the Great Dong himself. I wasn't too pleased when he gave it away to a foreign dog called, uh, Smacko or Whacko, or uh... oh, yes, Barco."

Whiskers jumped up, his eyes bulging.

Jackpot! Now I do believe that Barco Poocho wasn't lying about being with the Great Dong and having the Big Bone pointed out to him.

The armadillo stared at him.

"Oh, I'm sorry. I'll get back down in the dirt."

"Nay, stay as you are. You're dirty enough. Now tell me, why are you interested in this?"

"I need to get somewhere."

"Where you need to go is where you didn't know you were going."

"That may be, but at this moment I want to find the Big Bone. Do these markings give any clue to where it is?"

"You mean that thing that dogs are always yammering about? Offhand, I don't know. I'll have to study this bone again; it has been so long since I have seen it. Ah, here is the mark of the Great Dong. Too bad he passed away, but there are many interesting things on here relating to his empire. In fact, here is a mention of the Big Bone."

"What does it say?"

"Bite me."

"Well, yes, of course I'll do that when I get to it. But where is it? I need to find it before someone else does."

"Patience, Asshopper. Those who find something first would have been better to have found it last."

"Well, I need it first because I'm in a race. I have to beat another dog to it."

"When you beat another, you beat yourself. But if you help each other, you both win a new friend."

"Believe me, nobody would want a friend like him."

"The friend you have not made is not an unmade friend. He's just a different kind of friend."

"I'll make and unmake friends later. Right now I want to become Top Dog."

"When you think you are on top, and you look up, you will find that you are really looking at your bottom. Not a good view at all."

"The only view I want is of the Big Bone. Do the markings on that flat bone tell where it is?"

"I'll take a close look, but this part of the bone has been worn by so many teeth that what remains has gaps. My memory cannot fill them in; it has been too long. But I can read 'awful smell' and 'take heed of signs' and 'wonderful smell.' The smell part seems contradictory, but that's all I can make out."

"Well, I'll keep an eye and a nose out for those things. Please keep the bone as my thanks, and now I'll be leaving."

"Asshopper, how can you leave if you have not arrived?"

Whiskers didn't answer but posed a question of his own.

"Why do you turn everything around? Everything you say seems the opposite of normal sense."

"When you turn things around, you see the other side. And only when you see the other side can you see the first side for the first time. Asshopper, you have not seen any sides. You are very turned around."

"Maybe I am, I don't know, but before I go, can you give me a straight answer to one question?"

"What is it?"

"Why do you call me Asshopper?"

"When you meet new dogs, what do you do?"

"Go from one to another smelling butts, of course."

"You have found your answer."

"Oh."

52

PLATONIC, NOT GASTRONOMIC

"*Oh, wow! This is a big one.*"

"*I am so going to chew on this dog.*"

"*I want the gizzard.*"

"*Dogs don't have gizzards.*"

"*Look, guys, let's try sharing for a change rather than tearing at it in a crazy free-for-all. What do we start with first: heart, guts or spleen?*"

They were voices in his dream world, but whether they originated in it or were filtering into it was undetermined. His survival instinct told him to start waking up.

As he did so, the voices became louder. A rustling sound grew beside his head. Something brushed against his back.

He opened one eye. Strange, ugly feet tapped across his vision.

Bam! Something hard jabbed him in the side.

Pulling his legs in and rolling from his side onto his stomach, Scut sprang up. Turning quickly and snapping wildly, he caught a buzzard's wing, swung the bird up in the air, slammed it on the ground and stepped on it with his front paws. Snarling and pulling back his lips to reveal his fangs, Scut pivoted his head from side to side, fixing his eyes in turn on each of the four other buzzards who were backpedaling in fright.

"Kill him! Kill him!" shrieked Wegg, the pinned buzzard.

"We don't know how!" Squod screamed back. "We never learned!"

"Kill me? You'll all be dead," Scut growled.

"We're so sorry," Noggs said, eyes wide and breathing hard. "We didn't know you were sleeping. We thought you had succumbed to some unfortunate circumstance. It's a common mistake in our profession. We make it all the time. We've yet to have advanced training in determining the tipping point."

"Please, oh please, let Wegg go," begged Squeers. "You don't want to eat him. We taste horrible. It's because we have to eat so much rotten meat all the time."

"And we really didn't want to eat you, because we don't like dogs," Smike said.

"Whoa, don't take that wrong," Squod said quickly. "We do like dogs. We like them very much. What Smike meant to say is that it's a sad day when we have to eat a dog. It's not because we want to, and it's not a matter of taste. It's because we have to do it. Orders from headquarters. Mother Nature gets on our asses if we don't. So please understand and let Wegg go."

Scut took his feet off the terrified buzzard, who jumped up and quick-stepped over to his buddies.

"Oh, thank you," squawked the shaken Wegg. "Whew, my heart is beating so hard."

"Yes, mine too," said Noggs. "I guess now the joke's on us, unlike when we played a joke on that other dog."

"Other dog? What other dog?" Scut demanded.

"Just some terrier we ran into," replied Squeers, "but I assure you that we did not harm him. Like we just said, we love dogs, but only in a platonic way, not in a gastronomic way."

"What color was he?"

"White," said Smike. "I think he turned even whiter when I took a lucky guess and told him his name."

"Which was?"

"Whiskers."

"Whiskers? I've been looking for him. Where did he go?"

"He wanted help in figuring out something," Smike answered. "So, I sent him over to Shady Mountain. We can tell you how to get there. You're not too far behind him. With those long legs, you'll catch up in no time."

"Friend of yours?" inquired Squod.

"Not at all," Scut said. "Just a pain in the ass, and one that I intend to get rid of real soon."

"Hey, we understand," Noggs said. "Although we've liked all the other dogs we ever met, we didn't like that Whiskers from the moment we came across him. We couldn't even stand the sight of him. In fact, I almost threw up when I saw him. So, give him a good bite in the ass for all of us, and maybe we can clean up after you're done. Hey, now that's the way to go. Dogs and buzzards, cleaning up the countryside together. Teamwork. It's a beautiful thing."

"Hey, buzzard."

"Yeah, good buddy?"

"Shut up."

~

"WELCOME TO THE HOALIN TEMPLE. Aaaaoooo! Aaaaoooo! A stranger comes to see the master. Proceed stranger, with eyes closed and crawling on your belly."

Instead of obeying, Scut walked over to the Lhasa Apso, pushed his nose against the much smaller dog's face and said, "No."

Taking a step back, the Lhasa Apso asked, "But don't you come seeking wisdom from the master?"

Taking a step forward, Scut said, "No. I want information."

"About life?"

"No, about a snotty white terrier that came here."

"He left."

"Where did he go?"

"He went down the trail on the other side, which leads to the forest in the valley."

"That's all I need. You can go back to making your weird noises."

"Are you sure you don't want the master's advice for changing your life? He's the wisest of all in the entire Animal Kingdom."

Scut looked around.

"Are you kidding? The wisest animal chooses to live on this pile of bare dirt and rocks? What a dumbass."

With that, Scut left the small herald and headed off, wondering how another dumbass always seemed to be ahead of him.

PART IV

BAD TO THE BONE

53

PSYCH YOURSELF OUT

D r. Sid was frantic.

His shtick had gotten old, and his ratings were dropping. He was mortified when Tojo Motor Cars dropped his show, and the Ham-Wow slicer and dicer became his main sponsor.

Dr. Sid needed a savior, and to him that was Janvier. Ever since her explosive appearance on his show, he had entreated her by phone, fax, voicemail, email, texts, tweets, telegrams, bicycle messengers and skywriting to come back.

She had ignored everything.

It irritated him no end that the hottest property in the country considered her duty to save the nation to be more important than being on television.

I have never met such an ungrateful bitch. Before my program, she was a nobody. I'm the one who discovered her.

Actually, Peephole magazine had featured her story first, but Dr. Sid knew that live-action talking, finger-pointing, blaming, arguing, physical scuffling and emotional meltdowns on television are what count, not a bunch of boring words stuck together on stupid pieces of paper.

He psychoanalyzed Janvier from afar and concluded that she was traumatized by the demands of her celebrity and desperately needed counseling on his show so that a large portion of that celebrity could rub off on him, thereby providing her with psychic release.

I've got to find a way to make her understand how much she needs me.

Then he heard that the FBDI was going to have Janvier take time from her investigation to stop at a nearby animal shelter. The agency saw the national panic as an opportunity to change its image from that of being a persecutor of dogs to that of being a dog's best friend.

Dr. Sid showed up at the shelter uninvited and unnoticed by the throng of spectators ogling Janvier as she walked among all the dogs brought out for display in the shelter's parking lot.

"My offer still stands," he boomed over the crowd while trying to barge through with a camerawoman in tow. "Personalized counseling based on the groundbreaking insights in my newest video, 'Crawl Around Inside Your Own Head with Dr. Sid.'"

Janvier ignored him, taking her sweet time to pet all the dogs while conversing pleasantly with the shelter staff, signing FBDI posters and posing for pictures. Finally finished, she hugged the staffers and began walking toward her van.

Dr. Sid jumped in her path, hoping that she would have a change of heart about appearing on his show or, if nothing else, at least zap him with an electro-shock collar on live television.

Maybe I can win the Gimmee Award for Best Dramatics by a Daytime Talk Show Host.

Here she came.

His heart was aflutter as Janvier got closer, not just because she was ratings gold but, he had to admit, she was hot, she was strong, she exuded confidence, and she took no shit.

We're the perfect pair—an alpha male talk show host and an alpha female A-list celebrity.

Janvier closed in as if she had something to tell him.

Dr. Sid steeled himself. This was it. Either she would commit to him or do something outrageous to him.

Give it to me, baby. I'll take it all, whatever it is.

Janvier stopped to look back at the shelter attendants and their array of canines.

"Goodbye, everybody, goodbye, doggies," she said in her sweetest voice.

Facing forward again, she took a step, smiled, patted Dr. Sid on his bald head and kept walking without a word.

Dr. Sid panicked.

"Cut! Tape delay! Roll it back! Stop the press! Battle stations! Dive, dive! Go to a commercial! I can't have my television viewers seeing her petting me like a dog."

"It's too late," the camerawoman said. "It was live. I can't roll back what people saw."

If nothing else, Dr. Sid was a professional. Recovering quickly, he told the camerawoman to put him back on the air.

If she won't come on my show, she can still help me sell product.

"Yes, you saw it live, Special Agent Janvier, national hero extraordinaire, touched her exquisite hand to my high-capacity intellectual head, signaling her endorsement and by extension the Federal Bureau of Dog Investigation seal of approval to the entire brain-expanding line of Dr. Sid self-improvement products, including my most popular home study course, 'Psych Yourself Out To Pretend That You Are Better Than You Really Are So You Too Can Have More Fun, More Love and a Better-Than-Minimum-Wage Job.'"

54

LIKE TV STARS

"Hello, everyone. Welcome to The Spew."

The television camera zoomed in tight on the program host perched on a sofa. She wore a thin, white dress decorated with a variety of country flowers, all their colors purposely faded to give the brand-new garment the appearance of years of hard wear and many washings.

"If you're a regular viewer, you know I'm Sally Sass. But where are my four in-your-face co-hosts? If you tuned in for yesterday's squabble, you know that all their disagreements about politics finally came to a head. On the big screen behind me, you can see the replay of Jenny Scorn spitting a wad of lumpy mucous into Misty Wrangle's right eye. Now we see Misty retaliating by ripping Jenny's blouse open and snapping her bra. Bam! Ooh, I bet that left a mark. Of course, Starla Mock and Cindy Twit couldn't stay out of it. There they go, jumping on the backs of Jenny and Misty, clawing at their faces and pulling out clumps of hair.

"After the show was over, our network psychiatrist tried to hold an intervention but gave up. He said my co-hosts were so far beyond help that they might as well knock the shit out of each other. All four are now being trained in mixed martial arts so they can settle their feud in a televised death match.

"As for today, forget about nasty politics. We're going into the world of fashion. That's why I'm wearing this fabulously expensive dress as part of the look that has taken New York City by storm. And we just happen to have with us the lovely people who started it all…"

The television camera drew back to reveal two figures sitting on the sofa to the right of Sally.

"…Ma and Bud!"

"We's glad to be here," Ma said.

"Yessum, we is," Bud added.

"And we're thrilled to have you back by popular demand for your second visit to The Spew. I know you've been very busy since arriving in New York, but have you had a chance to see any of the sights?"

"We saw a feller in the street wearin' nonthin' but his underwear while playin' a geetar," Ma answered. "I told Bud he could do that wif his banjo and I could play the spoons."

"I'm sure you could," Sally said, "but underwear is old news. What's hot is Country Hick, the hip style that has swept New York fashionistas off their stilettos. Take a look."

With that, the picture on the large screen switched to the street scene outside the building. Office workers and shoppers hustling along sidewalks were dressed like Ma and Bud in faded flowery dresses and blue overalls with artfully applied splotches of mud.

"This fabulous return of fashion to our rural roots got started after your captivating first visit to The Spew," Sally said. "Ma, can you refresh our viewers' memories on how that appearance came about?"

"We were what you call character witnesses fer our dog Whiskers on the Dr. Sid show. His producer folks felt so sad about us losin' our faithful companion that they give us free tickets to the Jerry Sphincter show."

"We love Jerry," Bud said, "and we yelled louder than anyone in that audience."

"I 'spose that's why you brought us on your show the first time 'cause all you gals like to yell at each other," Ma remarked.

"As a reminder for our viewers," Sally said, "we spent that first show commiserating about the heartbreak of losing a pet who some say is a hero while the FBDI considers him a fugitive from the law. But little did we know that your country charm would make sophisticated New Yorkers go wild about you two."

"We're like TV stars," Bud said with a lopsided grin.

"That you are," Sally agreed as she reached across Ma to rub the thick, curly orange hair on Bud's closest arm.

"By the way," Sally said, "my inquiring mind wants to know: What brought you to town this time?"

"We got flown here by TV big shots. We's talkin' wif them right here in this building," Ma said.

"That's right, on one of them top floors," Bud added, "but we's sworn to secrecy, so we can't say nuthin' fer now 'cause their lawyers made all kinds of threats if we do."

"Ooh, how intriguing, but let's not get lawyers after us," Sally said. "Instead, I know you want to talk about your dog. Guess what? We have video from that turbulent time when he was in New York. Let's watch the replay."

The large screen switched to an overhead view shot by a drone. In it, a crowd gathers around a police officer performing CPR on an elderly man. A younger man and two dogs stand close by until one dog begins barking at the officer. A woman reaches for the dog's leash, but he runs out of camera view.

"Golly bejiggers! That's him!" Ma whooped. "That little scutter done come all the way to this here Big Apple lookin' fer us. But when he don't see us in that crowd, he takes off to keep a'lookin'. Poor thing—just lost and miserable. We so needs to get a'holt of him and put him out of that misery."

"How truly sad," Sally said, "so let's cheer things up. We've got a big fashion surprise for you."

She looked to her left, beckoned at the offstage area and said, "Strut your stuff!"

Out walked Coco Siliconoli, twisting and turning salaciously in skintight thong overalls to give equal display to each piece of her body pumped up by plastic surgery.

"Let's give a big hand to Coco," Sally said, "while we marvel at this incredible rethinking of overalls by the world-famous designer Foufou Spaghettini. In the front, below Coco's waist, the traditional blue denim is splendidly cut into a severe V-shape designed to reveal maximum skin in her party zone because it barely covers the hoo-la-la. As Coco turns around, we see that the thong strip on the backside goes into deep hibernation somewhere in her bounteous booty. Now, as she comes full circle, we can't keep our eyes off the chest area where two large, circular cutouts in the fabric allow for maximum external projection while Coco's modesty is maintained with tastefully applied blue denim pasties.

"Ma and Bud, what do you think of this fashion-forward-take on the Country Hick look that you inspired?"

"What I think is that someone done tore up her overalls!" Bud exclaimed, eyes bugging out. "I'd be happy to help her find the pieces."

"Lord, have mercy!" Ma squawked. "Them ain't overalls, 'cause they ain't hardly over anythin'. Bud, stop starin' at that big city hussy."

"But, Ma, she's pretty."

"Pretty dang loose, you mean, 'cause most of her stuff has fell out and what's left is bound to follow."

"Ma, I could marry a woman like that. Look at the size of her butt. She could drive a tractor all day long sittin' on that thing."

"I thought everyone would be pleased," Sally said, frowning.

"I'm very pleased," Bud said, waving with both hands for Coco to come back as she stomped offstage.

"We didn't come here lookin' fer that," Ma spat. "We just lookin' fer our Whiskers dog to eat."

"To eat?" Sally said, sitting up straighter.

"To eat with," Bud jumped in. "You know, to share food with, like what you all get in doggy bags at those fancy French restaurants—snails, slugs, leftover frog parts. We wants only the best to fatten up our fine dog."

"Oh, I'm sorry I misunderstood," Sally said, letting out her breath in relief. "My apologies. How sweet of you."

"Yes, we is and it'll be sweet to get our Whiskers dog back—a real sweet treat fer us," Ma said, wiping a little saliva from one corner of her mouth.

"On that note and before we close today, I understand, Ma, that you and Bud have set up a fund to help in your search for Whiskers."

"Yessum, Miss Sally, we has. It's at GiveUsUrMoney.com"

55

AND THE TWAIN SHALL MEET

"Have you seen this dog?"

"No, I haven't."

She had shown the photo and asked the question hundreds of times to folks like this woman gardening in her front yard.

"Well, how about this other one?"

"No. I wish I had so I could help you, but could you come inside the house? I want my dogs Twinkie, Cookie and Shitass to see you in person, and I want you to scare the bejesus out of 'em. Don't worry, Miss Janvier, they haven't bitten me yet so I ain't no zombie. That's because I don't let 'em out at night when spaceships are flying around trying to get control of their brains."

"Well..."

"Oh, look, there are the little bastards now, watching us through the screen door. Hey, you dogs! You better behave and stop that weird stuff you all been doing or Miss Janvier here is going to throw you in her van and take you away to the FBDI and you'll never come back. And she's got pictures of some other no-good dogs that she's gonna catch and ship their butts to one of them overseas places where folks are gonna wok 'em good.

That's exactly what's gonna happen to you three if you don't shape up right quick!

"Oh, whew, Miss Janvier, I'm out of breath after chewing their little butts out. I hope you don't mind me making that stuff up, but I got to scare 'em to keep 'em in line. And would you be so sweet as to give me your autograph on my gardening glove? Just inscribe it to: Muriel, my biggest and bestest fan."

Instead of writing all that, Janvier took a permanent marker from her pocket and scribbled a large "J" across the woman's forehead.

"Sorry, but that's all the time I have," Janvier said while walking quickly back to her van.

Another dead end.

Of course, showing photos of Whiskers and Scut to people wasn't why the FBDI had sent Janvier on the road. Quelling the national panic over weird canine behavior was her official mission.

But her obsession with Scut and Whiskers was never out of mind.

As long as I'm out here, I'm going to take every opportunity to track them down.

Autograph signing, however, seemed to be the only thing she accomplished with humans.

So, she had been asking dogs as well.

After parking her van out of sight and removing her utility belt so as not to arouse suspicion, Janvier would walk up to a mutt with a treat in her hand and show the pictures of Whiskers and Scut, asking, "Have you seen this dog? How about this one?"

Although they couldn't speak English to her, she was hoping for some kind of reaction. Day after day, though, she got none.

Driving slowly one afternoon, she spotted an Irish Setter. Janvier stopped her van, got out and approached the animal.

"Have you seen this dog?"

No reaction.

"Well, have you seen..."

The Irish Setter's eyes widened and its jaw dropped. After studying the photo of Whiskers for a few more seconds, she ran in circles around Janvier until she stopped, out of breath, chest heaving, tongue panting, tail wagging hard.

Yes! I've got a hit!

She began to have similar results the more she drove and the more dogs she approached. Sometimes it was a Scut hit, other times it would be a Whiskers hit. To make sure these weren't false identifications, Janvier mixed in photos of other dogs. Those photos got only a blank gaze or a cursory sniff while the photos of Whiskers and Scut drew wild, enthusiastic reactions. Janvier jotted down the Whiskers and Scut hits on a map that she dedicated solely to them. Their hits were not together, but the more she gathered, the more they were converging in the same direction.

On a different map maintained for her FBDI mission, she marked data pertaining to movements in the general canine population. The data included reports of dogs running away from their homes, sightings of dogs moving through the coun-tryside, and the finding of abandoned canine encampments. The state of petrification of leavings at those encampments indi-cated how many dogs had passed through and when.

After days of driving and recording more data, Janvier noticed similar patterns emerging between the hits on the offi-cial FBDI map and the hits on her map. Placing the Whiskers-Scut map on top of the FBDI map, she stepped outside her van and held them up to the sunlight. The hits on both maps were converging with one another.

This is not a coincidence.

She lowered the maps and stared up at the sky.

I'll use this evidence to crush those idiotic rumors about space aliens using dogs to bite people and turn them into zombies so they can take over the world.

Janvier raised the maps back up to the sunlight, separated them, then placed them back together. She did it over and over. Each time, she shook her head as she contemplated the gravity of what they revealed.

One master criminal and one vicious brute were behind the whole national panic. They were agitating and organizing dogs for some nefarious purpose, including perhaps the worst of all —no longer being man's best friend. Nor a woman's. Nor a child's.

How would life change if people's lovable fur babies suddenly became snarky, snarly and surly—much like human teenagers? No longer obedient, having transferred their allegiance to canine overlords, they could be called upon to wreak havoc using their superior physical traits of four-legged speed, incredible hearing, unbelievable sense of smell, and pointy teeth that really hurt.

No longer secure and confident in their own homes, Americans could lose that sense of can-do optimism that had buoyed the nation through all its prior trials and tribulations. If that were to happen, then America truly would have gone to the dogs.

One thing was for sure: Janvier's personal obsession and her official mission were no longer separate. They were now one.

But where were these two upsetters of the natural order?

I need better information than I'm getting from excited dogs panting their hot breath at me.

Somewhere, I'll find a human who can provide it.

56

PLEASED TO MEETCHA

"Is he stupid or what? How come he can't get the job done?"

"He's been trying, and I mean real hard," Phelonius answered.

"Excuses! I don't need excuses," Scratchy fumed. "Can't anybody play this game?"

"I, uh, don't know if that's a rhetorical question, but I thought you might make a comment in that vein, so I brought along somebody who can help our game plan, so to speak."

"Another stupid dog, I suppose?"

"No, you'll like this guy, I promise. He gives us a different approach, and he's big enough and strong enough to do the job."

"I can't wait," Scratchy said, sighing and rolling his eyes.

"Hey, we're ready for you. Come on over," Phelonius squawked, waving a wing toward a patch of bushy ground a ways off.

A bird, much larger than Phelonius, stepped from the bushes. Big, bold and intimidating, it crossed the distance to them almost instantly, braking in the air with wings spread. Even Scratchy flinched as it thumped down.

"May I present Vito the eagle. Vito, this is Scratchy. He's in charge of everything."

"How ya doin'?" Vito said. "Real pleased to meetcha. It's an honor."

"Well, you certainly are big. Did Phelonius tell you what the situation is?"

"Yeah, I got the idea. Nuttin' to it. Whatever ya want, I'll do it. Count on it. Guaranteed."

"Maybe," Scratchy said, pursing his lips.

"Now that we've all met," Phelonius interjected, "why don't you wait over there again while Scratchy and I talk a little more."

"Yeah, of course. Oh, uh, once again, nice meetin' ya, and ya can fuhgeddabout needin' Mutt to do the job, or whatever it is ya call him."

With that, the eagle flew back to the bushy patch to wait.

"I don't know about this," Scratchy said, pushing out his lower lip and scrunching up his forehead. "Eagles are known for being hard-headed."

"I assure you that Vito comes highly recommended. A real professional. Think about it. With Scut on the ground, Vito in the sky, and me coordinating everything, Whiskers' days of running in that ridiculous race will soon be over."

"Okay, do it. But this better work. I don't want to feel like I'm depending on a crew that might as well be called the Three Stupids."

57

YOU'RE NOT VERY BRIGHT

After leaving Shady Mountain, Whiskers had set about finding the clues that could help him track down the Big Bone and become Top Dog.

But he was clueless as to how to find those clues. Trudging up a hill, then plodding wearily down the backside, Whiskers perked up when he came across an animal run at the bottom.

Maybe it will lead to a water hole where some animal might have information that can help me.

Whiskers scooted along with his nose nearly touching the ground, eagerly smelling the scents of the different types of animals that had used the run.

"Well, hello there."

Whiskers stopped.

Looking up, his head jerked back.

Oh no, not again. What's going to happen to me now?

Each time he had seen her, he had been in a struggle for his life.

For her part, Rosie the spoonbill was thrilled.

"Oh my gosh, imagine meeting you again. The first time I saw you, you were just taking it easy in the quicksand, which wasn't very smart of you, and the next time was at your trial in the swamp for being a bad boy. Whiskers, I'm sorry to say this, but you must not be very bright, because you are always in some kind of trouble."

Don't I know it.

"Anyway, I was trying to catch up with that nasty crow, the one that carries messages everywhere. You know, the one they call Phlegmonius, Flumonius, Spumonious or whatever. But gosh he's fast. It's almost like he was trying to get away from me, or maybe he just doesn't know how to handle a big bird like myself, but I don't care because he's not my type—kind of small if you know what I mean. Anyway, he was making so many twists and turns that I got dizzy and set down here to take a rest. But I guess it's okay, because although I wanted him to carry a message for me, I forgot what my message was in all the commotion, and so it must be true what my momma said, that if you can't remember something, then it wasn't important. So, I guess it's just as well that I didn't catch up with him because what was the point in trying so hard to do something that's unimportant? I don't think there is a point to it. And if there's no point to something, then obviously it's meaningless, right?"

Whiskers didn't even try to answer. He just stared blankly at her.

"Anyway, here's the best part," Rosie continued. "I came to that conclusion all on my own, and that makes me very proud of myself, because the realization that it was meaningless was very meaningful because it meant that I'm actually a very deep thinker, not flighty at all. Still, I wish I could remember what it was that I forgot, even if it's not important. You wouldn't know, would you?"

"No, sorry."

"That's okay, but if you happen to remember, please let me

know because, oh my gosh, it may have been about you, and I owe you everything."

"You do?"

"Yes. You gave my life new meaning."

"I did?"

"Yes. I found Peter Crabcake. And it happened! We had lots of baby birdy bambinos like you predicted! Too bad I couldn't marry you too, because then we could have had baby bird-dogs. Wouldn't it have been so cute to see them flapping and barking at the same time?"

"That sounds great, Rosie, and I'm sorry I missed that opportunity, but you could help me right now."

"Yes, of course. Anything for you. Do you want me to save your life again?"

"Not at the moment. I just want you to get me somewhere."

"That's easy," Rosie said, stepping behind Whiskers and whacking him on the rear with her bill in scooping motions that bounced him forward.

"Oww, oww! What are you doing? Stop it!" yelped Whiskers.

"Is that far enough, already? Gosh, that was easy. Well, call me the next time you need anything," Rosie said, turning and preparing to fly away.

"Wait, wait!" cried Whiskers. "Yes, that was far enough on the ground, but now I want you to carry me through the air."

"Where do you want to go?"

"To the Big Bone."

"I don't know where that is."

"That's okay. Just fly me around until I spot the clues that will help me find it."

Suddenly, Rosie stiffened up, her eyes widened, and her beak fell open.

"Whiskers, do you think that was the message I was trying to send, to let you know that I could give you a ride?"

Whiskers mimicked Rosie's look of surprise.

"Yes! I'm sure that was it."

"Then let's get going. I'll squat down a little bit so you can climb aboard."

Whiskers stood up on the left side of Rosie, laid his front legs on her back, sprang up with his hind legs, slid on the smooth feathers past the center of her back and nose-dived headfirst off her right side onto the ground.

"Owwww!"

"Whiskers, I think you're the silliest dog I ever met, although I can't be sure about that because so far you're the only one I've met. Anyway, try getting on from behind me."

After blowing dirt out of his nostrils, Whiskers got behind Rosie, jumped aboard and clamped his legs tightly against her sides.

Rosie adjusted to his weight and lifted into the air.

This is the way to find the Big Bone.

As they flew across the sky, Whiskers eagerly scoured the earth below. After a while though, with no sighting of something that might help him, his mind began to drift.

Is it cheating to have a bird fly me to wherever the Big Bone is? Nah. Nobody said we had to stay on the ground. Besides, this isn't a competition about who can run the fastest, it's really about who has the intelligence to finally solve the mystery of the Big Bone. Taking to the air shows that I'm the one who has that intelligence.

Besides, my big dummy opponent is too heavy to fly. That's the advantage of having a normal-size dog as Top Dog. In fact, when I receive that title, I'll fly around to drop in on dogs everywhere, granting boons and privileges while accepting the applause and thanks of all dogs simply for being myself and making their lives better by allowing them to bask in the glory that radiates from me and which should help warm them on cold winter days.

"Oh, look, there are your friends."

Startled by Rosie's voice, his reverie broken, Whiskers looked down. He had a topside view of a large pack of dogs facing one lone dog cornered against a rock face.

"Uh, no, those aren't my friends," he said anxiously. "I don't know them. Let's just keep going."

But Rosie wasn't listening. She circled down in steeply angled spirals.

Aaah! We're going to crash!

A few feet above the ground, Rosie leveled off and gave a half-twist to her right.

Starting to slide off, Whiskers clawed desperately with all four paws to stay aboard, but his toenails couldn't get any purchase on the smooth feathers.

He was going, going, gone, dumped in the dirt on his back beside the lone dog.

Rosie righted herself and flapped her wings to rise above all the onlookers who stood transfixed with eyes wide and mouths open at having seen a bird dropping off a dog.

"Bye," Rosie called down to Whiskers. "I'm so glad I could help my very best friend find his friends, but I have to be on my way because I forgot there's something else I must do although I don't remember what it is but I'm going to do it anyway. Love you. Come see us sometime."

Still on his back, all four paws in the air, his abdomen exposed to attack, Whiskers quivered as a large head moved into view, blotting the ascending Rosie and the sky from his sight.

58

WHO'S YOUR PET?

"Where did you come from?"

Flat on his back, Whiskers stared up at Scut.

"I-I-I j-just dr-dr-dropped in, b-but it looks like you're b-busy, so I d-don't p-p-plan to st-stay. In f-fact, I'll b-be leaving r-r-right now."

Catching his breath, Whiskers rolled over onto his stomach, stood up and took a few shaky steps away.

"S-sorry for the intrusion, everyone. Don't m-mind me. Proceed with your meeting. Just f-forget I was ever here. As humans would say: chow and vayaconcheetos."

"What the hell is that?"

The question came from one of the seedy dogs in the pack of mongrels. Directed at Whiskers, it prompted the other dogs to start catcalling.

"Don't look like a dog to me. More like a cat."

"Talks like a cat. Walks like a cat."

"Looks like he's scared."

"I don't even think he's a he. I think he's a she. A sweet little pussycat."

"Come over here, pussycat. We got your litter box. Need to pee-pee and poo-poo?"

"Don't make her mad, she might show her itty-bitty claws."

Whiskers tried to ignore the gibes, but he couldn't. Each one stung. It was bad enough to be called a cat, but to be called a girl cat was too much.

Stammer gone, he looked at Scut and asked, "Who are these idiots?"

"We are the Black Patch Gang, at your disservice," piped up the leader, a huge, brownish, mixed-breed with a long snout, sharp-pointed ears, rough fur and a bushy tale.

Scanning across the lineup of miscreants, Whiskers saw that each had a black patch of fur somewhere, whether on the head, neck, side, rump, leg or tail.

"That loudmouth is Crud, who I thought was dead," Scut said.

"I came close to it," replied Crud, "but as you can see, I'm back and I brought some old friends of yours."

"Are they really your friends?" Whiskers asked Scut.

"Not at all. Crud sought me out more than once in the past to take me down and get a reputation as the toughest dog, but I whupped him every time. After this race started, I knew dogs were trailing me from the shadows. Now they've come out because Crud thinks he's got me boxed in. As for help, it looks like he's scraped the grime from the bottom of the dog bowl, the kind of curs you never want to see again."

"So, you do know them?"

"Yeah, on that end is Weed, then Scuffle, Loopy, Grudge, Smelly. Next is Sunflower; he's extra mean because he hates the name that his daddy gave him. Then Anus..."

"Anus? Really?"

"Yeah, he's a real asshole."

"And the last one?"

"Peoplebreath."

"Oh dear, it must be really gross."

"You don't want to find out."

"Now that we're all acquainted," Crud interrupted, "who's your pet cat?"

Scut ignored him and whispered to Whiskers, "This isn't your fight. You said you were leaving. Now's your time to run away."

Rats! All I need is for Scut or one of these morons to tell everyone in Dogdom that I ran from trouble. Even if I bring back the Big Bone and get named Top Dog, nobody will respect me. Then I might as well wear a dog tag that says "Top Coward" on it.

"No. I'm staying."

Scut stared at Whiskers for a few seconds and smirked. "I never would have believed it."

To present a united front, Scut turned his gaze back to the Black Patch bunch and said, "Meet my little friend, Whiskers."

"Whiskers? That's a cat's name!" yelled Anus.

"No, it's not! And it's better than yours," Whiskers yelled back.

"Shut up, kitty cat," Crud growled. "After we finish off Scut, you're going to be our new play toy."

Oh, no! I don't like the sound of that. We've got to get out of this, but even for Scut there's too many of them to take on. We need help.

Under his breath, he whispered, "Oh Rolls-Royce Crazy, patron saint of mixed marshmallow farts, help me and my temporary ally Scut against these uncaged dogs, pain without end, amen."

At that moment, the fear in his veins vanished. Calm and inspired, Whiskers stood up on his hind legs and raised his front paws to shoulder level. Shooting his left paw forward, he slowly turned to his left, then slowly turned back to his right, shooting his right paw forward and whipping his left paw back, all the while yowling eerily as he snapped his head from side to side and looked upward, staring into space as if his mind were somewhere else.

The Black Patch Gang was stupefied. What they were witnessing wasn't normal. Not even a cat should behave that way. It was downright weird and unsettling.

"I think he's gone crazy," Sunflower said.

"No, I've heard tell about it," Weed shuddered. "That there ain't no regular dog named Whiskers. That there is the Whiskers that knows that super-secret carrot-rotty way of fighting."

"I heard about it too," said Loopy. "He's beaten all comers with it. No one gets out alive."

"After he kills you, he brands you with carrot juice that burns your hide when he pees it on you," Grudge added.

"It just ain't right for a dog to eat carrots," Peoplebreath grumped.

"And now we've done gone and got him all mad at us," Smelly pointed out.

"Say, Crud, I don't know about this anymore," half-whimpered Scuffle. "We've been making fun of Whiskers the famous carrot-rotty dog who got flown in to help Scut."

"What's wrong with you? They can't take us all on," Crud snapped. "That's just a bunch of play-acting, and he's playing you for fools."

Then Whiskers stopped turning and yowling. Still standing, he cocked his head to the right and then to the left, listening.

From behind boulders and dense brush came the rumbling, deep-throated growls of predators much larger and more powerful than any dog.

Glancing around, the puzzled members of the Black Patch

Gang saw nothing. Legs trembling, their breath came in gasps as panic welled up.

Scut seized the moment and charged into them, slashing fiercely with his huge canines.

Down goes Anus.

Down goes Peoplebreath.

Down goes Sunflower.

Unnerved by Scut's sudden attack and fearful of the unseen monsters, the still-standing Black Patchers yelped like puppies and ran away, followed by the fallen who got up and limped after them.

"Come back and fight, you cowards!" Crud demanded. But the louder he barked, the faster they ran. Or limped.

Although abandoned, Crud was still game, circling Scut and looking for an opening. He found it when Scut made a quick turn toward him only to stumble on a rock. Crud bounded forward and lunged at Scut, opening his mouth to bite him in the neck.

But something landed on Crud's back.

Whiskers.

Way overmatched in size, Whiskers had danced around, looking for a chance to help. Now on Crud's back, he wrapped his front legs around the brute's neck and bit into the right ear, sinking a canine inside and breaking the eardrum. Crud screamed, shook Whiskers off and started running in circles.

Scut and Whiskers stood side by side, watching the wretched dog run in larger and larger circles trying to escape the pain in his head until he ran off into brush with only fading screams to mark his retreat.

"Up against that many, I thought this might be my last dogfight," Scut remarked. "I know that carrot juice stuff was just a rumor gone wild, but where did those noises come from? They sure unnerved those clowns."

"Speaking of clowns," Whiskers answered, "it's a trick I learned from a circus dog. Listening to lions and tigers every day, we passed the time by trying to imitate them. The neat thing was when he showed me how to throw my growl, to make it seem like it was coming from somewhere else. Like I said, it's just a trick, but it sure fooled those dopes."

"You really do surprise me," Scut commented.

"So, are we friends now?"

Scut stared thoughtfully at Whiskers. He had stood up when it counted. He hadn't run like a coward.

"Let's just say we'll race fair and square for Top Dog, and we'll go our separate ways when it's over. As for now, I can see a fork up ahead in the trail. I'll go one way, and you can take the other. I have no idea which one's better."

"That's fine with me," Whiskers said.

Yes! I can breathe again knowing that this monster won't be coming after me anymore.

Whiskers started to take the first step away but paused because Scut was silent, unmoving, and still staring at him. Finally...

"Crud's not the only one who's been after me," Scut said.

"Oh, really?"

"Yeah. While waiting for this race to get started, I was told that a dogcatcher was questioning lots of dogs, trying to track me down."

"So what? Dogcatchers are always after dogs," Whiskers said.

"This one's different. They call her the human she-bitch. They say she's relentless, that she never quits, that she always gets her dog."

"Oh, yeah, I've heard of her. Gee, that's too bad for you."

Whiskers didn't like the thought of any dog being taken by a dogcatcher, but...

If he does get caught, at least he won't be able to change his mind and come after me again.

"It's not just me she wants," Scut said sharply.

"What do you mean?"

"The word is that she's after you too."

Oh, no! Just when I get one enemy off my butt, I get a new one.

59

BABY ON BOARD

The black van drove into the Mal-Wart parking lot, sped to one side and parked near a large recreational vehicle.

Two outdoor chaise lounges of cheap plastic strapping were set up on the asphalt beside the RV. An elderly, balding, potbellied man in a white tank top undershirt and plaid shorts reclined on one. On the other lounger was an elderly, thin-haired, potbellied woman in a brightly colored muumuu.

They raised themselves on elbows to gaze with wide-open mouths at the pink lightning bolt on the side of the Dogster and the red flames shooting off its golden name. Sharp chrome spikes covered the wheels' lug nuts.

The woman who stepped out was a perfect match for the van with a tight black blouse, black pants, black motorcycle boots, studded dog collar, utility belt, stun guns with pearl handles, and black spiked hair with a pink stripe on each side.

"Oh, mercy me," said the gent, "it's that dog-getter gal. We can't let her see Beggar. As sure as the day I was born she'll take him away."

He scooped up a sleeping Dachshund puppy from under his lounger and pulled up his wife's dress.

"Good Lord, you old fool, what are you doing?" the woman said, trying to slap his hand away.

But he pushed her hand aside, plopped the dog on her potbelly and dropped the dress back down, making her stomach appear huge.

"Shhh, don't say nothin'. Maybe she didn't see him."

Now awake, the dog could hear the footsteps of the newcomer and started kicking its legs.

"Danggit, Hubert, he's a'wrigglin' like all get-out."

"You got to hold him tighter, Maybelle. Try to keep him still the best you can. Now shush up."

Janvier walked over to the couple.

"How are you folks today?"

"We be fine, thank you. I'm Hubert and this here is my wife, Maybelle."

"We know who you are," chimed in Maybelle. "You're that famous dog police lady, and you're right real pretty in person, I can tell you that."

"Thank you," Janvier said. "You two look mighty comfortable. Planning on spending the night in the parking lot?"

"Oh, yes, that's what we do," said Hubert. "We always stay at a Mal-Wart when we're traveling around. Plenty of room to park our big hunk of steel at no charge."

"Do you travel a lot?"

"That's all we do," Maybelle answered. "Sakes alive, me and the old man have been everywhere in this country."

"How nice for you. Tell me, have you noticed a lot of dogs around this area?"

Suddenly, the puppy under Maybelle's dress began squirming harder. She clamped her hands down tighter, but the little pooch's frantic movements made her hands and dress move up and down and all around.

"What's wrong?" Janvier asked.

Maybelle didn't know what to say.

"Uh, she's pregnant," Hubert blurted out.

"Pregnant, you say? She didn't look pregnant when I was driving in, but she certainly looks it now. How is that possible?"

"I get pregnant just being near Hubert, even at my age," Maybelle said. "Most potent man I ever did know. He don't even have to touch me. One minute you're not pregnant, and the next minute there you are with a baby on the inside who's a'kickin' like it's field goal time."

"Mind if I feel it?"

Maybelle flinched. She was scared of losing her baby.

"Oh, lawdy, please stand back. You don't want to get too close or Hubert might get you pregnant."

"Yeah, it's kind of like a force field," Hubert said proudly.

"Okay," Janvier agreed, smiling, "but since you two drive everywhere, I've got some pictures of dangerous dogs I'd like you to look at. I'll get them."

As she walked the few steps to her van, Maybelle leaned over to Hubert and whispered, "Danggit, I think he's peeing on me."

Coming back, Janvier spotted liquid dripping from the gaps in the strapping of Maybelle's lounger.

"What's that?"

Maybelle looked very worried.

"Uh, my water broke," she said.

"Then I promise I won't keep you long. Tell me, have you seen either of these dogs?"

Maybelle and Hubert took a good look at the photos.

Hubert's eyes widened.

"Yessiree, we have," he said excitedly. "We saw that dark one first, over by Miner's Crotch. That white one, we saw him in the countryside near Mule Butt. Each one was just scootin' along like he had a big-ass dog shindig to get to."

"Are you sure it was them?"

"Yes, indeed. The big one is so scary-looking you can't forget him, and the other cuss was just as cute as he could be."

"Were they both going in the same direction?"

"No, they weren't. That big one was going southeast. The other one, he was more on a south-by-southwest heading."

"Are you positive?"

"Yes, ma'am, because I'm a curious type, especially about dogs these days. I remember looking at the compass on the dash each time and saying to myself, 'What's that dog up to? And why's he going that way'?"

Yes! I've finally gotten the information I lacked—confirmed sightings of the pair by a human being.

"Anything else?"

"Well, that great big one was by himself, but the smaller one had a huge number of dogs with him, and he was out front leading them, like a general leading an army. And all of them dogs were barking like crazy with excitement. Kinda scary, if you ask me."

Whiskers has an army of dogs? This is very bad. There's no telling what major criminality he's planning. At least now I've got a bead on him and Scut. All I have to do is triangulate their directions of travel from Hubert's place names to pinpoint their common destination.

"Not to be impolite, but are you through with us?" Maybelle piped up, looking anxious.

"Yes, thank you very much."

"Well then, pleased to have met you, but I've got to run. I can't hold him in no more. Baby's startin' to come out."

Maybelle eased up carefully, clenching her hands tightly

against the wriggling beneath her muumuu. She waddled to the RV's door, dripping all the way.

"I can drive you in my van to a hospital," Janvier called out.

"Thank you, ma'am," Hubert said, getting up and following Maybelle, "but it's going to be a home delivery."

60

NICE TRY, DOG DIP

After the fight with Crud's gang and parting ways with Scut, Whiskers had traveled in silence until...

"How ya doin', dumbass?"

Startled, Whiskers froze, the paw for his next step still in the air.

"I said, how ya doin'? Whatsa matter, cat got ya tongue? Hey, if a cat got ya tongue, ya ain't much of a dog, are ya?"

Whiskers looked to his left, but all he saw were large boulders that had piled on top of each other in a landslide. Craning his neck, he looked up to see a bird perched above him on top of the pile.

Yikes! It's an eagle!

Until now, Whiskers had heard of eagles but had never come across one. This meat-eating predator was huge. The white feathers of the eagle's head contrasted dramatically with the body's dark-brown feathers. The most striking aspect was the fierceness the bird conveyed through its piercing yellow eyes and its powerful hooked beak.

"Ya some kinda dummy?" asked the eagle, lifting his wings

slightly and hopping off his rocky perch to land easily on the ground.

"The name's Vito, and yours is... hey, ya so ugly ya mutha shoulda named ya Buttface."

Whoa! What's his problem? Maybe he doesn't like dogs. Or maybe he's having a bad day and wants to take it out on someone. Or maybe he's just a jerk who likes to bully others. Whatever it is, I've got to find a way to calm this fool down.

"If you're looking for directions," Whiskers ventured, "I really can't help you because I'm a stranger here myself, but I know a place where you can get some. I suggest you fly to get there rather than walk because it's faster. Oh, wait, silly me. Of course you would fly, because you're an eagle, not a dirt-pounder like me who has to walk."

Vito took a step toward Whiskers.

"Wait, wait, wait! There's no need to come closer. I can see you're in a hurry, so let me give you the directions to the place that I mentioned. You just point yourself that way, flap your magnificent wings and take off like a bat out of..."

"I don't need no stinkin' directions, and I don't fly like no stupid bat," Vito snapped as he took more steps toward Whiskers.

Whiskers glanced down at the claws on the eagle's advancing feet. They were large, curved, pointed and frightening.

"Well, in that case, how about something else? There are some buzzards around these parts. I ran into them not too long ago and not too far away, and I recommend that you make their acquaintance. I understand they get a bad rap, but once you get to know them you'll be surprised. They are funny guys, a bunch of practical jokers. They played a joke on me, but it was all in good fun. In fact, I laughed so hard that I fell apart and had to put myself back together. So, you might want to look them up right now, have a few laughs, and swap some great stories and flying tips."

"Buzzahds? Are ya outta ya mind? Ya think an eagle is goin' to hang out wid buzzahds?"

"No offense. I just thought since you are all birds..."

"Shut up. Ya comin' wid me. Take ya choice: the easy way or the hard way."

"Whoa! Wait! Hold up there. I don't know what you want or where you're planning on going, but I'm in a race and I don't have time for sightseeing or whatever other kind of service you're running. Don't get the wrong idea, though, I'm not disparaging it. I'm sure it's a very good service, but I just don't have the time today. I've got to leave now, so please wait here for my assistant. She'll be along soon, and she can set up a day when I can go with you. By the way, she's a real cutie, unattached and, get this, she's a bird, a real big one just like yourself. She is really sweet and good to look at, if you know what I mean. Say, if the two of you want to get something going, don't worry about me, because there's nothing happening between us. In other words, no jealousy on my part. I'm glad we got that settled and I'll see you later because I'm late for my next appointment."

During his monologue, Whiskers had been slowly backing away, hoping that his effort to befuddle the eagle was working.

But Vito wasn't buying.

"Nice try, dog dip, but ya still comin' wid me, and ya comin' right now."

Whiskers stopped moving backward and held up a paw.

"Hold on. Did Scut send you? Has he gone back on our deal? Is this his way of stopping me from winning the race?"

"Scut? I thought his name was Mutt. Anyway, fuhgeddabout him. I'm doin' the job he couldn't do, which is to get a dog named Whiskers."

Vito opened his wings and ran at Whiskers.

"Stop! Don't come any closer, I get closetphobia when I get crowded."

"Tough," Vito grunted.

He swung a wing and struck Whiskers hard on the head, spinning him sideways.

"OWW!"

How could a wing hurt so much?

Then he rallied.

What am I afraid of? It's just a bunch of feathers and a goofy mouth with no teeth. Nothing but an overgrown chicken.

Whiskers growled, spun back around and opened his mouth to crunch down on a leg or wing, whichever was closest.

But Vito was quicker. He jumped on Whiskers' back and sank his claws through the hair and into the hide.

"OWWWW! OWWWW!"

Flapping his wings, Vito lifted Whiskers off the ground and flew up until they were thousands of feet in the sky.

"Listen up, Buttface. Don't ask no questions, and if I hear any growling out of ya, I'll drop ya. Dey want ya alive, but I don't mind if ya have an accident along the way."

Who's he talking about? Oh, no, please don't let it be...

As his brain filled with the fear of flying to a new confrontation, pee squirted out of Whiskers in short, rapid bursts.

He watched it fall so very far below.

61

BIRD OF A DIFFERENT FEATHER

S crunched uncomfortably into the bird nest, Whiskers stared at two sets of eyes.

Baby eagles stared back at him.

Even though they're young, their beaks look hard. What if they think I'm dinner and start pecking at me? I can't bite back, because Vito might rip me to pieces and really feed me to them. I've to get on the good side of these birdbrains.

"Hello, little ones. You were asleep when your father brought me to your nest. He took off kind of fast, saying he wanted to brag about something to a mutual acquaintance of ours. By the way, do you remember me?

The eaglets shook their heads.

"I remember both of you and, wow, look how you've grown. The last time I saw you, you were just a couple of hard eggshells, but I'd still know you anywhere. That's because I'm your Uncle Whiskers."

"How can you be our uncle? You don't look like an eagle," said Baby No. 1.

"Oh, my gosh!" exclaimed Baby No. 2. "He doesn't have any wings."

"That's easy to explain," Whiskers assured them. "I'm a greagle."

"What's a greagle?" asked No. 1.

"I'm surprised your dad didn't tell you. Anyway, a very long time ago, eagles stayed in the sky and never went to the ground, but they could see very bad things happening down there. When it got so bad that it could not be ignored anymore, some eagles declared that they would patrol the ground. They turned in their wings and became ground eagles, also called greagles, like me.

"There's something else, kids. Ground eagles also are called dogs. Why? Because it's a dog of a job that we have to do. To do that job, we had to develop bigger noses to smell better and bigger ears to hear better. We also had to grow all these legs to help us swim across rivers, climb hills and crawl under thorn bushes. That's why we look so different from you, but we'll always be eagles at heart. Like you, we stand for truth and freedom as we patrol and fight against vicious and poisonous animals every day."

"Wow, Uncle Whiskers. You're really brave," said No. 2.

"Tell us a story, Uncle Whiskers," chirped No. 1.

"Well, once upon a time, all the eagles were under attack by horrible things called hippoliposuctorises and highene-masquirtyasses. The eagles shrieked, 'Help us, doggy greagles,' and we answered by climbing the highest peaks to fight tooth and nail until we chased those bad things away for good. That's how dogs saved eagles from becoming extinct. And that's why your dad left me here to protect you from bears and mountain lions and catfish and woodchucks and billy goats and something the English Setters call spotted dick, which sounds very bad."

"Uncle Whiskers, you're the best uncle in the whole world," gushed No. 1.

"Oh, look, here comes Momma," said No. 2.

Whiskers twisted his head to see.

Oh, no! She's even bigger than the brute who brought me here!

Flying in with wings wide, the eagle dropped a fish in the nest and exclaimed, "What is this?"

"Momma," said No. 1, "it's Uncle Whiskers. He came to visit us."

"Uncle? What are you talking about? How did he get here?"

"Daddy brought him," piped up No. 2. "Uncle Whiskers was protecting us while you and Daddy were gone."

She stuck her beak against Whiskers' nose. Trying not to show fear, he attempted to stare her down, but her eyes were so narrowly set that his eyeballs had to rotate toward the inner corners of their eye sockets.

"He's no eagle's uncle. He's a goofy cross-eyed dog. I'm going to throw him off this mountain."

"No, Momma! He's special," said No. 2. "He's a greagle. A ground eagle. He told us all about how we're related and how the greagles stay on the awful ground doing a dog of a job so we can keep our talons nice and clean."

"Uncle Whiskers is our hero!" screeched No. 1. "He kept all the horrible beasts away while we were sleeping. We would have died without him!"

She looked at her pleading twins, then at Whiskers, and sighed.

"Unbelievable. You have filled their heads with more crap than I would have ever thought possible."

"Momma, he doesn't have his wings anymore. You have to fly him down," urged No. 2.

"And you can't hurt him. You have to take him wherever he needs to go to get back on patrol duty," said No. 1.

"Promise us!" both kids yelled.

"Fine, okay, just so we can get back to normal and get this dog smell out of here. Now, eat your fish."

She glared at Whiskers.

"Let's go, greagle."

62

FUHGET WHAT I SAID

"Hiya, Mutt, ya loser."

Scut glared at the smug eagle as it flew circles around him in a show of disrespect before finally landing.

"Who are you?"

"Not dat it's none of ya business, tough guy, but the name's Vito."

"You're pretty mouthy for a pile of feathers. What are you doing here?"

"Just lettin' ya know dat ya services are terminated. Dey ain't needed no more."

"What are you talking about?"

"I'm talkin' about a big dumb dog who couldn't catch a little dumb dog. I've already got him."

"Got who?"

"Dat dog ya been chasin' forever called Whiskers. The bosses dat hired ya called me in 'cause dey got tired of waitin' on ya."

"What have you done to him?"

"Nuttin'. But I offered. I said to dem, whaddaya want? Just

rough him up or put him to sleep wid the fishes? But naw, dey said take him to dem. Anyway, a job's a job, and ya do what the bosses tell ya. And now I'm goin' back to finish the job."

"I don't think so," Scut snarled as he lunged at Vito and knocked him to the ground.

The startled bird tried to scramble up, but Scut put one foot on his chest, bit into a wing and ripped out feathers, sending them flying into the air. Vito bent his head forward to sink his beak into Scut's leg, but couldn't reach it.

Scut quickly switched his feet on the bird's chest and ripped feathers out of the other wing.

Unable to free himself, Vito stopped struggling.

"Where did you leave him?" Scut growled, dripping saliva onto Vito's beak.

"I ain't talkin'."

Scut clamped his teeth around Vito's neck and began pulling with a force sufficient to pop his head off his body.

"Fuhget what I said! I'm talkin', I'm talkin'!"

Scut stopped and stepped back.

"Get up."

Vito stood, spread out his wings and examined the large holes in the middle of each.

"Look what ya done. Now I can't fly. What'd I do to ya? I thought we were on the same team."

"Not anymore," Scut said. "Now tell me where he is."

"I stashed him on a mountain."

After finding out the location, Scut growled, "If I find out that he fell off the mountain, I'll be back. In the meantime, you've got a chance to practice."

"Practice what?"

"Running for your life."

63

STINKS TO BE YOU

"I should drop you on those rocks far below," Vito's wife said, "but I promised the kids that I wouldn't hurt you. So, I'm just going to put you down on the ground and say good riddance to you."

"Wait, what's that smell?" Whiskers asked as he swayed in the clutch of her talons.

"I don't smell anything," she answered.

"It's very light, but for it to reach this high in the sky, it has to come from a really big smell," Whiskers said. "The amordildo told me there was a clue on the flat bone about such a smell. Please take me to it. Maybe there I can get answers to the other clues."

"Why should I waste my time?"

"Because you also promised to take me wherever I needed to go, and especially because you never know when your husband, who is a dear friend of mine, will bring me back to watch the kids again, and then I'll have to tell them if you were nice or not nice to me."

"Are all dogs as conniving as you?"

"Only the smart ones. By the way, there's something else."

"What?"

"I don't think you're really as cold-hearted as you act. You're just too pretty to be that mean."

"No, I'm not."

"Oh, yes, you are. I've been to the zoo, and I've lived in the circus. That makes me an expert because I've seen more pretty birds than you can imagine, like the bird of parasites and the peeincock. You, though, have a regal bearing they can't match. No one would look at them with you around. You are like a queen among all birds. In fact, if I wasn't a dog, I'd be on you like a fly on a fresh turd."

"That's the sweetest thing anyone has said to me in a long time."

"I mean every word of it."

"You mean you're full of it, but I still like hearing it. Vito never says anything nice to me anymore. Just comes home and grunts and complains about the idiots he works for and gripes that he should be running everything. So, you false-charmer, call me Doreen, keep telling me sweet nothings, and I'll take you where you need to go."

Whiskers flexed his nostrils rapidly, inhaled deeply, rolled the air molecules through his highly sensitive nasal receptors and said, "Turn left."

On they flew, farther and farther, the odor increasing in strength until Doreen said, "Whew, now I can smell it. I think we'll be there soon."

As they flew over a mountain, they saw far below an enormous, motionless, prone figure. Gray in color and furry with pointed ears, the head was huge. The top of it was level with the tallest trees. The body was covered in black fur with two brilliant white stripes running the length of its back, one on each side. The back legs were pulled in tight to the body, while the forelegs were stretched out.

The smell that came up was powerful and awful.

"Oh, my word," Doreen said. "I've heard about it, and now I'm seeing it. It's the Stinx."

"I know it stinks. That's how I navigated us here," Whiskers said. "But what is it? Is it alive?"

"Yes, it's alive, but they say it never goes anywhere, that it always stays in the same position, almost stone-like."

They drifted down in front of the Stinx's face. Its enormous eyes had elliptical, vertical pupils. The cheeks were fat and fluffy, but the nose was smallish. Prominent feeler-hairs stuck out horizontally.

Oh, no! It's a giant cat's face!

"Whoa, whoa, whoa!" Whiskers shrilled. "Take me back up high!"

"Sorry, no can do. I've been away from my babies long enough. Now hold on, the landing might be bumpy for you."

"I can't hold on. You're the one holding me," squealed Whiskers.

Doreen let Whiskers go a few feet above the ground, then she landed.

"What is this thing?" Whiskers asked, his voice quavering.

"Like I said, it's the Stinx. Head of a cat, body of a skunk."

"What does it do?"

"It talks, which is good because you came for answers. Feed it the same dogshit you fed me and the kids. You're very good at it."

"Will you come back and check on me?"

Doreen rolled her head in disbelief, opened her wings and said, "So long, Uncle Whiskers."

As she flew away, the Stinx rolled its eyes upward, watching the eagle climb higher and higher until it faded from sight. Then its cat eyes rolled down, fixing themselves on Whiskers, whose own eyes were open so wide that he looked dopey.

"Hello, traveler. I see you're a dog. I won't hold that against you. I always play fair."

"Play fair?" Whiskers half-questioned in a shaky voice.

"Oh, please, don't be scared," the Stinx said soothingly.

"Me? Scared? I've never been scared in my life," Whiskers responded despite the visible trembling of his legs.

"So you say, brave fellow. Well, I'm glad you dropped in. First off, are you a quester? Yes? No? Maybe so? Make up your mind, you're running out of time."

"A quester? If you mean looking for something, yes."

"Ah, a quester on a quest. The question now is, what's your quest, quester?"

"I'm looking for the way to the Big Bone. Do you know where it is?"

"Of course, I do. I know everything. You cross the first two mountains directly behind me, and then you..."

The Stinx interrupted itself, cocked its head to one side, scrunched up the fur on its forehead and stared hard at Whiskers.

"Why am I telling you this? What do you want with it?"

After Whiskers explained about the race to become Top Dog, the Stinx rolled its eyes.

"Pooh on that. Typical dog folly. But if you beat me, you'll win much more fame and glory than you can get from that nasty, greasy thing."

"Beat you? What are you talking about?"

"I'm so glad you asked. Here are the rules. I ask questions. If you don't get the answers right, I will devour you. Are you ready to play?"

"By devour, do you mean like eating me up with hugs and kisses? You know, being overly affectionate? Smothering me with love?"

"No."

"So, you mean like tear me apart, chew me up and swallow me?"

"Exactly. Sounds like fun, doesn't it? For me, of course, but not you. Sorry about that."

"But what if I beat you?"

"That's never happened."

Oh, catshit! I've got to get away. Surely this ponderous thing can't move quickly enough to catch a nimble dog. Besides, the eagle said it never went anywhere. Let me just glance around for...

"Oh, what's this? Looking about, are we? Methinks you want to leave. Naughty, naughty. We haven't played a game yet."

With that, the Stinx shot out one huge paw that whizzed by a stunned Whiskers and reached a point far behind him. Further emphasizing the foolishness of trying to escape, the Stinx slowly retracted the foreleg while gently brushing it against Whiskers in a show of controlled power.

"Ready to play?"

To counteract his trembling, Whiskers closed his eyes and inhaled deeply.

Mr. Professor told me that I am the smartest dog in the world and even smarter than people, which means I am definitely smarter than a screwed-up mess of a cat marinating in skunk juice.

Opening his eyes, Whiskers said calmly, "Looks like I have no choice, but I warn you, I know a lot too."

"Oh, getting your confidence back, are you? I like that. Now, let's play Name That Toot."

The tail end of the Stinx let out a puff of smell and a squidge of sound.

Puuupppppuuuppp!

"Cow."

Wwwwhhhhwsswhhhhhoooo!

"Horse."

The Stinx appeared peeved.

"No more easy ones. Try this."

Fffffwwwwwaaaagggggggffffffffwwwaaaagggffffwwwaaaaggg.

"Giraffe."

Wrinkling its face, the Stinx eyeballed Whiskers hard and asked, "How did you know that?"

"I'm a dog. We know a lot about toots, and in my travels, I've become a connysewer of them."

"We'll see about that," harrumphed the Stinx.

And then it began. Toot after toot.

Rrrrrrrroooooopepeppepwwwiippiippiiippaaahhh.

"Lion!"

Ssssuuuussssuuuusssshhhhhhrrrippppwwaaarppp.

"Tiger!"

Ttttwoeetttwoeeeppweefffhhhhwaaakkffffhhhwaakkk.

"Zebra!"

Vvvvwwaaaajjjjjaaagggaappwwaahhggggwwwapp.

"Elephant! Possibly with a hemorrhoid."

"Enough of that!" commanded the Stinx.

Thank you, circus.

"That was just a warm-up," the Stinx said. "Now, we're going to play Bassackwards. I'll give you the answer. You have to give me the question. Understand?"

"Sounds dumb, but yes, I'm ready."

"This lover has a feast."

Whiskers thought a moment, then said, "What does a black widow spider do to her mate?"

The Stinx frowned and muttered, "Stupid dog is kind of smart," then fired supposed stumper after stumper.

"A real butthead."

"What's a ram?"

"Prefers not to sing."

"What's a hummingbird?"

"Dining with a twist."

"What's an alligator death role?"

"Oh, never mind, never mind, never mind!" groused the Stinx.

Wow, I'm getting under its hide.

"You think you're quite clever, don't you? Let's see how you like the next game, Taxisquirmy."

I can do this, whatever it is. My mind is on fire.

"What do you get when you cross a pig and a tree?"

"A porkypine."

"A wolf and a tangerine?"

"A wolverine."

"A turd and a monkey?"

"A turkey."

"A frog and a smile?"

"A croakadile."

"A duck and..."

The Stinx stopped in mid-question.

"Never mind. Something's wrong here. You're either cheating or the luckiest guesser ever or smarter than you look. That's why we're going on to the next game, and I expect you to lose big because it's called Riddled to Death. Scared?"

Despite its aggressive language, the Stinx looked worried.

"No, I'm not scared. Are you?"

"Shut up! Here's the first question: What bird has wings but cannot fly?"

"A chicken."

"Nope."

What? Everybody knows it's a chicken.

"The correct answer is the dodo bird. That means you lose, and now I am going to make you as extinct as the dodo bird."

"Hold on. You said 'has' wings, and that means like right now. A bird can't have anything if it doesn't exist. Remember, you said that you play fair."

"Hmm, so I did. Okay, forget that one. Let's move on with this riddle: "What do you fly the friendly skies on?"

"An eagle."

"Wrong! Passenger pigeon. Get it? You're a passenger."

"But you saw me fly in on an eagle. And you said 'you,' meaning what do I, Whiskers, fly on? I can't fly on an extinct bird."

"You did use an eagle, didn't you? I'll have to give you that one also. Damn technicalities. Now, get ready for this one."

"STOP!" shouted Whiskers. "How many more questions do you have?"

"Stop? You're telling me to stop? That's quite a change in your demeanor from when you first showed up. But if you must know, I have an infinite number of questions."

Infinite! If it's got that many trick questions to ask, I'm sure to get one wrong and then it's going to eat me. I've got to go for broke.

"Let's make a deal."

"A deal?"

"Yes. Skip all this easy stuff. Hit me with your toughest question. If I don't get it right, devour me immediately. But if I do get it right, then I get to ask you a question."

"To what purpose?"

"If you don't know the answer, I get to walk away unharmed and…"

"And what?"

"Actually, several more things, starting with…"

"Nope, one thing only."

Gee, I really want exact directions to the Big Bone, but a hero must help others first, so…

"You never again bother any animal."

The Stinx frowned and shook its head.

"Oh, come on," Whiskers taunted. "You aren't scared of a challenge, are you? Besides, you said you know everything."

"I'm not and I do. So, I accept, but there won't be any mercy given for technicalities like 'has' and 'you.' You can forget about that, you little quibbler. Therefore, with great pleasure on my part, I present to you a question from antiquity. It's never failed."

When he heard that, Whiskers' stomach convulsed. His butt-hole began squeezing and releasing over and over.

Oh, my heart, please stop pounding so hard. I need to hear the question.

"What walks on four legs in the morning, two legs in the afternoon, and three legs in the evening?"

Whiskers' stomach and butthole relaxed. His heart took a breather.

"I'm waiting," the Stinx said with a smirk. "Give up? Don't even want to take a little guess?"

"I do have an answer."

"What is it?"

"A human."

The Stinx shuddered.

In a triumphant tone of voice, Whiskers explained, "A human crawls on all fours when a baby, walks upright on two legs in middle age and adds a cane in old age."

The Stinx swallowed hard and gasped, almost choking.

"How... did... you... know... that?"

"I used to live with a human who asked it of kids walking by his house. They didn't have any idea what he was talking about. He would laugh and shout out the answer. He was a university professor, smarter than anyone, and he taught me everything."

"How fortunate for you," said the Stinx, looking downcast. "I suppose you still want to ask your question?"

"Yes, I do, and here it is: What walks on five legs, hops on two legs, and does it with two heads?"

"That's downright weird," grumped the Stinx. "Are you sure this is a real question?"

"Realer than your dodo bird."

"I'll have to take an educated guess."

"Okay, what's your guess?"

"A mutated rabbit?"

"No. A kangaroo. I watched one in the circus. It uses all four legs and its tail to walk, hops on its two back legs, and does it all with the head of its baby poking out of the pouch."

"But a tail is not a leg."

"Neither is a cane."

The Stinx looked up at the sky and screamed. Its eyeballs rolled wildly in their sockets. The head jerked down, then back and forth and side to side. The rear end scrunched upward and blasted out clouds of brown smoke and a disgusting odor. Body parts began changing color to a dark brown, starting first with the paws, then the legs which were followed in turn by the sides, the tail, the back and the neck. As the brown color moved up into the gray head, the eyes stopped rolling and the head stopped jerking. The blasts of smoke and odor at the rear ceased, and the Stinx froze in place.

Whiskers stood still, wondering if something else would happen, but nothing did. The Stinx was no longer alive. It had turned into an enormous statue of dried manure.

That wasn't so difficult, and I did get a general idea of where to head for the Big Bone.

Walking away, Whiskers took one look back and said, "Stinks to be you."

64

LOUSY TRAITOR

"He got away?"

Scratchy threw up his front paws and shook them at Phelonius.

"I'm tired of being nice. You tell that doofus eagle to go find that jerk and drop him in a volcano. And it better be an active volcano with lots of boiling lava, not a dead one."

"Well, that's going to be kind of difficult," Phelonius said. "You see, right now Vito can't fly."

"Why not?"

"Uh, Scut chewed up his wings."

"What? Why?"

"It seems that while flying on his way here, Vito saw Scut. So, he made an unscheduled stop to rub it in about getting Whiskers and…"

"Oh, please, let me guess," Scratchy interrupted. "Hmm, what happens when a vicious dog gets together with a fatheaded, bragging bird? A picnic, perhaps? 'Might I have a taste of your birdseed, birdy old boy?' 'Why, of course, doggy old fellow, and I just might take a nip of that scrumptious-looking dog food, if you don't mind.' And then doggy says, 'This birdseed tastes like shit. I'd rather eat you.' Tell me, is that how it went down?"

"Not really. They didn't have any food, and neither one talks like that."

"Idiot! That was sarcasm."

"Oh, sorry. Anyway, it seems that Scut was concerned about what Vito did with Whiskers."

"Concerned? I thought you recruited that dog to work for me, not against me. What's wrong with him?"

"Apparently, Whiskers had helped him out of a very bad situation with a pack of curs, and Scut seems to have a sense of honor."

"Honor, shmonor! How about a sense of duty? I guess it doesn't exist when you're surrounded by nitwits, nincompoops and knuckleheads. They're not smart enough to have it. Now tell me, where was Whiskers while all this stupidity and sabotaging was going on?"

"Vito had stashed him way up high on a mountain."

"So, you and the rest of your wing flappers go get him."

"We would, if we could, but there are some problems."

"Like what? You get altitude sickness? It's your day off?"

"Only an eagle has the strength to fly him off there."

"Then go get another eagle."

"They won't venture into each other's territory, but Vito said to talk to his wife. She could get him off the mountain."

"And?"

"That's the other problem. As soon as I said Whiskers' name, she went crazy and started screeching that he wasn't there anymore and not to say his name again because her babies keep whining for him, saying he's a hero and their uncle. I didn't stick around to make her any madder because she is one big bitch, even bigger than Vito. But don't worry, I've got all of Flapper Express looking for Whiskers. We'll locate him soon."

"Well, thank you for that reassurance, but all I've seen so far is nothing but incompetence!"

Rather than provoke Scratchy even further with a response, Phelonius just stared blankly.

"You know, the more I think about him, the angrier I get," Scratchy fumed, as some fumes seeped from his ears.

"And that would be...?" Phelonius ventured cautiously.

"Scut, the lousy traitor. That turncoat has just joined Whiskers at the top of my shit list. I need some way to get both of them, but so far not a damn thing has worked to get just one dog!"

"I could contact some bears."

"No, it's about time for them to get ready for hibernation. They'll be too slow and sluggish."

"Well, I do have another idea. Something very different."

"It better be good," Scratchy warned.

Phelonius laid out his plan.

"Ooh, that is different," Scratchy said, pursing his lips and nodding his head. "Do you really think you can pull it off?"

"It won't be easy, but I think I can."

"Okay, I'm ready to try anything. Get after it."

65

AS THE CROW FLIES

After she had left Hubert and Maybelle in the Mal-Wart parking lot, Janvier began to have second thoughts about the couple.

Unlike most people who were star-struck upon meeting her and wanted to enjoy her presence as long as possible, the old folks had seemed very nervous.

She wasn't fooled. She knew the "baby" under Maybelle's dress was really a puppy.

Why were they trying to hide it? No registration? No tags? No shots?

That made her wonder about Hubert's truthfulness.

Did he really see not just one, but both Whiskers and Scut? And in places so far apart? Or did he make it all up, telling me what I wanted to hear so I would go away? Still, this is the only real lead I have, so I've got to follow it up.

After triangulating Hubert's compass directions from Miner's Crotch and Mule Butt on a map, Janvier saw that the paths of Scut and Whiskers would intersect far out in the country.

Why that spot? And for what reason? Perhaps it's their headquar-

*ters where they stir up the minions and give out orders for social
disruption. Whatever it is, I'm on my way.*

Janvier fired up the Dogster and drove for hours until the
standard GPS—Global Positioning System—took her off the
highway and down a two-lane asphalt road deep into the countryside, then for miles onto a dirt road that eventually petered
out. The Dogster's GPS became befuddled and useless, so
Janvier punched in a code to switch over to the BPS—the federal
government's highly classified Boonies Positioning System.

The BPS came alive and began guiding the Dogster over
rugged terrain. The van bounced and jounced over hard-baked
ruts, forcing Janvier to put a death-grip on the steering wheel to
keep it from ratcheting out of her hands. The ground finally
smoothed out as the van came to a large meadow backgrounded
by dark woods—the end spot of the triangulation of Hubert's
information.

Stepping out of the van, Janvier sighed as she surveyed the
scene.

Dammit! They're long gone.

It was obvious from the piles of dried poop and the
yellowing spots of dying grass that thousands of dogs had been
there. Her eyes followed the slim path that led into the densely
packed woods. Fine for a dog, but impassable for the Dogster.

Stumped, Janvier got in the van and made her way back to
the dirt track, then the two-lane asphalt road. When she came to
the highway, she got on the feeder road that paralleled it.

She drove slowly in a southerly direction, looking for dogs
that might still be loitering around. Coming across a palm tree,
she began imagining "wouldn't it be nice" scenarios for the
elusive pair.

*Wouldn't it be nice if a couple of coconuts fell off a palm tree and
bonked them on the head for easy pickup?*

Wouldn't it be nice if they gorged themselves so much on food spilling out of a dumpster that they couldn't move and all I had to do was just roll them into the van?

Wouldn't it be nice if the space alien rumor had been true, and they were taken away to another planet?

While Janvier indulged herself in such pleasant thoughts, something flew off a sign on the other side of the feeder road and into her peripheral vision.

A bird. A black one. A crow.

She glanced at it, then went back to looking ahead. But when she again looked out her side window, the crow was flying near the van. Janvier rolled down her window and waved her arm at the crow to encourage it to fly away, but it stuck with her, coming closer.

What if this bird distracts me at the very moment that I could have spotted one of the fugitives?

She turned the steering wheel left and back, left and back to scare the bird away, but the crow dodged sideways and back with the van's movements.

Irritated, Janvier yelled at it.

"Get away from here! Go annoy a scarecrow! Get baked in a pie with those other blackbirds!"

With her attention locked on him, the crow flew into the center of her lane, forcing her to slow down even more despite Janvier honking the horn incessantly for it to get out of the way.

What is this bird doing? Has it lost its mind?

As they came upon a house, the crow left the road and headed for the front yard. It flew low over some dogs, stirred them into a barking frenzy, then flew back to the van. As Janvier drove on, the crow repeated that action over some yards, but ignored others. In each one that the crow flew over, there was a dog. In the ones the bird ignored, there wasn't a dog.

Birds don't like dogs, but why does this one go out of its way to tick them off? And what does that have to do with me? Maybe it's trying to tell me something about dogs, but what dogs? What the heck, I'll give it a shot.

Janvier drove onto the shoulder and stopped the van. With her right hand, she slapped the photo of Whiskers up against the inside of the windshield. The crow landed on the hood, walked up to the windshield, stared, then began pecking furiously at the picture. Janvier replaced it with Scut's photo. The bird jumped at the windshield, trying to scratch up Scut's face with its claws.

That's it! This bird knows them. I think it wants to lead me to them. But why? Maybe they did something awful to him. Whatever, it looks like I've got myself a partner.

Janvier honked the horn. The crow stifled its attack. This time, instead of hearing angry shouts and seeing a shaking fist, the bird saw a smiling and nodding Janvier giving a thumbs-up sign followed by pointing down the road.

Phelonius wasn't knowledgeable about human hand signals, but the change in expression and attitude showed him that he had crossed the communication gap.

He had told Scratchy that he thought he could pull it off. Now, he had actually done it. He had gotten the dogcatcher that Flapper Express agents had identified from their sources as the one most feared throughout Dogdom, the one they called the human she-bitch.

They were a team. All he had to do was lead the way, and she would follow.

As Phelonius flew on ahead, Janvier started up the Dogster and pulled back onto the road.

On they went, mile after mile, occasionally stopping for the bird to take a breather. Seeing how hard he was working, Janvier rolled down the Dogster's windows at their next rest stop and motioned to Phelonius. He flew inside and perched on the top of the passenger seat. When she got back on the road, he stayed there. Whenever a turn needed to be made, he would fly out the window to show which side of the intersecting road to take.

Coming to the end of the day, it was time to stop. Janvier took a room at a Snore More Inn. Phelonius preferred a branch high up in a tree overlooking the parking lot.

The next morning when she came out, he was perched on an outside mirror, waiting for her to open the passenger door. They traveled for miles until Phelonius flew out of the van and took a sharp right down a gravel road.

They went down the road for a while until taking a left onto a dirt trail. Up ahead, Janvier could see that the trail dead-ended at a hedgerow about ten feet tall.

Well, he screwed this up.

Phelonius could fly over the hedgerow, but she was ground-bound. There was no way the Dogster could break through. With tough, thick branches densely intertwined and knotted together like heavy rope, the hedgerow was a giant sponge that would flex a little if rammed, but nothing more.

As Janvier started to turn around, Phelonius landed on the hood of the Dogster and pecked at the windshield. Once he had her attention, he flew straight at the hedgerow rather than over it. The vegetation opened up just enough for him, and he winged through.

He came back out, and the hedge closed. He repeated the performance several times, the hedge opening and closing each time.

Stroking her chin, Janvier stared at the hedgerow and the darting bird.

Am I really seeing this?

Phelonius landed on the hood of the Dogster, spread his wings, cawed at Janvier, and turned his head toward the hedge.

Is he nuts? It only opened enough for him. The Dogster can't go through there, but I'll roll up to it to humor him.

Janvier let the Dogster creep forward. The hedge started to open from top to bottom. As the Dogster got closer, the opening spread wider and wider until it was large enough for the van to go through.

Wow! This crow really does know what he's doing. I've followed him this far, and I'm not stopping now.

She gunned the engine and the van rumbled over a tangle of roots, its tires kicking back rocks and raising a cloud of dust.

Janvier checked the rearview mirror. The hedgerow was closing behind the Dogster. She turned on the Boonies Positioning System to determine her coordinates, but the screen was totally black and the controls wouldn't respond.

Fixated on her goal, she didn't care. She had only one thought.

Look out, you bastards. Special Agent Janvier is coming.

KING OF THE PILE

W hiskers plodded along. He had skirted around the two mountains mentioned by the Stinx, but once again had no idea where to go.

According to what the armadillo had read from the flat bone, he still needed "signs" of some kind and a "wonderful smell."

There was only one thing to do—keep walking while daydreaming about the joyous moment when he would return with the Big Bone to a hero's welcome.

I can hear it now: All hail Whiskers, the triumphant adventurer who...

"ANTS UP HIS LEG!"

Wh-wh-what?

Whiskers froze.

A sharp little voice had burst into his reverie.

He looked straight ahead. Nothing.

"ANTS UP HIS LEG!"

Whiskers jerked his head to the left. Nothing there.

"ANTS UP HIS LEG!"

Whipping his head to the right, he saw it.

A Chihuahua. A dancing Chihuahua. A twisting, jerking,

shaking little thing standing up on two legs with its eyes bugged out and screaming the same thing over and over.

"ANTS UP HIS LEG! ANTS UP HIS LEG! ANTS UP HIS LEG!"

What ants? Whose leg?

Angrily, the Chihuahua pointed a paw down the trail and screeched, "Dammit, how many times do I have to yell at you to wake you up? Stop staring and move it, move it, move it! The next one's waiting for you. Go!"

Puzzled but curious, Whiskers began a slow trot down the trail, then stopped to look back at the fervently dancing Chihuahua who yelled one more time, "ANTS UP HIS LEG!" while adding, "Go faster or you won't get it!"

As he resumed his trot, more Chihuahuas were coming out of the brush ahead to stand alongside the trail. Spaced equidistantly a ways from each other, they were dancing and jerking and shaking like tiny, crazed monkeys.

They were waiting for him.

Wow. This is weird.

Warily, he trotted toward the second Chihuahua who squeaked out, "Made Fido run" and waved him on toward the third Chihuahua who was motioning to him.

They don't want me to stop.

Speeding up, Whiskers ran past the third Chihuahua who said, "When they bit him."

The fourth one added, "In the bum."

That was the last one.

As he trotted on, Whiskers recalled and put together in his mind the lines spouted by the spaced-out Chihuahuas:

Ants up his leg
Made Fido run
When they bit him
In the bum

Well, that's kind of cute, but why are they doing this? Wait, what exactly was it that the amordildo read to me from the flat bone? "Take heed of signs." Maybe these crazy Chihuahuas are signs!

Eventually, Whiskers came to and ran past another group of herky-jerky Chihuahuas.

Around a tree
Bowser ran so fast
He bit himself
In the ass

Wow. I bet that hurt.

Farther on, he hit another patch of the frenetic shouters.

Rover rolled in
So much poop
He wound up in
A pooper scoop

Is that true? I better watch it the next time.

And so it went, living sign after living sign, some humorous, some cautionary, placed there by the late Great Dong whose diminutive messengers carried on.

As Whiskers continued on the trail, he looked forward to seeing them.

Snoozer dared
To sniff a skunk
Now his nose
Is useless junk

What a dummy. Without a working nose, he might as well be a cat.

There was one saying he particularly liked.

He took a bite
With a smile
Now he's the new
King of the pile

Those others were fun, but that one sounds like me, the dog who's going to be the official Top Dog of all Dogdom.

Inspired by the thought of his coming coronation, Whiskers came up with sayings of his own.

Big
Bone
Is
Mine

... followed by ...

Top
Dog
Is
Me

67

WHENCE COMETH THY HELP

S cut looked down from a pass in the high hills.

Getting here had taken some detective work. First, he had gone to the foot of the mountain where Vito claimed to have left Whiskers. There, he talked with Doreen.

When she inquired about her husband, Scut told her that Vito had preferred to walk home since his wings seemed to have lost their usual lift. In turn, she assured Scut that Whiskers was safe, at least when she last saw him.

Combining her directions with his superior sense of smell, Scut found his way to what had been the Stinx. After surveying the massive statue of dried manure, he had given it a long squirt. It was definitely worth claiming.

Whiskers, of course, was no longer there.

Knowing that Whiskers had a facility for becoming airborne, Scut decided not to depend on tracking him by scent. Instead, he had lifted his eyes to the hills and headed for them.

Scouting from the high land, he had worked the canine bark code. His message had gone out across hills and ridgelines, passed from one mountain dog to another. Answers came back with sightings of a terrier matching Whiskers' description.

Now, Scut stood beside a Great Pyrenees, the latest in the string of mountain dogs who had helped him out.

"You're sure he's down there?"

"Yeah, I saw him last evening. He just wandered in there and lay down. Never got up again. He's either dead tired or just dead."

"I'll go down and find out which. Thanks for your help."

"Sure. Anytime."

Scut began angling his way down the steep incline. Now that he had located Whiskers, he shook his head in disgust as he recalled all the boneheaded sightings he had received from Phelonius' winged associates.

I should never have wasted my time with them. Flapper Express, my ass. More like Flying Fools.

68

THE SMELL OF BACON

Lying flat on his belly, chin on his front paws, Whiskers flared his nostrils. The strange scent of last night was much stronger this morning.

His ears began to twitch. They were picking up grunts. Definitely not dog sounds. Definitely not good.

Dog-tired the night before, he had lain down in this field bordered by woods next to a slope. Full of green, leafy plants, the field seemed like a good place to sleep, hidden from view so nosy animals wouldn't disturb him.

Daylight, however, had brought visitors.

After trembling his limbs to get the stiffness out of them, Whiskers raised himself up on his front legs until his eyes were just high enough to peer cautiously across the tops of the plants.

Uh-oh.

Javelinas, about fifty of them, were scattered throughout the field, grunting as they munched on mouth-burning jalapeños. Streams of saliva dripped off their tusks. Their eyes were turning from white to pink to red. Their rear ends tooted out smoke and steam to a rhythmic PAH-poo-PAH-poo-PAH-poo beat.

The more they munched, the more fired up they became,

belching and pooting in a communal rhythm, working their way from plant to plant, moving closer to Whiskers' spot.

He was becoming surrounded.

I'm in big trouble. I can't talk my way out of this, because there's nothing in their heads to reason with.

Frantic, Whiskers swiveled around on his butt, looking for a way out, but finding none. Surprisingly, though, a dog was walking toward the jalapeño field.

I guess he's come to watch them rip me open with their tusks, smash my bones into splinters with their hooves, and eat my dead body's sweet meat garnished with hottalottapainyo poopers.

Instead of taking a spectator position and waiting for the show to begin, Scut stepped quietly into the field. Moseying along, he leaned his head into a plant, jerked up as if in pain, shook his head sideways a few times as if to clear it, forced his head back down into the plants and took a few more steps.

Ever so slowly he made his way toward Whiskers, shuffling through the ranks of the grunting, pooting, snuffling javelinas. Self-absorbed, they ignored him and kept their heads down to continue gorging.

Finally, he sidled over to Whiskers, who stood up and whispered, "Why did you come in here? Why didn't you just keep going?"

"Because I don't have any idea where the Big Bone is. If it even exists, I think you have some clue how to find it, and when you do, I'll just outrace you to it, fair and square."

"That's a nice plan, but it's not going to work."

"Why?"

"Because I'm going to die in this field. And so are you. Obviously, you don't think things through very well."

Scut didn't respond. He didn't seem concerned.

"Wait a moment. How did you get through these javelinas?"

"I was acting like them—moving along snuffling, grunting and eating jalapeños all the way to you."

Scut paused and exhaled full force in Whiskers' face.

"And my breath is on fire, so it smells just like theirs."

From his other end, Scut let out some gas in the same PAH-poo-PAH-poo-PAH-poo rhythm of the javelinas.

"Ooh, that's better," he said. "This stuff is tearing me up. I don't see how they stand it."

Scut stared hard at Whiskers.

"You've got to blend in, moving like them and eating like them so you can smell like them from both ends. That's how we're going to get out of here."

"I don't know if I can do it," Whiskers balked. "I've never eaten poopers. I hear they're killers."

"So are these crazy, wild pigs. Now eat one, and then we'll shuffle out of here."

Whiskers bit a whole jalapeño off the closest plant and held it in his mouth.

That's not too bad.

Three seconds later, his eyes got wide.

Oh, dear!

"Start chewing and swallow it," Scut urged. "You've got to get the gas going."

Whiskers chopped up the green jalapeño and forced it down. Almost instantly, his gums, tongue and cheeks were burning. Saliva poured from his mouth. Snot ran from his nose. His stomach jerked convulsively.

"AAAOOO!" Whiskers screamed, tears pouring from his eyes.

Immediately, the porcine grunting, snuffling and tooting that had provided a most pleasant background music for the mass consumption of peppery edibles ceased. Jerking their heads up, the javelinas saw two dogs standing in their beloved field of jalapeños.

Bewildered, the javelinas simply stared until instinct kicked in and told them something dreadful: the dogs were going to eat all their jalapeños. Scrunching up their top lips to reveal their teeth, the infuriated pigs grunted en masse as they closed in for a mass attack.

"They are really mad!" Whiskers squeaked. "Just look at the smoke blasting out of their butts. I'm so sorry, Scut. You had a way out for us, and I screwed it up."

Scut didn't respond. He turned his head quickly, surveying the arrangement of the javelinas, looking for an alley between them that might offer a chance to escape unharmed.

But with so many javelinas all over the field and the gaps between them closing rapidly, there wasn't a straight line anywhere. If they tried to dodge around the wild pigs, most likely the javelinas would latch onto their legs and rip out the tendons, causing Whiskers and Scut to fall helplessly under the tusks of the enraged creatures.

At that moment, something black flew swiftly past Scut's head. Before he could identify it...

"GET AWAY FROM THOSE DOGS, YOU PORCINE PUNKS! THEY'RE MINE!"

The shout from the public address system startled the javelinas, freezing their advance. Their heads ratcheted back and forth until they found the source—a black van tearing down a dirt trail.

The van flew off the trail with siren screaming, ahooga horn honking, red and blue lights rotating on the roof, white strobe lights flashing in the grill and pink laser beams sweeping across the jalapeño plants.

Barreling into the field, the van crushed scores of jalapeño plants as the sound of machine gun fire erupted from the loudspeaker, followed by a medley of Beethoven's "Fifth Symphony," "Ride of the Valkyries," and "I Am Woman, Tread on Me No More," all played up-tempo and backgrounded with heavy-metal power chords.

When the display of light and sound reached its crescendo, the music cut out and a woman's voice boomed from the public address system, "I LOVE THE SMELL OF BACON IN THE MORNING!"

With those words the Dogster skidded sideways, stopping so abruptly that the driver's door and the passenger's door flew open.

FBDI Special Agent Janvier jumped out, jerked open a storage panel on the side of the van, and pulled out a tank of liquid with a spray gun. Facing the javelinas, she pointed the high-pressure sprayer at them.

"You like peppers? Then get a load of habanero!"

Janvier pulled the trigger and blasted the porkers with the excruciating pepper spray.

Shocked and awed by the sudden human intrusion and screeching from the pain in their eyes, noses and mouths, the squealing javelinas abandoned their intended victims and scattered into the woods.

Whiskers and Scut watched the wild pigs disappear, then turned their attention back to the human who had saved them.

"Oh, catshit!" Whiskers said.

"Double catshit," said Scut.

There was no doubt about who she was. Her appearance and aggressiveness matched the descriptions told and retold throughout Dogdom. It was the relentless, fearless, human she-bitch who drove the machine that took dogs away from their happy lives.

They were within easy reach of her powerful spray gun.

"You're mine now!" Janvier yelled. "You thought I'd never get either one of you, but I'm taking both of you back to face justice!"

Whiskers and Scut glanced at the woods. The angry javelinas in there would rip them apart. The slope next to the woods was a mystery. If it ended in a drop-off, they could fall to their deaths. There was no other choice. They had to get past the she-bitch and her spray gun.

Their muscles tensed and their eyes shifted about.

"Don't try it," she warned. "Lie down and put your paws over your eyes, or else I'll nail you."

They bolted forward.

Janvier pulled the trigger of the spray gun. Nothing happened. The tank was empty. She dropped the sprayer and whipped out her pearl-handled stun guns.

Seeing the weapons, Scut and Whiskers dodged as she fired. The contacts flew past them, zinging into pepper plants that shook and trembled from the jolts of electricity.

Janvier tossed the stun guns aside and reached for the net gun on her belt to wrap up both dogs in one shot.

But Whiskers and Scut were too fast and now too close. As Janvier brought the net gun up, they split to opposite sides and went around her.

To avoid running headfirst into the Dogster's body, Whiskers skidded to a stop, flailed his legs to get traction and then bolted to the right.

Seeing the opening of the driver's door directly in front of him, Scut leaped toward it as Janvier whirled around and shot the net gun.

Blasting forth, the wide-open net smashed Scut's tail against his butt. Before the bungee netting wrapped around him, part of it snagged on the open driver's door, causing the net to halt in mid-air. As Scut disappeared into the van, the net collapsed. A wad of it lodged in the crack between the door and the van's frame while the rest fell to the ground.

Landing off-balance on the driver's seat cushion, Scut lurched heavily against the back of the seat, caromed off it to hit the steering wheel, then fell against the gearshift lever, knocking the van into gear.

The motor hadn't been turned off. The van started moving. Regaining his feet, Scut scrambled across the seat cushions and leaped out the door on the passenger's side as the vehicle rumbled toward the slope.

"Dogster!" screamed Janvier.

Running through the jalapeño field to catch up, she grabbed the part of the bungee net trailing on the ground just as the van reached the slope and picked up speed, jerking her off her feet. As Janvier fell, her body corkscrewed and the net wrapped around her arms. The Dogster rumbled deeper down the slope, dragging Janvier out of view.

High up in a tree, Phelonius slowly shook his head from side to side as he watched Janvier disappear while Whiskers and Scut ran pell-mell to get away, each taking a different trail.

Rats! What rotten luck. If I hadn't brought her, the javelinas would have done them both in. Scratchy would have been so pleased.

I'M YOURS, FOREVER

As he ran from the jalapeño field, Whiskers did a quick head turn to see Scut flying down another trail. Whiskers, however, stayed on the Chihuahua trail.

Eventually, new sets of the creepy, jerking little dogs began to appear. But their sayings had become somewhat disquieting:

Swift of foot
Poochie won the race
But then he fell
On his face

...and...

He took a leap
To take a bite
Now they call him
Jojo lite

The next ones puzzled him:

Is what you seek
What you find?
Especially when
You run blind?

...and...

Arfie wanted
Fame and glory
Now he's just
An alle-gory

What does that mean? It doesn't matter. At least I know I'm going the right way.

A little later, Whiskers picked up whiffs of something. The farther he went and the more he inhaled, the better it became. Better than anything he had ever smelled in his life.

This has to be it, the last clue from the flat bone! It's the "wonderful smell!"

He ran faster.

That is, until he had to slow way down for a large group of particularly strident Chihuahuas. Unlike the small groups who had shouted slogans while standing on the side of the trail, these Chihuahuas were cutting back and forth across his path, crowding him while they yelled in his face again and again and again:

Up or down
What you choose
May see you win
Or see you lose

Forced into a walk among the yellers, Whiskers noticed that the trail had a branch to his right going up a steep, massive hill.

Hmm, this Chihuahua sign is different from the others. Rather than hastening me on, they've slowed me down for a reason. I need to figure it out using the unused matter in my brain just like the fizzycyst that Mr. Professor told me about, Einsign, so that I can create an ipopacyst.

Obviously, any nonthinking dog would go straight ahead, since that's where the smell is coming from. However, no dog who set out to get the Big Bone has ever returned. Why? Either it's not straight ahead or something happens there or both. What if it's really somewhere on top of this hill and its aroma is so thick and heavy that it rolls down one side into a giant pile at the bottom? Maybe when dogs go straight ahead and get inside the aroma it is so strong they overdoze on it and never wake up. Or it drives them wild looking for something that isn't actually there and they go insane. Or they sniff themselves into such a frenzy that their noses overheat and catch on fire and they are burned alive.

Having conjectured such improbabilities, I must conclude that I popped the cyst and have divined that going straight ahead has to be the wrong choice. Therefore, I'm going upward to fetch the Big Bone.

Off he went, chugging up the hill. Finally, arriving in a white heat of panting, Whiskers shouted out, "Made it, Mr. Professor! Top of the world!" Eagerly looking around for the Big Bone, he saw…

Nothing.

Rats! I thought I had it all figured out, but I guess I outsmarted myself by coming up here. Now, I've got to go back down, but first I need to take a break.

While pausing to catch his breath, Whiskers studied the trail far below. Following it from his high vantage point, he could see that farther along something was on the trail.

Rather than running blindly down there to it, I'll check it out from up here.

Whiskers began trotting along the ridgeline until he came to the far end of the hill. Peering down, he saw that the trail ended at a cliff. He also saw:

A bone.

A big one.

Much bigger than he'd ever imagined.

It's the Big Bone!

It wasn't lying on the ground. The Big Bone was levitating above the trail, doing a slow shimmy that in effect said, You know you want it. You want it bad. So, so-o, so-o-o bad.

And why not? The reddest meat was attached to the whitest of bones, a bone as tall as the tallest of dogs and as long as five large dogs stuck nose to tail, with the purest of clear grease dripping off like raindrops while layers of the creamiest, most gorgeous fat cooked and smoked in the heat of the sun, forming a translucent, sparkling brown crust that cracked in places with a popping sound that tantalized, Come and get me. I'm yours, forever.

It's even better than all the stories I heard!

Transfixed, Whiskers couldn't stop staring at the Big Bone. Suddenly, his eyes widened, and he began shaking all over.

Then a great noise arose, causing Whiskers to turn so he could look back down the trail.

The mob of Chihuahuas was frantically screeching out their cautionary message as a dark shape moved toward them.

Oh, no! He must have gotten a whiff of the Big Bone and nosed his way here.

Scut was covering ground rapidly, running as if possessed, drawn by the siren smell of the Big Bone, its waves of aroma increasing in intensity with every step.

Screaming forward like a missile, the dog who had once

doubted the existence of the Big Bone was now crazed with lust for it, running full force at the Chihuahuas with no recognition of their presence. The Chihuahuas stopped yapping and started yelping in terror of being trampled beneath his paws. Before Scut smashed into the group, they dropped to all fours and scattered for the sides of the trail as fast as their tiny legs would move. To hell with the message.

From on high, Whiskers surveyed the distance Scut still had to cover to reach the Big Bone.

He's way faster than me, but I'm a lot closer and I'll be running downhill. I've got to get there first or stop him somehow.

Whiskers charged down the hill, aided by gravity so much that he was barely touching the ground, all the while eyeballing Scut who was running even faster than before.

As the two dogs closed in, the Big Bone rose higher and began to float straight back.

Cutting his eyes to the right and seeing Whiskers arriving just below the Big Bone, Scut put on a furious burst of speed and leaped above Whiskers.

As Scut passed over him, Whiskers jumped up and clamped his jaws on Scut's closest back leg. Sailing forward with mouth wide open, Scut snapped viciously at the Big Bone, but the weight of Whiskers dragged him down just enough to miss it by inches. Passing underneath the Big Bone, they sailed onward, cartwheeling through the air with Whiskers still holding on and Scut snapping his teeth mindlessly. Losing momentum, they stopped cartwheeling and began to fall, accelerating toward a river far below.

Smacking into the water, the dogs plunged deep below the surface. Stunned from the impact, but recovering their senses, they paddled upward until breaking the surface. Gasping for air, it took a few moments for each to get over the shock of being in the water.

Growling angrily, Scut glared at Whiskers.

"You idiot. I almost had the Big Bone. It was mine, not yours. I beat you to it, fair and square. Now I've got to find my way out of here so I can get back to it. But first, I'm going to drown you. And that's too bad because I was starting to think you were okay even though you're a little shit of a dog."

"W-w-wait, before you do that, look over there," Whiskers said, motioning with his head.

A wide rock ledge loaded with sharp-edged boulders jutted out from the base of the cliff. The ledge was covered with bones piled high on top of one another. Some skeletons were intact.

"Scut, those are the bones of dead dogs."

Scut shook his head in wonderment.

"What happened to them?"

"I guess they got a bite of the Big Bone but found themselves stuck in the air, hanging on with their teeth until they couldn't hold on any longer. Then it was all the way down onto those rocks."

"So you weren't trying to get it?"

"No. I went on top of the hill. When I got to the end and looked down, I could see the Big Bone and far below it all those bones at the bottom of the cliff."

Looking upward, Scut and Whiskers saw the Big Bone still hovering in the air. They watched it float forward, back into place near the end of the trail.

"Big Bone, my ass," Scut snarled.

Looking once more at the ledge of broken bones and pondering what might have been, Whiskers and Scut paddled quietly in place until they heard:

"YOU BASTARDS!"

70

THAR SHE GOES

napped out of his contemplation, Scut stared upstream and sneered, "Look, it's the human she-bitch."

"Wow!" exclaimed Whiskers. "She caught herself."

Janvier was trapped against the side of the Dogster, bound tightly to it by long strands of torn bungee net crisscrossing from the rooftop communication antennas to the rearview mirror, outside equipment brackets, and spiked lug nut covers.

The bulky van pitched and yawed in the water. Rolling to the opposite side, it raised Janvier up in the air. Rolling back, it plunged her below the surface, then rolled up again, raising her out of the water.

But she seemed to have no concern for herself. One arm was free, and she reached toward a bracket that held a long pole with a loop on the end of it. Janvier jerked the pole out of the bracket, pushed a button to extend it and then pointed it at the dogs while yelling, "Look what you two did! This van is government property. You refused to obey a lawful order, and now it's flooded. I'll get you for this and everything else you've done. Both of you!"

Realizing her helplessness, Whiskers and Scut barked and

howled, delighted to see every dog's nightmare caught and tied up. But their joy didn't last long. Although she couldn't get them, the Dogster could. The van was bearing down on them. If they didn't move, they would get run over in the water.

"Let's go!" Whiskers said.

Facing downstream, they paddled hard. As they neared a bend in the river, the current's speed increased and whip-snapped them around it.

Whiskers and Scut yapped in exhilaration to find themselves moving so quickly away from Janvier and the Dogster. That is, until their forward progress became sideways progress, which turned into rearward progress, then forward again. They looked at one another, puzzled to find themselves trapped on a wall of whirling water that led downward in a cone shape.

"Yikes! I don't like this," yelped Whiskers as he watched swirling leaves and broken tree limbs get sucked into the point of the cone and disappear.

"That's not our only problem," Scut said, looking off to the side.

Barging around the bend, the Dogster got caught in the rotating water and entered the whirlpool close to the dogs.

Trapped together, swirling around and around, they stared at one another—Janvier with fire in her eyes, Scut with disdain in his, and Whiskers' filled with the terror of being sucked into oblivion.

"Swim over here!" commanded Janvier, poking at them with the long pole, trying to drop the loop over one of their necks. But each time she almost got Scut or Whiskers, the van would rock and she would miss.

Prompted into action by the loop swinging about their heads, Whiskers and Scut turned onto their bellies and paddled hard until they got up and over the edge of the whirlpool.

Catching the natural river current, they started to float gently downstream.

"COME BACK HERE!"

They turned around for a last look. With each revolution in the whirlpool, the Dogster and Janvier would come into view on the far side. The heavy van was sinking lower and lower while she continued waving her pole at them.

Whiskers and Scut resumed paddling away, listening to their dogged pursuer's commands grow fainter and fainter.

71

NO MORE SNIGGERING

Scratchy and Phelonius stared at a body floating face-up beside a strip of land in the swamp.

"Is this her?" asked Scratchy.

"Yes."

"Alive-dead or dead-dead?"

"Alive-dead."

"Call the alligator for transport. Notify the rabbit to prepare for trial."

"Why, Scratchy? She's not an animal."

"Oh, no? Technically, for your information, humans are animals, and animal lore says that in ancient times they even had tails, but for some stupid reason they decided to stand on two legs and then they kept stepping on their tails and tripping themselves, so they gave up their tails instead of going back to four legs. Idiots! That's why they can't run worth a damn. Anyway, stop your quibbling and notify the bailiff to draw up a list of charges."

"Charges? Like what?"

"In general, dereliction of duty, failure to perform, incompetence and did not meet expectations. Specifically, she allowed two known criminals to get away, and they are, to wit: the escapee from exile known as Whiskers, and the duplicitous turncoat known as Scut."

"But, Scratchy, she didn't know anything about you. She was acting on her own behalf."

"Phelonius, you twit, she should have done her due diligence, such as: Who is this bird? Where did he come from? Who does he work for?"

"Scratchy, that isn't possible. Communication with humans is really limited. You should have seen the pantomiming I had to do. Even if I had taken a parrot along to translate, we couldn't have gotten all those concepts through to her."

"Doesn't matter. She accepted your help. She became indebted and under contract. Besides, I love a new challenge. Just think about it: prosecuting our first human. Doesn't that excite you?"

"Actually, maybe you should reconsider," Phelonius cautioned.

"Why would I do that?"

"Frankly, you've been losing respect in the swamp. Ever since Whiskers got away, the other animals have been sniggering behind your back. He's kind of like a hero to them. Plus, they heard about Scut and how he wasn't afraid to switch sides on you. By putting her on trial for letting them get away, it's an unstated but obvious admission that there is an escape from Scratchy."

The nutria stuck his lower lip out and rolled it over his upper lip, then flapped the upper lip on top of the lower lip, all of which was repeated over and over while scrunching and unscrunching the skin around his eyes as he thought about the implications.

"That's not good," he finally said. "Suggestions?"

"Send her back."

"Next suggestion."

"That's the only one."

Scratchy sucked in air and flared his cheeks, then blew the air back out tinged with saliva.

"Are you kidding? Just let her go? Like I'm suddenly some kind of a nice guy? Have you lost your mind? Forget about losing the respect of all the animals here, I'd lose respect for myself. You must have flown headfirst into a tree to come up with an idiotic idea like that."

Suddenly, the frown on Scratchy's face changed to a big smile.

"Wait, I've got it. There won't be a trial. Instead, I'll levy some administrative punishment. We'll use it as a teachable moment to get everyone back in line. They'll see that ignorance is no excuse and we don't reward failure with the idea that learning is taking place. Now, I just need to think of a good punishment to wow the public."

Scratchy furrowed his brow as his eyes rolled from side to side.

"Ooh, how about this? We'll have the beavers bury her in quicksand for a couple of days but with nostrils up for air. Sounds good, doesn't it? Besides, the beavers need the practice."

"I don't know, Scratchy. Her presence will raise lots of questions. It could backfire on you. Really, the quicker she's out of here, the better."

Frustrated, Scratchy looked down at Janvier, slowly shaking his head back and forth.

"I can't just send her back, I've got to punish her. It's my job, it's my nature, it's what I love to do."

Phelonius didn't comment. Instead, he looked around theatrically, as if to make sure that no other animals were near enough to listen.

"You know, I do have another suggestion."

"Bury her secretly? Cover the nostrils? Oh, Phelonius, if that's what you're thinking, my faith is restored in you. I was starting to suspect that you had a crush on her, a human, of all things."

"No, that's not what I was thinking."

Scratchy dropped his chin, cocked his head to one side and blew hot air out of his mouth.

"Then what is it? It better be good."

"Whiskers and Scut are out of our range. We've lost our chance to get them, but she can go anywhere they go. In fact, she wants them so bad that she charged into a field full of insane javelinas."

Squinting his eyes and pursing his lips, Scratchy took an appraising look at Janvier.

"Hmm, that does take a lot of moxie. Shows real determination. Single-mindedness. Hell-bent, you might say."

"If she gets them," Phelonius said, "maybe she'll put them in dog prison or something even worse."

Scratchy nodded and smiled as Janvier began to come around, coughing up some water.

"There's another advantage for you," Phelonius said. "After she's sent back, we'll tell the whole swamp about her, that she's your special agent going after Whiskers and Scut. We'll say she's the human she-bitch not just from dog hell but from animal hell, pursuing any animal anywhere. Then the others will know there is never any real escape. They won't be sniggering anymore. Total respect will be yours again."

"You know, I like that," Scratchy said, grinning. "Yes, let's do it."

He looked around furtively, saying, "She's got to go back now before anyone sees her. Otherwise, we won't be able to sell this soggy lump as the human she-bitch of their nightmares."

PART V

AFTERMATH

72

STICKHOLDERS

As time went by, dogs everywhere went from a heightened sense of excitement to one of deep concern.

Whiskers and Scut had not returned. Theories abounded: Perhaps bears or a pack of wolves had jumped them. Or maybe they were buried by landslides. Or the earth cracked open and swallowed them.

As more time went by, the anguish about predators and natural calamities began to change into disparagement of the mental and physical attributes of the two competitors.

Some of Scut's fans said they had made a mistake, that he was too stupid to find the Big Bone, that he got lost and was too embarrassed to return. Whiskers' backers berated themselves for supporting a dog who was too weak to drag the Big Bone back to them.

Next, rumors of selfishness and maliciousness began to spread.

One was that Whiskers had found a hiding place to which he dragged the Big Bone and ate so much meat and fat off it that his stomach exploded.

Another was that Scut did away with Whiskers and chewed the Big Bone into tiny slivers out of sheer meanness.

The tales of tragic fates sent many dogs into mourning. Their grief, though, wasn't for Whiskers or Scut. Their grief was for the dashing of the vicarious fulfillment that was to be had from backing a winner, which would have made themselves winners.

So, the elation and excitement that the great race had brought to Dogdom dissipated. There was no more eager running and barking to share canine-only messages while cutting sly, knowing, smirking glances at nearby clueless humans.

In other words, dogs drifted back into their normal state of lying around, even on their day off.

As DOGS CALMED DOWN, humans calmed down. Still, humans could not shake a latent fear that someday in the future Rovers, Fidos and Pookies all over the nation might rise up again.

Lazy people had a particular problem. They were under suspicion by their neighbors. Perhaps they weren't naturally lazy, but instead had been bitten during the national panic and might actually be zombies waiting for a signal to get on their feet and stalk the living. This was a great problem because there were so many lazy Americans.

To help restore harmony among the general public, their pets and the energetically challenged, the President proclaimed in his annual State of the Mess address to Congress that a dog was still a woman's, man's, undocumented citizen's, political donor's and corporate fat cat's best friend.

Next, after handing out participation trophies to each

member of Congress who showed up, the President put a parrot on his shoulder, saying that it was his new pet, Ike. Soon, Americans were wearing T-shirts that proclaimed "I Like Ike" and mobbing pet stores for parrots. Eventually, all parrots formerly in Central and South America wound up in North America, helping everyone to happily forget all their concerns about dogs and lazy neighbors.

AS A REWARD for having been smart enough to be the boss of Janvier, the FBDI's J. Egbert Hooter was tapped to be the director of the newly created FBBI—the Federal Bureau of Butt Investigation. His agents immediately began using butt-sniffing dogs at airports to detect anyone trying to carry illegal substances or objects up their rear ends.

A lawsuit was quickly filed by ASS—American Suppository Services—to disband the FBBI, claiming that the new agency was driving down sales as well as violating an individual's constitutional right to be secure anywhere inside his or her person absent a search warrant. "Stick it up your ass" became the company's rallying cry.

Hooter countered by contracting with Coco Siliconoli to do a public service commercial in which a German Shepherd gave her a cold nose up close and very personal inside her oversized celebrity booty, followed by a sneeze and a bark to indicate she was contraband free. The spot ended with Coco cooing sexily, "Ooh, that nose is so cold and wet it gives me goosebumps you know where."

That did it!

From then on people enthusiastically lined up to drop their drawers, followed by a photo of them hugging life-size cardboard cutouts of Coco and a German Shepherd while sporting a T-shirt reading, "I've Been Cold-Nosed." Each person also got a participation trophy and a free suppository from ASS.

WITH THEIR ATTENTION-GETTING appearances on the shows of Dr. Sid, Jerry Sphincter and The Spew, Ma and Bud became hot properties for television producers who signed them up as contestants on the Grub Channel's rural cooking show, "Country Bumpkin Can Cook," which they won with their expert preparation of the mystery ingredient—skunk—in a variety of dishes: skunk soufflé, skunk casserole, skunk sushi, skunk flambé, skunk a la Francaise, skunk tacos, skunk baby back ribs, skunk jambalaya, skunk mousse, skunk a la mode and a skunk margarita to wash it all down. In other words, they skunked the competition.

As their grand prize, they were given their own show, "Roadkill—It's What's for Dinner." The program's logo depicted a large cooking pot with a furry tail hanging over the edge. The show was canceled, however, when Ma and Bud advised viewers that if roadkill was in short supply all they had to do was go to the local humane society and adopt a dog.

But the American taste for colorful characters and bad behavior got them a second chance. Being country folk and therefore familiar with a wide variety of animal poop, Ma and Bud were signed on as technical consultants to set up the obstacle course for a reality show, "Doo Drop In."

Because their profound knowledge helped that show get sky-high ratings, Ma and Bud were rewarded with executive positions at the Hick Network. At the last report, they were engaged in high-concept strategy meetings and focus groups to determine which of the following titles for a new reality series would get more of the coveted fifteen- to nineteen-year-old age bracket off their four-wheelers and in front of their TV sets:

"Rubes with Boobs"

"Boobs and Rubes"

"Rubes Rubbin' Boobs"

"Boobs Rubbin' Rubes"

SCRATCHY SEETHED for quite a while over the failure of his efforts to wreak justice, punishment and vengeance on Whiskers, all thanks to a pipsqueak mouse, a muddle-headed rabbit, a double-crossing dog, a dimwitted eagle and a blame-deflecting crow.

After their fiascos, the human she-bitch had remained his only hope that the infuriating Whiskers and the traitorous Scut would suffer, if not in the swamp, at least somewhere.

Scratchy perked up when Phelonius relayed exciting news.

Pausing on a windowsill, one of the Flapper Express field agents had looked into a room and seen Whiskers' and Scut's faces displayed on the thing that people stare at all day long, followed by the face of the human she-bitch.

Conclusion: She was still pursuing them or, better yet, she had caught them.

The next day, Phelonius himself spotted the restored Dogster slowly rolling through large, cheering crowds of people. It drove up to a huge building that had tall, thin, pointed things on its roof as well as a lot of big round things. The human she-bitch left the Dogster and entered the building, followed by many other humans with cats in crates, guinea pigs in cages, dogs on leashes, fish in bowls, and parrots on shoulders.

When that news hit the swamp, several monkeys said it sounded like the same type of place they had escaped from—a building where humans prodded, poked, stuck, drugged, cut and otherwise tortured caged animals.

The evidence was clear: Whiskers and Scut had been captured and incarcerated, and the human she-bitch was presiding in that building over their torture sessions. Scratchy was so excited that he called a special swamp meeting at which he had the chattering monkeys eagerly embellish upon all the horrors that Whiskers and Scut would undergo.

Scratchy also made sure that all the swampsters knew he was the mastermind of the whole operation, the one who had sicced the human she-bitch on the odious canines. Obviously, his power now extended beyond the swamp. All the animals were tremendously impressed. Scratchy really could get you anywhere.

UPON HER RETURN from the river encounter, Janvier had stepped up the search operation by offering a sizable FBDI reward on cable and broadcast television stations. Hundreds of professional hunters and thousands of eager volunteers—especially taxidermists—went after Whiskers and Scut, but the pair was never spotted. After a sufficient amount of time, the culprits were presumed to have drowned and the search was called off.

Media jabberers on CNN—the Canine News Network—interviewed and debated with dog trainers, river pilots and animal psychics as to how the dogs could have met their demise, whether they became alligator food, were caught in a whirlpool and sucked out sight, had their heads smashed between floating logs, were chopped up by the propellers of fishing boats, got carried over a waterfall to be crushed on the rocks at its base, or simply became too exhausted to swim anymore and glided below the surface to the muddy bottom.

No matter how they perished, the public knew it had weathered the crisis thanks to Janvier. She was hailed as a national hero whose dogged pursuit of the two criminal canines had foiled their plans, causing the collapse of the Great Dog, Zombie and Space Alien Conspiracy theory. Peephole magazine featured her on its cover to show that she had replaced the long-missing earring with a reproduction.

Before a guest appearance on the crime show "Dognet," she was mobbed in the CNN parking lot by excited employees bringing scores of animals with them on National Take Your Pet To The Office And Do Less Work Day. Even a pesky crow flitted about her head, trying to get her attention, acting as if it knew her.

Naturally, offers flooded in for Janvier to endorse products ranging from flea powder to dog food, dog collars, canine tanning beds and luxurious pet resorts, but she wasn't interested.

She turned down millions of dollars to replace the Hillbilly Can Can Dancers as the halftime act of the National Footloose League's Super-Kick-the-Can Bowl, which wanted to feature her capturing trained lions and tigers and twerking them into cages, all the while having multiple wardrobe malfunctions sponsored by Boobweiser Breakaway Bras with their new slogan, "This Boob's For You."

Janvier soon found that her national celebrity and the paparazzi who followed her everywhere made it nearly impossible to carry out investigations for the FBDI.

It became clear there was only one workplace in America where her celebrity would be a major asset and not a major distraction—television. After resigning from the FBDI, she put out feelers and got an unexpected offer from Dr. Sid.

Unable to get Janvier out of his private imaginings and mindful of her value as a ratings skyrocket, he shockingly crashed the set of the early morning talk show "What's Up, America?"

Dr. Sid plopped his butt on the news desk between Janvier and her interviewer to propose marriage while extolling all the benefits that would come with it. She would get a job as a production assistant on his show and top guest billing once a month, plus up-close and very personal counseling with him in a new mansion to be built for the two of them. Shaking her head and rolling her eyes, Janvier declined his offer but countered that she would co-host his show at a salary equivalent to his plus one dollar.

Getting half of what he wanted at the moment and calculating that he would get the other half later through his alpha male charm and hypnotism, Dr. Sid eagerly accepted but soon found that his analytical mind was no match for her street smarts. With the extra dollar as equity leverage, she took over the show and remade his role into that of a sidekick. Each telecast started with Janvier leading Dr. Sid on a leash while he scampered on all fours with his tongue hanging out to the whooping delight of the females and vulnerable males in the audience.

If Dr. Sid's academically grounded advice disagreed with Janvier's real-world knowledge when counseling their messed-up guests, she would whack him with a rolled-up newspaper. It was just what the long-buried, non-analytical part of his brain had desperately needed. He was a very happy man.

With the highest ratings in daytime television, their show won the Gimmee Award for Best Afternoon Program, beating out Poperah, Jerry Sphincter, Judge Floozy, and Trailer Park Gourmet.

That's when the President came calling, offering the directorship of the Federal Bureau of Dog Investigation to Janvier. Dr.

Sid begged her not to go, and the network offered an enormous amount of money to stay.

Janvier took time off to reflect on what she should do.

All I ever wanted when starting out in life was to be a nice girl doing a good job, but now I know what my real job is: to kick ass and shake things up.

I like that.

73

A NEW U

After leaving their nemesis to her fate in the whirlpool, Whiskers and Scut had swum out of the placid lower reach of the river. They traveled together for a while, but each had different interests, so they parted.

Later, Scut began to hear stories that Whiskers had quit wandering. More than that, he was hanging out with strange characters and had taken up a new occupation. Intrigued, Scut journeyed from the high country to see for himself.

He arrived late at night on a bluff overlooking the grove where Whiskers now stayed. After taking a path down from the bluff, Scut had searched by smell in the dark, found what he was seeking, and left what he had been carrying in his mouth. He then retraced his steps up the bluff and went to sleep.

After awakening in warm sun, Scut walked to the edge of the bluff to scan the terrain below. Whiskers was sitting under a tree and conversing with three other animals. Scut made his way down the path, walked quietly toward the oblivious conversationalists and then let out a sharp bark.

"Scut! What a surprise!" Whiskers said, jumping up, his tail wagging in a blur. "Meet my friends!"

But upon seeing the fierce, imposing canine, Whiskers' friends scuttled a few steps back, unsure if they should stay or start hopping, flying and running away.

Looking at the group in puzzlement, Scut admonished Whiskers, "Have you forgotten that you're a dog and that you're supposed to run off birds and chase rabbits?"

"I don't care if they're a bird or a rabbit. They're nice, they're fun, and they're my friends," Whiskers said, motioning for them to come forward.

"Well, what's with that dog? He keeps bobbing his head around like he's looking for something. Either that or there's something wrong with him."

"Do you remember me telling you about the other dog in the swamp, the one who was always swimming and looking for his mind? I was worried about whether he could make it on his own outside the swamp, so I got word back to Sylvilagus asking if he could help find him."

"That's me," said the rabbit. "It wasn't difficult, because this poor, sweet, gentle dog was still poking around on the outskirts. Rosie, bless her big spoonbill heart, guided us to Whiskers from the air while I kept Loser from running mindlessly off track on the ground."

"But Loser won't be my name for long," chimed in the Labrador. "That's because Whiskers is the best friend I ever had, and he says he knows exactly where to find my mind, and he's going to brave extreme danger to get it while I stay here safe, and then he's going to put it back in my head using something he calls hipponoses. Then I'll remember my real name and where my real home is, and I'll finally be able to go back where I belong."

"And I'm going to make sure he gets there," Rosie spoke up, "using my own flying service—Rosie's Rosebuds—that I started with my baby birdy bambinos who are quite bigger now and

which Whiskers encouraged me to have with Peter Crabcake, or
is it Peter Clambake or Peter Cupcake or Peter Pancake? Well,
sometimes I get confused about his name because everybody
calls him something different, so I'm never sure what it is.
Anyway, we're the kinder, gentler alternative to that nasty crow
and his Freaking Flapping Floundering Flipping Floppers or
whatever he calls them."

"How interesting," Scut said, deadpan, "but what about that
lousy, puffed-up rat the stinking crow worked for?"

"Ah, so you know about our local egomaniac," said Sylvilagus. "He keeps popping up with so many devilish schemes that
it's like playing whack-a-maniac. And I'm dreadfully sorry to say
that I played a part in his machinations for so long. Be that as it
may, it was Whiskers' trial that was a revelation to me. His spirited, learned and courageous defense against what now seem to
be debatably spurious charges in light of the circumstances in
which he found himself made me realize that I had become too
wrapped up in the intricate and entangling details of precedent,
practice and procedure, all to the detriment of justice.

"That realization set me on a course to see how we could
rein in Scratchy," Sylvilagus continued, "and I am most pleased
to say that we've finally got him neutralized so that he's not
hurting anyone anymore. Here's the good part: he doesn't know
it. You see, I came up with a plan that puts that scheming manip-
ulator Phelonius to good use. Each day, he flies off out of sight
and lazes around doing nothing at all except hanging out with
other disreputable birds until flying back with phony progress
reports about the dastardly deeds that human recruits are
carrying out for Scratchy. You may ask, what human recruits?
Actually, none. They're all imaginary. Now, Scratchy is so busy
thinking up new orders for Phelonius to carry to his supposed
human lackeys and boasting about his power over them that he
no longer bothers to prosecute animals. As a result, the swamp

has become a pretty decent place to live, if you like swamps that is, which I do because that's my home, and so I'll be heading back now that Loser has gotten here without getting lost."

Scut shook his head in wonderment before commenting, "I guess your friends are okay, Whiskers. Now, show me what you've been spending all your time on."

"Sure, it's over there on the other side of those trees."

As they came to the copse of trees and walked around them, a large expanse of dirt came into view. Exceptional displays of turds in varying sizes, shapes and coloration were laid out in neat rows.

"It's magnificent," Scut said. "I've never seen anything like this."

"Once word got around about this turd garden, dogs of all kinds have been coming through and dropping off contributions," Whiskers said, nodding with pride.

Something caught Scut's eye. A gray cat was creeping into the garden at its farthest edge.

"Want me to run him off?" Scut asked.

"No, I let them use a little piece back there. It's easier than constantly chasing them away since they always sneak back. Besides, there's nothing to see, because they cover it up. They just don't get the concept, which is fine with me."

As they watched the cat finish and run away, clouds drifting in the sky unblocked a ray of sunlight that caused a sparkle in the garden.

"What's that?" Whiskers asked.

"It's a surprise I brought for your garden. I dropped it off last night."

"Show it to me!"

They headed to a major pile among all the other offerings.

"Whoa!" said Whiskers. "That's one of the biggest here, but what's that shining on top?"

The sun was glinting brilliantly off a small, metallic object.

"It's one of those things that lots of humans wear in their ears," Scut said. "I got it when I ambushed a dogcatcher."

"You actually ambushed a dogcatcher?"

"Yes. I wanted at least one of them to know the fear that all dogs feel when they try to get us. After I took it from her, I stashed it as a souvenir."

"Her?"

"Yes, someone we both know."

"Who?"

"The human she-bitch."

"Wow! Are you sure it's hers?"

"I knew it the moment I caught her scent in the jalapeño field, and after what you and I went through together, I felt this was the place for it."

"Scut, this is incredible. I'm going to make it the centerpiece of my garden. Dogs will come from everywhere to see it and hear the story."

After pausing for a moment, Whiskers' eyes widened. He bounced around on his feet, wagging his tail hard.

"Scut, I'm going to make this garden even bigger, so when those visitors come they'll find special participation sections—one for rolling around, one for artistic expression, one for those who partake, and one for leaving personal calling cards.

"That's not all," he panted, his eyes growing even wider. "I want to say one word to you. Just one word."

"What?"

"Frencheyes."

Scut studied Whiskers closely.

"Is that what you call the crazy look you've got in your eyes?"

"No. A frencheyes is something that Mr. Professor talked about. He said it's a way that shit gets spread around. Now I understand what he meant. I'll teach others how to do turd gardens. They'll sprout up everywhere. The dogs running them will take in bones, balls and toys from visitors. I'll get some of what they take in. That's how it works."

Whiskers was on a roll.

"Ooh, ooh, ooh, I've got another idea," he whooped. "When I get enough toys, bones and balls to go with the poop already here, I'll start a university with lots of professors to study all of it and give lectures to students."

"What are you going to call it?"

"Dogshit University."

"That's a good name."

"I know. It should draw a lot of applicants."

Whiskers looked down, then up, as if remembering something.

"Mr. Professor told me that when all the jerks he worked with come to apply for jobs, I should bite them in the ass. However, I'm going to be very busy organizing everything. Scut, you would be perfect for chief ass-biter. What do you say about sticking around and helping me with all of this? We'll be a great team."

The big dog shook his head.

"I've satisfied my curiosity and done what I came to do. Now I'm going back to the high country. That's where I fit in better. There are very few dogs and very few humans, which means a lot less foolishness. I must say, though, you seem to have found something that agrees with you."

"Candidly," Whiskers said, "I'm very happy tending my garden."

"At least it will keep you out of trouble."

"Oh, believe me, I used to think that's what I wanted, but I've had enough of it."

Scut cocked his head to one side, a half-smile on his face.

"From the things I heard about, you didn't do too bad."

"Really? You're not just saying that?"

Scut didn't answer. It was time to leave. He turned around and began trotting away.

"So long, friend," Whiskers called out.

Scut stopped and glanced back.

"So long, little hero."